Kai

A Bargain in Silver

Solis Invicti: Book I

Find your freedom!

JOSIE JAFFREY

By Josie Jaffrey

The Solis Invicti Series

A Bargain in Silver
The Price of Silver
Bound in Silver
The Silver Bullet

The Sovereign Trilogy

The Gilded King
The Silver Queen
The Blood Prince

Short Stories

Living Underground

For Jessie

PROLOGUE

The music pumped into the club around me, loud enough to drown the noise of the top cracking off the bottle I was opening. Goth metal again, unsurprisingly. I handed the drink to the vampire on the other side of the bar and collected his token, posting it through the slot in the wall safe.

One thing you could say for the new world order: the currency is a hell of a lot simpler. It's good to have a positive to hold onto when you're drowning in a sea of negative.

I'm actually one of the lucky ones. My name is Emilia, I'm twenty-eight and I'm still alive. I work as a barmaid at Sol's, a multi-roomed club in central London.

The hours are crappy, the outfits are insultingly misogynistic and the clientele are dangerous as hell, but being... close to Solomon, the eponymous proprietor, gives me a level of protection I couldn't even hope to achieve elsewhere. This wasn't what I had wanted for myself, but it's how things are.

I'm hardly in a position to complain, and I don't flatter myself that I have the freedom to do so. This is my assigned position and like it or not, I do it or I die. It has been made crystal clear to me that I'm not going anywhere. I'd tried to once before and it hadn't worked out well.

The vamp I'd just served started eyeing me up until he registered the black choker around my neck, which was intricately embroidered with silver thread in a detailed lily pattern. It was the international symbol for "hands off or suffer the dire consequences". The style and decoration changed depending on the identity of the protector, but the black choker marked me as off-limits for those hoping for a sip straight from the source.

Although I might serve the drinks here, I'm no one's hot-running blood bar. Well, nearly no one's. In any case, it's not like we don't have it available both bottled and on tap.

The choker's helpful when I'm working in such a high-risk environment, particularly when my protector is not only the club owner but also the Primus, the top vamp in charge for the entire country. With that sort of power protecting me even my work uniform, a strapless corseted top and a tiny skirt (all in black, of course), couldn't tempt the club-goers enough that they'd actually lay a hand on me.

I'd toned the look down as much as I could by leaving my dark brown hair long and loose to cover my neck and by rocking knee-high, flat-soled boots, but the management would only let me go that far. I was surprised they allowed me even that much latitude given that they pretty much owned me.

Some of my workmates aren't quite so modest. At the other end of the room, my fellow human barmaid Alice was leaning provocatively across the bar towards a vamp with blond hair tousled back from his face. The style was far too affected to be the genuine bed-head article he was doubtless aiming for.

Alice was dressed in the same uniform as me, minus the choker, but she'd upped the stakes with four-inch patent spike heels. She had also managed to construct a hairstyle that effortlessly poured her blond curls down one side of her neck, leaving the other side exposed.

Alice was truly stunning in her own right, with huge blue eyes and the cutest nose you've ever seen, but the thing that made her so irresistible to the vamps was the paleness of her skin. Practically translucent, her skin allowed you to trace the delicate, dark lines of the blood running in her veins.

Bed-head Vamp was practically drooling as he raked his eyes up her chest and along her neck. Alice clearly loved the game. She knew he couldn't touch her without one of the Solis Invicti guards smashing his head in for the vicarious insult to their lord and master, but she loved to be wanted, made to feel special and important now that humans were little more than slaves and donors.

I've only been at Sol's for a few days under the new management, so the Solis Invicti are a bit of a mystery to me. They work as bouncers in the club, and act as a sort of pseudo-military, but that seems to be incidental to their role as Solomon's guard. The vamps have played their cards close to their chests when revealing details of their hierarchy and history, so their society is relatively opaque to those of us outside looking in.

Whatever their true purpose, it's clear to me from the respect the other vamps in the club show them that the Solis Invicti are much more than glorified bodyguards. I'd seen them in action in the club, thankfully only once so far, and their agility is beyond anything I have ever seen, even living in a city packed full of vamps. No wonder we had so little trouble at Sol's.

When I first started working at the club, it was called Parker's and catered to a distinctly less toothy group of trendsetters. Jeff Parker was a pain in the backside, but he was a nice guy. He took me on with no references and no experience when every other employer in the city wouldn't give me the time of day.

It was just over six months ago, and we didn't even know vampires existed. I was just trying to make enough to live on. I hadn't realised how stiff the competition would be until I arrived in the capital, a few hundred quid in my wallet and no plan except to escape, to be new, to be better, to be strong. I'd had some setbacks and I didn't want to be myself anymore.

London's full of people with no credentials: people trying to find a better life, trying to run away from the one they have or just trying to escape from themselves. I'd been an idiot because I had been trying to do all three. Needless to say, it didn't work.

It had been my third week in the city and my carefully-saved money was all but gone. I was on my third club of the night when I walked into Parker's and found my safe haven. One of the bar staff had just left to have a baby and Jeff was kind enough to take me on. On my first night at the club, Jeff set me to work behind the bar with Cassie. Within half an hour, she'd offered me a room in her rented flat. Just like that, I was part of the Parker's family.

I hadn't had much time to enjoy my good fortune before all hell broke lose. Now Jeff was gone. Cassie was gone. They were all gone.

It started in America. They call it the Revelation now, but at the time it felt more like a world war, probably because it was. It claimed billions of human lives, the vast majority of the population of the planet, and only seventeen vampires. At least, that's what we're led to believe.

It changed our lives beyond recognition, even though it was over in a little more than a week. Afterwards, it seemed inconceivable that we hadn't realised before how hopelessly outgunned we were by a race the majority of us didn't think existed.

It began quietly, a whisper through the public consciousness that was picked up and blared out through the media. A girl had gone missing from a little town in Oklahoma and, although this wasn't in itself remarkable, the circumstances of the disappearance were strange enough to arouse suspicion in such a small community.

Cara Alton, a nineteen-year-old college student, vanished from her parents' back garden one Tuesday evening in full sight of five members of her family. One minute she was enjoying a glass of lemonade, talking with her mom about her next semester's classes. The next minute she was gone, her glass falling to the floor and smashing on the terrace, three feet from where her mom was standing.

At first, the report made by Cara's parents was treated with understandable scepticism. No one else had seen the girl since she'd returned from college, never mind that day, so the police tried to contact Cara at her college campus. When there was still no news after twenty-four hours, there were mutterings about group hallucinations.

The police turned their suspicion on her family. They decided that their incredible story was a facile attempt to conceal either a deliberate disappearance by Cara or a crime by one or all of their number.

The Oklahoman sent reporters. KFOR-TV sent news cameras. The community started to turn on the Altons.

On the Saturday morning after Cara's disappearance, the New York Times received a USB storage stick in the post. It contained an apparently genuine video of the moment Cara disappeared. Now you see her, now you don't. Her family's reaction: their shocked disbelief, their panic and finally their horror. The national press were on board and a small proportion of their audience was starting to believe what it saw.

Cara was found by a morning jogger three days later in the middle of a small park in a suburban neighbourhood, fifty miles from her parents' house. She was propped up against a tree in a seated position with her legs crossed. Her T-shirt was missing, her short skirt bunched up around her hips, her femoral artery punctured and her blood drained. Her body was perfectly preserved and freezing to the touch, even in the middle of the summer in Oklahoma.

But the thing that really sent the press into a frenzy was the mark across her stomach: a perfect handprint shimmering under the surface of her skin like frozen mercury.

CHAPTER I

Thursday

For me, it started two days after Cara was found. I'd heard about her murder, we all had. I'd even heard some of our customers in the club discussing it after the news had broken. Despite the fact that a lot of the odder details had been published, perhaps even because of it, the truth is that no one was taking the mystery surrounding Cara's death very seriously.

We heard about murders in America all the time: kids going on rampages through their schools with guns from their dads' personal arsenals, beheadings on the subway and pseudo-political assassination attempts. It was old news.

A few die-hards in the media argued that the handprint was weird enough to hint at something supernatural, but the British are born sceptical. As a nation, we were having none of it. It had to be a hoax.

As far as I was concerned, Cara was barely a blip on my radar. I did my job, got paid and lived my life. I didn't care enough to keep up with the news. That's why I was stupid enough to find myself walking home from work in the early hours of Friday morning after my shift at Parker's. I knew it wasn't a clever thing to do in any circumstances, but I was strapped for cash and it was difficult to track down a licensed black cab after last call on a Thursday evening, the capital's big drinking night. A lot of the city workers left London on Friday afternoons to spend the weekend at their country homes, so Thursday was the night for socialising.

All told, I was safer walking than taking my chances in an unlicensed taxi.

Jeff tried to dissuade me from walking on my own, but I insisted. He was forced to relent or risk implying I was unable to take care of myself, an error he knew I would be slow to forgive.

Jeff was a big guy and he was incredibly protective. He had a kind face: all boyish charm, soft lines and big brown eyes. He must have been about forty five, but he treated all of his staff like they were his wayward children. He gave us hell when we stepped out of line, but in a strange way I think he loved us. He looked out for us, his odd little family.

There were just ten of us and I was the newest addition, which was strange for a city club. Usually staff churn is insanely high in the nightlife industry, even more so in central London. I think it worked so well because each of us was, in our own way, looking for a new family; one that worked, even if it was a bit dysfunctional at times. Jeff glued us together, kept us loyal and kept us safe.

Usually.

By the time I hit the road that night, the bankers and lawyers had already cleared out of the Square Mile, back to their overpriced, concierge-guarded, managed flats on the river. It was the end of July and the city was already quieter than normal because everyone was on holiday. The Courts had practically shut down for the summer and anyone who could afford to do so was avoiding central London like the plague.

It was just as well in the circumstances.

I pulled my hair up off my neck in deference to the heat

and shucked my handbag onto my shoulder. I was wearing my normal summer work outfit: black shorts and a white cotton short-sleeved T-shirt with "Parker's" embroidered over the left breast, but I had changed out of my black flats in preference for some knee-high, flat, chunky-soled boots. They were soft black leather and much more comfortable for the distance I was going; definitely boots made for walking. I threw my redundant black leather jacket into my shoulder bag and set out from St Paul's.

My boots thudded quietly into the pavement. The street was completely empty. The odd cab rumbled past me through the night, but there was not a person to be seen in the road.

After the crush of the club, I relished the peace. I tipped my head back as a light breeze rushed down the street, bringing some brief respite from the heat. The darkness wrapped around me, blurring the edges of the world in the soft streetlight. The atmosphere was heavy with the lingering scent of hot tarmac and car exhaust.

As I walked towards one of the entrances to the underground station, a wave of fetid air washed across my face, making me glad that taking a tube at this hour of night wasn't an option. In night-time heat like this, I couldn't think of anything worse than plunging into the dark, sulphurous cocoon of the London underground.

I had taken the tube into work earlier that afternoon and as a result had arrived for my shift feeling like I'd been rolling in a skip. It hadn't helped that the carriage had been so packed that I had spent the journey with my face being intermittently pressed into some guy's armpit. I silently vowed to myself that I would walk into work until the heat wave broke.

I fumbled in my handbag for my iPod as I walked past the covered stairwell leading down into the underground. A noise from the bottom of the stairs caught my attention; a rustling followed by a couple of sharp thuds, then silence.

Strangely, the lights in the stairwell were off. The subway lights were never usually off when I left work. I wasn't sure they ever actually got turned off. I glanced down into the darkness then hurried onwards, telling myself it was just a tramp settling into his corner for the night, but feeling a bit on edge nevertheless.

I walked another hundred yards or so at a quick march, noticing with some trepidation that the pavements on the road ahead of me were both covered with scaffolding, making the walkways into painted plywood tunnels roofed with planks.

I glanced over my shoulder and, having reassured myself that I was alone on the street, I crossed over a silent T-junction and stepped into the long tunnel on the right hand side of the road. I relaxed as the tunnel encircled me in the scent of fresh paint and bathed me in warm, orange light from the lamps hanging above my head.

Chastising myself for being unnecessarily jumpy, I resolutely plugged my headphones into my ears, cranking up the volume on my favourite night-time playlist. The tunnel ran the length of the road to the next junction, about two hundred yards in total.

The storefronts to my right were interrupted regularly with small, winding alleyways leading back to ancient buildings. I glanced down one as I walked past, wondering what lay at its end. Although I'd been here for months, I still hadn't taken the opportunity to explore London and its idiosyncratic geography as much as I would have liked.

As I turned my gaze back to the pavement in front of me, I thought I caught a movement down the alley out of the corner of my eye. I stopped to look and realised it was just an urban fox, bolting away from me down the narrow passageway. Feeling guilty for disturbing his night-time foraging, I realised one of his companions was likely the cause of the noise in the subway.

I felt foolish for not connecting the dots earlier.

Relieved, I turned back to continue my way along the tunnel and stopped dead. A couple of the overhead lamps were out, but I could still make out a motionless, tall figure at the end of the tunnel. It was silhouetted against the streetlamp at the next junction.

Something felt off about it. The skin on the back of my neck prickled.

It simply stood there, immobile, blocking my way. There was something very wrong here, but I couldn't put my finger on it. I thought about calling out to it, but I would feel stupid if I created a scene over nothing.

Keeping my eyes on the end of the tunnel, I yanked the headphones from my ears and stuffed them into my bag. Heart pounding, I looked behind me and saw another figure blocking the way I had come. This figure was better illuminated than the first: she was a petite woman, slightly stooped, with dirt on her hands. Her shoulder-length hair seemed to be damp and was plastered to her face and head in places.

Panic surged through me, sending my heartbeat into overdrive. If someone wanted to attack me, I couldn't think of a better place. I was trapped.

I noticed an odd smell and I turned back to the alleyway. With a sinking feeling in the pit of my stomach, I realised the fox hadn't been running from me. I should've guessed. London foxes aren't timid; it would take something pretty terrifying to scare them away from their food.

It hadn't been me. It had been this third figure: the nightmare in front of me.

He was barely ten feet away, but I hadn't even heard him approaching. I'm five foot eight, but he was nearly a clear foot taller than me, a giant. His gaunt face loomed over me, with sunken eyes that were set too far apart in his head. He had gangly limbs and he was filthy from head to toe with dusty grime, but that wasn't why I was glued to the spot with terror.

His canine teeth were sharpened into points and his mouth was rimmed with blood. I would have thought he was on his way to a costume party were it not for his eyes. They drilled into mine, his pupils completely dilated, but it was the whites of his eyes that took me aback. They weren't white. They were so bloodshot they were mostly red, and they spilled crimson tears down his cheeks.

He stared fiercely at me, but his expression was slack and vacant. As he raised his hands towards me I saw that his fingernails were torn and that his arms were streaked with gore, ragged and bloodied. He reached for me, leaning his body closer, and exhaled, flooding the air with the odour of putrescence and earth.

I just stood there immobile and blinked at him.

This couldn't be real.

I was in a dream, unable to move my feet to run away and unable to open my mouth to scream: utterly impotent.

There was a thump on the scaffolding boards above me and I jumped with shock at the sudden noise.

The supports creaked and the wood splintered, sending a cloud of sawdust down onto me and my assailant. It snapped me out of the horror that had frozen me and I recoiled from the bloodied man, hurling my body hard into the plywood barrier separating us from the street. As I did so, I looked up to see hands groping through the gap in the scaffolding boards above us, levering the slats away.

It wasn't distracting the bloodied man and his friends. The first figure and the small woman had moved closer as they walked along the tunnel of the pavement towards us.

As the first figure drew closer, I saw that he was just a boy, a gangly teenager wearing a band T-shirt, Converse trainers and ripped jeans. He was so young that the woman could have been his mother.

They moved slowly in an oddly stilted, but determined, fashion. They reminded me of zombies.

I instantly regretted the mental association.

This was unreal.

"What do you want?" I croaked out.

All three simply continued staring at me as they moved silently forwards. It wasn't much consolation, but at least none of them had said "brains".

The bloodied man was quickly closing the gap and I glanced around me, desperately trying to identify something I could use as a weapon. I could accept that I probably wasn't going to be able to get out of this situation in one piece, but I'd be damned if I wasn't going to go down fighting.

Unfortunately, the tunnel was completely uncluttered. My handbag held only the essentials (keys, phone, wallet), my work shoes, my jacket and the normal handbag detritus that seems to accumulate on its own.

I looked desperately at the lamps lighting the roof of the tunnel and saw that the gap in the scaffolding planks was swiftly becoming large enough to admit a person. Any second I'd have more down on me from above, so the time to act was now.

I decided quickly that my best chance of escape was to run at the woman who had blocked the way I had come. I could then run back to Parker's and to Jeff.

I set my jaw and ducked as the bloodied man swiped a heavy arm across where my head had been. As he regained his balance, I leapt up and grabbed the trailing power cord supplying the lanterns above my head, ripping it down as I fell back to the ground. I hoped that the darkness would disorient them enough to allow me to overpower the small woman and make a clean getaway.

The lights went out, plunging the tunnel into darkness. My adrenaline spiked. I turned and made to run, when something grabbed me under the arms and yanked me upwards. The bloodied man's friends had finally made their way through the scaffolding boards.

I screamed and struggled, kicking my legs in my desperation to escape, but to no avail. I was lifted off my feet and upwards, out of the darkness of the tunnel and into the night air of the city, the light pollution hazing in the sky around me. I clawed frantically at the wood circling the hole in the scaffolding planks, trying to pull myself away from my assailant, but I couldn't even get a grip on the edge.

I was pulled relentlessly backwards out of the hole and onto the scaffolding walkway, my bag falling off my shoulder onto the boards beside me.

Once my legs were clear, someone wrapped their arms

around me from behind and held me firmly in a seated position on the boards. I started to struggle to release my arms, wriggling my shoulders from side to side in an effort to slide free, but there was no give at all.

A scent surrounded me, but it was startlingly different from the dirty, putrescent smell of the creatures down on the pavement. It was a rich smell of leather and wood, with an undertone of what might have been motor oil. The comforting, masculine scent calmed me as I breathed it in.

"Shh," said a male voice close to my ear. "If you're quiet, they'll forget you're up here and they'll leave. Short attention spans."

I went dead still.

The voice was warm and deep, rumbling and rich in tone. I was reassured by the fact that my assailant (or perhaps rescuer?) was capable of human speech. The monsters down in the alley didn't look like they could string a sentence together, and this guy had just said two in a row. At least that meant he couldn't be one of the zombies, I supposed.

"What the hell are they," I whispered, "and who the hell are you, for that matter?"

"Do be quiet, love," he said, securing his right hand across my mouth.

I fought my instincts to hit out at this guy and tell him I wasn't his "love", but I decided instead to sit quietly and listen to his advice. After all, he had just saved me from whomever or whatever those things were. We could quibble about presumptuous endearments later.

We sat in silence for five minutes or more, me sitting with my legs stretched out in front of me and he crouching behind me, pressed up against my back with one arm around my body. I felt my breath condensing on his fingers where he held them over my mouth and, as I stopped struggling, he removed his hand from my face.

We listened to the gentle shuffling search being conducted below us while I tried to calm my racing heart by concentrating on the rising and falling of the man's chest behind me. As he strained to listen to the movement in the tunnel beneath us, he leaned forward and stretched his head over my right shoulder. His breath rushed quietly past my ear in a steady stream of warmth, his hair tickling across my right cheek.

He was breathing slowly, his body moving in a soft rhythm that I tried to match with my own. His grip around my body softened as I relaxed, his left hand trailing across my stomach before coming to rest on my left arm. I breathed in the scent of him, starting to forget about the horrors beneath us as I fell back into the peace of my rescuer's embrace.

I told myself that just because he had saved me from those things it didn't mean he was worth trusting, but I felt safe enough with him. Besides, I didn't have much choice for now.

The silence of the city surrounded us as the breeze chased dust along the boards.

After what seemed like an age, he pulled his head back and released me, moving his body away from where it had been pressed against me. The sudden removal of his warmth from my back sent a shiver down my spine and I realised that, despite the heat of the night, I was freezing cold.

"They've gone," he said.

I breathed a sigh of relief, but anxiety continued to spike in my stomach. What the hell were they? My head was spinning and I didn't feel able to get to my feet just yet.

"So will you answer my questions now?" I asked cautiously, looking at him over my shoulder.

He stepped back into the shadow of the building supporting the scaffolding on which we were perched. He was standing in darkness, but he was tall and looked strong. I guessed he must have been to lift me from the tunnel on his own; I am not a petite woman.

"I guess you didn't catch the news this evening, then?"

"No, I've been at work since six," I said uncertainly, not sure where this was taking us.

What had I missed? Had there been some sort of epidemic?

"I'm not going to try to explain it to you here. We need to get you somewhere safe, and we need to do it fast. The streets are only going to get worse."

As he spoke, his attention was caught by something across the road and he stepped forward to the edge of the scaffolding to stare down over the barrier. The streetlamps from the junction caught his face and I got the first clear glimpse of my rescuer.

He was handsome in a rugged sort of way. His hair was dark and straight, mid-length, falling just below his ears at the front in a messy side parting. His jaw-line was strong and would have made him intimidating, but his brow was gentle and large eyes gave his face an open, approachable impression. He clearly hadn't shaved for a while as a dark shadow of stubble covered his cheeks.

He set his jaw and pressed his lips together, anxiety filling his expression.

"We're too late," he said. "They're already multiplying. We've got to get you out of here."

I stood up and moved to stand to the left of him at the edge of the scaffolding.

In the street below us, more shambling figures were appearing. They were joined by the teenager from the tunnel. They didn't seem to have a common purpose; they were just walking the streets in any direction that seemed to take their fancy. As they stepped into the light cast by the streetlamps I saw that each of their faces was streaming with bloody tears. These, then, were the same sort of creatures as the bloodied man.

As we watched, the bloodied man himself shuffled from the tunnel to our left with the small woman by his side. They walked off down different streets in the general direction of St Paul's.

I turned to face my rescuer as he followed the bloodied man's progress down the road. His face was turned towards me so I was afforded the chance to study it in more detail.

I didn't understand what I was seeing and I was unsure of

16

the evidence of my own eyes.

His irises were a shocking, emerald shade of green, but where you would normally expect to see the faint lines of blood vessels, the whites of his eyes were threaded with silver. They shone like silk in the lamplight. As I watched, the silver flowed into his irises in tiny strands of gossamer, surrounding his pupils in a shining halo.

I gasped and stepped away from him in alarm.

"Your eyes…," I said, my mouth opening in amazement.

Where the eyes of the creatures below us were lined in blood, his were lined in silver. His brow furrowed and he touched his fingers to the corner of his right eye, confusion spreading across his face.

"What…," he breathed, looking off to one side, as if he were speaking only to himself.

He looked shocked and slightly horrified. It wasn't very reassuring, but as he registered my expression he raised his hands towards me in a placating gesture.

"Look," he said gently, "just calm down."

"You're like them, your eyes, they're… wrong."

My feet were putting distance between us, but I found myself leaning back towards him to watch. It was mesmerising.

"But I'm not one of them," he said as he stepped slowly towards me. "I'm trying to help you."

I started to move back towards the hole in the floor through which he had dragged me. I wasn't sure whether I'd be better off trying to escape back the way I had come, or perhaps through the alleyway below us. As I was debating this in my head, the man held out his hand, but I moved away, backing up further towards the hole.

He shook his head at me and rolled his eyes.

"Come on, you stupid human! You're going to get yourself killed," the man hissed in exasperation.

I stopped, open-mouthed.

"What do you mean, 'human'?"

He sighed.

"Please calm down," he said softly with some effort, speaking through gritted teeth. "I'm not going to hurt you. I'm trying to help you. Please. I need you to trust me."

I paused again.

This guy had just saved my life. I examined him critically as he stood in front of me.

He didn't seem like he was dangerous. Well, he actually looked pretty fierce in his khakis and leather jacket, and I was pretty sure that was a knife slung on his belt, but I didn't feel that he presented a danger to me. Besides, what choice did I have? I wasn't going to be able to make it home on my own with the bloodied man and his friends thronging in the street below.

"Answer my questions, then we'll see," I said, folding my arms and leaning up against the building next to us. "Who are you and what are they?"

He sighed and mirrored my pose, leaning up against the edge of the scaffolding opposite me.

"My name is Andrew," he said, "Drew for short, and we call those 'Weepers', for obvious reasons. They... well, they eat people."

I made a face. Man-eating monsters on the loose in London.

"I'm Emilia," I said. "You haven't really answered either of my questions, though."

"I know, but it will have to do for now. Will you let me get you somewhere safe? Then there's something you need to see that will explain everything."

I hesitated.

"Emilia," he said, "I promise you that I'll keep you safe. I know you don't know me, but without my help the Weepers will kill you before you get fifty yards from here."

I believed him. I might be able to fight off one, but with the numbers of the creatures that seemed to be gathering in the streets I'd be dead in minutes.

Left with no other option that seemed viable, I reluctantly agreed.

"Fine," I huffed, "but if you try to eat me there'll be trouble. I once kicked a guy in the nuts so hard he needed surgery. I assume that, whatever you are, you still have the same vulnerabilities as normal men?"

"Don't worry," he chuckled. "I'm the same as any human male in that respect."

I eyed him suspiciously as I collected my handbag and let him lead me along the scaffolding to where it ended at the next junction.

"I've got a place near here," he said. "It's completely secure. You'll be safe there if we can just navigate the next few streets."

"What do you mean 'you've got a place near here'?" I asked, flabbergasted. "We're in the square mile. No one lives in the square mile."

I paused.

"Unless you're a zillionaire connected up the wazoo, that is."

He looked over his shoulder at me, raised his eyebrow and shot me a cheeky grin.

"You're shitting me," I muttered.

"Just keep quiet and follow me."

CHAPTER II

We arrived at Drew's place a few minutes later. It was down one of the small alleys that ran between the storefronts on the next street.

With his help, I managed to climb back down from the scaffolding and slip unobtrusively into the next street without catching the attention of three Weepers who were walking around at the road junction. I breathed a sigh of relief as we turned into the empty, dead-end alley and headed for a door set at its end.

He unlocked it and let us into an old, narrow stairwell that wound up for ten stories above us. It was a strange building, an odd fusion of ancient and modern architecture that teamed stained wooden beams with stainless steel and glass. Walking up through the floors I felt like I was walking through time as the building style changed around me. I wasn't sure I liked it, but I was intrigued.

I reached the top of the stairs out of breath and exhausted. Drew, who seemed untroubled by the climb, unlocked the door at the top and let us into a penthouse apartment.

The door let into an open plan living area with a kitchen and dining area at the end farthest away from us and sofas at the other. It was a large space with huge glass windows running its length. Beyond the dining area, a corridor led away to what I supposed must be the bedrooms.

The kitchen was pretty high tech, but the seating area looked cosy and well-loved, like it had been chosen for comfort and not appearance. The whole place was neat and tidy, but there were bookcases everywhere and it felt pleasantly lived-in. It was not what I had expected at all.

"Wow," I said, slightly lost for words.

Who was this guy?

Drew smiled, took my bag from my shoulder and extracted my jacket, hanging both on a hook next to the door.

"You'd better stay here tonight," he said. "The Weepers are only going to multiply overnight."

Then he shrugged out of his own leather jacket and hung it next to mine.

His and hers. Nice.

I mentally shook myself and tried to focus.

Yes, he was pretty hot, but now was not the time. Besides, I didn't even know what he was, much less who he was.

He strode over to the seating area and sat on one of the sofas. He picked up the remote control for the flat screen fixed to the wall and began channel hopping. The same thing was showing on each channel: an impossibly handsome, blonde-haired man speaking into the camera. Each channel seemed to be showing a different point in the broadcast.

"It's on a loop," Drew said, settling on a channel when he found one at the beginning of the programme.

"Just watch this," he continued, "it'll explain everything. After that, you can ask me anything you want. Just please believe me when I say I want to help."

Looking over at me, he raised an eyebrow and indicated the space next to him. Not wanting to encourage over-familiarity before I knew I could trust him, and slightly concerned that if I wasn't careful I might find myself forming unhealthy attachments, I took the armchair instead. There was enough crazy stuff going on at the moment. I could do without adding Stockholm Syndrome to my list of worries.

The corner of his mouth quirked up and then down again so quickly I wasn't sure I had really seen it. I was apparently amusing him.

The screen filled with the face of the handsome man. He was wearing a suit jacket and a shirt open at the collar. His golden hair was cut short at the sides and lay in loose curls on the top of his head. His cheekbones could have been chiselled from marble and his mouth was tipped into a slight smile. He had full lips and beautiful, piercing blue eyes.

Then I saw it: the whites of his eyes were threaded with silver, just like Drew's.

My eyes darted over towards him where he sat on the sofa to my right.

He met my gaze and nodded towards the screen.

"My name," the beautiful man said, "is Solomon. I am not like you. I am different: stronger, older, faster, better."

His voice was melodic and clear, but it lacked the warmth of Drew's rumbling tones.

"I and my kind have been living alongside you for many years, building our strength and numbers and securing our positions in your society. It is time for us to come out of obscurity.

"Many of you will have seen the creatures we call Weepers gathering and multiplying in the streets of your cities. They have forced our hand. They are a scourge that only our kind can contain. We will protect your country from the threat they present and build a new world from the ruins they will leave behind them.

"We will give you every necessity: healthcare, safe accommodation and food. We will protect you from the Weepers. In return, all you will have to do is perform the job assigned to you and provide monthly blood donations. This is the bargain between our races.

"I regret the circumstances that have made this action necessary, but this bargain will be our mutual salvation. If we are unable to work together, both of our races will perish, you at the hands of the Weepers and us from starvation.

"This reciprocity will found a stronger society, you dependent on us for protection and us dependent on you for sustenance, as the cattle and the farmer each depend on the other. I am afraid that it is the only way your race will survive."

I watched the beautiful Solomon in shock as he outlined his plans for the subjugation of the human race. Cattle?

This wasn't a bargain. This wasn't reciprocity. It was slavery.

"Your population has been more than decimated," he continued on the screen, "and there is a great deal of work to be accomplished in a short time to ensure your continued survival. Effective immediately, the governance of this country will fall to me as Primus of our people in England. If you will submit to our rule then we will keep you safe.

"In each town and city across the country, our people are establishing safe houses to receive you. At nine o'clock in the morning, each of you should go to your local safe house to receive sanctuary. Further instructions for each town and city will follow by regional broadcast at eight o'clock."

I turned to Drew in horror.

"Is this for real?" I asked him quietly.

He nodded at me, pressing his lips together with a grimace.

On the screen, the camera panned back from Solomon's face to show the room in which he was sitting. What was apparently the remainder of our former government sat at a table to his left. On either side of him, standing slightly behind him, were two imposing men who loomed over him like bodyguards.

The man on the left had short, brown hair pushed back up off his forehead and he looked like he'd taken a bunch of steroids. He was dressed in khakis and a long-sleeved T-shirt that was straining at the seams.

In disbelief, I recognised the man on the right of Solomon. I could do nothing but sit staring at the screen as the picture faded to black and the broadcast began to replay from the beginning.

"You?" I whispered quietly, watching as Solomon repeated his words.

"Yes," Drew said sadly, "me. It was recorded earlier this evening."

"And what exactly are you?" I asked him.

The dam broke and a tear slid down my cheek. I dashed it away in irritation, furious that my body was betraying me by showing weakness in front of this… whatever he was.

"I think you've worked it out, haven't you?" he asked me in a soft voice. "Like the Weepers, we feed on humans. Unlike the Weepers, we're civilised and not completely devoid of what you call 'humanity'. Whatever name humans give to us, to ourselves we're the Silver. We've hidden for many years, but it's been decided that now is our time."

"I see," I said, not seeing at all.

It was too much.

I just wanted to curl up into a ball, wake up tomorrow and have this all be over. It couldn't be real. It just couldn't. I looked at Drew mournfully.

When I spoke my voice was quiet and toneless. I was exhausted and I was beaten. I had escaped from one impossible enemy straight into the arms of another.

"What about me?" I asked him. "Am I just a midnight snack?"

His forehead creased in concern.

"That's not how it's going to work, Emilia. It's not like that at all. I want to help."

The arrogant little shit.

I couldn't believe he was sitting there telling me he was going to help me when he and all his race were preparing to serve us up as lunch. Just like that, I was livid.

"You want to help?" I jumped to my feet, shouting at him. "By eating people?"

There was a sound like a piece of fabric being ripped in two and the breath was knocked out of me.

In a fraction of a second, Drew had pushed me up against the wall of the sitting room, holding me suspended off the ground by my shoulders. My breath was coming quick and ragged and I began to regret taking my temper out on a creature clearly so much stronger than me.

Drew leaned into me, flattening his body against mine and meeting me eye to eye. His earthy scent of forests and leather filled my head, washing over me and setting light to something in my nerves.

I thrilled with fear and excitement, the two warring in my body for attention.

"Is that what you think I want, Emilia?" he whispered to me. "You think I saved your life just to make a meal of you?"

He leaned forward so his lips were just fractions of an inch away from mine, looking into my eyes as his emerald irises dilated to black.

I breathed him in, staring back at him wide-eyed as my breath caught. My eyes widened in horror as Drew lowered his face to my neck, running his cheek along mine as he did so. I felt my heartbeat in my throat and was filled with the sudden certainty that he could hear its thud.

He was going to bite me. He was going to sink his teeth into my flesh.

I tried to move, but I was pinned so securely to the wall by Drew's hands that I was going nowhere. I tipped my head back and away as his hair brushed against my neck, desperately trying to escape the reach of his teeth.

Then, incongruously, I felt the rumble of a gentle chuckle rising in his chest as he pressed against me.

"You think I'd bite you?" he whispered quietly, his breath warming my skin. "I wouldn't ever hurt you, Emilia. I promise you that."

As he said this, I felt his lips touch my throat in a kiss.

I froze in surprise.

He leaned backwards, arching his back so his chest separated from mine, and looked into my eyes.

"This isn't about your blood," he said, "though that experience can be fun. For both of us," he added, with the same cheeky grin he'd flashed me back on the scaffolding.

To my amazement, he released my shoulders, gently dropping me to the ground. He raised his hand casually to my face and brushed a loose strand of my hair behind my ear.

I didn't know what to say.

"I don't understand," I said with complete honesty. "What are you doing?"

"Do you have to understand?" he asked with a slight edge of desperation in his tone as he leaned into me again, pinning me against the wall with the weight of his body.

I put my hands on his chest and tried ineffectively to push him away.

"Do you really want me to stop?" he asked quietly, his breath tickling the fine hairs around my ear.

I paused, twisting my hands in his T-shirt, drawing in his scent as the electricity sizzled between us. Then his mouth was back at my neck, trailing kisses slowly and tantalisingly down to my collar bone. It felt wonderful.

Before I knew what I was doing, I ran my right hand up his neck and into his hair, intertwining my fingers with its dark strands. I writhed against him, twisting my hips beneath his weight, and he moaned into my neck.

I snapped back to reality. This was a truly awful idea.

"Drew…," I said, putting my hands back on his chest again to hold him back.

"Shut up, Emilia," he responded, curling his left hand around the back of my neck as he trailed kisses ever closer to my mouth.

"Get off me!" I shouted at him.

He let me push him away from me. I was flustered and upset. The last thing I needed was more complications.

"I'm not a toy you can pick up and play with until you're bored," I yelled. "I won't be your momentary distraction while there's nothing better to do. I may just be a human to you, but I'm not going to be your plaything."

"It's not like that…" he replied, but I cut him off.

I didn't want to hear his explanations. Maybe he got off on danger, or maybe he just fancied a quick tumble since we'd already watched the only thing that was on TV. Whatever the reason, I needed to keep things simple.

If I was being honest with myself, I was a bit freaked out at how much I had wanted him to carry on, and at how much I missed that intimacy now it was gone.

"I'm grateful that you saved my life," I said, "so thanks for that and all, but I've had a confusing enough night as it is and sleeping with the enemy is definitely not on my to do list."

To my enduring satisfaction, Drew looked a bit ashamed. He glanced down at his feet before looking back into my eyes.

He really was breathtakingly handsome. He was looking at me with regret in his eyes, contrite and apologetic. Guilt prickled in my chest.

"I'm sorry, Emilia. That was… inappropriate of me."

It had been, but part of me regretted stopping him when I did. This hardly seemed the time for propriety. It felt like the end of the world and if that was the case why not go out with a bang?

"Let me get you set up in one of the spare rooms," he continued. "We can talk in the morning."

He grabbed my handbag and led me through the corridor at the back of the penthouse to a surprisingly cosy spare room with a double bed and an en suite bathroom.

"There are clean towels in the bathroom if you want to wash up. I'll be just down the corridor if you need me."

I nodded gratefully. I couldn't think of anything I wanted more right now than to get clean.

"Look," he said to me as he made to leave, "you should know that not all the Silver are like me. I'm relatively… modern. The others can be a bit more old-fashioned, often cruel. None of this is going to be easy, but please believe me when I say I'm here to help you. To do that, I need you to be careful what you say and who you say it to."

Drew took a step back into the room, reaching out towards my face with an inquiring look.

I nodded my acquiescence: he could touch me.

He took another step forward and cradled my face in his

hands.

"But you can say anything to me, Emilia. I mean that. I'm going to get you through this. I'll look out for you."

Now I was even more puzzled.

"Why would you do that? Seriously, we just met."

Drew looked frustrated, shook his head, then sighed and pulled me into his arms.

"Just know I'm here. I'll always be here."

"Is this one of those 'I saved your life and am now responsible for it' things?"

"If you like," he replied with a smile.

"I still have so many questions…"

"Tomorrow," he breathed into my hair.

He kissed my forehead, almost tenderly, then left the room without a second glance, shutting the door behind him.

Today was turning into a complete headfuck.

CHAPTER III

I stayed standing where Drew had left me until I heard a door open and close further along the corridor, then fumbled frantically in my bag for my phone. I had to call the club, to check that everyone was okay. My heart sank as I checked the display.

No signal.

Looking around the room, I spotted an old-fashioned handset on the bedside table. With a premonition of disappointment, I picked up the receiver to a dead tone. The line was out. I'd just have to hope that everyone had already seen the broadcast and had got themselves to safety.

I walked into the bathroom to try to clean myself up a bit before I got into the bed, locking the door behind me, just in case. The bathroom was clean and neat, a small, bright space with a mirror running the length of one side above the basin and a deep bath with a shower suspended over it on the other.

I removed my boots then pulled off my T-shirt and shorts so I could give myself a quick once-over in the mirror. Barring a few bruises and scrapes from where Drew had hauled me out of the tunnel, I was in one piece. Physically, at least. Unfortunately, I was covered in grime where the dust from the scaffolding had glued itself to my legs. There was no way

I was going to embarrass myself by tracking that into the bed.

There were clean towels set out on a rail next to the tub, so I got the shower running, hoping the sound wouldn't disturb Drew. It was some ridiculous hour of the morning and I was exhausted, but all I wanted right now was to wash the day away before I dropped into bed.

I stepped into the tub and the hot water blasted my skin, strong and soothing. There was nothing for it; I was going to have to wash my filthy hair as well. I hadn't felt clean all day and I was damned if I was going to pass up what might be my last opportunity to wash my hair in a proper hot shower. Who knew what tomorrow would bring?

I felt that Solomon's broadcast this evening had been a little… misleading. As I poured shampoo into my hand and lathered it gratefully into my hair, I thought about everything he hadn't told us. He hadn't even named his people. He talked about blood donation and labour. He talked about strength and age. He himself was beautiful, but with a cool aloofness that had a certain otherness about it. He hadn't said the word in all our minds: vampire.

I wasn't sure what terrified me more, the Silver or the Weepers. To me, the new world order sounded like slavery by another name. A subordinate race, 'cattle' for the Silver's glasses. And then there was Drew and his pledge to protect me. Yes, he had saved me from the Weepers, but that was exactly what Solomon was also offering. For a price.

The 'bargain', he had called it. Where did Drew fit into this bargain? What was his place? He had been kind to me. He had looked at me with such intensity as he vowed to protect me and then, when I thought he was attacking me for my blood, it turned out he had something entirely different in mind. How could I even hope to process that?

He wasn't even human. He had stood by Solomon's side as he made his decree. I realised with a sinking heart that he was a part of this as much as Solomon was. And I was trapped in a tenth-floor penthouse with him, with the Weepers gathering in the streets outside.

I gasped to myself and had a small panic attack, my heart rate soaring as I broke into a sweat. I focussed on the heat from the shower and soon my breathing returned to normal, but I couldn't stop the tears. This was a nightmare. The end of humanity. The end of everything.

Pulling myself together, I quickly finished washing the dirt from my body and stepped out of the shower, grabbing a towel from the rail as I did so. I couldn't think of a way this was going to end well. I dried down quickly then put on a towelling bathrobe I found on the back of the bathroom door. It would have to do; I had nothing else to sleep in and I couldn't face putting my filthy clothes back on.

I opened the bathroom door and came face-to-face with Drew.

I let out a cry of surprise and stepped back, grazing my right arm against the catch of the bathroom door.

"Shit, I'm sorry, I heard... I just wanted to check you were alright..." he said, reaching towards me.

I took another step backwards and raised my hands up in front of me to tell him to stay where he was. I needed some space. As I lifted my arms a trickle of something ran down to my right elbow from my forearm and I looked down to see that I was bleeding where I had grazed myself on the door. It was a pretty big gash, but it wasn't particularly painful.

"Dammit," I said, rolling up the arm of the bathrobe so it didn't get stained.

He might be a vampire, but that was no excuse for trashing his stuff.

I took a breath and went dead still.

Vampire. Blood.

Oh shit. This was not my day.

I looked up to see Drew assessing me from the doorway of the bathroom, pupils dilated and nostrils flaring at the scent of the blood. He took a step towards me and slammed the bathroom door behind him. I jumped then carried on stepping backwards until I was pressed against the towel rail. He looked hungry and wild, his eyes flashing with urgency.

I was dead, I thought. This is the end. Bleeding in front of a vampire: clever move, Emmy. Shit.

The corner of his mouth quirked up into a smile and the small room filled with the gentle, earthy sound of his chuckle.

"What do I have to do to prove to you I'm not going to hurt you, Emilia?"

I looked at him quizzically as he took my right hand gently, pressing his body into mine. This guy had serious issues with invading my personal space. I tried to jerk away from him, but I was trapped against the towel rail.

"Shh," he said, fixing me with his big, dark eyes, "just let me see it."

He raised my arm to his face and his nostrils flared again. Here we go, I thought. I closed my eyes and waited to feel his teeth sink into my arm.

Instead, I felt his right hand slide around my waist and pull me into him as he pressed his lips to my forehead.

"Please, Emilia. Just trust me. I won't hurt you, but I can make it better."

I blinked up at him in surprise. As he gazed down at me, his emerald irises suffused with silver again as they had on the scaffolding in the city. Or maybe I only noticed it when I was this close to him. I only had a glimpse before his eyes dilated black, swallowing up the colour of his irises together with their glinting highlights.

Raising my right arm to his face, he looked down as he gently ran his tongue along the cut on my arm.

"You're getting nothing out of this, I suppose," I said, making an inane joke to try to hide my discomfort with the situation.

As he continued to clean the blood from my arm, his tongue gently rasping along my skin, he looked up into my eyes and I felt a thrill rush through me. Dear God, this was twisted. This should not be an enjoyable experience. I felt the blood rush to my face and my pulse began to thud in my veins as he held me close, my chest rising against his.

He released me abruptly and stepped back, putting his

hands on my shoulders to hold me at a distance.

"Enough. It is healed," he said roughly, his eyes glittering in the soft overhead lighting of the bathroom.

I didn't know what to say. I stood and gawped at him while my pulse returned to its normal speed and the blood drained from my face. He took his hands from my shoulders and turned to leave the room.

"Wait a second," I said, channelling my frustration and embarrassment into fury, "what the hell was that?"

"I healed your arm," he said, turning back to me and nodding to indicate my injury.

"What's wrong with a band-aid? Did you have to clean it with your tongue?" I said in an affronted tone of voice, trying to pretend that I hadn't enjoyed it.

Sadly, Drew was fairly astute. The wry smile returned to his face.

"It's a Silver band-aid, Emilia. Look at it."

I saw that the edges of the wound were drawn and held together with what looked like a filament of metal. The skin around the wound glinted like it was suffused with mercury. Not for the first time today, I was speechless. I gaped at Drew.

"It's a Silver thing," he said in answer to my silent question. "It's a gift."

"Cara Alton," I said on a whisper.

I couldn't believe it. My arm was shining where Drew had run his tongue over my skin. The mercury handprint was where Cara had been touched by a Silver.

Drew hung his head and sighed.

"Yes," he replied, "Cara Alton."

"Was that a gift?"

"No," he said, turning his head to the side, "that was a tragedy."

His face was full of sorrow and regret. He turned back and looked me in the eye like he meant it. There was a strange intensity to his gaze, like he was trying to make me understand something he wasn't willing to tell me.

He seemed to be taking Cara personally. I made another unwanted mental connection.

Oh no.

"Did you… was it…," I stuttered, looking at the floor as I tried to push through my fear to ask what I needed to know.

I ran my fingers into my damp hair, pushing it away from my face, and met his gaze.

"Was it you? You and Cara? Am I… is it… will this kill me?" I asked desperately, indicating my healed arm.

Drew's jaw dropped. He looked horrified.

"No! God. No. I would never… and I never even met Cara. Look, I can't explain it, but what happened to Cara, it was an accident. I promise you. I can't tell you that the Silver don't kill people, because we do. But Cara…," he stared off over my shoulder into nothing. "It shouldn't have happened like that."

I didn't find this as reassuring as I think Drew hoped I would. At least, not until I interpreted the expression on his face. It was intense and mournful, dark and broken. What the hell? He stepped towards me, taking my arm in his hands.

"This," he said, stroking his fingers gently across my healed graze, "is a gift. It's precious. It is never a weapon."

He looked at me like he was willing me towards comprehension. I shook my head.

"I just don't understand. There's so much I don't understand."

"I can't explain it, Emilia. I'm sorry."

He spoke quietly, looking away from me.

"I get it," I said, pulling my arm from his grip and tying the bath robe tighter around me. "I'm not one of you."

"No, you're not," Drew said, as a puzzled expression flashed across his face.

"Look," I said, "I'm tired. It's been an insane day, I don't know what's going on and you're clearly not going to tell me. It's too late at night for cryptic. Can you just leave me alone to try to get some sleep?"

He looked almost a little hurt.

"Of course," he replied, stiffly, "I'll leave you to sleep."

He turned and walked out of the bathroom, leaving the door open behind him. I followed into the bedroom. As he opened the door into the corridor, he stopped and looked down at the floor.

"You know I have to take you to the safe house tomorrow?"

Ah yes, I thought, as I recalled Solomon's broadcast. They were corralling their cattle.

"I guessed as much. Can't disobey the boss man, huh?"

"You shouldn't talk about him that way, Emilia. He has power over each of us. He decides whether we live or die."

I scoffed at his subservience.

"He's your king, not mine."

"You're wrong," Drew said sadly. "He's the Primus. He holds us all to his will and he always has: Silver, Weeper... and human."

With that, he met my eyes briefly before leaving the room, closing the door quietly behind him.

CHAPTER IV

Friday

I barely slept that night. The bed was incredibly comfortable, but I was alone and scared. The world was changing and I was away from every touchstone I had. I thought of Jeff and Cassie, and my other friends at the bar. Even the man in the memory I was running from, the reason I came to London. All I wanted was something familiar to hold on to, some reassurance to anchor me whilst reality was rebuilt around me.

I was feeling intensely ambivalent about Drew and my thoughts of him hounded me through the night. Part of me wanted to break my way out of the penthouse and take my chances with the Weepers, whilst the other part wanted him here with me, holding me, making me feel safe. Or, at least, not alone. That couldn't be healthy.

I finally dropped off to sleep as the sun crept above the horizon, so I hadn't been out long when there was a rap at the door.

"Time to get up, Emilia," Drew's voice sounded through the door.

I heard his footsteps tapping towards the living area and

swung my legs out of the bed. With regret, I put my grubby work clothes back on and tidied the bedroom and bathroom up as best I could before leaving the room.

"Tea?" Drew asked as I stepped into the kitchen dining area.

"You drink tea?" I asked, incredulously.

"Yes. I thought you might want a cup."

As soon as he said it, he seemed ashamed to have made the offer. He looked away from me and started putting the tea back in a cupboard in the kitchen.

"Tea would be great," I said quickly. "White, no sugar."

I had a feeling today was going to be a shitty day and I could do worse than having Drew on my side to help me through it. He paused for a second then started to make me a mug. Very domestic. I mentally chastised myself and took a seat at the kitchen table.

He finished up the tea and brought me over a huge mug.

"Thank you," I said, wrapping the mug in my hands.

He flashed me a quick smile and took the seat opposite me.

"So," I said, not sure where we went from here.

It was like the morning after from hell, only without alcohol or sexual indiscretion. Well, not much sexual indiscretion. Thinking about it doesn't count, and we hadn't even kissed. I shook my head at myself. Now was not the time to fixate on someone who was, effectively, my captor. I tried not to focus on the fact that he had been my rescuer as well.

"I'm taking you to the safe house in an hour," he said, staring at the tabletop. "There'll be another broadcast, more information. We'll take it from there."

I looked across the table at him.

"You mean I'll be taken from there. Into servitude. For the rest of my life."

"I'm not going to let anything happen to you, Emilia. How many times do I have to say it before you'll believe it?"

He reached across the table and pulled one of my hands

into his own.

"It's the only way we can keep you safe. You won't be a slave. It's not going to be like that. You'll each be assigned a job and given somewhere safe to live. We'll establish a border around a limited area of the city and keep the Weepers out. Life will go on. It will be normal, in time."

I looked at Drew incredulously. Normal. Wow. As if life was ever going to be normal again.

This guy was from another world, a world of superior beings that made me and my fellow humans insignificant, our worth judged only by our ability to sustain our new overlords. I felt like a beetle squashed under his boot, but he couldn't seem to understand what the fuss was about. He really was living in a fantasy land if he thought humanity wasn't about to become enslaved to the Silver. There was no other conceivable outcome.

This was insanity. I drew my hand out of his and stared into my tea.

"Let me get you a clean shirt," he said softly, pushing his chair back from the table and striding away down the corridor to the bedrooms.

He returned a few moments later with a stretchy black T-shirt, which he slung over the back of one of the empty chairs. I left my tea mug where it was and, not daring to meet his eye, took the T-shirt and returned to the bedroom I had recently vacated. The moment the door shut behind me, I started wracking my brain for a plan.

I couldn't live this life. Not again. I'd let myself be caged once before in my life and I was damned if I was going to roll over and let it happen now.

It would have been easier if I wasn't stuck with one of the Silver, then I would only have to find a way to avoid the Weepers and make some sort of break for freedom. As it was, I would have to manage that whilst also evading my Silver escort. How did I get into this situation and how the hell was I going to get out of it?

I stripped off my dirty Parker's T-shirt and eyed it critically.

The back of the shirt was ripped up from where Drew had dragged me through the hole in the scaffolding. Worse still, I saw that there was a smear of blue paint across the shoulders. It must have transferred to me from the fresh paint on the plywood boards lining the tunnel in which I had been attacked last night. Now that I had something else to wear, it was only good for scrap.

Sighing as I realised I might never have the opportunity to replace it, I chucked the Parker's shirt into the rubbish bin in the bathroom.

I shrugged the black T-shirt over my head and quickly checked myself over in the mirror. The T-shirt was too large, but it was serviceable. It must have been skin-tight on Drew.

The mental image was not at all unpleasant. I lifted a handful of the shirt to my face and breathed in the scent of leather and wood. It smelt like him. Hastily pushing myself out of my unwelcome reverie, I gathered up my handbag and returned to the living area.

Drew sized me up as I walked to the front door to collect my leather jacket from the peg.

"It's a bit big," he said, running his eyes up and down my body.

"It'll do," I replied, as monosyllabic as possible.

I needed to put some distance between the two of us, so I was trying not to engage him in conversation. Once I had thrown my leather jacket over my handbag, I stood at the door waiting for him.

He raised an eyebrow at me, sensing something was off.

I was desperate to get out of the sanctuary of the penthouse, back into the real world where I could see him for what he was. It was time for me to leave.

"You're ready to go?" he asked hesitantly.

"Yes. You said you'd take me to the safe house. For the broadcast."

He seemed a little thrown, both by my sudden docility and by my apparent eagerness to throw myself into servitude to the Silver. He clearly smelled a rat. Nevertheless, he walked across to the door and grabbed his jacket from the hook, shrugging into it even though the morning city heat was already verging on intolerable. He opened the door and ushered me out of the room in front of him.

"Things are easier in the daytime," he began.

I realised that we were about to go out into the daylight. Aren't vampires supposed to burst into flames in direct sun? I cast a concerned look over my shoulder at him and immediately regretted it.

"I knew you cared," he chuckled at me.

Damn, I hated that chuckle. Steely-faced, I fixed my eyes on the stairs in front of me and kept moving.

"The sunlight doesn't bother the Silver," he continued, "but it hurts the Weepers' eyes, makes them bleed even more, so they tend to stay under cover during the day. That's why we're moving you all now. I've had a team moving through the subterranean network surrounding the safe house since first light, clearing out the tunnels and blocking them off. We haven't pushed out to our designated final perimeter yet, but we'll do enough today to make sure that the central hub is secure, above and below ground. Nothing's getting near you or the Primus tonight."

"The Primus?" I asked, my curiosity overruling my desire to stonewall Drew.

"Yes, he's here. This is the capital, so this safe house will be his base. I go where he goes." Drew paused, adding in a low voice: "Usually."

That was it. I'd had enough of Mr. Cryptic. I rounded on him, my shoulder bag whirling out behind me as I turned.

"And what does that mean?" I shouted at him. "Are you incapable of having a single, simple conversation without going all Captain Mysterio? I get it: you're unfathomable and complicated. I'm sure all the lady vampires are really impressed by that routine."

The corner of his mouth quirked up and a smug expression flooded his face.

"Ah," he said, "there's my girl."

His chest was shaking with that bloody chuckle again.

"I'm not 'your girl', you arrogant shit."

I turned with a cry of anger and stomped off down the stairs. The man made my blood boil. Apparently I simply amused him. I could feel him smirking behind me all the way down to the ground floor.

I had to shake this guy.

As I reached the bottom of the stairs, Drew put his hand on my arm and stepped in front of me, pulling me behind him as he opened the door. The alley was clear. He closed the door, shutting us back into the stairwell.

"Before we go out there, Emilia, we need to set some ground rules."

He was straight-faced and more serious than I had seen him all morning.

"You have to be careful out there. The safest thing you can do is keep quiet and make yourself unobtrusive. I'm going to have to leave you when the broadcast starts and I'm not going to be able to see you again until you're in the safe house."

I tried to hide my excitement. This was the best news I'd heard since this whole thing started. Here was my chance to get away.

Drew could see my mind had wandered. He reached forward and took my face in his hands, staring at me with those big, silver-lined emeralds. I realised that it must always be there, the silver in the green, like daylight shining through the forest. They were so beautiful. How could something that beautiful be the mark of a killer?

"Please, Emilia. Don't do anything stupid," he said, fixing me with his gaze. "Just stay safe. Don't talk to anyone, don't make yourself noticed and I'll find you when you're in the safe house.

"Today is going to be hard. The other Silver, well… they're going to ask you to do some things you'll probably object to on principle. They'll probably want to take your blood, mark your skin, examine you. I'm begging you to be compliant. If you can just toe the line for today, I can make sure that things get better for you. I can give you a better position in there than most people will have. You just have to give me the chance to help."

He stared desperately at me, willing me to agree. He knew what he was asking. He knew I couldn't give in. I started to shake my head, but he held it steady in his hands.

"Please, Emmy. If you don't sign up with the Silver you'll die. You'll be prey for the Weepers. Don't you see that? This is the only chance we have."

He snapped his tongue and looked away in frustration.

"I mean, this is our only option. We have no other way to protect you."

I looked him in the eye.

"Alright," I lied, "I promise."

CHAPTER V

As we stepped out of the passageway onto the main road, I saw just how much damage had been wrought overnight. Glass storefronts were smashed and the morning breeze carried last night's copies of the Evening Standard swirling down the road.

The worst thing was the blood. It was everywhere. On the hood of a car that had crashed into a traffic island, smeared in a hand print across a bus shelter, congealed into perfect circles on the cement paving slabs. This was a nightmare.

"When did this happen?" I asked, turning towards Drew in surprise. "None of this was here last night."

"Mostly early this morning. Either people who hadn't turned on the television or who decided to try to make an early getaway, escape from the city. There are so many Weepers gathered in the city now that they're acting like a sieve, picking up every human who tries to slip through. They may not be smart, but sheer strength of numbers can stop a car when the supply of easier kills starts to dry up."

I started in horror at the detritus around me.

"This is why I'm being slightly neurotic about your safety," Drew added quietly as a faint smile played across his lips. "I know it's not in your nature to do what you're told, but can't you see the alternative is worse?"

Drew swept his arm in an arc, encompassing the carnage of the scene around us. This was the life to which I would be condemning myself. It was either the gauntlet of the Weepers or blood slavery. What a choice for a Friday morning.

We walked in silence the rest of the way to the broadcast, which was apparently taking place in Paternoster Square, a paved open space next to St Paul's Cathedral surrounded by the glass towers of banks and the London Stock Exchange. I knew the square well. I often cut through it on my way to and from work. The ground floor of most of the buildings was given over to retail: coffee shops, restaurants, gift shops and bars for the city workers in the floors above.

No one was working today.

There was a platform set up at the far side of the square with a huge screen behind it, and there were two smaller screens set to either side of the central platform. These guys were clearly expecting a lot of guests and they hadn't stinted on the AV equipment, but there were only about thirty people milling around in the square.

As we walked towards the centre of the square I raised my eyebrow at Drew.

"Most people are watching the broadcast at home," he said, guessing my question. "We're bussing them in afterwards from all over the capital. They'll gather here later."

"All over the capital?" I repeated. "How is one central safe house going to hold everyone?"

Drew lowered his gaze and took my hand. When he looked back up to me his eyes were full of compassion.

"Emilia… we've lost a lot of people. We couldn't save them all."

"Weepers?" I asked on a whisper.

"Weepers," Drew confirmed. "Their bite is infectious. It spreads through the human bloodstream in the space of seconds. It's how they multiply so fast and why they are such a threat to you all."

"And the Silver?" I asked.

"Don't worry, Weepers can't hurt the Silver. We're immune."

"No," I said, shaking my head, "I mean, is it the same for the Silver? Does a bite from a Silver make a human into one of you?"

He pressed his lips together and dropped his gaze.

"No," he said softly. "It's more complicated than that."

More secrets, I thought.

There was a scuffing sound on the paving off to our left and Drew dropped my hand, putting some distance between us as he did so.

"Drew," said the newcomer, "where've you been, mate?"

He was shorter than Drew, but that wasn't saying much, and it looked like he was his match in muscle mass. His hair was dark blonde and he had a friendly face with a broad, smiling mouth and twinkling brown eyes. He was dressed in the same style as Drew: khakis and a T-shirt with practical boots. It could have been a uniform.

"Rounding up strays," Drew replied with a laugh, tipping his head in my direction.

I was a little insulted. His attitude was a far cry from the intense 'I'll always protect you' spiel of the past twelve hours.

The new guy glanced at me briefly before joining in with Drew's laughter. I was barely a blip on his radar. I was less than impressed and huffed in irritation behind Drew's back.

He shot a warning glance over his shoulder at me. I supposed I had better behave until I could make a clean getaway.

The new guy did a double take and leaned in towards Drew, staring into his eyes.

"Is there something you want to tell me?" he asked Drew, rocking back on his heels as a smile spread over his face.

He was grinning like a cat.

"What were you really up to last night, you dog?"

"Drop it, Tommy," Drew growled.

"Alright, alright," he replied, raising his hands in a placating gesture, the grin still fixed on his face. "None of my business, I'm sure. Why don't you introduce me to your stray?"

"Emilia," Drew said, reluctantly ushering me forwards, "this is Thomas. He's a friend. Thomas, this is Emilia. I found her last night trying to take on three Weepers with her handbag."

Thomas laughed and looked me over appraisingly, offering me his hand to shake. I shot a quick glance at Drew before taking Thomas's hand and shaking it. I was about to pull it back out of his grasp when the colour drained from his face.

He held my hand fast, turning my wrist so he could see the outside of my forearm. He was looking at my graze from last night, knitted together with Drew's 'Silver band-aid'. His eyes went wide with shock then his brow knitted in incomprehension.

"What the hell, Drew?" he demanded in a rough whisper.

As Thomas spoke, he took a step further towards Drew, still holding my hand and pushing me sideways between them as they stood face to face over my head.

"Are you fucking crazy?"

"Tommy…," Drew whispered hoarsely back at Thomas, "just don't, okay?"

"What are you thinking?"

Thomas's grip on my hand grew tighter and, mindful of Drew's advice about not drawing attention to myself, I tried my best to suppress a cry of pain. Drew's gaze darted downwards and, as he saw my hand crushed in Thomas's, he narrowed his eyes at him and growled softly.

If I thought I had heard him growling before, it was nothing like this. The sound was terrifying and feral. Quiet as it was, it still reverberated through the air surrounding us, violent and forbidding. A shiver skipped down the length of my spine. Thomas immediately dropped my hand and stepped back. Drew's arms wrapped me into him, crushing me face first into his chest.

"I'm sorry, Drew," he said quickly and quietly.

For what seemed like an age, we all froze. Eventually,

Drew started to relax.

"I know," he replied softly. "So am I."

After a few seconds, Drew let out a shaky exhalation and released me, setting me a foot or so clear of him. I was confused again, but I knew I'd only rile Drew up if I opened my mouth and I never wanted to hear that growl again. Even the memory made me shudder.

Drew shot me a concerned look.

"Are you okay?" he asked me.

I just nodded, wrapping my arms around myself. Thomas's eyes flitted back to the wound on my forearm and he nodded his head towards it.

"You'd better cover up your stray," he said.

Drew looked down at my arm.

"You know I'll follow you, no matter what," Thomas continued, "but this is a shitstorm waiting to happen."

He looked meaningfully at Drew, who nodded unhappily in reply.

"I know that," he said.

"Alright then. I'll keep it between us?" Thomas asked him.

"I'd be grateful," Drew said with a sigh.

With one last glance at me, Thomas patted Drew on the shoulder and moved away across the square, where more people were starting to gather now in front of the stage. It was quarter to eight, nearly time for the broadcast.

Drew turned to me, pulling my jacket from my bag.

"Put this on Emilia, please," he asked quietly.

I was already warm, but I did as he said.

"What was that all about?" I whispered back at him, shrugging into my jacket. "He looked at me like I had three heads."

"It's a Silver thing. Silver don't usually do what I did last night. Not with humans anyway."

"You mean the healing thing?" I asked.

Drew looked into my eyes then turned away sadly and nodded. I got the sense that this was going to mean trouble for him.

"Then why the hell did you do it? It's not like it wouldn't have healed on its own."

Drew put his hands on his hips and gritted his teeth. He let his head fall backwards and exhaled loudly.

"It was stupid," he replied, "but I didn't think it was safe for you to be bleeding with all the Weepers about. They're attracted to the blood."

This explanation didn't really ring true to me. He had me locked away safely all night, ten floors up, and he was delivering me in daylight to the safe house. What danger did the Weepers really present to me at the moment? As I was working this through, a thought struck me. I inhaled sharply.

"You said I was going to get examined when I was admitted to the safe house. They're hardly going to miss this," I whispered urgently, indicating my forearm. "How am I going to cover it up? How long will it take to go away? Can't I just hole up somewhere until it heals?"

I was talking excitedly, hoping to jump on a solution to keep me out of the safe house, out of enforced servitude and monthly blood-lettings.

"Emilia, calm down," he said, hushing me. "It'll last a day or so, and that's too long for you to be out of the safe house. It's okay, I have some pull here, I can find a way around it. Just watch the broadcast, get yourself admitted and I'll take it from there."

He led me towards the stage and stopped me at the back of the crowd of people gathering there.

"Just stay here with everyone else," he said quietly, "and please do what you're told, just for a few hours. I'll be right there."

He pointed towards the stage and raised his eyebrow at me.

Damn. From that vantage point, he'd be able to see my every move. With that pre-emptive admonishment, he quickly scanned the square and slipped through the crowd towards where a group of people were gathering at the right hand side of the stage. This was my best chance to make a move, but people were starting to flow into the square in greater numbers now, cutting short any thoughts I had entertained of exiting unobserved.

At that moment, the microphone on the stage screeched into life. I turned in its direction to see that a lectern had been set on the stage and people were starting to line up behind it. There were Drew and Thomas. They were joined by two of the most imposing women I have ever seen. One had pale, freckled skin with fiery red hair and the other had skin the colour of caramel with piercing black eyes that darted across the congregated humans. They were both Silver and they both carried themselves like their bodies were weapons.

I had to get out. It didn't look like there was any chance I could get by the crowd on my right, but to the left of the stage the audience was growing outwards towards the buildings surrounding the square. There was an alley running between two of them. It looked like my only option.

I turned back to check the buildings to my right again and nearly jumped out of my skin. There was a guy standing barely a foot away from me, looking down with an expression of faint amusement on his face.

He was Silver. As I recovered from the shock, I realised that it was the brown-haired steroid monkey from the first broadcast.

"You know Drew and Tommy?" he asked me.

I thought about ignoring him, but realised he must have seen us talking. There seemed to be no point in denying it, so I nodded.

"Benedict," he said, offering me his hand with a smile, "but you can call me Ben."

Wary of what had happened last time I shook the hand of a Silver, I simply nodded and looked back at the stage. I didn't feel like chatting. The arrival of Drew's friend had thoroughly put paid to any notion I might have had of escaping the so-called 'safe house'. I suspected that Drew had asked Benedict to stand with me for precisely that reason.

I was starting to feel intensely claustrophobic. I had to get out of the square.

I was still trying to suppress my anxiety as a hush fell over the crowd. A tall man mounted the stage, beautiful and imposing, even from this distance: Solomon. He stood behind the lectern and waited a moment for silence to descend before he addressed the crowd, his voice powerful and cold.

"Shortly, you will each see a regional broadcast giving you directions for transport to your local safe house. However," he paused, his eyes glinting in the morning sun, "before we transmit those broadcasts, I want you each to appreciate the context of the regime we're going to be enforcing from this moment on."

Solomon lifted his hand, moving something that had been resting on the lectern, and the screens behind and to either side of him blinked into life.

I didn't know what I was looking at. The screen was largely dark, covered with rounded shapes illuminated by orange patches that could have been glowing flames.

"This is downtown Detroit," Solomon continued.

Now that he said it, I could sort of see where the streets should have been. It was an aerial shot, but the lines of the roads were disrupted by an aggregation of matter that blurred the lines between the buildings and the pavements.

The angle of the shot changed, bringing us down to street level. I could see the shapes were stacked against the skyscrapers like snow drifts, rising in peaks towards the smashed glass of office windows.

The hairs on the back of my neck stood on end as I realised that the drifts were moving. The street was churning with a writhing mass of Weepers. They were climbing over each other, stamping each other down, using each other's bodies as pyramids to reach the people sealed in the buildings and drag them down into the frenzy.

"It's the same all over America," he said as the pictures on the screen changed, showing us a cross-section of the country from cityscapes to prairie, crawling with Weepers.

As the pictures scrolled relentlessly on behind him,

Solomon turned to his audience.

"This is what we are trying to prevent. Our counterparts in the States allowed this to spread. We can contain it here, but you need us to do it for you. The Americans attempted to combat the Weepers with nuclear weaponry, but simply succeeded in destroying themselves and seventeen of the Silver along with them."

I looked around me to gauge the reaction of the crowd. They were mostly staring at the screens in shock. A lot of them had tears pouring down their cheeks. I noted with detachment that Benedict has slipped away at some point. I wasn't sure when; the man moved like a ghost. After a moment of silence, Solomon turned off the screens.

"Arrangements for admission and containment are to be directed by our military, the Solis Invicti, led by my Secundus. Andrew?" Solomon said, turning to Drew.

Holy shit. This just got worse and worse.

My Latin wasn't great, but even I could manage to translate that. He hadn't been kidding when he said he had pull here. My heart sank and a chill spread through my body as I thought about the implications of this development.

He was Solomon's right hand man. He wasn't just strong, he was powerful. More importantly, he was part of this, an integral part. The enslavement of my race wasn't just something he was failing to prevent. It was something he was actively working to bring to fruition.

Solomon stepped to one side of the lectern and Drew took his place, a grave expression on his face.

"We need to be very clear about the choice that is presented to each of you," Drew said, casting his gaze across the crowd as he rested his hands on either side of the lectern, "either you submit to our regime and present yourself for admission into a safe house or you will die."

He identified me through the crowd and caught my eye. He wasn't messing about, but I wasn't particularly surprised by the line he was taking. I'd been hearing this from him ever since the first broadcast last night. I rolled my eyes at him as he looked away.

"Most likely, those of you who fail to comply will be fed on or turned by the Weepers. For those who are not, we will have to assume that you are carriers of the Weeper plague."

He looked down at the lectern then looked up from beneath his brows, fixing me with a stare.

"To protect those humans within our care, we will be obliged to terminate you on sight."

My mouth dropped open in disbelief, but I suppressed my incredulity. The last thing I wanted to do was tip Drew off to my intended exit, and I had never been more sure that I needed to get out of this situation. Slavery or certain death? There was no choice to make.

Surrender is for the weak. I'd fight to my last breath.

Drew pushed away from the lectern and turned to the back of the stage as Tommy stepped forward to announce the regional arrangements for the London safe house. This was it.

As soon as his back was turned, I ducked my head and moved slowly and stealthily through the crowd to the left hand side of the stage. More people were arriving into the square all the time, jostling for a space up front, so it was fairly easy to blend in with the cover provided by their movement.

Eventually, I edged my way forward to the alleyway I had been aiming for, slipping along the back wall whilst Tommy outlined the admission procedure.

As soon as I hit the street I was gone, darting along the empty pavements at a flat-out sprint towards Parker's.

CHAPTER VI

I crashed up against the double door of the club and pounded on it with my palm.

"Jeff!" I screeched upwards towards the small set of rooms above the club that he called home.

"Open up! Jeff!"

My cries were met with silence. I pounded both hands into the door and yelled with desperation and frustration as anxiety ratcheted up in my chest.

I looked out of the recessed doorway of the club over my shoulder and along the street, but it was still deserted. That didn't reassure me as much as I hoped it would.

There was a clattering from the other side of the door. With a shudder I realised that I had no idea what was going to greet me when the door opened. The club was dark, windowless and cool, perfect for Weepers trying to find some respite from the heat of the day.

Cursing my idiocy, I started to back away from the door. With terrible visions in my head, I lost my nerve and turned to run, but instead I smashed straight into someone. Or something.

I fell backwards, stifling a scream, as my hand was grabbed and pulled. I struggled for all I was worth, kicking out in a panic.

"Emmy?"

I stopped dead and focussed. Incredulous, I looked into a pair of brown eyes as familiar to me as my own. They were set into a friendly, round face with pink cheeks and dimples and they belonged to a nineteen-year-old boy who was exactly my height.

"Danny?" I quavered, my voice cracking as tears pooled in my eyes.

I snapped.

"You bastard! You scared me to death!" I said angrily, punching him on the arm as the tears overflowed and poured down my cheeks.

My face screwed up with dismay and I grabbed him by the shoulders of his T-shirt, pulling him towards me. His brow furrowed in surprise and confusion as I buried my face in his shoulder and sobbed, my chest heaving.

"Pleased to see you, too, Emmy," he said softly into my ear, wrapping his arms around me, "but let's get you inside."

As he spoke, one of the double doors to the club opened.

I pulled away from Danny and looked over my shoulder. Jeff stood in the entrance, looking at me in disbelief. He looked like he had aged ten years overnight.

"Emmy?" he said softly.

I grinned back at him.

"Thank God," he said, "I've been worried sick since about ten minutes after you left last night."

He rushed towards me and gathered me up in his arms.

"Hi Jeff," I mumbled into his shirt, accidentally wiping my nose on his shoulder as I did so.

I leaned back and rubbed at the wet spot with my hand, hesitating for a moment before looking up into his eyes.

"Sorry about that," I said with a sheepish grin.

He laughed quietly and looped my arm in his, ushering me into the club. Danny followed us in, locking and bolting the door behind us. Jeff led me through the entrance corridor, past the cloakroom to the main downstairs bar.

The club had three different bars spread across two floors. The ground floor comprised the main bar, where we were standing, and a small VIP area accessed through double doors to our left. There was a stage in the main room for live bands and a door behind the bar led into a small taproom. The taproom for the VIP area was in a cellar underneath it. The first floor was taken up entirely by a dance floor with a bar running the length of one side. A taproom and office were accessed through a door to one side of the bar.

The second floor was where Jeff usually hung out. It was mostly given over to storage for the lighting and sound systems used in the club, but he'd sectioned part of it off as a living space and converted it into a flat. I thought that was where we'd been heading, but as it turned out they had holed up in the VIP area.

"This way," Jeff said to me, leading me towards the double doors with Danny in tow. "I've locked the top floor and sealed it off as best I can."

I raised an eyebrow at him in a question.

"Windows," he elaborated.

Clever. He'd locked us up in a windowless building that was designed to be secure and soundproof. And for me, it was home. I couldn't think of anywhere I'd rather be.

A smile spread slowly over my face. Jeff glanced my way and flashed a quick smile back at me, but it didn't reach his eyes. We were postponing the inevitable. I knew we had some catching up to do. However much I wished things were otherwise, we couldn't ignore reality forever. I sighed and Jeff jostled me closer to him in sympathy.

Jeff and I pushed open the door to the VIP bar. It was a much smaller room than the main bar, cosier, filled with padded chairs and leather couches scattered around small drinks tables. There were two flat screen TVs: one hanging above the bar and the other set into the opposite wall.

As we moved into the room, Sarah moved out from behind the bar to join us, a look of concern quickly replaced by a huge grin as she saw me. She was about four inches shorter than me with cropped platinum hair and a face traced with laughter lines.

"Emmy! You're alright!" she gasped, rushing up to me and holding me tight.

I laughed and unlinked my arm from Jeff's, squeezing Sarah tightly back. She pulled away and kissed me on the cheek, looking at me with a warm smile before returning to the bar and opening up one of the fridges.

"This definitely calls for a celebration. I don't know about you lot," she said, "but I could really do with a drink."

There was a general murmur of acquiescence as she fished four bottles of beer out of the fridge, cracking the caps off each of them under the bar, and handed one to each of us. I took my bottle and settled down onto one of the couches. Danny came and sat beside me while Jeff and Sarah took their seats on the couch opposite us on the other side of a small table.

"It's not even nine in the morning," I thought out loud, looking at the bottle in my hand.

"I think the rules are out of the window today, kiddo," Jeff replied.

I nodded my agreement and swigged at the bottle. My stomach grumbled in response and I realised that I hadn't eaten since before my shift last night.

Danny heard it and laughed, reaching down into a bag by the side of the couch to extract a packaged sandwich, which he offered me with a flourish.

"I had just returned from a supermarket smash and grab when you arrived. I stowed my haul in here and was just giving the outside of the building a once over when you bumped into me. Literally," he snickered.

I took the sandwich gratefully and bit into it with relish. Beer and a bacon sandwich for breakfast. I licked my lips and took another swig of the beer. Best make the most of little pleasures while we could.

As I ate, Jeff grabbed the remote for the TVs from the bar and switched them both on. He flicked through all the channels, but the same thing was playing on each one: the Paternoster Square broadcast from earlier this morning. Thomas was just coming to the end of his announcement about the London safe house as Jeff cranked the volume up and the broadcast returned to the start. Solomon stepped onto the stage.

"They've been showing nothing but this since eight o'clock on repeat. Last night it was just this guy," he said, indicating Solomon, "talking about how we need to work for them and donate our blood."

Jeff made a noise of disgust in the back of his throat and hit mute.

"I know," I said quietly, reaching forward to put my empty sandwich box on the table. "I've seen it."

Jeff looked at me in surprise.

"You have?" he asked.

He paused for a second.

"Where have you been?"

Curiosity infused his face and he leaned forward in his seat, resting his elbows on his knees, as if he had only just thought to wonder how I had turned up here safely, hours after leaving the club to walk home on streets full of monsters.

I sighed.

"You first," I said.

He opened his mouth to remonstrate with me, but I raised my hand to cut him off, trying to make him understand that I needed a break before I talked about it.

"Please, Jeff."

He subsided with a sigh, settling back into the sofa and taking a swig of his beer. Danny reached down into the bag containing his spoils and pulled out a few more sandwiches, chucking one to Jeff and handing another to Sarah. Sarah smiled at him as he opened his own packet and started to eat.

"Well," Jeff said, setting his half-empty beer bottle on the table and tearing at the packaging of his sandwich, "when I'd said goodbye to you last night, I locked up the door behind you and came back here. Danny was in the taproom upstairs," he said, nodding towards Danny where he sat next to me, "replacing a barrel and shutting off the gas for the night. I was in here running the mop round and Sarah was still here because…," he hesitated, looking at his hands, "well, Sarah…"

This was too painful. I interrupted him.

"Jeff," I said, as kindly as I could, "look, we all know you and Sarah have a thing going. We've known for months."

Sarah and Jeff looked at each other in surprise, Sarah blushing like crazy. Danny and I exchanged a glance. They'd not been particularly subtle about it and we'd been happy for them once we'd got used to it as a concept.

"It's a good thing," I continued in a gentle tone of voice, "we all think it's a good thing…"

I trailed off into silence. The others. Were we all that were left now? I stared into the bottom of my beer bottle.

"Have you seen…," I stuttered after a moment, looking at Jeff. "Cassie, Lisa… Do you…"

"We don't know, Emmy."

It was Sarah who replied, reaching out to her side to take Jeff's hand in hers.

"Right," I replied quietly.

They were probably dead. We were lucky to be alive as it was.

We dropped into silence, thinking thoughts we'd rather not say out loud. Jeff stood up and moved towards the bar, snagging four more beers to bring back to the table. I wasn't sure it was a good idea for us to have too much to drink while the forces of the Silver were setting up the perimeter for their safe house down the road, but I didn't think a couple of beers were going to do much harm.

A thought struck me.

"They were setting up a perimeter, pushing the Weepers out above and below ground," I said uncertainly, not wanting to give too much away. "We're inside the perimeter, aren't we? How did they not find you?"

"Yes," Jeff confirmed with a nod, "we're inside the

perimeter. They've kindly cleared out all the Weepers, for now at least, so we don't have to worry about them until dark. Shall I start from the top?"

"May as well," I replied, tipping my beer at him. "I've got drinking to do."

The three of them spent the next hour or so filling me in on their night. Sarah had gone up into Jeff's apartment when her shift ended earlier in the evening to wait for him. Jeff had been in the VIP bar mopping the floor. The TVs had been off all night because we'd had a private party in, but Jeff had turned them on to entertain him while he cleaned up.

He'd watched Solomon's broadcast through once then fetched Sarah down from his apartment to see it too. When Danny came downstairs to leave for the night, he'd stopped in to say goodbye and found Jeff and Sarah staring at the TV.

They'd debated about coming to find me. Finally, hearing thumping noises at the street door, they'd decided to climb out of a skylight in Jeff's apartment so they could see what things looked like from the roof. That's when the Silver had blown through the club looking for Weepers, cleansing the safe zone. Jeff, Sarah and Danny had crammed themselves into a recess in the building's roof created by the conjunction of the fire escape and the flues for the air conditioning system, managing to stay hidden from the Silver as they searched the roof. They hadn't needed to be very thorough. Weepers don't try to hide.

They'd been incredibly lucky.

Sarah picked up the thread of the story.

"When they'd gone, we moved out of our hiding place and lay on the edge of the roof, looking out into the street. I've never seen anything like it, Emmy. At least, not until the footage from America was released this morning."

We fell back into silence.

"So," said Danny, "what now?"

"Well, we know they're organised," said Jeff, "and they've clearly been planning this for some time. The water's still on and everyone seems to have electricity. That doesn't happen on its own. Someone's made decisions about what's necessary and what's not: they've got their TV broadcasts working, but I can't pick up anything on the radio and the Internet's utterly dead."

I thought about this. He was right. They would have to have designed everything well in advance to pull it off this smoothly. I corrected myself: Drew would have had to design it that way. My heart lurched in my chest.

"They wanted to control the information that's reaching us," Jeff continued "make sure it comes only through one channel: the broadcasts. Everything else has been disabled, though I don't know how they're managing that."

He paused to take another swig of his beer.

"They're not making this up as they go along," he continued, "and I think they've planned for the future. By bringing everyone into a central safe zone, they've effectively limited the area they have to supply with water and power. That has to make things easier in the long term."

"What about food?" I asked.

Jeff shook his head. We were silent for a few seconds.

"I don't know," Sarah said, "but I'm sure they do."

If the population was as depleted as Drew implied then feeding people from what was already sitting in the supermarkets around the country would probably be viable in the short term, but I couldn't imagine that they hadn't planned beyond that. Drew wouldn't be that short-sighted, particularly as the Silver needed us alive to feed them.

And Drew was one of them, I reminded myself.

I dropped my head into my hands and pushed my fingers back through my hair. It had started the day in the ponytail I had tied it in this morning, but after the past eventful few hours it was falling out all over the place.

"We can agree on one thing," asked Danny, looking at each of us in turn, "we're dealing with vampires, right?"

He shook his head and laughed.

"Man, that sounds crazy out loud."

"They're called the Silver," I said quietly, resting my chin in my hand as I stared at the silent TV screen.

There he was on the podium, the creature who had saved my life, telling us to comply or die. I just couldn't believe this was happening.

"The what?" asked Sarah with a confused expression.

"The Silver," I said, turning away from the screen to look at her. "It's what they call themselves."

"And you know this how?" asked Danny.

"I met one. Well, three actually," I corrected myself.

All three of them were looking at me in amazement.

"They didn't hurt you?" Jeff asked, sitting forward to look me over as he did so.

"No, I'm fine. It was the other ones, the Weepers. They attacked me on my way home last night. A guy, one of them, the Silver," I shrugged, "he saved me."

As I spoke, my eyes drifted back to the screen where Drew was stepping back to let Thomas take over.

"Can you turn the volume up?" I asked Jeff. "I didn't catch this bit."

He did as I asked and Thomas's voice filled the room, outlining plans for transporting people to the safe house from further afield. As I began to gain an understanding for the scale of this operation, I felt like I had hugely underestimated both the number of the Silver and how long they had been planning this. It couldn't have started with Cara Alton. This must have been in the works for a while, just as Jeff had said.

Thomas talked about testing procedures that would be undertaken at each transport site before departure to identify whether or not any humans were Weeper carriers. He didn't say what would happen to those who were, but given that Drew had spoken earlier about 'termination', and Solomon about 'containment', I couldn't imagine that they had bright, shiny futures ahead of them.

As the broadcast reached its conclusion and restarted, I picked the remote off the table and set the TV back on mute.

"You've seen the rest?" Jeff asked me.

"I saw it in person. They're in the square around the

corner. That's where I was running from."

We all fell silent. I didn't want to talk about it in any more detail than I had already and the others didn't ask.

"Why 'Silver'?" asked Danny a few moments later, in a tone of voice that implied he thought it was a girly name.

"Their eyes," I replied, "they have silver in the whites of their eyes. You've got to get up close to see it."

Danny and Jeff exchanged a look.

"Just how close were you getting, Emmy?" Sarah asked me, slowly and deliberately.

"Not that close," I said with a snort, trying to laugh it off.

This was my family. I couldn't face admitting to them that I'd spent last night pressed up against a vampire, or that it hadn't exactly been awful.

"Mind you," Sarah said, her eyes drifting to the screen as Drew took up his place behind the lectern once more, "they're not exactly repulsive, are they? I could get a little closer to him, for example…" she giggled, pointing at the screen.

Jeff faked a hurt expression then pounced on her, tickling her until she was laughing so much she was having trouble breathing.

I looked down at my hands, my cheeks flushing pink as I remembered just how close I had got to Drew. Jeff saw my embarrassment and stopped tickling, his face becoming serious.

"Sorry, Emmy," he said, "I know this whole thing with me and Sarah is fairly new. We didn't mean to embarrass you kids…"

"No, no Jeff. It's not that," I cut him off, smiling through my embarrassment. "You're not embarrassing me any more than you usually do."

Sarah looked between me and the screen and, unfortunately, the penny dropped.

"My god," she said, inhaling in shock, "that's him, isn't it? That's the guy?"

I nodded back at her.

"What," asked Danny, "the second in command guy? He's

the guy who saved you? The one who keeps talking about how they'll kill us all if we don't volunteer for their little people farm? Jesus Christ, Emmy!"

He jumped up from where he'd been sitting and strode over towards the other side of the room in irritation.

"Danny…" I began.

"Don't you get it, Em?" he stopped in the middle of the room and turned to face me, gesturing angrily with his hands. "He's the one calling the shots. They're going to kill people. Lots of them."

Danny had clearly had the same thought as I had. The best way for them to contain the Weepers would be to kill anyone carrying the Weeper plague, whether or not they surrendered.

"I know, the Weeper carriers…"

"No, not just them, Emmy. These creatures, these Silver, they drink blood. Human blood. Our blood. That's what he saved you for. Some salvation," he scoffed.

"But that's why they're making us give blood donations…" I started saying, but he cut me off again.

"Seriously? Are you really that naïve?"

"Danny…" Sarah cautioned in a low voice, concern painted on her face.

"I don't know what this guy has been filling your head with," he continued, pointing at the screen, "but you're living in a dream world if you think any of us are getting out of this alive. Say they impose a 'no killing people' rule. What happens when that rule gets broken? You think the vampires are going to give a fuck about what their cattle think?

"One more dead animal, Emilia, that's all it would be to them. Their only interest is in making sure there are enough of us around to feed them all. Beyond that, we're nothing to them, whatever they might say."

His mouth twisted in disgust and he exhaled loudly as he stalked off behind the bar to fetch himself another beer.

We all fell silent for a moment.

"Just ignore him, Emmy," Sarah said quietly, glancing over her shoulder at Danny, "it's not been an easy day for any of us."

"No," I said, shaking my head, "he's right. It is naïve to think that we're going to have any value to the Silver, to these vampires, other than as food. They might talk about a new society with a place in it for all of us, but it's a joke."

And it was. I must have been mad to let Drew get so close to me, to think that there was any truth in his promises to protect me. Yet he made me feel such confidence in his intentions.

I leaned back heavily in the couch and closed my eyes, feeling the seat depress as Danny sat down again next to me.

"Did this vampire guy tell you anything that could help us?" Jeff asked.

I thought about it for a moment. He hadn't told me anything I thought was relevant that hadn't already been put out on the broadcasts. I shook my head.

"Nothing we can use," I said, opening my eyes. "Sorry. I was too rattled to get much out of him and he wasn't exactly forthcoming."

Danny slipped his hand into mine.

"Sorry I went off on one, Emmy," he said softly.

I reached out for him and dragged him across the couch into my arms.

"It's alright. You were right," I sighed. "So, I guess we're agreed that surrender isn't an option?"

"Agreed," said Jeff as Sarah nodded beside him.

"Then we'd better make a plan."

CHAPTER VII

As it transpired, the plan was simple: stay hidden till the final perimeter was established, then strike out beyond the safe zone before we were discovered. We were hoping the delay would give the Silver a chance to clear out a fair portion of the Weeper population, so we'd have less to contend with when we made our break.

We thought it was likely that the vampires would wait until the safe zone was properly protected before they spread people around within it, so it should be a while before anyone came back to Parker's, particularly since they'd already been through here once. We reckoned it would take some time for the vamps to build and finalise their perimeter, after which we'd make our move. For the moment, then, we were watching them work.

The club office on the first floor had a load of security feeds from all over Parker's. A lot of them were internal, but there were a couple on the street and one on the roof. We had all of these trained on the end of the road, where we could see the vamps tearing down buildings to form a barricade. We were a bit puzzled by this. We'd all seen the footage from America and we knew a physical barrier wasn't going to present any challenge at all to the Weepers, so we weren't sure what they had in mind.

Every now and then, we directed one of the cameras towards the other end of the street, where vehicles were dropping people off outside the square. There was a steady trickle until about midday, when they became much more intermittent.

Jeff and I were upstairs watching the security feeds at about one o'clock when there was a shout up the stairs from Danny.

"Get down here! They've got a countdown running on the TV. Looks like they're about to make another broadcast."

We barrelled across the dance floor and down the stairs, crashing into the VIP bar as the countdown clicked down towards ten.

Sarah and Danny were sitting on one of the couches facing the screen on the wall opposite the bar. Sarah looked up at Jeff with an anxious expression. He sat on the arm of the couch next to her, sliding an arm around her shoulders. I looked around for a seat facing the screen, then shrugged and plonked myself down onto Danny's lap instead. Three... two... one...

They were broadcasting from the square again, but as the camera panned across the audience I saw that there were a great deal more people there than had been this morning. They were rammed into every available space, thousands and thousands of them. It seemed like a huge number until I realised that this was it. This was all that was left of London. Every single remaining human inhabitant could be crammed inside a fairly modestly-sized square. The survivors numbered in the tens of thousands, out of a city that had been home to millions.

It was unbelievable.

"If that's how many humans are left alive in this city," I said hesitantly, "how many Weepers are we going to be up against when we leave the safe zone? How many of them got infected?"

I looked around at my friends. Jeff looked haunted, Danny

71

resigned, but Sarah just shook her head and pressed her lips together, staring at the screen.

No Solomon this time. This time it was just him: Drew, the vampire soldier who was calling for the extermination of the insubordinate, the creature who had apparently saved my life just to feed me to the Silver. I tried to reconcile this image with my memory of a man who had risked condemnation from his kind by healing my wound, the man who had looked at me with passion in his eyes and had pressed his lips so softly to my neck it had made me tingle. He had been gentle and compassionate, full of humour and kindness.

It felt like I had dreamed it. As I looked at him now on the screen, there was no trace of the man I remembered.

"At five o'clock today, primary admission to all safe houses will close. All transports have now arrived at their destinations, so any humans currently outside a safe house holding zone must now make their own way to their nearest safe house. Those of you who fail to do so will be brought in by our search parties, who are tasked with locating all of you who remain, including those not capable of reaching a transport under their own power. If you refuse to submit, you will be terminated for the protection of those residing within the safe houses.

"I wish to impress upon you that it is in your best interests to join with us."

As Solomon had done earlier that morning, he pressed a button on the remote that rested on the lectern and the screen behind him lit up. After a second, Drew disappeared and the picture on the TV screen was filled with the same image. The screen was dark, the scene lit with street lamps, but I could just make out that it was a feed from a street I recognised. It was about a half a mile away over the other side of the square.

Buildings had been brought down on either side of the street and the rubble had been used to create a barricade several storeys high. There was a no man's land of razed buildings for what looked to be about thirty feet from the foot of the barricade on the external edge.

"This is one of the edges of the safe zone in London. You're seeing a recording from a stationary camera that was taken in the early hours of this morning."

As we watched, a figure darted out from where it had been concealed within the rubble of the barricade and plunged out into the no man's land. As it got about halfway across, a wall of Weepers flowed out of every alleyway and intercepted it. The runner hadn't even managed to go twenty feet before it was inundated with Weepers, obscuring it as they piled on top of it in a surging mass.

About five seconds passed before the Weepers drew apart, leaving a body on the ground, immobile.

A couple of Silver appeared on top of the barricade, moving faster than the camera could track them. As soon as the Weepers saw them they started to back away from the barricade, back into the cradle of the buildings, one of them dragging the corpse behind him.

"This is the fate that awaits you if you try to go it alone. This is the last warning we will give you. There will be no further broadcasts beyond the safe zone."

The screen turned dark and then, as with the previous broadcasts, it replayed from the beginning.

"You were right, Jeff," I said, breaking the silence.

"What's that?"

"You were right. They're limiting the power supply. Shutting things down outside the safe zones."

Jeff nodded back at me.

"It's not going to work," Sarah said quietly.

I raised an eyebrow at her in enquiry.

"The plan," she said, "to go outside the safe zone. There must be millions of them, the Weepers. The Silver aren't doing anything about the ones that are outside the safe zone. They'll kill us all if the Silver don't get to us first."

"So we make another plan," said Danny. "We stay inside the safe zone and hide."

I shook my head at him.

"I don't think that'll work either. At some point, they're

going to want to open up the whole area within the safe zone for people to move around in. They're even blocking all the underground tunnels at the perimeter. But they're not going to open up the safe zone until they've completed a thorough search of the whole area, and this time they're not just going to be looking for Weepers who are too stupid to hide themselves."

"Well, what do you suggest then?" he replied, his voice rising in exasperation.

I shrugged and said nothing. I couldn't think of an alternative. We were trapped.

Jeff sighed and stood up from the couch.

"I can give you a short term plan: a couple of us should get some sleep while the other two watch the cameras. Nothing's going to happen till after five o'clock now. When the next broadcast has been and gone, assuming there is one, we'll swap around and the other two can get a few hours' shut-eye."

We all agreed.

Sarah and I volunteered to take the first shift on the cameras because we'd each managed a few hours last night. We walked up to the first floor with the boys. Jeff and Sarah had managed to grab a few bits and pieces from the flat before they sealed off the top floor. Amongst them were a single and a double mattress together with some bedding, which Jeff and Danny collected to carry downstairs and set up in the VIP bar. We wanted to keep as much as possible in there because, although no one was articulating it, it was the most defensible room.

Sarah and I wished the boys pleasant dreams and locked ourselves into the office, just in case. The room was a small one, with a desk running the length of one wall. On top of the desk was a bank of monitors showing views from around the club, inside and out. There were three office chairs lined up along the desk making it a tight fit, but it was snug.

We settled in and focussed on the screens.

Nothing was happening outside. The barricade was half-built and empty. No one was moving at the end of the street where it led to the square. No one was coming out. They must all be waiting for admission into the safe house on the other side of the square. I wasn't even sure what building (or buildings) they were using as the safe house, but it certainly wasn't on our street.

Inside the club, we could see Jeff and Danny pushing some of the couches up against the walls so they could lay the mattresses on the floor of the bar. They started arranging the bedding and, after chucking the pillows at each other for a minute or so, they turned the lights down low and settled down to sleep.

We'd picked up a couple of chocolate bars from Danny's supermarket haul on our way upstairs and I tore mine open as I leaned back in my chair, putting my feet up on the desk in front of me. Sarah did the same. We sat in silence for a few minutes, chomping away quietly as we watched the screens. It was going to be a long afternoon.

"So," I said, "you and Jeff?"

"Yes," Sarah replied with a smile, "me and Jeff."

I turned to her and smiled.

"I'm happy for the two of you."

"He's a good guy," she said, softly.

A thoughtful expression crossed over her face.

"Is it weird at a time like this to say that I'm happier than I've ever been? Not with all the vampire stuff obviously, but nonetheless."

I laughed.

"No, Sarah, you're allowed to be happy, even if the world is going to shit around us."

"He's not like Pete. Or Sean," she said, offering me a wry smile.

I groaned and smiled back at her. With a sympathetic look, she turned back to concentrate on the camera feeds.

When I'd first started working at Parker's we'd bonded quickly and deeply over our horrible relationship histories, hers with Pete and mine with Sean.

After a long, unsuccessful battle with the bottle, Pete lost his job and took it out on Sarah with his fists. She hadn't hung around long enough for him to try to apologise.

Sean was different, or at least he had been different. I'd thought we were in love and when he left me I felt broken for a long time. It took six months for me to pull myself together enough to move to London and get on with my life.

I wondered how much differently things might have turned out if it hadn't been for Sean.

We'd met just over three years ago in Oxford, where we had both been living at the time. After failed forays into several different careers, I had been working in a bar and restaurant to pay my way through a foundation degree in graphic design. Sean had been finishing his PhD in some obscure branch of biochemistry and was out for drinks with friends one night in the place where I worked.

I'd been carrying a full tray of drinks to the table next to Sean's when one of his friends had pushed his chair back suddenly. It had caught me by surprise and I'd tripped on the chair leg, throwing the drinks into the air, where they hung for an instant before crashing down on top of me.

My injuries were largely superficial, except for gashes on my palm and the back of my thigh where I had fallen on top of broken glass. I was mortified, but Sean was even more embarrassed. His friend was incredibly apologetic and he and Sean both insisted on coming with me in the ambulance to the hospital. Once there, Sean convinced his friend that he would look after me and, with repeated apologies, his friend took his leave.

We chatted for hours. He held my hand as the doctors stitched me up, took me back to my parents' house afterwards and visited me on a daily basis, which he said was so he could make sure I was healing okay. He swept me off my feet. He was quiet and serious, but also kind and gentle. He treated me like I was precious and made me feel like I should, and could, be a better person than I always suspected I was. I'd never felt anything like it.

My parents loved him. They'd had mixed feelings about my announcement the previous year that I was moving back home to go back to college at the age of twenty-four and, although they'd said they loved having me around, I think they'd been secretly thrilled at the prospect that Sean might take me off their hands. As it turned out, I moved into his shared house with him that summer.

Sean had just finished his thesis, something to do with viral epidemiology, and had been immediately snapped up by a big pharmaceutical company who were so desperate to employ him that they offered him a massive golden hello, even when he insisted he was taking a few months off over the summer.

It was magical. I gave up my job at the bar, managing to secure a job at a small local graphic design firm that started a few weeks after Sean's did.

Then, two weeks before Sean was due to start work, my parents both died in a car accident as they drove back from the theatre one Saturday night. Everything stopped. I moved back into their house and Sean came with me, giving up his room in his shared house to a friend from university. There was the funeral, then probate to deal with and it was a month before I could tell which direction was up. Sean was there beside me every step of the way. He even got his new employer to postpone his contract start date so he could support me.

We both started our new jobs at the same time and, despite the continuing hell of the administration of my parents' estates, everything got better, and it was all because of Sean. He seemed to be enjoying his new job, which was challenging him as mine was challenging me.

Then, about a year into our relationship, everything changed. We'd just been through a rough patch: it turned out that the mortgage on my parents' house, together with their outstanding debts, was enough to eat up nearly all the equity in the house. We had to sell the house and move out into a small rented flat and we had no spare cash.

About a month after the move, Sean had started acting

oddly. It was nothing in particular, he was just not himself. Three months later he was becoming paranoid and anxious, constantly looking over his shoulder and thinking he was being followed everywhere we went. By the time Christmas came round, he begged me to let him escort me to work and asked me to stay inside the flat with the doors locked when I was at home.

By this point, I was becoming increasingly concerned. I thought there must be something wrong with him, that he had suffered a mental breakdown. I tried to raise the subject with him, to encourage him to see someone, but he wouldn't hear of it.

Eventually, his controlling behaviour became completely intolerable. Every day was a minefield of emotional blackmail and screaming arguments that broke my heart. I stayed because I loved him and I was worried about him, but I had no idea what to do. In the end, I just did what he wanted because it kept him happy.

I stopped going out of the house, I stopped seeing anyone and I picked up the phone to Sean every time he called, which had escalated to about once an hour.

Then, one day in July last year, he didn't come home from work. His car was at the office, his jacket hanging on the back of his office door, but he was nowhere to be found. I spoke to his employer, I spoke to the police, there were enquiries made all over the county, but no one had seen him. No one knew what had happened.

The police told me they suspected he had been borrowing large sums of money from unlicensed money lenders and that his disappearance might be related. I didn't believe them. They showed me CCTV footage of him meeting with known loan sharks and I broke down.

I guess you can never really know someone, even, perhaps especially, when you're in love.

As I turned my attention back to the monitors, I wondered for the thousandth time what had happened to Sean, what I might have done differently if I had a chance to change things.

I guessed there was nothing. I had played the cards dealt to me.

I knew the chances were slim, but I wondered if he was still alive. If so, I wondered if he had made it to a safe house. Probably not. I was grateful that my parents weren't here to suffer through this nightmare. They were not the type of people who were easily cowed and I reflected on the fact that they had, at least, died free.

The TV screens were still on in the bar so when the boys woke up they'd be able to see if anything had changed, but all we could see on the monitors was a fuzzy glow emanating from each TV. I fiddled with the monitor feed settings using the computer that was set up on the desk in front of us and, after about half an hour and fifty false starts, managed to get one to pick up the TV broadcast so we could see what was going on without waking Jeff and Danny. The short broadcast from earlier this afternoon was still going round and round on a loop.

On the camera feeds, we could see that the Silver had returned to the barricade at our edge of the safe zone. They were somehow smashing up buildings at the end of the street to make their perimeter. We could feel the ground shaking slightly from here.

As I switched my gaze back to the TV feed, I saw the lone figure strike out once more across the no man's land. My gaze flicked between it and the camera feed showing the barricade and I reflected that, without this broadcast, we would have rushed from our perimeter to the same end as that figure. As things were, I wasn't sure we were going to be any better off.

Drew appeared back on the screen.

At this point I'd probably spent more time watching him on TV than I had spent with him in real life. The vampire on the screen may as well have been a stranger. I never met him, I'd met someone different.

I sighed to myself and looked back to the camera feed. I had to stop thinking of him in human terms. I had to stop thinking about him full stop.

"I've got all the time in the world if you want to talk about it," Sarah said.

I shook my head at her and grimaced.

"I wouldn't know where to start."

"Well," she said, "what was he like?"

I thought for a second.

"He wasn't like that," I said quietly, indicating the screen.

"Like what?"

"You know," I said, looking back at the screen, "cold and militant. Heartless. He was…"

I puffed out a breath and looked at the ceiling. I couldn't tell her what he had been like. I wasn't really sure myself anymore.

We sat together in silence for a few minutes.

"Danny's right, you know," she said.

"About what?"

"About them, about the vampires. You look at that one like he's disappointed you, but he's one of them, Emmy."

"I know that."

"Do you?" she asked with concern in her voice.

I rubbed my hands over my face and looked down at the floor.

"He was different," I said.

I looked over at her, trying to make her understand. She looked back at me sceptically.

"He was kind, Sarah. And I know how crazy that makes me sound."

"And now?" she asked.

"That's not who he is now. Maybe he was never that person."

"But you miss him?"

"No," I said, "I don't miss him. I spent barely two hours with the guy, all told. How could I miss him? I just…" I struggled to find the words to express myself correctly.

"A lot can happen in two hours," said Sarah. "It's been less than a day since this whole thing started."

I nodded. It felt like a lifetime had passed in the last

twenty-four hours.

"When I was with him, when this whole thing started, he swooped in and took me somewhere safe, gave me a safe place in the eye of the storm. I was grateful for that."

I thought about his penthouse and the sense of security and peace it had provided. It was walking distance away from where we sat, but it may as well have been on the moon. I'd slept like a baby, despite the horrors of last night. He'd given me that, then he'd fussed over me: worried about my panic attack in the shower, healing my insignificant wound, making me tea this morning.

It wasn't anything to do with the penthouse, I realised. It was to do with him.

I did miss him. He was what had made me feel safe.

No wonder it felt like he'd betrayed me.

We sat in companionable silence for much of the rest of our shift at the monitors, each lost in our own thoughts.

Five o'clock came and went as we stared at the screens. The vampires worked on the barricade, building it up with such astonishing speed that the portion we could see was finished by the time the light started to fade at the end of the day. We let Jeff and Danny sleep on. There were no further broadcasts and it seemed like a good idea to let them rest while they could.

Just after nine that evening we saw Jeff waking up down in the VIP bar. He shook Danny awake and, after grabbing themselves some drinks and more sandwiches, they came to relieve us at the monitors. We had nothing to report other than the building of the barricade, so after a quick handover we gratefully went downstairs to get some sleep ourselves, planning to wake with the dawn in the morning.

When we reached the VIP bar, I located the bag of food and pulled out a couple of sandwiches for us to eat before turning in. I noted with concern that there were only a few packages left in the bag. At some point tomorrow we were going to have to go out to get more. We had only had enough to last us a day or so and we hadn't exactly been rationing.

We should probably stock up and start thinking more seriously about moderating the use of our food supply. We didn't know how long we'd be able to move around within the safe zone without getting caught by the vamps.

Jeff had had the foresight to grab a load of clothes from his flat before sealing it up and they were stacked in a booth in one corner of the bar. None of his trousers were going to fit me, but I grabbed a long-sleeved T-shirt and headed into the VIP bar toilets. I thought I'd have a quick wash at the sink before turning in.

Wary of showing my 'band-aid' to Sarah, I waited until the door shut behind me before I stripped off my jacket. I was left standing in my work shorts and the black T-shirt Drew had given to me. It had dissipated a little over the day, but I could still smell the warm wood-and-leather scent of Drew washing over me as I stripped the T-shirt over my head. I felt a pang of loss as I remembered him holding me in his arms the previous night. The smell of him brought it all rushing back.

Shaking my head in disgust at myself, I checked my injuries in the mirror. The bruises I'd picked up last night were turning an attractive shade of purple. They looked much worse on my pale skin than they had this morning.

My eye was caught by the flash of silver on my arm and I paused to examine the wound Drew had healed. The silver was already a lot less visible than it had been. There was still a fine line glinting along the main part of the cut, but a lot of the shining particles had bled out into the skin surrounding the area where the graze had been. It looked like I had wiped silver glitter on my arm. I would still have to keep it covered for now.

Sighing, I washed as well as I could then slipped Jeff's big T-shirt over my head. It would do nicely for sleeping in.

Hating myself as I did it, I carefully folded up Drew's T-shirt and slipped it into my handbag when I returned to the VIP bar. Sarah was already in bed. She'd taken the single mattress and left me the double. That was Sarah all over. She always put everyone else's happiness and comfort before her own.

I leant down and wrapped my arms around her. She returned my hug, wishing me a good night's sleep. I zipped off my boots and slipped myself under the covers, wrapping them around my shoulders, and curled up on my side, facing the TV screen as Drew appeared for the umpteenth time. I closed my eyes against the image and willed myself to sleep.

CHAPTER VIII

Saturday

I had a moment of disorientation when I woke before I realised where I was. Sarah was still asleep on the mattress beside me and the same broadcast was showing on the TV screens. I wondered how much time had passed as I zipped my boots back on. Although I was trying to be quiet, I woke Sarah in the process. She rolled off the mattress and we both headed upstairs to the office to check on Jeff and Danny.

As we crossed the dance floor, Danny opened the door to the office and beckoned us towards him.

"You'd better get in here and see this," he said, a serious expression on his face.

Jeff was leaning forward in one of the chairs as we entered the room, staring at the bank of screens. The sun was just starting to rise on the monitors. We must have been asleep for seven or eight hours.

"It started about an hour ago," he said, pointing to a central screen that was showing the feed from a camera trained on the building across the street from Parker's.

It was a huge, modern hotel that had been built in faux-

Georgian style, a beautiful building with a rather pedestrian name: The Palace Hotel. Quite apart from anything else, it was nowhere near Buckingham Palace, so the name didn't make much sense.

There'd been a pretty big fire in that location about a decade ago that had destroyed a lot of old buildings beyond repair. The land owner had managed to get permission from the planning authority to change the use of that plot in order to build the hotel. It had proved to be an incredibly successful venture, so much so that there had apparently been some speculation that the fire hadn't been entirely accidental.

Either way, Jeff was a fan. The hotel clientele had brought in a lot of business to Parker's. It was one of the reasons the club was so successful. It looked like the Palace was about to have a resurgence in popularity.

As we looked on, a stream of people poured in and out of the grand foyer of the hotel, carrying objects around. There was a lot more going in than there was coming out. I thought it was likely that, as the most luxurious building in the vicinity, they might use it as Solomon's headquarters. If so, I wondered if he had enough of a sense of humour to appreciate the irony in the name of the hotel: Solomon's Palace. Probably not, I decided.

"Great," said Sarah. "We're not going to be able to leave the building with all that rabble across the street. We're going to be stuck in here until things calm down."

"Look on the bright side," I said, "given how quickly they managed to establish the perimeter, I can't imagine it will take them very long to get themselves set up in the hotel."

"And then how long will it be before they find us here?" asked Danny.

We thought about this. Probably not long.

"What else happened in the night?" asked Sarah. "Were there Weepers on the streets? Might we have more luck leaving the building in the dark?"

Jeff shook his head sadly.

"There were a lot more than I thought there were going to

be. The other vamps cleared them out pretty quickly, but there are a lot still around."

"So much for the safe zone," scoffed Danny.

"It might not be an option at the moment," I said, trying to find an upside, "but if their work at the barricades is any indication, I don't think we'll have to wait long before it's safe enough for people to start walking around at night in the safe zone."

"That actually doesn't work entirely in our favour," Danny pointed out, with a withering look.

"I know," I responded in a sardonic tone. "They'll find us here sooner or later, but we should have a few days at least to come up with a plan."

"So," Jeff said, "going out at night isn't possible at the moment..."

"We're running low on food," Sarah interjected.

"Yes," he continued, "but we have running water so even if we can't eat we can stay hydrated. If we see an opening to make a food raid, we should go for it, but it will have to be during the daylight and with all the activity outside I think we're stuck here for the day."

We all agreed.

"I need to get out of this office," Jeff said, standing up and stretching his arms to the ceiling.

"Why don't you and Sarah go downstairs and spend some time together," Danny offered, "while Emmy and I man the monitors?"

I was a little surprised at Danny for making such a thoughtful suggestion. I wondered if Jeff might have been talking about Sarah while the boys were on watch duty together.

"Good idea," I agreed. "Maybe you could go through the stuff in the bar and bag up some essentials. You know, just in case."

Jeff's forehead creased in anxiety, but he nodded back at me. Sarah pulled me into a quick hug then they left the office together and headed downstairs.

"That was kind of you," I said to Danny when they had left.

He gave me the look I thought of as his 'little brother' look, the one that said I was being patronising. I got it a lot from him.

"I'm not a total idiot," he said. "If you had someone you were close to like that, wouldn't you want some alone time with him at the end of the world?"

I thought about Drew again. I reminded myself that he and his kind were the reason the world was ending. Well, I suppose it was primarily the Weepers, but I wasn't going to quibble between vampires.

"We'd better not look at that camera feed too closely," I said, a little weirded out.

"That's why I think we should be the ones to make the run for supplies," he continued. "They have each other and that's worth protecting. You and me…"

"It won't matter so much if one of us doesn't come back," I agreed.

"Also, we're young and nimble. Well," he paused for a second, offering me a playful grin, "I am at least."

I picked up a pencil from the desk and threw it at him then we settled into our chairs to watch the monitors.

For a long time, the vamps just carried on ferrying furniture and equipment in and out of the Palace. It was difficult to differentiate between them on the camera screen, but we thought we counted maybe twenty different vampires.

It didn't stop until it was past ten o'clock in the morning and the sun was high in the sky. They finished bringing the last loads inside and just stayed there, doubtless setting everything up. I could see the curtains in the front windows twitching and I imagined that they were inside, running around at super-speed, whipping up a breeze.

We swivelled one of the cameras up and down the street, looking for any movement, but there was nothing. Even the barricade was clear.

An hour later, five people came out of the front of the

hotel. I guessed from the way they moved and the fact that they were outside the safe house that they were probably Silver. They split off in five different directions and walked away from the Palace.

"Search parties?" I asked.

Danny nodded and leaned towards the monitor.

"Things are probably about to get interesting," he said.

We had to wait another half an hour, but he was right.

We had one of the cameras trained on the end of the road where the barricade was and another pointing across the street at the hotel. Then there was movement on the monitor showing the feed from the barricade. There were people walking in the middle of the street towards us. As they drew closer, I made out five figures walking side by side, with another on its own a few steps behind, bringing up the rear. They were walking straight to the Palace.

"He's found some stragglers," said Danny, frowning at the screen.

They appeared on the monitor showing the Palace feed and it was clear now that this was one vamp escorting five humans. I wondered whether or not they had been willing to be found. One of the humans was leaning on the shoulder of another, walking with a limp. Maybe he had been too injured to reach a transport.

The Silver raised his fingers to his lips and put them in his mouth.

Danny looked at me with a puzzled expression on his face as the front door of the Palace opened and a figure came out.

"I think he was whistling," I said.

We both looked back at the screen. The figure from the Palace came closer until his features could be vaguely distinguished.

"I met him," I said to Danny in surprise.

"You did? He was in the first broadcast, wasn't he?"

"Yeah."

It was Benedict, walking down the steps of the hotel and into the street to meet the small group gathered there.

"I think he's one of the guard, the... what did Solomon call them?"

"The Solis Invicti," Danny supplied.

"Yep, them."

Benedict stopped at the foot of the steps as a second figure emerged from the Palace and walked down to join him. My heart sank. It was Drew.

The humans had assembled into a line facing Drew, side by side with their backs to the camera. We saw Drew's lips move as he reached out his hand to the one furthest to our left, a young man. The man seemed to hesitate for a moment before offering his hand to him, palm up. Drew raised the proffered hand to his face and put his lips to his wrist.

"Ew," said Danny. "How do you like your vampire friend now?"

"What's he doing?" I wondered, gazing incredulously at the screen.

"I think he's tasting him. Probably trying to work out whether or not he's yummy enough to bother keeping alive."

He clearly was, because Drew had already dropped his wrist and moved on to the next human. I could see a dark mark on the first man's wrist and wondered why Drew hadn't bothered to heal him. He probably didn't think the man was worth his time.

"Maybe he's checking them for infection," I thought out loud.

As he finished with the second human, the penultimate figure in line, a teenaged girl, turned and ran in the opposite direction to that from which she had come, nearly out of shot of the camera. In a second, her vampire escort was beside her, grabbing her from behind and dragging her backwards, sinking his teeth into her throat.

I gasped in shock. It was over in an instant.

The girl arched her back then fell still, limp and lifeless in the vampire's grip. She dropped to the ground as he released her. I was grateful that the resolution on the screen was poor enough that I couldn't see the expression on her face.

Danny gave me a withering look.

"You're shocked?" he said. "Really? After everything that's happened, you're surprised that they're eating people?"

"No," I said with exasperation. "We've had this conversation. It's just a bit different seeing it happen right in front of you."

He didn't look convinced.

"I need to know that you're in this fight," he said, "because if we're going out there, just the two of us, I want to know that you have an understanding of what's at stake."

I smiled at him.

"No pun intended?" I asked.

"It's not a joke, Emmy," he said angrily, shaking his head. "Every time I think you understand what these creatures, these things, are capable of... you're still surprised when they don't act in accordance with your expectations. They're vampires, Em."

"I'm not a child," I said irritably. "You know I'm with you on this, even if it kills me, and I'm not the type to be controlled, Danny. You can trust in that."

He stared at the screen and we lapsed into silence for a few minutes as Drew bit into the last of the humans.

"Can you at least shift the camera over so we don't have to look at the body?" I asked.

He nodded and reached forward to the controls, shifting the camera a fraction to the left so the girl's body disappeared off screen.

Drew's head snapped up from the human's wrist and he stared straight into the camera for a second.

"Oh shit," I whispered through gritted teeth, thinking we'd been found.

But Drew quickly looked away, gazing around the street. He had heard the noise of the camera moving, but he couldn't work out where it was coming from.

Danny and I both exhaled in relief as Drew turned and walked back to the Palace with Benedict behind him, looking around over his shoulder as he went. The searcher walked off down the road with the four remaining humans in front of him, moving towards the square and the safe house.

"New rule," Danny said, looking me in the eye. "No more moving the cameras."

I nodded my enthusiastic agreement and, a little shaken, we settled back down to watch duty.

CHAPTER IX

A few hours later Jeff and Sarah came to relieve us and take their turn at the monitors. We filled them in on the Drew and Benedict episode and, most importantly, warned them not to move the external cameras.

"We found a couple of unclaimed backpacks in the cloakroom," said Sarah. "We thought they'd be useful when we go on the supermarket raid, so we've emptied them out and left them by the door."

"Good thinking," I said.

"So…," said Danny, "about the supermarket raid."

Jeff and Sarah both looked at him.

"What about it?" Jeff asked.

"We're going," I said, "me and Danny. The first opportunity that crops up, we'll go. We want you two to stay behind where it's safe."

"I know we're a bit older than you," Sarah said, "but we're hardly invalids."

I shook my head at her.

"That's not the point. The point is that you have to look after each other. So please, we've discussed it, and we want you to stay here."

Sarah started to protest, but before she could get a word

out Danny cut her off.

"Wait a minute, something's happening."

We all looked at the monitor showing the feed of the hotel. The doors had opened and the vampires were coming out in force. I identified amongst them all four of the Silver I could name: Solomon, Benedict, Thomas… and Drew. They were all leaving.

"What's going on?" Jeff wondered aloud.

At that moment, there was a crackle and the TV screen turned to black.

"Shit, they're gearing up to do another broadcast," Danny said, "this is our chance."

He looked at me with excitement.

He was right. Everyone would be in the square: all the Silver and all the humans from the safe house. It was still daylight so we shouldn't have any trouble from the Weepers. It was the perfect moment to grab what we needed while we still could.

I barely hesitated.

"Let's go," I said.

I paused to hug Jeff and Sarah in turn then we ran out of the office and down the stairs, pausing when we reached the door to the outside world. We gathered up the backpacks and each slung one on.

"Right," I said, "we move away from the square and head to the Marks and Spencer down the road running parallel to the barricade. Agreed?"

"Agreed," said Danny.

"We move quickly and quietly, and we stay in the cover of the buildings. When we reach the shop, we try to break in without attracting attention to ourselves."

"Odds are we won't even need to break in," he said, "I'd be amazed if it hasn't already been smashed up."

"Okay, then we pray no one else was interested in the tinned food. Ready?"

He nodded in reply.

I opened the door a crack and looked out carefully. There

was nothing moving in the street and everything was quiet over the road at the Palace. We slipped out of the door, pressing our bodies into the recessed doorway of the club, and closed it silently behind us. The latch caught on the other side.

We were on our own now. No retreat.

Raising my finger to my lips, I peered out along the road to our left, down towards the barricade. It was still deserted. I felt very exposed in full sight of the hotel. There was no guarantee that every last one of the vamps had emptied out of the Palace to watch the broadcast. In any case, the broadcasts were usually fairly short, so we had to act fast.

Staying tight in to the buildings lining the pavement, I ran as quietly as I could down the left side of the street with Danny following behind me. When we were only a couple of buildings away from the barricade, I side-stepped into an alleyway and pressed myself up against the wall, frantically looking around for any signs of danger as I did so.

Danny pressed himself up against the opposite wall of the alley so he had a view of the barricade while I looked back the way we had come. Nothing was moving. As we caught our breath, I scoped out the alley in a bit more detail. It was open at both ends, cutting across this block of buildings to let out on the next street over.

There had clearly been some Weeper activity here, which wasn't surprising given how close we were to the barricade. There was a woman's shoe in the middle of the alley, about halfway down its length, and bloody footprints led away from it to the end of the alley before stopping abruptly. I wished the story of what had transpired here wasn't so clear to read in the marks left behind it.

I'd seen a lot of horrible things in the past two days, but I still wasn't getting used to it.

Across the street from us was the road we were aiming for. It branched off from the main street just before the barricade and there was a line of shops along the side nearest the perimeter. We could just see the supermarket from where we were standing. Its position was more exposed than I would have liked. The buildings either side of it had huge glass frontages and those on the other side of the street were all office blocks standing flush to the edge of the pavement. There was nowhere to hide while we broke our way in.

As I pondered our next move, Danny waved at me to get my attention and mouthed something at me. I looked back at the front of the supermarket. It's open, he had said.

I looked closely at the swing door and saw the black edge of its seal. As I watched, it moved a fraction, showing a larger portion of the black, then moved back to its original position. Danny was right. The door was unlocked and moving slightly as the air pressure inside the store changed.

I shot Danny an anxious look. I wasn't sure this boded well for us. I supposed that the air conditioning in the store could be on, creating a breeze that was moving the door, but I was concerned that the movement might indicate the presence of someone already inside. The door wasn't moving in the steady rhythm that would be caused by a breeze. Instead, it moved in a single motion now and then, the kind of movement that might be created by someone opening and closing other doors in the same building.

Danny shrugged at me. Time was short and we were out of options.

Scanning the road once more, I took a deep breath and plunged across it to the cross street and our destination. I hugged the glass storefronts as I ran and Danny overtook me just as we reached the supermarket door. We peered into the store to check for obvious danger, but we had no time to make sure. We pulled the door open and slipped inside.

It was immediately obvious that the power was no longer reaching this cross street. The overhead lights were off, but the smell we encountered as we entered the store told us that the fridges and freezers were no longer operational. Another reason to get in and out as quickly as we could.

It also made me worry more about the movement of the door. It could have been the result of natural air currents moving around the building, maybe enhanced by the gases released from the decomposition of the food rotting in the fridges and freezers, but it certainly wasn't the air conditioning. My anxiety cranked up another notch.

We paused and looked around us, listening and looking carefully for any sign of movement. As we had suspected, the store had already been looted. There was fruit strewn across the floor where it had tumbled from displays and empty sections of shelving stared back at us from the nearest stands. I hoped the story wouldn't be the same in the rest of the store.

There'd also been some fighting in here. I wasn't sure that it had been Weepers because, although there was some blood, there was not as much as the Weepers normally seemed to leave behind them. Also, it was present only in defined drops on the floor rather than in smears that might indicate a tussle on the ground.

Either way, it didn't seem like there was anyone else here right now.

I looked at Danny and tipped my head towards the left hand side of the store, where I knew they kept the tinned and dried foods from previous visits in happier times. We stuck together like glue as we moved in that direction. This was no time to make ourselves vulnerable by separating.

We tried to make our footfalls as soft as possible as we crept to the back of the store, but they still squeaked slightly on the tiled floor. I was overcome with relief when we reached the shelves I had been aiming for. They were almost half full.

Danny stood watch whilst I took both of our backpacks and filled them each halfway to the top with tins of pre-cooked foods: beans and other pulses, stews, tunafish, fruit and vegetables. I grabbed a load of packs of noodles and threw them in too because they were compact and calorie-dense. We could use the kettle behind the bar to make them up.

We still had about half of one bag empty, so I zipped up the full bag and gave it to Danny for him to put on, indicating that we should move to the next aisle. We walked lightly round the corner into the biscuit aisle and I grabbed as many granola and cereal bars as I could fit into the remaining space in my backpack.

Once I was satisfied that we couldn't carry any more, I slung the backpack over my arms and hiked it up onto my shoulders. I tightened the straps as far as they would go so I'd be ready to run and Danny did the same with his. We looked at each other and nodded. We were ready to make a break back to Parker's.

We'd only been in the store for about five minutes so, I thought we'd probably only been away from the club for less than ten. We'd need to get a move on, but I thought we had a good chance of making it back before the broadcast ended.

We walked towards the checkouts as quietly as we had come. It was odd going to a supermarket, particularly one I had frequented fairly regularly in the past, and leaving without paying. It felt quite liberating, but I felt guilty at the same time. I didn't think most of the shareholders or directors of Marks and Spencer were likely to be in a position to give a damn about whether or not they lost forty quid's worth of produce, but it was a clear indication to me that the reality of our lives from this point on still hadn't yet sunk it for me.

Danny was right. I just wasn't facing the truth about our new world, in so many ways. It was time to get tough.

As we neared the end of the aisle, there was a rustling noise to our left and slightly behind us. It sounded like it was coming from the next aisle. My heart started pounding in my chest fit to burst. Danny and I exchanged a panicked glance and, wary of being cut off from the door back out to the street, we both broke into a run, all thoughts of moving stealthily abandoned.

Sprinting towards the door, I peered over my shoulder as we cleared the end of the aisle.

It was Weepers, four of them. They weren't in great shape. There were three women and a man, emaciated and bedraggled with their clothes hanging off them. I wondered how long it took for a Weeper to be starved of blood. I wondered if they ever died.

They were dragging themselves out of the open chest freezers on either side of the aisle. I supposed they must like the cool, dark, damp space amongst the decomposing food. It was an ungainly and incongruous display that would have been hilarious in different circumstances. As it was, I was simply grateful that we'd got a head start on them.

I put my head down and ran. I was confident that we'd have enough time to get out of the door before they reached us and I was pretty sure they wouldn't follow us out into the sunlight. Their eyes seemed to be reacting badly even to the small amount of daylight that was penetrating into the store from the glass frontage. Their eyes were already more bloody and inflamed than those of the bloodied man I had met two nights before.

We sprinted through the checkouts and burst through the door to the outside world. Looking behind us, I saw that the Weepers had stopped just short of the end of the frozen foods aisle. They weren't following us. I exchanged a glance of relief with Danny and my adrenaline levels start to dip.

We hadn't taken the time to check out the street before leaving the store, but it was thankfully clear. Finally, some good luck. We moved cautiously back to the junction where we were to rejoin the main road and stopped on the corner, peering around the edge towards Parker's and the Palace. The road was still empty so, nodding to Danny, I ran quietly across it and back to the alleyway in which we had hidden earlier.

It wasn't until I was pressed up against the wall, facing the barricade, that I realised Danny hadn't followed me. Gazing around in panic, I saw that he was still over the other side of the road, his backpack caught on a decorative metal railing that covered the lower portion of a window of the building on the corner. There was a soft tearing sound.

Danny's face fell.

My stomach lurched.

As I watched in horror, a tin dropped from his backpack onto the pavement with a thunk. He tried to catch it with his foot, but he was still caught on the railings and only succeeded in speeding its progress towards me.

A quiet whirring sound filled the street as it spun on its side then came to rest in the middle of the road. It felt like it was the loudest sound in the world.

Danny closed his eyes as a look of anguish crossed his face. He was going to have to try to extricate himself without releasing any more of his cargo.

I made to move towards him to help, but he held a hand out towards me and gave me a stern look. He wanted me to stay where I was.

He reached behind himself with both arms and started feeling around, a look of intense concentration on his face as he tried to locate the tear. As he did so, I heard a murmur up the street and saw that the vampires were starting to return from the square.

We were out of time.

I decided to throw caution to the wind and, tightening the backpack around me, determined to run back over to him, but just as I took a step towards the street to go to Danny's rescue a blur ripped past me. It resolved into Benedict, who stood in front of Danny as he groped behind himself desperately to try to get free.

It was too late. He was trapped.

I pressed myself as far up against the wall as I could and watched Benedict standing in the side street, reaching for Danny's wrist. Danny struggled, twisting his body around to try to avoid Benedict's grasp, but it was never going to work. One of Benedict's hands shot out, pinning Danny to the window pane by his throat with such force that it cracked behind him. With the other hand, he secured Danny's wrist and brought it to his mouth, biting into it with glinting teeth as Danny squirmed.

Instantly, Benedict's lip curled in disgust and he spat the blood out onto the street.

I went numb. I knew what was going to happen next.

"No…," I whispered.

Benedict heard the noise and looked across the road towards me. Recognising me, he smiled as, with a casual flick of the wrist, he snapped Danny's neck.

My mouth dropped open and I staggered back against the wall. I felt like my chest was imploding as I struggled for breath. Pressing one side of my face into the wall, I stared back across the road with tears pooling in my eyes.

Danny's knees crumpled as his body fell to the ground, his torso held upright where his backpack remained attached to the railings. He looked like a marionette, discarded by his puppeteer and lifeless.

It had been over in a second. One nonchalant gesture from a vampire and Danny was dead.

Rage washed through my veins and I glared at Benedict through my tears. With an expression of vague amusement and incomprehension, he began stalking across the road towards me.

My turn next, I thought.

Knowing I had no way in hell of outrunning him, I turned down the alley away from Benedict and ran anyway, my heart thumping in my chest as I sobbed and gulped down my tears. When I reached the end, surprised that I had not yet been intercepted, I turned fearfully and looked over my shoulder.

Benedict was gone. The alley was empty.

I looked back along its length to the side street. Danny's body had gone too. I supposed that Benedict had thought the risk of leaving an infected body lying around was greater than the risk I presented running around in the safe zone.

He wasn't just dead, he was gone. I would never see him again. I gasped at the shock. It was too fast, too sudden.

Deciding I was in no state to navigate the main streets right now, I crouched down in the cover of the alley to give myself a few seconds to recover. It would be stupid to hang around now that Benedict had seen me, but a few seconds would make no difference when he moved as fast as he did.

When I had myself a bit more under control, I stood up and peered into the main road. It ran parallel to the one on which Parker's sat. There was another alleyway that cut right through from one road to the other on the far side of the club. If I could get to that alley safely along this parallel road, I'd have less distance to travel in sight of the Palace.

I sucked in a deep breath. I had to hold it together for long enough to get back to Jeff and Sarah. We could make another plan. But how was I going to tell them about Danny?

I pushed the thought out of my mind and whipped round the corner of the alley into the street, sprinting as fast as I could towards my destination. This street was completely deserted and in much worse shape than the other. There were huge gouges out of the pavement where now absent objects had torn across it and street signs were hanging from their poles, which were crushed and mangled into bizarre angles. It looked like a battleground, a completely different world from the one from which I had come.

I was vaulting piles of rubble and twisting around crashed cars, the weight of the backpack tearing down onto my shoulders with every jolting step. I misjudged a jump and came down heavily on my left knee, skinning it on part of a breezeblock as I fell. I bit my lip to stifle my cry of pain and limped onwards, leaving drops of blood behind me for a few steps. I worried about leaving a trail for a second, but my blood was barely noticeable amongst the myriad stains already littering the pavement.

After what seemed like an age I finally reached the second alleyway and ducked inside, crushing myself through a narrow gap between the wall and a car that was tipped impossibly on its end, blocking the way. The alley wasn't in a much better state than the road I had just left. It was littered with lumps of masonry and twisted metal. A small kitten with long tortoiseshell fur, maybe three months' old, was digging through a rubbish bin that had toppled over on its side. Looking up, I saw that a fire escape had partially come away from the wall to my right, pulling chunks of stone down with it.

I negotiated my way slowly and tortuously along the alley

until I had navigated its length. I could see the Palace clearly across the road, but, once more, the street was silent. Everyone must already have returned from the broadcast. I would have to move quickly to avoid being spotted through the windows.

I took a minute to check my knee. The blood was now running freely down my shin and inside my left boot. I'd grazed off a large area of the skin and it hurt like a bitch. Shivering involuntarily, I wished I had something to bind it with. It was going to be agony if I accidentally brushed up against it.

Another worry struck me: could the Silver smell fresh blood? I hoped there were none wandering around outside, sniffing the air.

I took a deep breath and, taking a final peek around the corner to check the way was clear, I ran the short distance to the door of Parker's.

CHAPTER X

I knew something was wrong a second before I reached the double doors of the club. The right hand door was hanging very slightly open.

With a growing sense of dread, I stood on the threshold and pushed the door with the palm of my hand. It swung wide in front of me, thunking gently against the inside wall as it came to rest. It was dark and, with the light of the day behind me, I couldn't make out the inside of the club from the doorway. My hands shaking, I stepped inside.

I looked carefully from side to side as I passed the cloakroom, checking every corner as I went. As I walked into the main bar downstairs, the wide shard of light from the open doorway illuminated a path across the bar floor towards the stairs leading up to the second floor. There was no light in the stairwell. The chairs and tables remained arranged as they always were, neatly set around the edge of the floor. Everything was quiet and nothing was disturbed.

To my left, I saw that the light in the VIP bar was on, shining through the patterned panes of glass set into each of the double doors at head height. I crept across the floor and paused momentarily at the doors. If this was an ambush, I may as well get it out of the way. There was no way I was leaving without Jeff and Sarah, so I was going in that room one way or another.

I pushed both of the double doors open and strode through into the bar.

At first, I wasn't sure what I was seeing. The mattresses lay on the floor in front of the bar side by side, a pile of clothes heaped on one of them. Then I looked closer and realised in detached confusion that it wasn't a pile of clothes.

It was Sarah.

She was crumpled onto her knees with her body folded forwards away from me, face turned to the side at an awkward angle on the mattress. One arm was flung above her head and the other was twisted under her body. Her neck was marked with a bite from which blood had spilled onto the sheets below her, staining them red. With sightless eyes she stared off towards the back wall of the bar, her mouth slightly open, a small smear of blood wiped across her chin.

My throat tightened and my fingernails dug into the palms of my hands as I curled them into fists. I felt myself break into a sweat, but I was chilled to the bone.

I took a few steps closer to the mattress, bringing into view the seat of a couch with its back to me. Jeff was half sprawled across it, his shoulders resting on the couch with his lower body tangled in the legs of the table placed in front of it. He, too, had a wound at his neck, his empty eyes gazing up to the ceiling.

They were both dead. Danny was dead. Now Sarah and Jeff were dead too. The vampires had killed them all.

Everything was different now.

The world sharpened around me. It felt real for the first time in two days, but at the same time I felt like I was more distant, like I was stepping back out of myself. My skin tingled and I became dizzy with the sense of loss and change.

I had a brief impression of speed and weightlessness then I fell to my knees in front of the mattresses, my injured flesh thudding into the floor and sending a dagger of pain up from my knee and through my hip. It barely registered.

Gone. All gone.

There was nothing left for me to hold on to.

I was still for a while after that. I'm not sure how much time passed.

When I returned to myself with a shiver, I gently levered myself up from the floor. I had to grab what I needed and get out of here, find somewhere else to hole up until morning. I was on my own.

Moving quickly, I emptied a few of the tins and cereal bars out of my rucksack to make room for my shoulder bag, which I shoved into the top along with my leather jacket. I was still wearing Jeff's long-sleeved T-shirt from the previous night and I had Drew's T-shirt, but I grabbed a couple more from the pile Danny had left in the corner of the room and crammed them into the bag too.

There was a soft, white, cotton T-shirt in the pile that I thought would do well for bandages. Walking into the VIP bar bathroom, I tore the T-shirt into wide strips and ran a sink of warm water. I stripped off my boots and socks while I waited. My left sock was soaked with blood from my knee and the other had developed a hole, so I used the right sock to wipe the blood from my boots with a little water then chucked both of them away.

I really, really didn't want to rub a cloth over my skinned knee, so I had to find another way of getting it clean before I could bind it up.

Once the sink was full, I put my uninjured knee on the counter surrounding the sink and, putting my hands either side of the sink to balance myself, I put my weight on my good knee until it was supporting me as I hovered my left knee over the water. Very gently, I lowered my injured knee into the sink. Pain ripped through me, communicating along my spine, but I clenched my jaw and held my knee in the water until the sharp edge of the pain was gone, replaced by a dull ache.

I hopped down off the counter and, giving the injury a quick look over, decided it was clean enough. I wet one of the strips from the T-shirt and used it to wipe down my legs, removing the blood and grime from my fall. When I was satisfied that I was as clean as I was going to get, I wrapped several strips of the makeshift bandage around my knee.

Walking back into the bar carrying my boots, I averted my gaze from Jeff and Sarah's bodies. I returned to the pile of clothes and fished out a few pairs of socks. I put one pair on before once more donning my boots and put the others in the backpack along with the remaining strips of T-shirt. Finally, I walked around into the bar to find a water bottle.

As I did so, I noticed a white Parker's T-shirt lying in a heap on the bar. I thought about taking it with me as a memento until I saw that it was dirty and torn. With a growing sense of unreality, I reached out and spread it across the bar top. It looked to be my size. Flipping it over onto its front, I saw what I was dreading and yet expecting to see: a smear of blue paint across the shoulders.

It was my Parker's T-shirt, the T-shirt I had been wearing the night of the attack, marked with the blue paint from the plywood scaffolding tunnel. It was the T-shirt I had discarded in favour of Drew's black one, the T-shirt I had left in the bin in Drew's penthouse. I'd been a fool to leave it behind.

He'd used it to find me, but I hadn't been here when he came. So instead, he'd killed Jeff and Sarah.

A cold sense of purpose settled over me. There was no one left in this world I loved anymore. He had no power over me. I'd get out of this alive and I'd do it on my own.

Gritting my teeth in fury, I located a couple of large plastic bottles and filled them with water. I stuffed them into my backpack, adding a large bottle of gin for good measure. I might need it, I told myself, for medicinal purposes. A first-aid kit caught my eye from under the bar so I grabbed that too, cursing myself for not having thought to look for one before I bandaged my wound. I zipped up the bag and made ready to go.

Before I left, I had to move Jeff and Sarah. I couldn't leave them like they were. It just didn't feel right. Moving quickly,

I walked towards Jeff and grabbed him under the arms. He was still warm.

I blinked away the tears that were starting to form in my eyes. I just had to get on with this. There'd be time to mourn later. At the moment, every second I was in this building I was in more danger.

Dragging him backwards, I managed to manoeuvre him onto the double mattress next to Sarah. I took hold of her shoulders and gently rolled her onto her side, then onto her back, her side resting against Jeff's. I turned her head from its unnatural angle so it rested against his shoulder. Finally, I carefully placed Sarah's hand inside Jeff's and reached over to close their eyes. It was hardly a proper burial, but it was all I could do for them.

I had no one to pray to, so I simply swore to hold my memories of them and Danny close to my heart. For now, I had to push down my grief and coat it with steel so I could concentrate on my escape. With a final glance, I slung the backpack onto my shoulders and turned away, leaving them hand in hand together behind me.

CHAPTER XI

By this time it was early evening. The sun was still high in the sky, but when night fell it would come quickly.

I decided to strike off back the way I had just come, along the detritus-furnished alley. I made that decision on the basis that it seemed like the vampires had been doing less clean up work in that area, so they probably didn't go there as often as the more navigable roads. It wasn't that they had any trouble moving around quickly and athletically, because they certainly didn't, but from my limited encounters with them I thought they were the sort to keep their surroundings tidy.

The main street was still eerily clear as I left the club, turning right and slipping quietly back into the alley. I was disconcerted by the silence. I fully expected that more people, or at least more vampires, would be moving around after the broadcast had come to an end. It made me suspicious and, as a result, I was edgy and nervous.

I picked my way through the obstacles littering the passage until I found myself beside the precariously upended car once more, looking out into the battleground beyond. Crouching behind a pile of masonry and twisted metal, I was hidden from the street behind me. I needed to try to work my way as far from the safe house and the Palace as I could, whilst still remaining within the perimeter. Other than that, I had no plan.

I took a few deep breaths in an attempt to settle my nerves. If I went out there like this, full of panic and adrenaline, I was going to do something careless and get myself killed. I needed to move as silently as I could and, in a street as covered in shards of stone and metal as the one in front of me, it was going to take a great deal of concentration to avoid kicking or falling on something. I was conscious that any noise was likely to bring the vampires running.

As Danny had learned.

I pushed the unwelcome thought away and, taking another deep breath, peered around the vertical roof of the car to assess my best route. I scanned the opposite side of the street and, from my vantage point, I could see three passageways notched into the line of buildings that faced me. One was almost directly across the road from me and I could see clear through it to another main road beyond. Both of the remaining alleys, one to either side of me, looked like they were blocked to some extent, but because of the angle from which I was looking at them I couldn't tell whether or not they were dead ends.

My instinct was to move to one side or the other rather than blazing across to the next street moving on the same line. I was also nervous about being in the alley opposite for any length of time because if I were standing at any point down its length I would be in clear view of anyone standing where I was now. There was very little to choose between the other two passages.

Deciding that I would rather be a little further away from the barricade when night fell, and thus further from the Weepers amassing behind it, I resolved to take the alley on my left and, not wanting to hesitate any further, quickly scanned the road once more before squeezing out past the car and into the street.

The street was too cluttered for me to run. I balanced on the balls of my feet and, leaning forwards to counteract the weight of the backpack, I jumped over the bricks and scaffolding poles strewn across the road, dancing from side to side as I picked the clearest possible route. As I reached the middle of the road I found a drift of concrete chunks and stone before me, running the length of the street in both directions. There was no way around it and it was low enough to climb over, but I was going to have to do so carefully to avoid dislodging any of the pieces.

My progress was tortuous. As I placed my foot upon each block of shattered stone, I had to test that it would take my weight without moving before I could step fully onto it. After ten or so steps in this way, I reached a huge limestone boulder half-buried in rubble, which looked like it had been ripped from the side of a building. Judging that it was less likely to move under my weight than the scree either side of it, I decided to go straight over the top. Wedging one foot into a gash in its side, I slung my injured leg over the top and shifted my weight forward so I could drag the other leg over behind me.

Sitting on the top of the boulder, I had never felt so exposed. I was on one of the highest points of the wreckage in the street and would be clearly visible to anyone who happened to look this way. My heart was pounding. Suppressing a shudder, I slid down the other side of the rock and picked my way the remaining distance across the road until, with relief, I reached the alley I was aiming for.

The passage was narrower than I had first realised, not even wide enough to admit a small car, and its mouth was partially blocked with, of all things, a telephone booth. It had been uprooted and now lay in the street at an angle, footings jammed into a pile of rubble as it leant up against the wall on one side of the alley. I ducked underneath it and stepped carefully away from the street, scanning the alley in front of me as I did so. It seemed to be clear.

Other than the initial blockage, there was very little detritus in my way, so I had a clear view to the end. Unfortunately, I could see that the passage terminated in a small square of paving set in a recess to the left, in which a door was set. The door was dark wood, ornately carved and looked to be extremely old. I walked up to it and wondered whether or not I might be able to break through and find a hiding place in the building beyond.

I ran my fingers along the surface of the wood. It was so old it had hardened like stone. Even if I found some sort of makeshift crowbar and tried to force it open, I'd make so much noise that I could hardly avoid being heard.

I was just considering my other options when a small scuffling noise from the mouth of the alleyway caught my attention.

Shit. I was trapped.

I crammed my body into the small recess of the doorway with my back to the wall. From my right, the scuffing noise approached closer. Although I doubted it would do me much good in the long run, I wished I had thought to pick up a weapon. A stick, a brick, anything. It would have made me feel better to have something with some heft in my hand.

As it was, fear sparking through my veins, I gritted my teeth and curled my right hand into a fist. As I did so, I moved slightly away from the wall so I had space to draw my elbow back behind me.

The noise stopped about three feet to the right of the corner in which I was hiding.

"Are you there?" a voice whispered.

My brow creased in confusion and I relaxed my fist slightly as my arm fell back to my side. I peered cautiously around the edge of the recess. There was a young man standing there.

He looked to be in his early twenties, with a wave of dark blonde hair. He was tall, about six foot two, with wide shoulders and gangly limbs that reminded me of Danny. His eyes were a deep brown and his skin soft, a light tan in colour. It didn't look like he had to shave very often. I checked his eyes carefully, but there was no hint of silver in the white.

He smiled at me affably.

"I've been holed up in one of the shops over the way and

saw you crossing the street," he said, pointing over his shoulder with his thumb, "and I… well… I'm on my own."

He paused, looking a bit embarrassed.

"I was hoping I could come with you."

I looked at him with suspicion. I didn't know what to say. I hadn't thought I'd be coming across any other humans.

"I'm Cameron, Cam for short," he said eagerly, holding out his hand towards me.

"Emilia," I replied, cautiously taking his hand in mine and shaking it.

He grinned at me happily and I offered him a small smile in return. I couldn't say no to him. It would be like kicking a puppy.

"So," he said, looking at me expectantly, "what's the plan?"

Apparently I was in charge. I could barely look after myself, so I wasn't sure how I would manage to keep the two of us safe. Oddly, Cam's company made me feel even more isolated. I wished Jeff were here to take control, just like he always did.

I sucked in a breath and took a quick look around us. Other than the door, there was no way out of this passage except the entrance through which we had come. I wasn't going to hazard the third alley. It was approaching evening and it was too close to the barricade.

Returning to the mouth of the alley, I peered around the corner to the right, away from the barricade towards the other end of the road. Not far from where we were standing, the road was so congested with cars and twisted metal piled on top of each other that it had, in effect, become a second barricade.

"It's blocked the whole way across and it's precariously stacked," Cam said, tipping his head towards the pile. "The only way out is through."

I wasn't risking that. One accidental shift would bring the whole lot crashing down on top of us.

A feeling of claustrophobia settled over me. It was like the whole street was a trap, only one way out in the direction we needed to move.

"We take the next alley," I said, nodding towards the barricade.

Cam nodded back at me and a look of relief crossed over his face. I was the one calling the shots, but he hadn't wanted to crawl through the barrier either.

"Let's go," I said.

We crept along the road as quickly and quietly as we could. Surprisingly, Cam was stealth itself, which just made me cringe all the more as concrete pebbles crumbled under my boots, crunching into the pavement. In no time at all, we had reached the empty alleyway.

"We run it," I whispered over my shoulder at Cam, not wanting to be in the passage any longer than necessary.

The clear path made me suspicious and I was concerned to get through it as quickly as possible. As we turned into it, I saw that there was nothing on the paving for its entire length. Not even a small shard of rock. Not even a newspaper or a plastic bag. Adrenaline thrummed through my system, but we ran nevertheless, sprinting until we reached the end and lined up side by side against the wall.

The next street along was completely clear. It wasn't a good sign. Night was falling quickly and we needed to find somewhere we could hide from the Weepers, preferably somewhere high and secure. We could make more progress in putting distance between us and the Palace tomorrow.

I looked up at the buildings either side of us and saw a fire escape hanging from the building to our left just beyond my reach. I assessed the chances of us managing to climb onto it and break into the building quietly. Deciding to ask Cam for his opinion, I looked over my shoulder to see that he had put his thumb and forefinger into his mouth.

He whistled.

My mouth falling open, I stared at him in incomprehension.

He shrugged and, as I watched in disbelief, silver strands

gradually suffused the whites of his eyes.

"Sorry, Emilia," he said with a wry smile.

It had been a trap. Just not the kind of trap I had been expecting.

"You utter shit," I said, then turned away from him and ran blindly out into the road ahead of us.

Betrayal heaped on betrayal.

My heart sank as I scanned the street and saw that my options were seriously limited. I was faced with an uninterrupted wall of buildings from one end of the road to the other. The barricade cut across the street to my right, but it was dusk and the world beyond would be crawling with Weepers. My only option was to turn left and run down the main road. Bearing in mind, of course, that Cam was quite capable of catching and killing me in the space of a few seconds, just as Benedict had with Danny.

I still ran.

After five seconds passed I wondered why Cam wasn't trying to catch up with me. I looked over my shoulder and saw him still standing in the alley, following my progress but not making any move to stop me. A couple of moments later I heard engines approaching from the direction in which I was running and realised why. Cam was just the tracker. The collection crew were on their way.

I stopped in the middle of the road as two motorbikes turned into the road. I guessed that they were using them to pick up the stragglers instead of other vehicles because they'd be more easily manoeuvred in the cluttered streets. They came straight for me.

I slung the backpack from my shoulders and dropped it to the ground at my feet. I knew this was my last stand and I didn't need in weighing me down.

As the motorbikes came closer I saw they were a couple of vintage Triumphs ridden by two familiar Silver: Thomas and Drew.

I cursed under my breath. It had to be him.

The image of Jeff and Sarah's bodies flashed across my

mind. My blood roared in my veins and my fists clenched at my sides.

"Emilia?" he shouted in disbelief over the roar of the engines as he and Thomas skidded their bikes to a stop about twenty feet away from me. He stuck out the stand and jumped off, Thomas close behind him.

I stared at him with loathing in my eyes and ground my teeth together, moving onto the balls of my feet. I was fit to explode with anger and hatred.

"Oh shit," Thomas muttered. "Cam," he called, raising his voice, "get back to the Palace! Now!"

There was a blur in the left periphery of my vision as Cam sped back to the hotel. At least I now had one way out of here. Theoretically.

"Emilia, get on the bike," Drew said in a forcibly calm voice through clenched teeth.

I looked quickly over my shoulder towards the alley Cam had just deserted.

"Please don't run, Emilia," Thomas pleaded, moving a step closer.

I looked again and saw that Weepers were starting to make their way over the barricade behind me. As I watched, a couple stumbled out of the alleyway too, walking towards me.

I took a step backwards, away from Drew and Thomas.

Drew strode towards me.

"For Christ's sake, get on the fucking bike, Emmy!" Drew shouted at me, losing his cool.

Making up my mind, I flashed him a defiant look and turned on my heel, racing back towards the alley. The Weepers were slow moving and, if I was quick, I could dodge them and make a mad grab for the fire escape I'd spotted earlier.

At least that was the plan, a split-second before I felt a crack across the back of my head. Lights out.

CHAPTER XII

I awoke to a thumping headache, the sound of engines and the wind whipping at my hair and clothes. I decided not to open my eyes until my brain stopped feeling like it was trying to escape from my head. I was in an awkward position, curled forwards with my legs out in front of me.

"What else was I supposed to do?"

There was a vibration against my chest as Drew spoke, a strange reversal of the night we first met. How different the circumstances had been then. He was shouting over the wind and the engines as we roared along the road.

As I became more aware of my body, I realised that he had tied me to him like a backpack so he could carry me on the bike unconscious, one arm over his shoulder and the other under his arm with both legs crossed around his torso.

"She's not going to forgive you quickly for knocking her out."

"You saw her face, Tommy. I'm not sure there's anything I could do to make things worse at this point."

"If anyone finds out…"

"Are you going to tell?"

There was a pause. I wasn't sure what, if anything, was passing between them. The air stopped rushing past me quite so violently. We were slowing down.

"At least Cam didn't see."

I had pins and needles in my fingers and I couldn't feel my feet, so I wriggled around, moving my hands to try to get the blood circulating again. At the same time, I cautiously opened my eyes to find that we were pulling up outside the Palace.

Back here again. I felt crushed by the weight of my failure.

"She's awake," Drew said, the soft statement grumbling on the surface of my chest as we rolled to a stop.

I felt a brief pressure on my ankles then my feet fell from around him. He gently touched my hands and I flinched away, trying to yank them backwards, but only succeeded in pressing myself closer into his back.

"Shh," he said in a whisper, "I just want to untie you so we can both get off this bike."

That did sound like a reasonable proposition. Grudgingly, I held my hands out to him and quickly felt his fingers moving softly across my wrists. As he released my hands he took my left hand with his right and brought it to his lips, pressing a kiss onto the inside of my wrist. Horrified, I snatched my hand back over his shoulder and jumped off the bike away from him.

Unfortunately, the feeling hadn't yet returned to my feet, so I ended up sprawled on the pavement, cracking my skinned knee in the process. My healing wound split open and I felt blood soaking through the bandage. I clenched my jaw in agony and screwed my eyes shut for a couple of seconds until the pain passed.

Strong arms passed under my knees and shoulders, lifting me from the ground and pressing me into a warm chest that smelled of wood and leather.

My eyes snapped back open.

I elbowed Drew in the stomach and struggled out of his grip, managing to stand on my own this time. I rounded on Drew with fury in my eyes.

"Don't ever touch me," I hissed at him.

For a second, he looked stunned, a wounded expression

on his face. Then he nodded sadly and looked at the floor.

"I'm sorry, Emmy," Thomas said, stepping away from his bike and coming to stand beside me, "but we have to take you inside one way or another."

"Then I go with you," I said to Thomas, "not him."

Thomas looked at Drew with an anxious expression. Drew nodded at him and, without another word, turned and walked up the steps into the Palace.

"You shouldn't be so hard on him," Thomas said when he was gone.

I stared after Drew with vitriol and said nothing.

Thomas sighed then picked up a bag that was propped against his bike. He hoisted it onto his shoulder like it was as light as a feather. It was my backpack, so I knew it weighed a ton.

"Drew asked me to grab this before the Weepers got to it. He thought you might want to have it with you."

"Thank you," I said blandly, not really knowing how to respond to a kind gesture from a murderer and kidnapper.

"Ready?" Thomas asked.

I nodded in answer and we walked up the steps to the Palace together, side by side.

I'd been in the Palace a lot of times before. Parker's had a good relationship with the Palace, and we used to help each other out with change for till floats or by lending out bottles of spirits when either of the bars were short. In the reception area at least, very little had changed.

Plush seating was grouped around low tables either side of the atrium and doors led off from either side to a restaurant and a bar. The reception desk was set in the centre of an atrium with a high ceiling, a mezzanine circling above us that was accessed by a grand staircase rising at the back of the room, splitting into two branches halfway up its height. The reception desk was manned by two well-groomed women who looked to be human, though after Cam I wasn't sure I trusted myself to tell the difference anymore.

Six vampires were placed at regular intervals around the

atrium, standing stiffly with their arms crossed over their chests. Everything was shining marble, polished wood and leather. I felt like I was making the place untidy just by standing in it, grubby and bleeding.

Thomas led me past the reception desk towards a doorway at the back of the atrium, my knee dripping blood onto the perfect floor. I suffered a moment of guilt before remembering that this place belonged to the vampires now and that they were all bastards. I smirked childishly as my boots smeared the blood under my feet.

"Thomas."

The clear voice came from the mezzanine as we drew level with the base of the staircase. I turned to see Solomon standing at the balcony railing behind us. He was wearing a white shirt unbuttoned at the neck with navy blue chinos and smart black shoes.

"Primus?"

"I need you in the audience chamber," he replied.

"Yes, Primus," Thomas said, "I'll be with you momentarily after I have taken this human to admission."

"I'm sure someone else can escort her."

As he spoke, one of the vampires who had stood at the bottom of the stairs moved to my side, but Thomas put himself between us, shaking his head. He looked embarrassed but determined.

"Primus, I would really rather escort her myself."

Solomon's brow wrinkled in confusion. He shrugged.

"Then bring her with you."

"Primus?" Thomas asked hesitantly.

Solomon tipped his head and clicked his tongue in irritation.

"Just come on, Tommy."

Thomas looked at me uncertainly then, taking my arm at the elbow, started to lead me up the stairs. I shook my elbow free and stepped up the stairs ahead of Thomas, glaring at him over my shoulder.

He raised his eyebrows at me and held his hands up in a

gesture of surrender before following behind me.

We took the stairs in silence, our footsteps muffled by the carpet running along the centre of the marble staircase. We turned right at the first landing then followed the balcony around to an open door leading into a large, grand room. It looked like it had been designed as a ballroom, with beautiful wooden parquet flooring, but there was now a small semicircle of chairs arranged around a table at the head of the room. Solomon sat in the central chair with Drew on his right hand side.

I took a deep breath and strode across the floor towards them, Thomas at my side.

"Tommy, what the hell is she doing here?" Drew said angrily, getting to his feet.

"I told him to bring her," Solomon said calmly.

Drew turned towards him, incredulity on his face.

"Primus?"

Solomon shrugged with a nonchalant expression.

"Sol," Drew said with a hint of desperation in his voice, "she shouldn't be here."

"Why not?" he asked, his voice suffused with confusion. "What's up with you two this evening?"

Solomon raised an eyebrow and scrutinised Drew closely. Drew opened his mouth as if to speak, but thought better of it, shaking his head and retaking his seat.

Thomas and I reached the table, Thomas setting down my backpack before taking the seat on the other side of Drew. Solomon indicated the empty seat to his left with a smile.

He was dazzlingly good looking. The broadcasts had hardly done him justice. I was a little stunned, if I'm honest. His blue eyes danced with life and, unexpectedly, good-natured mischief. In real life he had a great deal of charisma and, where his beauty had seemed cold on a TV screen, in person I felt bathed in warmth by my proximity to him. I was surprised to find that I was drawn to him.

Turning to Thomas, Solomon got down to business.

"I want you heading up the search and destroy party

tonight. I need Drew here. Can you coordinate with Ben and Viv? They'll be taking the first and third units, you take the second."

Thomas nodded and the three of them began a painfully detailed discussion of the streets and subways, sewers and underground tunnels to be searched this evening and the best order in which to search them to ensure every Weeper was located and eliminated. I confess that I was so shattered I tuned out after the first few minutes.

I was ambivalent about them being so organised. It gave me confidence that they had the ability to protect those under their care, but I didn't trust their judgement as to who was worthy of protection. That being the case, I wanted to try to get out of here. It would have been easier if they'd been a little more inept.

I watched them as they talked, taking the opportunity to examine them whilst they weren't paying attention to me. They were all three of them striking in their own ways, having a certain otherworldliness about their appearance. I noted that Thomas and Solomon both had silver threading in the whites of their eyes, but Drew was the only one for whom that shining filament flowed into the iris.

Drew looked over at me and caught me staring at his eyes in interest. Their tactical conversation had come to an end whilst I was lost in thought and he caught me off guard. I looked away in embarrassment, but was immediately angry at myself for doing so. I returned my eyes to his and stared him down. He rose to the challenge.

"Yes," Solomon said to me with a knowing smile, "I had noticed that too."

Drew broke my gaze and looked at Solomon in alarm.

"Drew's… circumstances have rather changed in the last few days. You are seeing the expression of that change in his eyes."

"Sol, please…" Drew interrupted, indicating me with a tip of his head then looking away in what looked like shame.

Thomas glanced at Drew with panic.

"Alright, then," Solomon replied. "Keep it to yourself."

"Don't feel offended," he said to me in a confiding tone, "he won't talk to me about it either."

"Primus," Thomas said, standing from his chair, "if there is nothing else I should get the human admitted and prepare my team."

Solomon waved his hand at him.

"By all means, Tommy, but no need to delay yourself. You can leave the human here. We'll see her safely through admission."

Damn. I really would rather have gone with Thomas. Drew and Thomas looked like they would have preferred it too.

He paused for a second then effected a small bow. He shot a helpless look at Drew before leaving the room, his long legs striding quickly across the vast expanse of the ballroom floor.

Solomon turned to me when Thomas had shut the door behind him.

"You will probably have worked out that I am Solomon, the Primus," he said, extending his hand to me.

"Emilia," I replied uncertainly, putting my palm in his and shaking.

He smiled and squeezed my hand as if to reassure me. Turning it over, he looked at my wrist then reached for the other and did the same, as if he were looking for something. Still holding both of my hands in his, he raised a quizzical eyebrow over his shoulder at Drew.

"As you can see, Primus," Drew said, indicating a trail of bloody footprints across the room, "she was already injured. There was no need to take blood from the vein. I assure you that she has been tested and I can vouch for the purity of her blood."

My stomach fluttered. Everything was starting to come together. That was why he had been so solicitous when I had injured myself back at his flat. That was why he had healed my wound. He had been trying to bring me in and didn't want to alert me to the fact that he was testing my blood to see whether or not it was tainted with the Weeper infection.

I wondered what he would have done had I not serendipitously grazed myself. Maybe he had been there outside the bathroom that evening specifically to engineer such an accident. Maybe I would have woken up the next morning with an unexplained cut. My mind boggled at the depth of his deception.

I glared across the table at him, my eyes flashing with fury.

Solomon caught this and looked between the two of us with interest.

"I don't think she's your biggest fan, Drew."

Drew said nothing, gritting his teeth together and looking down at the table top.

"I don't much like any of your kind," I replied frankly.

"And why is that?" Solomon asked.

"You killed my friends. A boy in the cross street by the barricade. A man and a woman in the club across the road."

I felt hollow, dissociated, saying the words whilst trying not to think about their reality. Solomon looked at Drew in enquiry.

"The boy was a carrier, Primus. The man and woman… resisted."

Solomon nodded sadly and sighed.

"I am sorry for your friends, Emilia. We are trying to protect your kind, to save as many as we can, but not all are willing to cooperate and not all are in a position to be saved."

"It's tyranny," I replied defiantly.

"If one rebels and we fail to punish, we risk letting a carrier spread the Weeper plague. If we do not control the situation, if we allow anarchy to run rampant, we let this country fall as did America. I wish it were otherwise, but we are walking on a knife edge and we cannot tolerate resistance."

"I resisted," I replied.

"I am not at all surprised," Solomon returned with a ghost of a smile. "It is fortunate that you were unconscious when you were located."

I glanced at Drew. I hadn't started out unconscious. I had run.

Drew looked back at me with entreaty in his eyes. I decided to drop it for the time being.

"So will you kill me now that you know I won't submit?"

Solomon paused for a couple of seconds, a thoughtful look on his face. He shook his head.

"I hope not."

Drew looked at him anxiously.

"I know that it seems heavy-handed," Solomon continued, "but we have a moral duty to protect the humans in our care. That is the nature of our bargain."

"This is not a reciprocal social arrangement, Solomon," I sneered at him. "This is slavery. You said it yourself: we are your cattle."

His beautiful blue eyes bored into mine.

"What would you have me do?" he challenged. "Would you rather I lied? That I use clever arguments to convince you this is something you want? That I manipulate you into believing the reality of this arrangement to be other than it is?"

I looked down at the table.

"We have to drink blood to live," he continued, "and it has to be human. There's no way I can make that concept more palatable to you, if you'll excuse the pun. Life as you knew it has changed, Emilia. We have always been here, moving amongst you, it was just that you weren't conscious of our presence. Now, with the Weepers multiplying, consuming and replacing your kind, we can no longer hide."

"Isn't that a little disingenuous?" I said, remembering Jeff's theory about the lead time that would have been required for the level of organisation the vampires had displayed. "Aren't the Weepers just an excuse for you to act?"

"We have been waiting for an opportunity for some time," Solomon acknowledged with a tilt of his head.

"I know you want things to return to how they were," he continued, "but that is not in my power to give. Your world is gone. You're fighting for a life that no longer exists. There are difficult decisions to make, sacrifices, simply to save what little remains to us. I am trying to salvage an existence for your race, a new world for both of our races. There could be a place in that world for you, if you're willing to look for it."

I looked back at Solomon, suddenly unsure.

It was true. I was trying to find a way to get back to the life I had before the vampires. I was unable to adapt, unable to accept the vampires for what they were, to accept our lives for what they now were.

Danny had tried to tell me: I couldn't judge them as if they were human. Unlike Solomon, he hadn't wanted me to be okay with it. But Solomon was right too. The world had changed and I couldn't expect things to remain the same. This was not the time to deal in absolutes. My self-righteous rigidity was condemning me, had condemned Jeff and Sarah.

I just didn't know whether or not it was right for me to bend, whether I could do so without breaking. Submission felt like a betrayal of everything I had fought for, of Jeff and Sarah and, more than anything, a betrayal of Danny.

Danny, burning with the inflexible sense of injustice that comes with youth, sentenced to death by his tainted blood.

"Give it a week," Drew interjected, leaning over the table towards me.

I glared back at him.

"I'm truly sorry about your friends, but please at least give me... give us a chance to prove to you that we aren't the monsters you think we are."

I shook my head and Drew sighed in frustration. He reached over to me and grasped my hand in his.

"Please, Emmy," he begged, his eyes brimming with emotion.

Solomon raised his eyebrows at him in surprise.

"Perhaps I might venture a suggestion?" Solomon said quietly.

We both turned to him.

"The club, Parker's, I wish to reopen it as a gathering place for the Silver, perhaps for the humans too in time. We will all need somewhere to relax and its position across the road is fortuitous. Perhaps you would like to be part of that operation, Emilia? It might give you… purpose."

I thought in horror of Jeff and Sarah's bodies in the VIP bar. Drew saw the look on my face.

"They're gone, Emmy. We've already cleared the bar."

In a flash I was angry again and Drew guessed why.

"We buried them," he said quickly, "just like all the others. Beyond the perimeter to prevent infection. I laid them together."

I didn't know what to say. A tear slipped down my cheek as the image of the two of them hand in hand returned unbidden from my memory. My fury abated and I was left feeling defeated and alone, without even my righteous indignation to warm me.

Had I misjudged the Silver? Had I misjudged Drew? I had no idea anymore and I was too tired to think.

I wondered whether working at the bar would give me some continuity, help me to find some peace, or whether it would haunt me with the memory of a life that no longer existed.

"Just try it," Drew continued, "just for a week."

Part of me wanted to refuse simply because Drew was the one asking, the vampire who had killed my friends for refusing to submit. Who had followed my trail to Parker's to find them.

But most of me wanted to give in, to say yes for the sake of the man who had rescued me, who had held me in his arms until my heart calmed with the gentle rhythm of his breath. I saw that man in the vampire across the table from me, his eyes pleading with me.

I was exhausted and my anger was only going to sustain me for so long.

Hesitantly, I nodded.

He looked to Solomon.

"Primus?"

"A week, then," Solomon agreed.

CHAPTER XIII

Solomon and Drew spent another hour or so discussing logistics for securing and revitalising the safe zone. I was filthy and exhausted so, much though I probably should have been following their conversation keenly, I nodded off. I felt utterly deflated. All the fight had gone out of me.

When he saw that I had fallen asleep in my chair, Solomon decided that my admission could wait until tomorrow.

"Come on," he said, rising to his feet, "let's get you settled in. You'd better stay here, at least for tonight."

I stood unsteadily, leaning on the table to support myself. My knee had seized up while I was sitting and putting any weight on it was agony.

"Here, Primus?" Drew asked with surprise.

I gathered that humans were not usually accommodated at the Palace.

"Why not?" he replied.

"Sol, I'm not sure it's appropriate for her to bunk with the Solis Invicti."

"Of course not," he replied with a toothy grin, "that's why she should have the spare suite on the fifth."

Drew paled.

"I don't know why you're looking at me like that,"

Solomon said. "You know as well as I do it's the safest place in London. Well… except for my apartments of course."

Drew acquiesced quickly at that, bending down to retrieve my backpack from where Thomas had left it on the floor.

"I shall escort her there," he said.

"Unnecessary," Solomon replied. "I'm going that way shortly myself."

Solomon looked like he was suppressing a smile. Drew clenched his jaw.

"I insist," Drew said. "It's no trouble."

Solomon scrutinised him for a second. I felt like he was prodding Drew, testing him to see how he would react. He shrugged.

"Very well, then. I shall see you tomorrow, Emilia."

He eyed Drew with interest as he strapped on the backpack then, to my surprise, swept me up sideways with one arm under my knees and the other under my shoulders.

"Drew," I said in outrage, "I'm perfectly capable of walking."

"No, Emilia," he replied in a long-suffering tone, "you're not. You don't have to act tough, so just shut up and let me help you."

As he reached the door of the audience chamber with me in his arms, I looked back over his shoulder at Solomon, who was standing by the table watching us leave.

"Sorry I bled on your floor," I shouted back at him as Drew opened the door into the corridor.

Solomon let out a bark of laughter and smiled at me as Drew stepped through onto the mezzanine balcony, shutting the door behind him.

"You know, it wouldn't hurt you to show a little respect to the Primus," Drew said to me as he carried me round the mezzanine.

I said nothing.

He was heading for an ornate stairwell leading up to the remaining floors of the hotel. It was enclosed and wasn't as grand as the main staircase by which we had ascended to the mezzanine, but it was still pretty impressive. It was on the opposite side of the atrium from the main staircase, set over the front door to the Palace.

"Okay," he continued, "maybe it would hurt your pride."

"Don't make it sound like I'm being petty," I snapped back, "and it isn't about my pride."

"I know it isn't, Emmy, but…"

"You killed them," I whispered.

I couldn't get the image of Jeff and Sarah's vacant eyes out of my head or the last time I saw them: hand in lifeless hand. Whatever Solomon and Drew said, I didn't think I could accept an excuse for that.

Danny… Danny had been infected. To my mind, it was entirely different to kill someone who presented a real threat than to kill someone who might. I felt Jeff and Sarah had a right to resist, that regardless of their ability to carve out a life without the help of the Silver, they had a right to try. I had a right to try.

But what if what Solomon said was true? What if there was no safety for us beyond the barricade? Maybe any attempt I made to escape would see me engulfed in a wave of Weepers. Maybe killing rebels was necessary to contain the Weeper plague. To save humankind from itself.

Perhaps I was so upset by Jeff and Sarah's deaths because they were at his hands, at Drew's hands. At the hands of someone I had trusted, however irrational or misplaced that trust may have been. Whatever Danny and Sarah had said to me, I had still been holding on to my impression of him as a saviour. At the beginning of the night I could only see him as a murderer. Now I just didn't know what he was.

"Emmy, I…," he started, before falling silent.

Neither of us spoke as he carried me up the four flights of stairs that brought us to the fifth floor. I was so tired I started to drop off again.

When we finally reached the fifth floor I saw that it was also the top floor of the building. The stairs went no higher. Drew carried me out into a small but richly-decorated corridor running directly ahead from the top of the stairs. It was adorned with plush burgundy carpet and bold, crimson and gold wallpaper.

There were three sets of double doors leading from the corridor, each marked with a room number. The first was set directly opposite us, about ten yards ahead of the stairwell. The other two doors were set on either side of us, halfway down the corridor.

"That one's empty at the moment," he said, nodding towards the door on the right. "The Weepers got in just after the Revelation and it's not been repaired yet."

"I'm not picky," I said sleepily.

"It's only got three walls."

"Oh," I replied. "Walls are important."

"Yes," he said with a brief burst of the chuckle that had so irritated me two nights ago. "This one's yours."

He lowered my feet gently to the floor in front of the door on the left and pulled a keyring from his pocket. Unlocking the door, he swung me into his arms again and carried me over the threshold. The oddity of the symbolism was not lost on me. It was incongruous enough to be funny to me in my addled state and I huffed out a short laugh.

"What?" Drew asked, looking down at me as he walked into the suite.

"Rites of passage," I replied incoherently.

He looked back at the doorway contemplatively as he flicked on the lights.

"Don't worry," he said with a smile, "our marriage rites are very different from yours."

I looked around the room. It was a beautifully furnished, cosy suite with soft light blue carpet and cream curtains patterned with small blue flowers. Straight ahead of us as we entered was a comfy-looking seating area with a small fabric sofa and two armchairs set around a low wooden coffee table.

On the right, set against the wall opposite the door, was a queen-sized, four-poster bed with a small pedestal table on either side of it. There were two doors in the wall to the far right, one of which I presumed was a wardrobe and the other the en suite bathroom.

Drew walked over to the sofa and lowered me down carefully over it.

"I don't want to bleed on it," I said with concern.

Drew rolled his eyes and, wrapping one arm around me, pulled me close to him with his right arm as he reached with his left for a blanket that was folded on the back of the sofa. He spread it quickly over the seat then set me gently on top of it.

"There will be other rites of passage for you to worry about tomorrow," he said to me darkly as he shrugged out of the backpack and his leather jacket, setting them on the floor next to the sofa.

Admission. I wondered what it entailed, but I wasn't sure I wanted to talk about it. Certainly not with Drew.

He knelt down in front of me and looked at the sodden bandage around my knee. It really was revolting. Well, to me anyway. As far as I knew, it was like melted chocolate to the vampires. I shuddered at the thought.

"Will you let me heal it for you?" he asked, looking up at me.

I remembered him healing the wound on my arm two nights ago, of which there was now no sign at all. My cheeks warmed as I remembered the trail of his tongue on my skin, the intensity of his gaze as he looked up into my eyes. My stomach flipped.

I shook my head.

I was concerned to find that my primary reason for not wishing him to heal me was not that I wanted to avoid him touching me in such an intimate way. Instead, I was concerned about the possible repercussions for him if he broke the unwritten 'no healing humans' rule.

Part of me actively wanted him to touch me that way again.

It was irrational and it was wrong. I was all over the place: both disgusted and enflamed by him. I needed to get some sleep and then deal with it tomorrow, when I could think straight.

"I need to sleep," I said, moving to stand.

He stood quickly and took my hands, supporting my weight.

"Emmy, please let me help."

I ignored him, looking down at myself.

"I'm filthy," I said plainly. "I can't get into that clean bed like this."

"It doesn't matter."

"Yes, it does," I insisted.

I started hobbling towards the doors on the far side of the room, assuming one led to the bathroom. Before I'd moved more than two steps, Drew picked me up again.

"I don't need your help!" I shouted at him in irritation.

"Well, you're getting it anyway," he growled down at me, his eyes flashing.

I glared back at him. I was feeling impotent enough with my whole situation. The last thing I needed was him making me feel even more powerless by denying me even the independence to walk across a room on my own.

It was an extra kick in the teeth that it was Drew who was helping. Drew, who had murdered Sarah and Jeff.

He strode towards the doors on the other side of the suite with me in his arms. Opening the door on the right, he stepped into a beautiful marbled bathroom with a wide tub. I could have wept at the sight. There was nothing I wanted more at that moment than to soak in a scalding hot bath. It was probably a really bad idea to soak my knee, but I just didn't care.

I looked up at Drew.

"Bath?" he asked.

I nodded, trying to keep the joy off my face.

He set me down on the side of the tub and reached over to get the water running.

"Hot," I urged him.

He smiled as he fiddled with the heat settings.

I frowned at him.

"I don't know what you're smiling about," I snapped. "If you think you can make up for the murders of the few people in this world I loved by running me a bath then you're sorely mistaken."

He looked at me mournfully.

"I know that, Emmy."

"You're the author of all of this," I glared at him. "I'll never forgive you for their deaths, or for bringing me here."

"The Weepers would have killed you," he replied, shaking his head. "I wasn't just going to just stand by and watch you die."

"I resisted," I said quietly. "You should have killed me too."

"How many times do I have to tell you: I'm never going to hurt you."

"You already have!" I yelled at him, trying to get to my feet.

He caught me before I fell, enveloping me in his arms, and settled me back on the edge of the bath. I thumped at his chest with my fists to no effect, screaming at him in rage. He just wrapped his arms more tightly around me as my screams turned into sobs.

Why did I have to keep crying all the time?

I pushed him away, wiping the tears from my face as I turned away. There was a line of bottles on the edge of the bathtub and I rifled through them, looking at each of the labels in turn. Anything to avoid looking at Drew.

After a few moments I selected a lavender bubble bath at random and leaned towards the taps so I could put a dose into the bath, but Drew gently took the bottle from my hand. I flinched away from him as he wordlessly poured a generous measure under the running water.

"What else have you to wear?" he asked me as he screwed the lid back on the bottle and returned it to the side of the tub.

"Just leave me alone," I said quietly.

"I'm sorry, but I can't do that. I need to make sure you're safe."

I sighed. There was no way I could force him out of here if he was unwilling to leave on his own. I was just too broken.

"Clothes are in the bag," I said.

He left me in the bathroom with the bath running and I watched him through the doorway as he walked back to the seating area to retrieve my backpack. He brought it back with him and, putting it down at my feet, looked at me in enquiry.

My forehead creased in surprise. He didn't want to go through my stuff without my permission.

I nodded at him and, kneeling in front of me, he unzipped the bag. He pulled out the first aid kit, water bottles and strips of T-shirt and placed them on the floor next to him, raising his eyebrows at me as he found the gin.

I shrugged back and, grabbing it from him, unscrewed the lid and took a swig. Then another, bigger one.

"Enough, Emmy," he said, taking away from me.

I looked down at my hands where they lay in my lap. A tear slipped unbidden down my cheek and splashed onto my wrist. I was furious at myself for crying again, but I didn't seem to be able to stop.

"It's been a shitty day," I muttered through my tears.

"I know."

"It's your fault."

"I know that too," he replied on a sigh.

He hesitated for a moment then placed a hand on my tear-sodden cheek and looked up into my eyes.

"I'm so sorry, Emmy."

I shook my head at him in despair, my face creasing up with grief. I don't think I had ever cried so much in my entire life as I did that day. And for it to be in front of Drew... I was burning with frustration and misery.

His brow furrowed in anxiety and, running his hand round to the back of my neck, he moved towards me. He took me into his arms, holding me sideways in his lap on the floor, pressing my body closely into his chest. He wrapped his arms around me, cocooning me in the scent of leather and sawdust.

I tried to push away from him, but I started sobbing

uncontrollably, deciding instead to bury my face into his shoulder as he rocked me gently back and forth. I concentrated on the steady pulse of his heartbeat and, gradually, my breathing calmed.

"I said I'd get you through this and I will," he whispered into my hair, "I promise. I'll keep you safe."

"How can I ever trust you," I mumbled into his T-shirt, "after what you've done?"

"Time," he said simply, kissing me on the forehead as he lifted me back to sit on the edge of the tub.

I wasn't so sure.

He reached over and turned off the water, the bath now full of steaming hot water and bubbles. Kneeling back down in front of me, he pulled Jeff's T-shirts and socks out of my backpack, along with my leather jacket and handbag.

"You can have your T-shirt back," I said. "It's in my handbag."

He shook his head and gave me a small smile.

"Keep it," he replied.

He left the food in the backpack and surveyed the small pile of belongings around him on the floor.

"Well," he continued, "apart from your jacket, none of these clothes are going to fit you properly."

"They'll do."

"No," he replied, "I've got a better idea: I'll go out and find you some clothes that will fit while you have your bath."

"You don't need to do that," I said, not wanting to be indebted to him.

"It'll only take a moment," he replied. "I'll grab something from the shops around the corner."

I sighed heavily. This was ridiculous.

"I'm going to lock you into the suite," he said, "but I'd like to take the keys with me, if you don't mind?"

Whatever. He could get in here anyway if he really wanted to, so what did it matter? I nodded at him. Smiling at me, he gathered up my belongings from the floor and took them back to the seating area.

"You'll be alright on your own?" he asked, shrugging into his leather jacket as he moved towards the door to the suite.

I rolled my eyes at him through the bathroom doorway and he let himself out, the key turning in the lock as he left.

I blew out a breath.

This was all a bit too domestic for me. He ran me a bath, for Christ's sake.

Sighing, I bent down to unzip my boots. I just wanted to get clean and get some sleep. I wasn't sure what time it was, but it felt painfully late. I guessed it was irrelevant really. It's not as if Drew was going clothes shopping, he was just taking clothes from a shop.

I had a brief moment of anxiety as I realised the Weepers would now be out in force, but realised that he could doubtless look after himself. More importantly, I probably shouldn't care.

I pulled off my right boot and peeled the left one carefully from my foot. There was blood everywhere. I wasn't sure if I was going to be able to salvage the boot. I kicked myself for not asking Drew to grab me some footwear while he was at it.

I stripped off Jeff's long-sleeved T-shirt and my bra then pushed my shorts and my underwear to the floor, balancing as well as I could on my right foot to keep my weight off my left knee. Worried that Drew might return before I was out of the bath, I pushed the bathroom door shut and threw the lock.

I sat back on the side of the tub and tentatively touched the bandage on my wound, recoiling as pain stabbed through it. I swore and bit my lip until the agony subsided. Taking a deep breath, I untied the bandage and carefully started to unwrap it. It was stuck together unpleasantly, pulling at the wound where it had dried. Scooping some water from the bath with my hand, I gently dribbled some onto the bandage to help release it.

Finally, after a lot more swearing, I had the wound fully unwrapped.

I swivelled around and swung my legs up, lying my left leg

along the side of the bath as I dipped my right foot into the scalding water.

It was heaven.

The bubbles were heaped on top of the water, completely obscuring it, a fluffy pillow about a foot deep. They enveloped my leg as my right foot hit the bottom of the tub. Leaving my left heel where it was, I put my arms either side of the bath and scooched sideways, lowering my body into the water whilst leaving my left leg as far out as I could. I sucked in a breath as my injured knee bent with my descent.

When my body was fully in the water, I very, very gently lifted my left leg and started to inch it into the water. My wound burnt as it hit the water, but the relief as it soaked away the congealed blood and the stiffness in the joint was amazing. I closed my eyes in pleasure as the heat warmed my aching limbs.

Reaching behind me, I pulled out my hair band and put it on the side of the tub. I slipped down into the water and lay down on my back putting my head under, combing my fingers through my hair. I stayed under until I ran out of breath then broke through the bubbles to the surface, pushing them from my face with both hands.

I settled back, resting my head on the lip of the tub and closing my eyes.

I must have dropped off, because the next thing I knew Drew was pounding on the bathroom door. I started and opened my eyes.

"Emilia!" he shouted, just before there was a colossal crash as the door swung open, tearing the bolt from the wall.

"What the hell?" I yelled at him, sitting up and crossing my arms over my chest.

"Shit," Drew muttered, his eyes dropping briefly to my chest before he turned his back to me.

"What do you think you're doing?"

"I was knocking on the door and you weren't answering," he said. "I got worried."

I exhaled loudly and lay back down in the tub.

"You can turn around," I said on a sigh, "I'm covered in bubbles."

He turned to me with a sheepish look on his face.

"Sorry," he said.

There was a knock on the door to the suite.

"What now?" I asked, exasperated.

Drew walked out of the bathroom and opened the door to the corridor a crack. He conducted a brief conversation in a hurried whisper with whomever was on the other side before locking the door again and returning to the bathroom.

"The Primus was worried," he said simply on his return.

I was finding it a little difficult to adjust to the concept of vampires being worried about me. I stared at Drew levelly from the bath.

"The door at the end of the corridor," Drew said, "that's Solomon's apartments. He heard me break the lock and was concerned there was something wrong."

I raised my eyebrows at him in surprise. Apparently, I was to have an influential neighbour tonight.

"Whatever," I sighed. "I just fell asleep, that's all."

"Oh. Sorry," he repeated.

"Just go away and let me wash. I'll be out in a minute."

He nodded and left the bathroom, attempting to shut the door behind him but succeeding only in dragging it until it was ajar. The bolt was hanging off at an angle, stopping it from shutting.

"Sorry, Emmy," he mumbled again from the other side of the door.

"Go away!"

I heard his steps padding away towards the other side of the suite.

Stupid vampires.

I dunked my head back under the water and shampooed and conditioned quickly. I washed my body, avoiding my knee, then finally cleaned the blood away from around the wound. It looked pretty revolting and I doubted that soaking it had been a helpful thing to do, but at least it was a clean as it could be.

Pulling the plug from the tub, I stepped out and towelled off carefully, wrapping the towel around me under my arms. My hair was falling in wet strands past my shoulders and there wasn't much I could do without a brush. I did my best to untangle it with my fingers then plaited it, securing the braid at the end with my hair band.

When I was sure it was as good as it was going to get, I gathered my dirty clothes from the floor and wrenched the door open, limping over to the bed.

Drew was standing over by the coffee table, a huge number of clothing store bags strewn around him. There was everything from designer labels to high street to boutique.

"What did you do?" I asked incredulously.

"I wasn't sure what you'd want to wear," he said, looking at me helplessly.

"At the moment," I replied, "I'd settle for pyjamas."

Drew smiled and reached into one of the bags, pulling out a pair of soft, cotton pyjamas with long trousers and a stretchy, lacy top. I chucked my dirty clothes in a pile under one of the pedestal tables and sat on the side of the bed as Drew grabbed the first aid kit and walked over. He put the pyjamas on the bed then sat down next to me.

"Lie back," he said, opening up the first aid kit.

"I can do it," I replied.

"Will you just let me help?"

I sighed with irritation but shifted back on the bed, swivelling so that my back lay propped up on the pillows behind me. As Drew opened it up, I saw that there were a few bandages and, to my relief, some wound dressings in the kit. He gently took my left foot in his hands and, raising my leg a little, moved along the bed so that when he lowered my leg back down it was resting in his lap.

"Are you sure you won't let me heal it?" he asked.

I shook my head at him again.

"I don't want you to."

Sighing, he reached for the wound dressing and used a pair

of scissors from the kit to cut it to the right size. He pressed it gently to the wound and I flinched, sucking in a breath.

"Is it okay?" he asked solicitously.

I nodded back.

At least the bleeding seemed to have slowed for the time being.

I felt the roughness of his fingertips as he wrapped the bandage around the dressing, holding it securely in place, but he was so gentle that I barely felt it. He was treating me like I was made of glass.

"It's a bad injury," he said as he tied off the bandage. "It'll take a pretty long time to heal properly."

"It's fine."

"Look, I know you don't want to trust me, but please think about letting me heal you. It would make things easier for you."

"It's not that," I replied. "Drew, tomorrow…"

He looked at me curiously.

"It's admission," I continued. "They'll see it."

"You're worried for me?" he asked with a small smile.

"Let's not get carried away."

He grinned at me.

"Look," I snapped at him, "just because I don't want to get caught up in some ridiculous Silver intrigue about how healing humans is wrong doesn't mean I hate you any less. Got it?"

"Right," he replied, chastened.

I bent my right knee up and swivelled back around, reclaiming my leg from Drew and putting it over the edge of the bed.

"I'm going to go to sleep."

"Okay," Drew said, making no move to leave.

"I'm really tired."

"I imagine you would be."

"Will you go away, now?" I asked him in exasperation.

"I'm not leaving you alone, Emmy," he replied. "Not in a house full of Silver. Not with Solomon next door."

"You're Silver," I pointed out.

"I know," he said, "but I trust me, even if you don't."

"Telling me that you distrust not only your Primus, but your entire race is not a good way to instil confidence in me. What are they going to do, kill me in my sleep?"

"No!" he replied in outrage, "nothing like that. That's not how the Silver are."

"I don't believe you."

He sighed.

"Just let me stay, please. Just let me watch over you."

Creepy, I thought. Or, at least, that's what I should have felt, but, much though I wanted to deny it and despite his actions, I did feel safer with him around. Nevertheless, he needed to leave.

"No," I replied.

"Well, I'm staying anyway."

I let out a yell of frustration.

"Fine, but I can get changed on my own!"

With a satisfied smile, he stood up from the bed and walked into the bathroom, jamming the door shut behind him.

I put my head in my hands, completely overwhelmed.

Standing gingerly from the bed I threw off the towel onto the floor. There was blood on it from where it had touched my wound, but I couldn't bring myself to care. There'd been so much blood today, mine and other people's.

I carefully pulled on the pyjama trousers, trying not to pull at my bandage as I did so, then dropped the top over my head. They were beautifully soft and warm. Sighing with relief, I pulled the covers off the bed and slipped between the sheets, wrapping them around my shoulders.

"You can come back in, but you stay on the other side of the room," I called to Drew. "And turn off the lights."

Rolling onto my side, I closed my eyes as the room dropped into darkness. I was asleep in moments.

CHAPTER XIV

Sunday

I woke in a wonderful, warm bundle. In my semi-conscious state, I revelled in the toasty embrace of the blankets around me. The sheets were soft and clean, smelling comfortingly of washing powder and... something else. There was a wonderful heat on my back.

Sighing with pleasure, I tried to roll over from my left side, only to come up against an obstruction at my back. A pressure tightened around me.

My eyes flew open with alarm. I slid my hands to my waist, away from where they were pillowed under my head, and encountered an arm around me. Inhaling deeply, I breathed in a distinctive leather and wood scent: Drew.

There was a rumble behind me that reverberated through my rib cage as he stirred. He pulled me closer to him, tucking his arm around me, and rubbed his face into my neck. His lips were pressed against my skin under my ear, his breath tickling the back of my ear.

Outraged, I tried to pull away, but his arm was completely unyielding.

"What are you doing?" I asked incredulously.

"Hmm?"

"What are you doing?"

"Snuggling," he said with a smile in his tone, slipping his other arm under me so I was fully enclosed in his embrace.

"Get off me!"

I wriggled around trying to free myself, but only succeeded in turning myself in his arms onto my side to face him. I glared at him, but he just pulled me closer to him, burying his face in my shoulder as he wrapped one hand tightly around my waist and the other around my shoulders.

He was so warm, the smell of him rich and exciting. My body was pressed closely against his.

He moaned in pleasure and rolled slightly onto his back, pushing his leg between mine to rub up against me. My breath caught in the back of my throat and I inhaled shakily, my chest pushing upwards into his. My hands moved towards him, one wrapping around his neck and the other pushing through his hair.

Growling his approval, he rolled on top of me and, planting his arms either side of my shoulders, pinned me to the bed with his hips. It would have been difficult not to notice that he was enjoying himself. He stared into my eyes, his silver irises disappearing behind his dilating pupils.

My mouth fell open as I gasped for breath.

He moved his gaze to my lips.

Heat pooled at the top of my thighs and I shuddered with excitement.

This was moving too fast. How was I even in bed with him?

"Let me go," I said with my teeth gritted as I shot him a look dripping with loathing.

He rolled off me immediately.

"Emmy?"

I slid across the mattress and turned my back to him, sitting with my legs hanging over the side of the bed.

"What's wrong?" he asked, anxiously.

"What's wrong?" I asked angrily. "What do you think is wrong? What the hell was that?"

"But," Drew said in confusion, "you were... it was..."

He seemed lost for words.

"No," he said vehemently, "you can't try and tell me you weren't into that, Emmy. You were right there with me. You felt it. I know you did."

He was right, but I said nothing.

"Fuck, Emmy," he said in desperation, moving closer behind me, "don't do this to me. Don't pretend there's nothing between us."

I shook my head.

He put his hand on my shoulder and pulled me roughly back towards him, turning me to face him.

"You felt it too," he growled at me.

I had to get myself out of this situation.

"Let go!" I shouted at him.

He dropped his hand and looked at me with sorrow and disbelief. A weight settled in my chest as his gaze bored into me.

"Say what you like, but you feel it."

Yes, I did. And it had scared me senseless. This was the creature that had murdered my friends.

Time to change the subject.

"What are you even doing in my bed?" I asked indignantly.

He paused for a moment and gave me a look, as if to say that this topic of conversation would be revisited at a future time.

"You were screaming in your sleep," he replied quietly. "You wouldn't calm down until I held you. I tried to move away," he said, looking at me meaningfully, "but you just screamed again."

I looked away from him.

"It's been a traumatic few days," I said, brushing it off. "It doesn't mean anything."

"You screamed for me to help you, Emmy," he said softly. "You screamed my name."

Shit.

I shook my head, but it made sense. He'd become my safe place in this new world, screwed up as that was.

"No," I said stubbornly.

He laughed bitterly.

"Deny it all you like, I heard it," he said. "Hell, half the Palace probably heard it."

That was going to make today so much more difficult. I groaned and put my head in my hands. He cupped his hand around my cheek, using it to raise my face to his.

"Don't touch me!" I hissed at him, batting away his hand.

His eyes burned into mine, mercury circling his pupils and veining his irises.

"You were screaming for me in fear, like you needed to be saved. I want you to scream for me, Emmy," he said, the tone of his voice softening, melting, "but not like that."

Just like that, I was breathless again, my heart thumping in my chest. A slow smile crept across his face as he registered my response.

"It doesn't mean anything," I repeated in an irritated tone of voice. "I think I've made my feelings for you perfectly clear."

"Whatever you say," he whispered. "I know it's there, and that's enough for now."

CHAPTER XV

While I slept, Drew had put all of the clothes he had acquired the previous night into the wardrobe next to the bathroom. There was an insane breadth of choice, from beautiful designer dresses to scruffy outdoor wear. Not only had he secured a range of footwear, he'd also found an amazing range of underwear, somehow divining my sizes correctly, or at least closely enough.

I had been delighted and surprised to find that he had arranged for my dirty clothes to be laundered. He had also managed to clean the blood from my left boot until it was as good as new. I couldn't believe he had been so thoughtful. Or manipulative, I told myself.

In the end, I decided on shorts, a new pair of flat black boots that fitted below the bandage on my knee and a casual, green T-shirt, paired with my old leather jacket. I also indulged myself by choosing the softest cotton knickers and bra I could find in Drew's selection. This was no time for lacy undies.

It was actually very late in the day, nearly midday. I'd slept long and deeply, despite the screaming. I was grateful to Drew for letting me sleep, but I resented even that emotion towards him. I wasn't willing to accept what I felt. Part of me wondered whether it was a trick or a trap.

Drew and I met Solomon coming out of his apartments as we left the suite, so we walked downstairs together. I was starving, but I wanted to get the admission process out of the way before I did anything else.

Drew wanted to take me through admission, but Solomon wanted him to sort out the security teams for the Palace and Parker's. Solomon won. I breathed a sigh of relief. I really wanted some space from Drew.

To my surprise, Solomon offered to take me through admission himself. Drew didn't look very happy at the prospect.

"I suppose always winning arguments is a perk of being an evil dictator," I said sarcastically to him as the three of us walked together down the stairs to the atrium. There were a lot of them.

"Emmy…," Drew growled in admonishment.

"I prefer to think of it as supreme executive power," Solomon replied with an indulgent smile. "It reminds me that my control is limited, that such power is not absolute, that it is transient, even for the Silver. I lead only because people choose to follow."

"It's easy to make your people compliant if you kill everyone who makes the 'wrong' choice," I replied petulantly.

Drew glared a warning at me.

In my frustration and my confusion about my feelings for Drew, I was directing my anger at Solomon instead. I knew I was doing it, but it didn't stop me from feeling irrationally angry towards him. I just decided to go with it.

"You've effectively decimated the remaining human population," I continued, "leaving alive only those humans who are too weak in character to challenge you."

Solomon looked at me appraisingly as we reached the third floor.

"You see everything in black and white, Emilia," he replied. "For you, humans have either stood against us and so are strong or have acquiesced to my bargain and so are weak. You paint your defiance as a moral necessity and cast judgement on those who fail to throw themselves on their swords for your cause. You do them a disservice."

"They gave away their freedom," I said harshly. "Freedom is worth fighting for, worth dying for."

"There is no prize at the end of the battle you seek to fight, Emilia. There is no freedom for the dead. For someone so bent on dealing in absolutes you fail to appreciate the most obvious one: either you give up your freedom, as you call it, or you will die."

"You mean you'll kill us."

"No," Solomon said, shaking his head, "we won't have to. The Weepers will. You call me an evil dictator, but it is not in my nature to fill that role. I would not lightly enslave an entire race of people, and I know that is how you see it: slavery. Without our intervention, without the loss of the lives we have taken, every human on the planet would be dead.

"For you, it is easy to oppose us. You have only yourself to lose. Would you be so eager to throw your life away if you had family to look after, children to care for? Would your morals require their sacrifice to escape what you perceive as your subjugation?

"There is no virtue in giving yourself up to certain death, Emilia. It is the ultimate surrender: a grand, empty martyrdom. True strength lies in those who struggle on in the face of adversity for the sake of those they love, who strive to build a better life."

"You killed everyone I loved," I ground out through my teeth.

Solomon sighed.

"Refreshing as it is to engage in such lively debate with you, Emilia," Solomon replied, glancing sideways at me, "I'm not going to keep covering the same ground. You may disagree with my methods for containing the Weepers, but you know very well that the reasoning behind them is sound."

We walked the rest of the way in silence, skirting round the mezzanine when we reached the first floor.

Drew left us at the base of the stairs and walked off across the atrium to what I gathered was the security office, casting an anxious glance over his shoulder at me as he did so. When he was out of sight Solomon turned to me, indicating the door to admission through which Thomas had been intending to take me last night when we had been called upstairs.

"You don't have to escort me, Solomon."

He smiled at me in amusement.

"I thought I would take the opportunity to get to know you better, since you seem to have both my Secundus and Tommy in a bit of a flap. Why is that?" he wondered aloud.

"How should I know what goes on in the pretty little heads of your lackeys?" I asked with a saccharine smile.

He leaned a little closer in to me and dropped his voice to a whisper.

"Although I'm quite happy for you to be as defiant as you like with me one-to-one whilst you wait out your week," he breathed close to my ear, "I'd appreciate it if you'd tone it down in front of the lackeys, as you call them. Reputation is a precarious thing."

I looked at him with a raised eyebrow.

He sighed loudly, pushing open the door to admission and holding it open as I stepped through, following after me. We walked into a large room that had clearly once been a library. Now, chairs were arranged in lines at the end into which we entered, like a waiting room. Several sets of ornamental screens were placed at the other, separating that portion of the room into three cubicles. Between us and the screen was a desk, behind which sat two chatting women, both Silver.

As Solomon stepped into the room a hush fell. One of the women gasped in surprise and rushed out to intercept him.

"Primus!" she gushed at him, "what an unexpected surprise!"

I looked over my shoulder at him, raising my eyebrows. He tried to give me a stern look in return, but he was unable to keep his face solemn.

"Hello, Rena," he said to the preening woman with a slight

smile.

She giggled back at him, clearly delighted that he knew who she was.

"Another one to be admitted?" Rena asked brightly. "I thought we were all done. Well, anyway, I'll take care of her."

She reached out to take my hand.

"Actually," Solomon interrupted her, "I'll see her through admission myself, if that's not too much of a disruption."

"Of course not!" she crooned. "You go right ahead. Take any cubicle you like, they're all free."

He smiled kindly at her and held his hand out towards the screens, inviting me to choose one. At random, I walked towards the one on the left with a little trepidation and paused at its edge. I wondered what happened next.

"Rena, might you give us a little more privacy?" he asked quietly.

"Oh yes, of course! We'll be right outside if you need us, Primus."

She ushered her colleague out of the room with a confidential glance at Solomon, shutting the door behind them.

Solomon turned to me with an apologetic smile as he moved towards the screen.

"I'm afraid she thinks I want to snack on you."

My eyes widened a little.

"Don't worry," he said, "much though you intrigue me, you're safe with me. I derive no pleasure from drinking from the unwilling."

My skin tingled with fear.

"You're saying there are people who want you to drink their blood?" I asked, putting as much revulsion into my tone of voice as I could.

Solomon stopped in front of me and gave me a level look.

"You know there are, Emilia. Don't pretend you don't understand the attraction."

I looked up into his eyes, disarmed by his forthrightness.

Despite his unnatural beauty and movement, he was so

human I found myself forgetting what he was. But, however much my mind might forget, my body knew. It thrilled with his proximity, with the danger my senses knew he presented to me.

The worst thing was that it didn't even feel wrong.

I couldn't deny that I could imagine how someone might give in to that. I remembered the feeling of Drew's lips on my throat, the excitement in the anticipation of his bite. Given more time alone with him before I'd run, maybe I would have given in.

"I understand it," I admitted, grudgingly.

"It can be an intensely enjoyable experience," he said huskily, leaning forward to speak into my ear, his warm cheek brushing against mine.

I was too surprised to move. He smelt delicious: like Christmas and spring all rolled into one. I shivered involuntarily and he pulled back slightly, a teasing glint in his eye.

"Just let me know when you're ready for it."

"When?" I replied.

"I can see it in your eyes and hear it in the beat of your heart: the thought excites you."

"It's fear, not excitement," I responded breathlessly, Solomon's face inches from mine.

"I heard you in fear last night in your dreams," he said. "This is not fear, and my Secundus is not here now to come to your aid. Or to restrain you."

Shit.

I looked back at him in panic.

The corner of his mouth jerked upwards in a smile and he moved away, side-stepping me to walk into the cubicle. I followed his movement with my eyes, looking over my shoulder.

"As you wish," he said, his icy eyes shining, "but the more you resist, the more you will desire it. Making it forbidden ultimately just increases the thrill of transgression, even within your own mind. Your obstinacy makes you weak."

He was not trying to provoke me. He simply stated it as if it were fact. Although there was no judgement in his tone, I dropped my head in shame nonetheless. I felt like he could see into my soul, scouring me clean. He had known me for less than a day and my mind was an open book to him. He knew things that were not yet clear even to me.

"I'm sorry, Emilia," he continued, "I didn't mean to upset you."

I turned towards him, shaking my head.

"I'm not upset," I said quietly. "I just… you're essentially telling me that freedom is a matter of perception. That I can accept this bargain for what it is and be liberated, or that I can swim against the current and drown."

He sighed.

"No, Emilia, you're missing the point. I'm not just telling you that you can break through the cage in your head, I'm telling you that you want to, that the choice is already made. That the more you stay inside your cell, the more you yearn to be free."

"That doesn't make it right."

"No," he replied with a smile, "but just because you decree it so doesn't mean it's wrong either."

I exhaled loudly. For someone who claimed not to manipulate with his words, Solomon had a certain turn of phrase that made it difficult to argue against him.

"Come on," he said, beckoning to me as he stepped behind the screen.

I followed him, turning the corner to see a low bed with a chair set beside it, a rolling tray of medical instruments nearby. He motioned me towards the bed as he sat in the chair.

I looked nervously towards the needles, scalpels and other various torture devices.

"What exactly does this process entail?" I asked, my voice rising as concern tightened my chest.

Solomon stood again and took my hands in his.

"I'm not going to lie to you: this is going to hurt. Quite a lot. But it's something every human here has had to go through."

I looked back at him, trying not to show my fear in my eyes.

"I'm sorry," he said, "I would break this rule for you if I could, but it's for your safety."

I closed my eyes and took a deep breath.

"If it has to be done then just get it over with."

He paused for a second as a thoughtful expression crossed his face.

"I can make it easier for you if you'll let me," he said, looking at me intensely. "I can make it so you barely feel a thing."

"Is it a blood thing?" I asked suspiciously.

He smiled a slow, feline smile.

"Even better than that," he whispered, closing the distance between us.

Then his lips were on mine with a gentle pressure. I was overcome with shock.

I opened my lips slightly in surprise and breathed in his scent, an intoxicating mixture of warm spice and fresh dew. I closed my eyes as my head spun with the aroma and a wave of dizziness overcame me. He leaned me gently backwards, bearing my weight down onto the bed.

Every nerve in my body was tingly with sensation, fire and ice jumping from the tips of my fingers and toes, converging at the back of my neck where his fingers teased tantalisingly across the surface of my skin. He moved his mouth against mine and starbursts fired across the insides of my eyelids. I groaned and reached my arms around his neck, hungrily drawing him down towards me.

As I did so, he captured my wrists, pinning them above my head and holding them there with one hand. He drew away for a moment and, opening my eyes, I looked straight up into the cool, blue pools gazing down at me with desire.

My mind wanted to tell me this was wrong, to move away, to tell him to get off me. Much though I was unwilling to admit there was anything between me and Drew, this felt like

I was betraying him. Mind you, he'd done worse.

What I actually did was very different from my intended action.

"Sol…" I murmured, arching my back and entwining my legs around his as I tried to get him to come closer to me.

His pupils dilated as he stared down into mine and a feral moan rumbled from his throat. He moved his hands so that both were now above my head at my wrists then lowered his face back to mine, pushing my lips open with his as I moved my body up to meet him.

He pulled away from me, doing what I had failed to do.

I was confused, not sure what had happened.

He was flustered and clearly disconcerted. He moved off the bed quickly and walked a couple of paces away from me, standing at the edge of the screen with his back to me.

"Enough, Emilia," he said breathlessly. "It's done."

I stared after him in disbelief.

"That was the distraction?"

He turned back to me and nodded.

"It was a little more distracting than I was expecting," he said with a rueful smile.

"Great," I said, rolling up to a seated position on the bed, anger and shame chasing each other through me. "You could have warned me."

I glared at him. He looked perturbed.

"Is this a thing with you vampire guys? Do you have a thing for playing with humans?"

"Emilia, have I upset you?" he asked, looking at me solicitously. "It wasn't my intention."

I huffed out a breath.

"And what do you mean 'vampire guys'?" he asked, raising an eyebrow at me. "Who else has been kissing you?"

I nearly told him about Drew, but it felt like it was a bad idea. I didn't want to pit these two against each other, besides which Drew hadn't kissed me, not properly, and Sol had only kissed me as a distraction.

I shook my head and looked at my feet. Sol came and sat

beside me on the bed to my left, taking my hand in his.

"You know, we do consider the word 'vampire' to be something of an insult," he said, stroking his thumb across my fingers.

"Then I'm glad I used it correctly," I retorted, snatching back my hand.

"Emilia," he said, "I'm sorry. I got carried away. Kissing you was… enjoyable."

"You say that like it's a surprise."

"I wasn't expecting it to be quite that enjoyable," he replied with a smile. "Silver don't usually engage in romantic liaisons with humans. When we do, I'm afraid that to some extent one type of hunger excites the other. It is difficult to stop ourselves from indulging once we have developed a particular… appetite."

I looked at him in horror.

"You mean you would have killed me?"

"No, Emilia," he said, touching the back of his hand to my cheek. "Simply that I wanted to taste you."

My stomach fluttered. He gazed into my eyes.

"Admit that you want me to and I'll do it right now. You have only to say the word."

My mouth dried. This was just too much for one day.

I shook my head.

"I don't."

He ran his fingers under my chin, tipping it up to his face, and kissed me. My mouth opened as I inhaled his scent.

"You lie," he breathed, his lips moving against mine as he spoke.

I felt like I was going to melt. He pressed his lips to mine in a final kiss before withdrawing.

I didn't know what to say or feel. I gaped at him, worried about Drew despite myself.

Looking down, Sol took my hands in his and turned them over so I could see my wrists.

"What the hell?" I exclaimed.

The inside of each wrist bore a black, raised mark. Inside

an oval outline on my left was the legend "O+", my blood type, I realised. On my right was a stylised representation of the letters "SI". The 'S' was topped with a radiate crown and the 'I' slashed down through its centre like a blade. I looked at Sol in incomprehension.

"They're tattoos," he said, picking up a couple of round boxes from the rolling tray to show me.

I took one from him, turning it over so I could see the underside. There was an ink well in the top of the device which fed hundreds of tiny needles arranged in a circle along its bottom edge. It was like a stamp, only it looked vicious.

"The oval bearing your blood type is permanent," Sol continued. "The other one, that means you're under my protection as part of my house. It will last for only six months before it will need to be replenished. Each safe house has a different brand because each has a different leader, although ultimately they all answer to me."

He said this with no arrogance at all. It was simply a fact he was conveying to me. He was effectively king of the country, but it was no more exciting to him than was the colour of the carpet. Which, incidentally, was green.

I examined my wrists in some detail. Although the wounds were clean, they were large and they burned.

"How did I not feel this?" I asked in confusion. "It was a good kiss, don't get me wrong, but these look like they should have been agony."

"It only happens to the strongest and oldest of us. Our kiss," he replied, "when we choose it, can release a drug that heightens sensation and turns pain into pleasure. It's a secret we guard closely from the humans, so try to keep it to yourself, my little dissident," he added with a smile.

I was silent for a moment, feeling violated. I wasn't sure whether or not to be insulted by the endearment.

"You drugged me?"

No wonder I'd felt so out of myself.

"I told you I could make it easier. We are very physical creatures, Emilia, even more so than humans. That physicality is reflected in some of the abilities we carry. Touch can be incredibly powerful for us, it evokes strong emotion, so while we crave it, we use it sparingly."

I looked at him in incomprehension. I thought he had been fairly liberal with his hands as far as I was concerned. He seemed to guess my thoughts and smiled.

"I wanted to touch you," he said without artifice.

Like I was his to do with as he wished, like it didn't matter what I thought at all. Maybe it didn't now, I thought, staring down at the brand on my wrist.

"Does it matter what I wanted?"

"Touch forges a bond, Emilia," he said, taking one of my hands in his and pressing it to his chest, "and it is reciprocal. We only form that bond where it is welcome."

He looked at me pointedly.

"You welcomed it," he continued.

"Because you drugged me," I replied.

"Because you welcomed it," he said forcefully. "For us, there is no such thing as an empty gesture. Every touch has meaning. It can be a pledge, a solace, a prayer or a proclamation, but it is always given with purpose."

"And what meaning am I supposed to take from this?" I asked, indicating the two of us.

He smiled slightly.

"I said my touch had meaning, but not that I would tell you what that meaning is."

I raised my eyebrows at him, unimpressed.

"I smoothed your admission, Emilia," he said to me. "It need not be more than that."

If he thought a magic kiss was going to make me eager to offer him my jugular, he had another thing coming.

His head snapped up and he looked towards the door of the library.

"You have an escort for lunch," he continued with a rueful smile.

CHAPTER XVI

We left the library to find Drew standing outside waiting for us. He scrutinised me carefully, his expression clouding over as he registered something. I looked down at myself surreptitiously, but I couldn't identify anything that might have upset him.

"Secundus," Solomon greeted him.

"Primus," he responded stiffly.

"Why are you not supervising the security teams?"

"I have drawn up the strategy and schedule. Tommy is looking after the team at the club and Eveline is putting my measures in place here."

"I see," Solomon said with a hint of a smile. "And you would escort the human to lunch?"

Drew's jaw clenched.

"We actually consider the word 'human' to be something of an insult," I shot at Sol.

He raised an eyebrow and locked his gaze with mine.

"Then I used it incorrectly and I offer you my apology."

Drew glanced between the two of us furiously.

"Would you like to go with Drew?" Solomon asked me intensely, seeming to convey more in his words that their superficial meaning.

His ice-blue eyes bored into mine, willing me away from the rest of the world as Drew looked on. Sol unsettled me. It was as if he had power over me, irrational power that pulled me towards him.

"Or would you rather remain with me?" he continued.

I forcefully snapped myself away from his gaze, shaking my head as I turned to Drew. He looked at me with a measure of relief in his eyes.

"Very well," Sol said, the vague smile playing once more on his lips, but never reaching his eyes. "If you will excuse me?"

He turned to climb the stairs up to the mezzanine.

"Oh, Drew," he said abruptly, "before I forget: I'm not sure it's appropriate for the Secundus to be away from the rest of the Solis Invicti overnight. Your place is with them on the fourth floor."

"Yes, Primus," Drew replied, his tone compliant but with fire in his eyes.

Sol's smile inched up a notch as he turned away and headed upstairs.

I couldn't work out whether this development was good news or bad news.

Drew was livid, his fists clenched by his sides. He watched Sol, fuming, until he entered the stairwell up to his apartments on the other side of the atrium, then he took my hand in his and stalked across the floor to a doorway on the other side of the staircase. Wrenching it open, he dragged me inside.

It was a fairly small room that looked as if it was used as a private dining room. A large, polished oak table took up most of the space, circled with straight-backed chairs. A couple of dressers sat on either side of the room, presumably to hold serving dishes and drinks.

Drew slammed the door behind us and spun around to face me, pushing me up against the back of the door.

"You let him kiss you?" he asked me incredulously in a husky whisper.

I was taken aback.

"You were spying?"

"No," he said in irritation, "I can smell him all over you. And I can smell the stench of his kiss."

Wow. I was never going to adjust to that. I thought for a moment.

"So that means…" I started saying.

"Yes," Drew interrupted angrily, "he could smell me on you. He knew."

"Well, you did spend last night carrying me around."

He nodded grudgingly.

"But why would you let him do it?" he asked me in despair. "Why would you let him kiss you?"

"What the hell has it got to do with you?" I replied. "Anyway, I didn't know he was going to do it."

"But you let him, Emmy. You let him do it."

I said nothing. I couldn't deny it; I had let him kiss me. I'd even tried to get him to kiss me more.

Drew shook his head in anguish.

"He said it was a drug," I said, "that it soothed the pain."

"That's not all it is. It's a brand, Emmy. A mark of ownership as plain as this."

He grabbed my right wrist and showed me the symbol marking it, the stylised 'SI'.

"Solis Invicti," he continued. "Property of Sol the Invincible."

My eyes widened. I hadn't known that.

"You're his Secundus, you're one of the Solis Invicti. You belong to him as much as I do."

"No," Drew replied, "we are his invincible army, but we have our freedom. We choose to follow him. You are his to own, to the exclusion of all others."

"What?" I asked, horrified. "But I didn't ask for that!"

"Sol wouldn't have been able to make the mark if you hadn't accepted it," Drew said sadly. "It's just how it works."

Touch forges a bond, Sol had said.

"That bastard!" I screamed. "Why the hell would he even want to impose that on me? Doesn't it work both ways?"

"Usually," Drew said.

I raised an eyebrow at him.

"You're not Silver," he said. "No other Silver will be permitted to drink from you or try to claim you, but I don't know what it means for him."

Drew released me, turning away and stalking towards the other side of the room. He ran his hands through his hair with his back to me.

"What do you mean 'claim me'?" I asked softly. "What does that mean?"

He turned to face me from across the room.

"I can't touch you," he said with feeling, his forehead creasing in consternation. "Frankly, even this conversation is probably out of bounds."

I shook my head, not understanding at all.

"You let him take you away from me," he whispered. "The one person I can't challenge."

"Why would he do it?" I asked again.

"I don't know," he replied. "Maybe to keep you safe, because he knows I have been concerned about your wellbeing and his name carries authority. Maybe to piss me off, because he realised I care for you. Maybe for no reason at all, simply because he could and he wanted to."

He looked at me from the other side of the table with longing in his eyes.

"I should have kissed you first this morning, but I wanted to wait until you knew. To wait until I could tell you what it means and have you still want it."

I was surprised to find that I wished it was Drew instead of Sol. I slapped the thought down. An entanglement with any vampire was a bad thing.

"Is this forever?" I asked.

Surely vampire relationships could be as transient as human ones. You couldn't be locked to one person forever, just because you kissed them once and they put their mojo on you. It made no sense.

"No."

"Then how long does it last?"

"It depends," he replied.

"On what?"

"On how many more times you let him kiss you," Drew replied, gritting his teeth. "Because you'll do it again and again. You've let him in and now you'll crave him. Soon you'll be begging for him."

I shook my head in disbelief.

"And you've just told him you'd rather be in my company than with him. That's a challenge he won't resist."

Drew gazed at me sadly.

"I can't believe this is over before it's started," he said.

"You're giving up pretty easily," I snapped back at him without thinking.

"Suddenly you're encouraging me?" he laughed bitterly. "Why couldn't you have done that this morning?"

This morning was a different proposition entirely. This morning I had a choice between a vampire who had killed my friends or no vampire. This afternoon it was a choice between one vampire who made me feel safe and another who sent fear rushing through my veins.

Better the devil you know. Or, at least, better the vampire I knew better than the other vampire, but that didn't have the same ring to it.

Now I was backed into a corner, only one option in front of me, I wished I had the luxury of choice. I wanted a different option from that which had been chosen for me, but I didn't think I would have chosen either if the choice were truly mine.

The impotence made me feel suffocated, but I also had to be realistic. I was livid at the way Sol had behaved, but I hadn't refused him. I wasn't sure what I would have done had my decision been better informed.

Drew saw the look on my face.

"You wanted him anyway?" he asked, his expression collapsing into resignation.

"I don't know."

"Well," he said, "either way, he is the Primus. Whatever his motives, whatever he decides to do with you, he has claimed you."

"How long? How long before it wears off?"

"If you don't kiss him again," he replied, "it'll be a day or so."

"Can you help me avoid him for twenty-four hours?" I asked.

He shook his head sadly.

"You heard what he said: I'm back in the Solis Invicti rooms on the fourth floor tonight. You'll be sleeping right next door to his apartments again. He'll come to you and you'll let him mark you again."

He paused, pain crossing his face.

"You'll want him to do that, and more."

I swallowed tightly, my throat sore and dry. I was afraid that he was right.

We stood looking at each other in silence.

I felt helpless, like there was an inescapable fate bearing down on me over which I had no control. I wasn't used to being defined by who I belonged to. I wasn't happy with the concept that I apparently had to belong to someone at all, but the fact that such ownership could extend to whom I was allowed to kiss, or rather who was allowed to kiss me, sent a hot, scratchy wave under my skin.

And he was just letting it happen.

I was on my own in this.

"I should get you into the restaurant," he said quietly after a moment. "You need to eat."

I was so shaken up by the events of the morning, not to mention the grief from yesterday, that I was too numb to feel hungry. Nonetheless, I nodded at him.

A thought crossed my mind.

"Will everyone else be able to tell?" I asked anxiously.

"Yes," Drew said with a snort of derision, "that's kind of the point."

"But... why would he be okay with that? Won't the Silver

be, well, surprised?"

"Emmy," he said sadly, "I don't think this is going to be the same as it would be were you Silver. A lot has changed recently and Sol makes the rules."

"What do you mean?"

"The Silver aren't going to think you mean anything to him beyond your ability to provide him with blood. They'll smell the blood on you from your knee and just assume he's drinking from the vein. They'll think you're a toy."

This just got worse and worse.

"We're a proud race," he continued, "and a lot of Silver think he's being too lenient in the measures he's introduced to control the humans. He's convinced the majority of them that an element of reciprocity is the best way to protect our food source, but some have seen his stance as an indication of weakness. They'll probably think more of him for taking a human plaything, not less."

"Shit," I said. "Is that what I am?"

Drew shook his head.

"I don't know. I follow him because he's generally a good leader, but I don't know what he's up to."

He looked helplessly down at his feet for a moment before looking back up to meet my gaze.

"Either way, no other Silver will bother you in the restaurant."

The thought of everyone looking at me, leering, knowing that Sol had kissed me, thinking he'd probably done more… I shuddered, my cheeks flushing. This was going to be a nightmare.

I sucked in a breath and gritted my teeth.

"Okay," I said, "let's do it."

CHAPTER XVII

As we walked across the atrium towards the restaurant, I tried to avoid the gazes of the Silver around me. It wasn't particularly busy, but there were the usual guards placed at intervals around the room. I saw a couple register surprise as I passed and realised it was going to be a long day.

I put my head down and we quickly arrived at the open double doors to the restaurant. It was a large, open room with huge, multi-paned windows pouring light in from the street. The ceiling was high and ornate, with chandeliers falling down into the room at regular intervals. The floor was a rich, burgundy carpet.

There were perhaps thirty tables of differing sizes in the main room, but I could see that a door on the right hand side led through to a further dining area.

I was surprised to see that the place was full of Silver.

"You guys eat?" I asked.

"Of course," he replied.

"But the blood?"

"Is just something else that we need. We're not that different from you, Emmy."

I raised my eyebrows at him sardonically.

As we entered, a figure stood up from a table by the wall

on the other side of the room and waved at us enthusiastically. It was Cam. I got the feeling from the reactions on the tables around him that it wasn't normal for the Silver to behave like over-excited children in a school canteen.

Despite his betrayal yesterday, I was quite taken with his screw-you-all-I'm-happy attitude. I smiled back at him and he grinned.

But we'd have to pass every table to get to where he was sitting.

Drew looked at me anxiously. I took a breath and started walking across the restaurant, Drew at my side. There was a Mexican wave of murmurs and indrawn breaths as we did so. I was mortified, but I ignored them and kept going.

When we finally reached the small, round table, I was bright pink.

"Hey there, Emilia!" he said with a smile.

"Sorry about yesterday," he added, his face falling a bit.

His puppy-dog charm was so endearing that I couldn't help myself from smiling at him cheerfully.

"That's okay, Cam."

He grinned back at me happily. He was an uncomplicated vampire. He just wanted everyone else to be happy.

"How the hell did you do that thing with your eyes anyway?" I asked.

"We can cover up the silver," he said with a shrug, "just as we can move at speed, but it's exhausting. It's nice not to have to do it all the time anymore."

So that's how the Silver had hidden from the humans. I wondered whether this ability to manipulate the silver in their eyes meant they were able to make it flood their irises on demand, as Drew had.

Thomas sat at the table next to Cam. I'd been so distracted by Cam that I hadn't even noticed he was there.

"Emilia," he said, standing to greet me.

"Thomas."

"Tommy, please," he said with a small smile.

I nodded my head in acknowledgement. Apparently I was

now chummy with all Sol and Drew's vampire friends.

His face froze.

"Woah," Cam said loudly. "Been spending some quality time with the big man, huh Emilia?"

My blush deepened and I looked down at my feet. Ground: swallow me up.

"Cam," Drew growled through gritted teeth, "shut up."

He held his hands out in a placating gesture and sat back down.

"Calm down, Drew. It's not like everyone doesn't already know."

A growl rumbled through Drew's chest and he moved towards Cam, leaning over the table, with a thunderous expression.

"Shut your face, Cam," Tommy interjected, "or I'll shut it for you."

He looked between Drew and Tommy in incomprehension then pressed his lips together, crossing his arms over his chest and sliding down in his chair.

Drew subsided, holding a chair out for me. I sat quickly, taking the opportunity to make myself a little less conspicuous in a room full of curious Silver. I was grateful that my chair faced the wall. Nonetheless, I rested my elbows on the table, hiding my face in my hands with a groan.

Drew took the chair to my left, opposite Tommy. I was opposite Cam.

"How did this happen?" I heard Tommy ask Drew.

"Admission," he replied. "Sol took her through himself. The pain…," he trailed off.

"Why?"

"I don't know," Drew replied.

"Does he know about… you?" Tommy asked.

I lifted my head from my hands and looked at Drew.

"What about you?" I asked.

Drew just shook his head at me and turned away.

"I don't think so," he replied to Tommy.

"Then what?" Tommy asked.

Drew shrugged.

"That shitstorm I told you about?" Tommy said, raising an eyebrow. "This is it."

"You think I don't know that? What am I supposed to do?"

"Getting her out of here would be a good start," Tommy replied.

"I'm sitting right here," I interjected.

They ignored me.

"It's too late for that and you know it," Drew said. "He's got her set up in the suite on the fifth and he's made it clear I'm not welcome there."

"Fuck."

Silence settled over the table. Cam looked curiously between Drew and Tommy, trying to work out what was going on.

"What about the club?" Tommy said eventually.

Drew looked at him.

"We've turned the whole of the second floor into sort of a human dormitory and we're opening the place up tonight," he continued.

Tommy turned to me.

"You could be with them, instead of here," he said. "You'd have to convince Solomon. There'll be little opportunity for you to be alone with any of us over there, even the Primus."

I glanced at Drew. He had a pained look on his face.

"What if he just renews the mark?" Drew asked. "You know how this works."

"It's the only way," Tommy said to him.

He nodded reluctantly.

"Emmy?" Drew asked me.

I was intimidated at the prospect of returning to the club, of finding it so different from how I had left it, of working there without my little Parker's family. But it was better than being Sol's toy.

"Okay," I said, "I'll talk to him."

The food in the restaurant was simple but amazing. Human servers gave us a choice of three different meals: steak burgers, pasta or salad. I opted for the burger and it was delicious.

They'd clearly implemented the blood donation policies as well. There were bottles of fresh blood available or, more disturbingly, volunteers were able to give blood straight from the vein: table service.

I found the whole thing distinctly distasteful, not just because of the blood drinking, or the fact that there were humans queuing up to fulfil the needs of the vampires, but because the entire procedure was very intimate. And the noises the humans made… it felt like I was eating lunch in a brothel.

It was nothing like blood donation, which I knew was rather cold and clinical, nor like I imagined being fed on by a vampire would be. The humans weren't scared, they weren't attacked.

They took a seat next to the vampire they were destined to feed and offered them a wrist. The vampires didn't seem to get emotionally involved in the situation, simply taking what they wanted then dismissing the humans.

But for the humans it was clearly a different experience altogether. At the first pressure from the vampire's teeth, their eyes rolled back in their skulls and they began moaning, writhing, lost in an ecstasy known only to them. I was horrified, but I couldn't look away.

None of the vampires on my table seemed to mind, but they could see I was uncomfortable and so none of them had any blood themselves, not even bottled.

"Why do they do that in here?" I asked in disgust.

"Would you rather they hid it away?" Tommy replied. "Better they do it where we can all see, so they won't get carried away and so you are under no illusions as to what we are. This is how we survive."

"We can sanitise it all we want," Drew said to me, "bottle it and store it, but we need to drink human blood to survive.

And, yes, it can be a pleasurable experience."

"Just for the humans though. It's so… one-sided," I struggled to express what was bothering me.

"It reminds you of prostitution, only the humans pay in blood," Tommy supplied.

I thought for a second then nodded.

"It's not always like that, Emmy," Drew said to me, looking intensely into my eyes. "It can be a pleasurable experience for both parties."

I could imagine just how pleasurable Drew would make it. I thought about the night in his penthouse, his tongue cleaning the blood from my arm as he healed it. That wasn't exactly awful. My cheeks flushed and my heart beat faster in my chest.

I bit my lip involuntarily.

Drew caught the movement and his pupils dilated. He gazed into my eyes longingly as a murmur rose from across the table.

"Drew…" Cam warned.

He started to reach out his hand as if he was going to touch my face.

"Drew!" Tommy whispered urgently. "Everyone's watching, listening… smelling," he said pointedly.

With one last mournful gaze, Drew dropped his hand to his side.

"Smelling?" I asked incredulously.

"I didn't know you two had a thing," Cam said, sounding almost a little hurt.

"We don't," Drew said, looking away. "That would be ridiculous. I need to go and check in with Eveline."

He stood abruptly and strode across the room, leaving me feeling oddly bereft. I looked around at Cam and Tommy helplessly. What now?

"Silver can smell arousal," Tommy explained apologetically. "They can also smell whose mark you bear. It would have been… awkward."

Shit.

I could imagine all the Silver in the room turning against Drew to enforce Sol's 'hands off' mojo. I was glad Drew had left.

"I don't know what the Primus is after from you, Emilia, but please take care," Tommy said, "for Drew's sake. He can't help how he feels."

"And Sol?" I asked.

"I doubt he feels anything, but if he does, we're all in trouble. Hopefully he'll just quietly forget about you if you're out of sight."

"Tommy," I said hopelessly, "I don't understand why this is happening."

"None of us do."

"I do," Cam piped up.

Tommy raised an enquiring eyebrow at him.

"You're feisty," Cam said. "I like that."

He grinned at me.

Tommy shook his head at him in exasperation.

Cam shot an irritated look back.

"Seriously, Tommy," he said, "when was the last time anyone said no to the Primus?"

"On that note," I said, standing to leave before the argument really kicked off, "I'm going to go and tell Sol where he can shove his…"

"Emmy!" Tommy whispered.

"Well, fine," I said, sulkily, "I'll just go and talk to him then, shall I?"

Cam smiled at me cheerfully as I waved and, turning away, walked back across the restaurant to the atrium. There were vampires everywhere, but I decided I was probably safe given that I apparently reeked of Solomon. The sentries around the atrium eyed me cautiously as I stomped up the main staircase and round the mezzanine, quickly climbing the stairs to the fifth floor.

By the time I got to the fifth floor corridor my knee was agony, but I wasn't going to let it show. I limped painfully towards Sol's door at the end of the passage then straightened myself up so I didn't look like I was in pain when he answered the door. I was raising my hand to knock when the door opened to reveal Sol himself.

"Emilia," he said with a smile, "I thought that was you. I recognised the limp."

Bastard.

"How dare you!" I yelled at him.

A hint of a smile crossed over his face, like my anger amused him. My fury instantly trebled.

"You marked me, like I was some sort of possession? Do you have any idea what I've just had to tolerate from your fellow Silver in the restaurant? You didn't even have the courtesy to warn me!"

"I see Drew filled you in on the details," Sol replied.

"Why, Sol? Why would you do that to me? Why would you even want that?"

He looked at me appraisingly.

"There's something indomitable about you that I find quite appealing," he replied.

"So you marked me as yours? On the basis of a casual appeal?"

He raised a sardonic eyebrow.

"As I told you earlier today," he replied, "our kiss need be nothing more than a balm to your pain during admission. But please let's discuss this inside like civilised people."

As he spoke, he stepped back and to the side of the door, ushering me in. I decided that the rest of the Silver knew enough already of what had gone on between me and Sol, so I reluctantly acquiesced.

I stepped through the door then looked around me in amazement. The place was huge. The front door let straight into an enormous open plan room with double-height ceilings and floor-to-ceiling windows on the side facing me. There was a spiral staircase to my left leading up to a mezzanine level (apparently a feature of the hotel).

There were doors leading off from the main room to left and right. The room I was in contained four different areas arranged on the multi-levelled floor in front of me: to my left a low seating area with leather seats around a coffee table; behind it a study area with a large desk and chairs on either side; to my right a dining area set with a large glass-topped table and metal chairs and finally a snug sunken nook with a television behind that. It was four rooms in one.

Sol walked towards the low seating area on the left, dropping down two steps. He picked a bottle of wine off the table and tilted it towards me.

"Can I offer you a glass?"

"I'm not here to cosy up to you," I hissed at him.

Sol sighed.

"I don't have to tell you my reasons, Emilia."

"I'm asking you to."

Sol paused. He didn't seem to have considered this.

"Alright then," he said, the corner of his mouth twitching up slightly. "At first, I was just trying to put the pieces together, to work out why Tommy and Drew were fussing around you. I was uneasy that my Secundus appeared to be withholding information from me."

"You were trying to provoke him."

"Yes, to start with. But then, I found I was unwilling to let you suffer. I've seen many humans go through admission and it is not dignified nor is it easy. Those who do not pass out from the pain vomit copiously. It was in my power to save you that so, for both of our sakes, I did."

He didn't want me throwing up on him. I wasn't at all sure how to take that.

"You barely offered me a choice and you did it without telling me what it meant."

"I didn't want you to refuse."

"I had the right to if I wanted to!" I yelled at him.

He put the wine down on the table and stepped towards me, cupping my cheek in his right hand.

"And did you want to?" he asked huskily. "Would you have refused me?"

My blood rushed and I fought the urge to reach out to him.

A smirk flickered on his face.

"You arrogant bastard," I hissed at him.

"You say that, Emilia," he whispered, sliding his other hand around my waist and leaning in to my ear, "but all I can hear is your heart racing."

He pulled me close to him, running his right hand around the back of my head to twist around my braid. He wound it around his hand and pulled, forcing my face up so my lips tilted to touch his. I moaned as I inhaled his fresh, spicy scent. Shivers ran down my spine and I flattened my palms against his chest, meaning to push him away.

"Tell me to stop," he breathed, his lips grazing over mine as he spoke. "Tell me not to touch you."

His breath was intoxicating. His left hand stroked down the side of my waist as he pulled me closer to him, lighting a fire under his fingertips, his hips pressing into mine. My hands twisted in his shirt and instead of pushing him away I pulled him towards me, willing his lips towards mine.

"Tell me not to kiss you," he whispered.

My lips parted, but I remembered Drew's words.

"It's self-perpetuating," I whispered.

A wave of confusion crossed over Sol's face.

"The mark," I breathed. "Your kiss."

Sol took his lips away from mine and unravelled my braid from his hand, stepping away. He sat down heavily in one of the chairs.

"Straight from the mouth of my Secundus I presume?"

I just looked at him.

"I found the scent of Drew on you... displeasing," he said.

"That doesn't make marking me with yours okay."

"I didn't say it did," he said, shaking his head at me. "But I won't apologise for it."

He met my gaze steadily.

I sighed and took the armchair opposite him.

"Sol, I'm not staying next door. I want to go back to Parker's."

"Where?" he asked, confused.

"The club across the road. Remember? I used to work there, before all this. Before you, before the Weepers."

"You can work there again, but it doesn't mean you can't stay here. It's safer."

"No," I said adamantly, "I don't want to stay here. And I don't want this mark from you."

A brief look of hurt crossed over his face, but it was replaced so quickly with one of haughty self-possession that I wasn't sure I had seen it at all.

"I've told you before that I don't enjoy taking what is not freely given."

"So you will let me leave?" I asked.

"Yes, you can leave. To wait. Wait until the mark is gone." I sighed in relief.

"But you will feel the same."

"What?" I asked.

"The mark cannot bring emotion into existence, Emilia. It simply intensifies and enhances what is already there. The bond is self-perpetuating only because it founds itself in something real."

He looked at me for a moment then reached into the pocket of his chinos, pulling out a scrap of black lace.

"I want you to have this," he said, holding it out to me.

I took it from him and spread it between my fingers. It was decorated with lilies picked out in silver thread. How appropriate.

"It's a choker," he explained. "I would like you to wear it. It signifies that you are under my personal protection, even after the mark is gone. It also means that you need not make blood donations with everyone else and any person who drinks from you directly will have to answer to me."

I stared at him.

"Sol," I said, shaking my head at him.

"This is not a bargain, Emilia. It is not a bribe. It entitles me to nothing from you and I will ask for nothing from you except that which you wish to give to me. It is a gift."

Drew's words of three nights ago echoed in my head. The

night he healed my arm. It's a Silver thing. It is a gift.

"Nothing's free, Sol."

"No," he answered quietly, "but sometimes the price is fair."

CHAPTER XVIII

I spent the rest of the afternoon getting my head together and packing up a few essentials from the suite next door. I took only what I had brought with me and the clothes I was wearing. I just didn't feel right taking all those new clothes with me. I packed everything away neatly into my backpack and set it by the door to the suite.

I still had a couple of hours to kill, so I decided to curl up on the sofa and enjoy a little luxury and tranquillity while I could. I grabbed a book from the coffee table in front of me, some mindless trashy novel, and settled in.

I was just getting to the good bit when there was a knock on the door. Sighing with irritation, I put the book down beside me on the couch. Sol had insisted that I be escorted over to the club by the Solis Invicti, despite the fact that I was going over before night fell, but I didn't think it was late enough in the day for this to be my guard.

"Come in," I called.

Opening the door, Benedict walked into the room.

"What the hell do you want?" I asked him in shock.

I hadn't seen him since yesterday afternoon. Not since... Danny.

"Emilia, I...," he paused, apparently unsure how to

continue. "Emilia, I'm one of the Solis Invicti, and the Primus has asked me to escort you to your new home."

Great choice, Sol.

"However," he continued awkwardly, "I suspect that you have a low opinion of me, so I wanted to speak to you, to reassure you of my faithfulness to the Primus, before he leaves you in my care."

"You killed Danny," I said blandly.

"The boy in the street?" he asked. "When you were there?"

I nodded back at him, stony-faced.

"He was my friend," I said.

"I'm sorry," he said, "but he was carrying the Weeper plague. If he was your friend, it's a miracle he didn't pass it to you. It is something for which we should all be grateful, seeing as you are... to the Primus's taste."

I glared at him.

"The less said about that the better, Ben."

He looked confused at my response.

"I would have thought any human would be happy for his protection," he said.

"Well, I suppose most of them would. But I don't understand it. I didn't have any choice in it and between the two of us: I'm not sure I like it."

"And Drew?" he asked.

My eyes snapped to his.

"What about him?" I asked cautiously.

"Well, you were with him that day we met and earlier today in the restaurant..."

"You were there?" I asked.

He nodded.

"I was there. I thought there was some... tension."

I blushed and looked away, praying he hadn't thought it was more than an argument. Surely if he'd known what was really going on he would have told Sol?

"I found the environment difficult. The blood. The humans."

"Of course," Ben replied sympathetically. "It can be a little overwhelming."

"Yes," I said quickly, keen to change the subject. "Look, Ben, I'd really like to have a bit of time to myself before we leave. Would you mind?"

"Not at all," he said kindly. "I'll come back in a little while."

"Thank you," I said gratefully.

"Oh, before I forget," he said, reaching back into the corridor to pick up a paper carrier bag, "here's your uniform for the club."

"Uniform?" I asked.

"Yeah, the Primus wanted to have the staff be easily recognisable so you'd be protected from the Silver's... indiscretions."

"That's not very reassuring, Ben."

He handed me the bag and flashed me a quick smile then, stepping through the door, closed it softly behind him.

Exhaling heavily, I sank back down into the sofa and picked up the book again. When I'd read the same sentence five times, I decided I wasn't going to be able to lose myself in the story and returned it regretfully to the pile of books on the coffee table.

I grabbed my handbag and rifled through it until I found the choker Sol had given me. It really was a beautiful object. I walked across the suite and, going into the bathroom, carefully fastened it around my neck in the mirror. It was about two inches wide, a band of gossamer filaments wrapping around my throat in an irregular silhouette, the pointed edges of petals interrupting the border of the lace.

Sighing, I removed the choker and put it away in my handbag. I didn't need it yet.

I thought I may as well get into my uniform while I was at it, so I retrieved the paper bag from where I had left it on the couch. Opening the wardrobe so I could use the full-length mirror that was fixed to the inside of the door, I tipped the contents of the bag onto the bed. Then I looked in the bag again, shaking it upside down to make sure I hadn't missed anything.

Nope, that was it.

I picked up one of the two miniscule, black items of clothing and held it out in front of me. It was the tiniest pleated skirt I had ever seen. Strictly speaking, it was probably a belt. I picked up the other item: a black, strapless corset with lace and burgundy trim. As far as I was concerned, it was underwear. Sexy underwear.

My mouth fell open in horror.

This was a serious surprise. Up until now, vampire fashions had seemed to me to be pretty similar to human fashions. They tended towards the utilitarian, which I supposed was appropriate for the war zone in which we found ourselves: khakis and T-shirts were very much the norm.

But maybe that was just what they wore when they were in fight mode. Maybe I could expect Bela Lugosi and eighties goth for their casual wear. Or maybe they just wanted their food dressed in lace. I repressed a shudder.

I told myself it wouldn't be as bad when it was on. Taking a deep breath, I shed my comfy clothes then shimmied into the skirt and tied myself into the corset.

It was worse. The top barely met the skirt and I couldn't bend over without showing my knickers.

This was completely unacceptable.

I zipped myself back into my boots and, slamming the door of the suite behind me in a rage, stomped over to the door to Sol's apartment and hammered on it with my fist.

He opened it in a flash, obviously having zipped to the door at superspeed. Before he even had it fully open, I was yelling at him.

"What the hell is this?" I shouted, indicating my outfit. "How is this supposed to protect me from being eaten by vampires? If I bend over they'll be able to see my fricking ovaries!"

But he wasn't listening. His eyes were travelling the length of my body before slowly returning to my eyes. His pupils dilated and an intensely serious expression settled onto his face.

"Sol?" I asked uncertainly.

A split-second later I was flying backwards and thudding into the wall of the corridor, Sol's body pressed tight against mine, holding me in place. This was starting to be a theme with me and vampires. I wasn't sure whether or not I minded just at the moment.

"There are plenty of things I can do to you that don't involve kissing," he murmured, rubbing his lips across my ear as he spoke.

His fresh, spicy scent filled my head and I gasped as he pushed his left leg between mine, rubbing against me. My head swam. My blood was rushing in my veins and I couldn't breathe. In a second my anger turned to desire. I wanted him, badly.

My hands wrapped themselves around his neck, one of them burrowing into his hair as I pulled his head round, directing his mouth towards mine, consequences be damned.

"Emmy?" a voice said in a tone of disbelief.

I became vaguely aware of movement at the end of the corridor by the stairwell.

Sol went still, his expression clouding but his eyes still boring into mine with desire.

"What do you want, Drew?" he asked in a low rumble.

My head snapped towards the stairs and there he was, framed in the corridor walls, staring at me with fire in his eyes.

Sol sighed and stepped backwards, releasing me to slip back onto my feet. He glared at Drew.

"Your timing leaves much to be desired."

"Apologies, Primus," he replied, looking like he wasn't sorry at all, "but I heard a thud and I was concerned for your safety."

Drew looked back at me and noticed what I was wearing. He went still for a second, his silver irises sparkling at me.

"Emmy," he said huskily, "what the hell are you wearing?"

"My uniform, apparently," I replied, crossing my arms

over my chest. "It's for the club."

Drew made a rumbling sound in the back of his throat, sort of a cross between a growl and a purr.

Sol looked at him in surprise for a beat then started laughing. Proper, all out laughing. I couldn't recall ever having heard him laugh like that before.

"Well, you chose the bloody thing!" I shouted at him, not understanding what was so funny.

"Sol…," Drew said in a warning tone of voice.

"It beggars belief," he said to Drew with an enlightened smile. "It's Emilia isn't it?"

"What's me?" I asked, looking between the two of them in confusion.

"It's nothing," Drew said through gritted teeth, still looking at Sol, "just go and put some clothes on."

"Not until someone tells me what's going on."

Drew's look turned to one of pleading. Sol paused in thought for a moment then seemed to relent. With a tilt of his head to Drew, he turned towards me.

"It's nothing that need concern you, Emilia. Go and get your things together. Benedict will arrive shortly to escort you to the club."

I glared at them both then, groaning in irritation at the two of them, returned to the suite, slamming the door behind me.

I furiously gathered up the comfy clothes I had been wearing and stuffed them violently into the top of my backpack, using the action to take out my frustration.

Sol had clearly realised that Drew and I 'had a thing going', to quote Cam, but I still felt like there was something going on that they weren't telling me. As a member of the subordinate race, I supposed I had better get used to it.

I pulled a full-length, fitted, black leather coat from the wardrobe and shrugged it on, deciding I may as well go the full dominatrix look since I didn't seem to have a choice about my work attire. It was actually a beautiful piece of clothing: soft, buttery leather with a burgundy lining. It matched the corset, so why not? At least it would mean I could bend over without showing off my knickers.

Neither Drew nor Sol were anywhere to be seen when Ben arrived to help carry my stuff over the road. Part of me was irked at the implication that I couldn't manage on my own, but I was actually grateful for the help. My knee was still sore and I didn't think I could have managed five flights of steps whilst hefting my backpack.

"So," Ben said to me as we started the walk down, "you used to work in the club?"

"Yeah," I replied.

"Is this going to be weird for you?" he asked, concern evident in his voice.

"Yep, all kinds of weird. I practically lived there. Without Jeff, it feels wrong to call it Parker's."

"We're not," Ben replied. "We're calling it 'Sol's' now."

"Of course you are," I muttered grumpily. "Everything's Sol's."

Ben smiled at me and snorted with laughter.

"Yes it is," he said, "but you don't seem very happy about it."

I grunted back.

We walked together in silence for a couple of flights of steps before I decided it wasn't fair to take my anger at Sol out on Ben.

"Anyway," I said, "what's your role in all this, Ben? Why have you been volunteered to ferry my baggage around?"

"Well," he replied, "in answer to your first question: as I said, I'm one of the Solis Invicti. A lieutenant actually. In answer to your second question: the Primus asked me to help you, so that's what I'm doing."

"And how does that work? The Solis Invicti, I mean?"

"Well, it's not something we really talk about," he replied evasively.

"You must be able to tell me something."

He thought for a moment, pausing briefly on the landing of the second floor.

"Okay, I can tell you a bit," he said, starting down the last flight of stairs to the mezzanine. "The Invicti are split into four branches, headed up by the Secundus: that's Drew. Each of the four branches is led by a lieutenant: that's Eveline, Karina, Lorelei and me. We protect the Primus and we protect the Silver under his rule. As you can imagine, our role is somewhat more challenging since the Revelation."

We walked round the mezzanine to the main staircase.

"And…?"

"That's it," he said ruefully, "that's all I can tell you. If you want to know more, you'll have to ask your friend the Secundus."

He paused.

"Or the Primus, for that matter. How did you manage to make such influential friends so quickly?"

I shrugged.

"Bad luck, I guess."

Ben laughed as we made our way down the main staircase.

"You're not enjoying their attention?" he asked.

It was confusing as hell. They were both very different people and although they seemed to have the same thing in mind as far as I was concerned, it was in quite different ways.

Drew had a frantic sort of concern for me, possessive and controlling. But it made me feel safe. It warmed me. Being in his arms felt like a homecoming, assuaging the emptiness in my chest, wrapping us up in a world of our own. But then I'd remember Jeff and Sarah, and the glass bubble would shatter.

It was different with Sol: fresher, fierier. Dangerous. And Sol himself was just… different. He was so other. Although he seemed to want me to make my own decision about him, I had a feeling it wasn't so much out of concern for me as it was a result of his interest in the power of choice. If this mark, this bond, made me want him, then where was the fun? Where was the power? But if the bond was gone and I still wanted him… then he'd won the game.

But I wasn't going to tell Ben any of this. Instead, I just smiled at him and shook my head as we reached the marble floor of the atrium.

"Shouldn't you be horrified about it?" I asked Ben. "Isn't there a big taboo about Silver and humans being... together?"

Ben looked at me in confusion.

"Not at all. Where did you hear that?"

Now I was confused. Drew had told me that it was taboo from vampires and humans to get romantically involved.

"Humans and Silver hook up sometimes," he continued, "but it's not a great experience for the humans. You must have realised that, for us, blood and sex are inextricably linked. When Silver get together with humans, it doesn't mean anything to them. It's shallow and empty, often brutal. The Silver can't help but get a little... rough."

But Sol... Sol had told me that every touch had meaning. That it was special and not given lightly.

But then he had also told me that touching me made him want to taste me. He said he wouldn't have killed me, but there were a lot of horrendous things he could do that would fall short of leaving me dead.

"It's not something you want, Emmy," he said quietly, stopping and turning towards me. "It's not romance, it's a violation in every way you can imagine."

I reflected on my encounters with Sol and Drew. It wasn't like that.

"Thanks for the warning," I replied, embarrassed, "but... things... haven't been that way."

"We're not moral creatures. However you might think things are, the only reason we don't simply take what we want is that sometimes the chase, the competition, is more fun."

He looked at me sadly then turned away and carried on walking.

I was speechless, but for the first time since the Revelation the pieces fell into place. Drew and Sol had both treated me like a toy. It was the only explanation that made sense. There was nothing that distinguished me from any other human being, except that I apparently presented more of a challenge. Cam and Tommy had said as much at lunch.

Shit.

How could I have been such a fool? I'd done exactly what Danny had warned me against. I'd forgotten what the vampires were: monsters.

I was the game. I was a prize in a power struggle between Drew and Sol, and if I carried on letting myself get played then one way or another I was going to end up dead. I shuddered with horror as I thought of how close I had come to giving in to Drew on the night of the Revelation, or to Sol just this afternoon.

I needed to start thinking like them, to learn how to manipulate this situation to my advantage, or I was going to get used and spat out.

I was on my own.

We walked down the steps of the Palace and out into the evening sunlight onto the road. It was a beautiful night, the setting sun glinting off the glass in the windows of the buildings on the street. The sign that had until recently hung over the door of the club was gone. Parker's was no more.

I looked towards the barricade and saw a couple of Silver walking along the top of it, one of them the caramel-skinned woman I had seen on the stage at the first broadcast in Paternoster Square.

"That's Eveline," Ben said, noticing my interest. "She's leading the patrol tonight."

"She's terrifying," I replied.

"I'll let her know. She'll be delighted that you think so."

I raised my eyebrows at him.

"She's of the view that humans should know their place, that you should be grateful that we have a reason to keep you alive."

"Do a lot of the Silver feel that way?" I asked, a lump in my throat.

"More than you might think," he answered softly.

I looked down at my feet as we crossed the road.

"Don't worry, Emilia," he continued, "that scent mark you carry means anyone who bites you has to answer to the Primus. We're almost impossible to kill, but you can imprison us for centuries and torture us with silence. You're safe from those who might snack on you."

He paused, thoughtfully.

"Apart from Sol, of course," he added.

I narrowed my eyes at him.

"Ben, you're not helping."

He laughed again. We reached the door of the club and he held it open for me.

"Come on," he said, "let's get you assigned to a bunk."

He led me past the cloakroom and walked across the main bar on the ground floor, heading towards the stairwell. I started to follow him, but my eyes were drawn towards the door leading through to the VIP bar. Last time I walked through those doors, I left Jeff and Sarah's drained bodies behind me.

I stopped in the middle of the main bar. It had been a really bad idea to come back here. How was I going to live with the ghosts that would haunt this place for me? Every corner I turned I'd be expecting to see Jeff, or Sarah, or Cassie. Each shift behind the bar would seem lonely without Danny.

Every inch of this place had meaning for me beyond its substance. The notch in the wood on the edge of the main bar wasn't just a random mark, it was the notch Jeff had made the night we all had too many Jagermeisters and he bet me twenty quid he could open another bottle by smashing it cleanly at the neck. I got twenty quid and he got a trip to accident and emergency.

The multicoloured shot glasses under the main bar weren't just normal shot glasses, they were the glasses Sarah and I had bought for Danny's nineteenth birthday party. We'd taken over the VIP bar for the night and lined the shots along the length of the wood, trying all the most hideous combinations we could concoct from the bottles behind it.

The stains on the floor of the VIP bar floor weren't random marks either. They were blood stains. Jeff's blood. Sarah's blood.

"Emilia?" Ben asked quietly.

"Sorry," I said, "this place has...memories."

"They were your friends, weren't they?"

"Who?" I asked cautiously, not really wanting to talk about it with Ben.

"The humans, the ones through there?" he replied, pointing towards the VIP bar.

I turned to follow the line of his finger and nodded slowly. They had been my friends, but they'd also been more than that. They'd been my family, my support, my home. They'd made me feel safe and loved even after the world had fallen to pieces around me. Now the only person who made me feel safe was the man who'd killed them.

How fucked up was that?

"If you want to take some time, we still have a few minutes," Ben said.

I looked at him gratefully then stepped slowly towards the double doors to the VIP bar.

I had to see it. I knew their bodies had gone and I was sure that the Silver would have cleaned the place till it was immaculate, but I just couldn't rest until I'd seen it for myself. I reached my hands out in front of me and pushed the doors open, a horrible feeling of déjà vu stealing over me. In the second it took for the doors to swing apart, I had convinced myself that I was about to see Sarah's body again, lying lifeless and contorted on a mattress on the floor.

But the bar had been completely cleaned. It was back to its normal self, couches and chairs arranged artfully around low tables. No mattresses, no piles of clothes, no dead loved ones. I felt an odd mixture of relief and dissociation, as if seeing their bodies would have made everything feel real again, as if it would have given me a shred of (albeit horrific) normality to which to cling.

"I'm sorry, Emilia," Ben said.

He'd followed me into the VIP bar, but I'd been so preoccupied I hadn't even noticed.

I nodded, staring straight ahead in a daze.

"I was here when it happened," he continued. "I couldn't

stop him."

"What?" I asked, whirling around to face him.

"I was here," he said grimly. "We came in and they were sleeping. The Secundus was out of control, he just… I couldn't stop him."

He shook his head regretfully and looked down at the floor.

The floor dropped out of my world. They were sleeping?

"They didn't resist?" I asked, my voice breaking.

"They didn't have time to, it was too quick," he replied.

I thought about how I had found them, Sarah's body on the mattress and Jeff's on the couch. Their positions made sense, more sense than if they had been putting up a fight. He had fallen asleep on the couch watching the TV. She had been pulled from the bed, the blood drained from her, then unceremoniously dropped back onto the mattress.

By Drew.

I couldn't believe it. He'd not only killed them, he'd done it for no reason. I wondered whether Sol, so hung up on his moral justifications, was aware that his Secundus had broken his edict, making a mockery of his bargain.

I had just been starting to convince myself to forgive him, or at least to start trying to. And now: betrayal heaped on betrayal.

"He was furious," Ben added, shaking his head. "Then when I came in here to clear the bodies and I saw how you had left them… I'm just sorry it happened."

"So am I."

But I wasn't going to start crying over it in front of him. I was a gullible idiot to have believed Drew's story. I turned without another word and left the VIP bar, Ben following closely behind me.

He led me up the stairs from the main bar, straight past the double doors to the first floor bar and up to the second floor: what had been Jeff's apartment and the storage area for the club.

I gasped as the doors opened to reveal the new layout of

the floor. It had been completely gutted and remade. To my left, where Jeff's bathroom and kitchen had been, there was now a large bathroom with a line of shower heads and toilet cubicles on one side and a line of sinks on the other. To my right, there was a new open kitchen area and a long wooden dining table with benches on either side of it. It was all pretty basic, but it was serviceable and clean.

The rest of the floor, which was as big as the large dance floor on the first floor, was split lengthways into two long rooms, each filled with two rows of beds. There must have been about fifty bunks in total and nearly all of them looked occupied.

"You did this in a day?" I asked, incredulously.

"You've seen how quickly we can move," Ben answered. "These dorms are to house all the humans who will work in the club and the Palace. We moved them over from the safe house this morning."

"Where's the safe house?"

"It's one of the office blocks in the square," he replied. "It works for now, but it's cramped and it's not really kitted out for long-term residence, so we're gradually converting other buildings in the safe zone and allocating bunks on the basis of where each of you is going to be working. We're stepping up that activity because we've spent today bringing humans into London from all over the country."

"And the Silver?" I asked.

"Most of us are at the Palace. You actually outnumber us quite considerably. We're a small, select population," he added with an unpleasant smirk.

"There will be a few other safe houses," he continued, "Leeds, Glasgow, Oxford and Norwich are all confirmed for the moment, but otherwise we're consolidating them. The vast majority of the remaining human population, and the Silver, will be based here. We're expecting a total of about five hundred Silver and less than a hundred thousand humans."

I had no idea the disparity in numbers was so great. It was

mind boggling to think that the whole country had been taken over by what had to be a total of fewer than a thousand Silver.

Ben walked into the dorm on the right and led me the length of the room to the bed on the very end of the row, pushed up against the wall under a window. He put my backpack down at the side of the bed and I added my handbag to it.

"Here you go then," he said. "Laila, the Silver in charge of running the club, will be up in a moment to get you settled in and assign your duties. I'll leave you to get settled in."

"Thanks," I replied quietly.

He gave me a small smile then strode back the way he had come, leaving me in the dorm alone.

The whole place was fairly Spartan. There wasn't even a curtain on the window above my bed. It was a far cry from the Palace, but at least here I wasn't at risk of romantic (or, apparently, entirely unromantic) entanglements with vampires. At least here I could be amongst human beings.

I wondered what day of the week it was. It must be Sunday night, I thought. It had been Thursday the night I stayed at Drew's apartment, then one night here in the club with... and then last night at the Palace.

I pushed my rucksack and bag under my bed and opened up my handbag, drawing out the choker. I might not trust him as far as I could throw him, but there was nothing to stop me from availing myself of the protection afforded me by Sol's 'gift'. I fastened the scrap of lace around my throat and sat down on the bed to wait for Laila.

I didn't have to wait very long.

Only about ten seconds had passed when a sharp clicking sound emanated from the stairwell and, a few moments later, a tiny Indian woman walked through the door to the dormitory. She had a long braid of jet black hair down her back and she wore a bright red dress with matching heels. She was very pretty, but possessed nothing of the regal beauty I had come to associate with the Silver. I found that quite comforting, although as it transpired that was an irrational reaction.

"You're Emilia?" she asked brusquely as she walked towards me.

"Yes."

"Come here."

She stopped halfway across the floor and folded her arms across her chest. Feeling slightly affronted by her rudeness, I stood up and made to cross the room towards her.

"Lose the jacket," she said as I stood.

Reluctantly, I shed the garment and, folding it over my arm, dropped it onto the bed before walking over to her.

She put up her hand and moved her finger in a circle, indicating that I should spin around. Raising a sardonic eyebrow, I rotated on the spot as she looked me up and down.

"You'll do," she said, "but let's have less of the attitude from now on."

Wow. She thought a raised eyebrow was attitude? I opened my mouth to give her a large piece of my mind, but before I could do so she held up her hand, cutting me off.

"I don't want to hear anything from you unless I ask you to speak. And just so you know where we stand: let me make it crystal clear to you that the bit of lace you're wearing around your throat might prevent me from drinking from you, but it's not going to stop me from snapping your neck if you piss me off. Got it?"

I stared at her in shock. I really hadn't appreciated quite how worthless we were to the vampires. Despite the fact that I reeked of Sol's kiss and despite the fact that I was wearing his necklace, I still wasn't safe from the vampires.

Apparently he had just placed me in a state of 'dibs', but my life itself wasn't meaningful enough to warrant protection. He might be a conniving bastard, but he could have warned me.

Apparently it was to be an evening of betrayal and disillusionment.

Laila tutted at me in irritation.

"You may speak, human."

"Got it," I replied simply.

"You've worked in this club before?" she asked. "You know your way around?"

I nodded.

"Then I'm putting you behind the bar on the first floor. We weren't going to have any humans working on that floor because... well, you'll see. With that thing around your neck, you should be safe enough. You'll be working the bar on your own. We open in an hour. Follow me."

With that, she turned on her heel and sashayed out of the room towards the stairs.

That bar had a capacity of eight hundred people. I knew from my talk with Ben that there wouldn't be more than five hundred Silver, but it was still pretty intimidating. Talk about in at the deep end.

CHAPTER XIX

I followed Laila as she walked down the stairs to the first floor and pushed through the double doors onto the dance floor. I was disconcerted to note the 'no humans' notices stuck to the panes of glass set in each of the doors.

There was a stage across the wall at the other side of the dance floor and the bar ran the length of the right hand side of the room. Walking through the access hatch to the bar, Laila impatiently motioned for me to follow her.

At first glance, everything looked exactly as it always had done. Then I noticed that a large number of the taps and bottles behind the bar had been replaced.

"Alcohol and soft drinks are free to all Silver," Laila said, "but the bottled blood is one token and the warm blood on tap is two tokens. Tokens go in the slot," she said, indicating a box fixed to the back wall of the bar between the optics.

I gaped at her. Blood on tap?

"What's wrong with you?" she asked harshly. "Are you broken?"

"Blood?" I replied, incoherently.

"From our donors," she replied impatiently, "a service you are apparently too good for, not that I would wish to question the wisdom of our Primus. It is rationed."

"Will there be donors here?"

"The blood is taken in advance, just like your human blood transfusions. The environment here is… not conducive to the safety of humans. There will be no live donors. There will only be one other human on this floor tonight."

I looked at her in enquiry.

"You will see," she replied dismissively. "Prepare the bar. You are in charge."

With that, she strode away and through the doors into the stairwell.

I felt a little lost. Apparently I was running the largest bar in the club tonight, on my own, serving a load of vampires. I wasn't sure whether I should be flattered that Laila was apparently confident in my ability to manage on my own or insulted that she was quite happy to leave me in such a dangerous environment to get mauled to death.

I realised I was kidding myself if I thought she cared at all for my safety. I was a resource to be used until expended, then discarded. I was nothing to her. No different from a battery or a tube of toothpaste.

I needed to pull myself together and get on with it. Things could only get better after tonight, I told myself. Predictably, I was entirely wrong.

I walked around the bar and into the taproom to check the gas and the barrels. Things back here had changed a bit more substantially. A few of the barrels were now surrounded with some heavy-duty machinery, which I imagined must be the mechanism for keeping the contents of the barrels warm. I didn't want to think about it. I quickly noted that the gas was all fine and the barrels were ready to go then left the taproom to go back to the bar.

I wasn't sure what I was supposed to do until the punters started arriving, but I took the opportunity to check the glass washer and the optics. When I'd done all the busy work I could find behind the bar, I bent down in front of one of the glass-fronted fridges to familiarise myself with our new product range.

One fridge was filled entirely with unmarked bottles containing a dark liquid. I opened the fridge and picked one out, tipping it towards the light so I could see the colour. Yup. It was a glutinous, blood red liquid. It was a fair bet that it was probably blood.

I sighed and replaced the bottle. Turning round to face out onto the dance floor, I noticed that a few of the beer taps now had new labels, marked with a capital B. It looked like I was going to be a valued employee of our new metropolis's main blood distribution network. Lucky me.

I crossed my arms and leaned my elbows on the bar. After about five minutes of wondering how long I'd have to wait for something to happen, the lights went down. I guessed things were about to kick off.

There was a loud whirring sound that seemed to be coming from all around me. I looked around in panic. As I watched in open-mouthed fascination, the entirety of the wall facing me began to lift slowly upwards. I discerned an area beyond the wall set with tables and chairs.

In the space of a day, the Silver had not only demolished the wall and replaced it with a sliding substitute, but they'd also extended the first floor of the building to make a terrace. There was no guard rail around the edge. The terrace simply dropped away, revealing an uninterrupted view of the city beyond. The scope of the work was insane.

The bottom edge of what had been the wall rose higher and higher, finally disappearing above the line of the ceiling to reveal the vista of the city in front of us. I stared at it in wonder.

It was nothing like the city I knew, the buildings visible only in outline by the scant moonlight. No streetlights, no lights in the tower blocks silhouetted in the sky, no flashing aircraft. The only light I could see outside the small circle of the safe zone was rising in orange flashes through the smoke of innumerable fires blazing across the panorama.

It was utterly terrible and yet heart-breakingly beautiful, the guttering flame glorying in the ruin of the machine.

The sight of the night-inked skyline crushed reality down on me. Everything we'd built, everything we'd been, crumbling into obscurity. We'd thought we were the dominant race on the planet. Now the race was done and the humans had lost. Our world had been consumed in the flame and we weren't going to rise from its ashes.

This was their world now: the world of the Silver, of the Weepers, of the vampires. But there was such majesty in its decrepitude, the points of light glowing through the destruction they illuminated.

"May I assume from your expression that you approve of my modifications?" a voice to my left asked quietly.

I turned from the open cityscape to see Sol standing on the other side of the bar, his arms resting on the wood.

Mindful of Ben's words of earlier in the day, and aware of the desire for him that his kiss had elicited in me, I eyed him with suspicion. My look was returned with one of curious amusement.

"Would you care to tell me what I have done to merit such blatant mistrust?"

I didn't know what to say. I wasn't expecting to see him here tonight, so I hadn't even begun to plan out how I was going to play our next meeting. I hadn't expected to see him until after the kiss had worn off. I didn't want to end up being a casualty of his bloodlust.

Frankly, it wasn't as if I'd ever really trusted him, so I thought I may as well act how I felt.

"I'm unsure of your motives," I responded noncommittally.

"My motives towards you," he asked, "or my motives for modifying this room? I can assure you that in relation to the latter, I only wished to share this beautiful view with the patrons of this establishment."

As he spoke he swept his arm around behind him, indicating the city beyond the wall. As if responding to his cue, strobe lighting started flashing across the dance floor. It was like watching the city through a lightning storm.

"In relation to the former," he continued as he leaned further over the bar towards me, his voice pure silk, "I'll admit that my motives are somewhat… impure."

I was not in the slightest bit reassured by his words, but I couldn't stop my heart racing.

"Sol…" I started.

"I know," he interrupted, "you trust neither me nor your own feelings. But come tomorrow afternoon, you will know that both are true."

The silver in his eyes danced in the strobe lights, magical and hypnotic. With a hint of a smile, he turned from me and raised his voice towards the double doors.

"You may enter, Secundus."

If I thought I was going to escape the Sol and Drew show here at the club, I had clearly been mistaken.

Without a glance at me (thankfully), Drew entered the room followed by six other Silver, whom he began directing to various posts around the room: three by the stage, two by the bar and one by the door.

As they took their places, music started pumping through the speakers that hung from the walls and ceilings around the room.

"Drink?" I asked Sol.

He looked at me for a beat.

"Bottled or on tap," I added quickly, "not from the vein."

"Am I your first customer of the evening?"

I raised an eyebrow at him, casting my eyes to either side as I invited him to take in the emptiness of the dance floor.

"Thank you, Emilia, but no. I consider blood-drinking a private activity. It's not a habit I choose to indulge in public. I would, however, enjoy a scotch."

"On the rocks?" I asked.

He inclined his head at me with a smile.

"Just the one cube, if you would be so kind."

I grabbed a short glass, adding an ice cube to it from the cooler under the bar. Turning my back to Sol, I slammed a couple of shots of whiskey from an optic into the glass. I was surprised to see the good stuff up on the wall, but I guessed Sol had something to do with that.

"Here you go," I said with a small smile as I plunked the glass down on the bar in front of him, "that'll be totally free."

"Are you actually enjoying yourself?"

I shrugged a shoulder grudgingly.

"I love this place," I replied. "However much it's changed, however much it hurts, it'll always be home. It's good to be back."

As I said the words, I was surprised to realise that they were true. It was good to be back behind the bar, serving people, even if they were vampire people. It made the world seem a little more normal, a little less like it was spinning off its axis.

"You have purpose," Sol said.

I nodded in reply. It was a crappy purpose, but at least I wasn't completely aimless. And it wasn't life or death, either. It was my comfort zone. Well, sort of.

Sol picked up the glass delicately and tipped it to his mouth. As he did so, the Silver by the door to the stairwell opened it wide, letting in my customers for the night. There were only about thirty so far, but I imagined there would be more of them later.

Half were dressed in the practical military gear of the Solis Invicti, all dark khakis and boots. The other half were a complete mixture: everything from power dressing to what I considered 'normal' casual wear. I noted with dark amusement that a significant proportion was dressed in a distinctly gothic style. Leather and black were definite themes.

I took a deep breath. Here we go, I thought.

To start with, the vampires completely ignored the bar. They each paid their respects to Sol where he was propping up the bar then walked around the dance floor greeting the Invicti, but once the pleasantries were dispensed with they all gravitated back my way, intrigued by the availability of blood. Cold, bottled blood must have been a familiar experience for them (surely they stored it?), but I could only imagine that the prospect of warm blood on tap was something of a novelty.

A group of three men were first to line up, dressed like they'd just walked out of an Anne Rice novel. They all had hair down to their shoulders, which looked to me as if it had received more attention from a hairdresser in the past week than mine had in my entire life. They were all dark-haired (though I wasn't sure that was their natural colour) and wore loose shirts teamed with tailored jackets.

"Well hello there, little human," the first said, his eyes twinkling at me.

"Hey there, Lestat. Who are your friends? Louis and Armand?"

'Lestat' went bright red in indignation.

"Why, you impertinent..!"

He clocked the choker around my neck and his eyes flicked towards Sol, who was standing to my left over the bar from me, watching our exchange with interest. I got the feeling that he was anticipating the opportunity to put the three of them in their place with relish.

I knew now that the choker didn't protect me from being murdered by a vampire, just from being drained by one, but Sol's presence clearly had some sway.

Sol nodded at the three of them and Lestat simmered down immediately. I thought Sol looked a little disappointed.

Clearing his throat, Lestat turned back to me.

"What are you serving?" he asked me.

"We've got the usual array of alcoholic and non-alcoholic beverages," I replied, "then we've got cold bottled blood or hot blood on tap."

I grimaced slightly with distaste.

Lestat's pupils dilated hungrily.

"A pint, on tap," he said, nearly drooling.

He was utterly repugnant. This is the type of creature I thought of when someone said 'vampire': a pretentious idiot who dribbled when he caught the scent of fresh blood. He couldn't be further in character from Sol if he'd been born on a different planet. Hell, maybe he had been. If vampires were real, why not aliens too?

"Two tokens," I replied, my upper lip curling in disgust.

"Two?" he asked incredulously.

"Yep," I said, "two. If you want it bottled it's one."

He looked over his shoulder and held a mumbled conversation with one of his friends, who grumbled at him before reluctantly handing over a token. Lestat passed both his and his friend's token to me, trying to pretend he wasn't embarrassed about it. These guys were clearly on the very bottom rung of the ladder if they could only scrounge up two tokens between them. Either that, or they'd already blown their tokens in the restaurant in a bout of profligacy they were now regretting.

I smirked at him as I took the tokens, dropping them into the box fixed to the back wall of the bar. I grabbed a pint glass and took the hot blood tap on its inaugural run. I put the glass under the nozzle and threw the tap, but nothing happened. After a few seconds, when I was just starting to wonder if there was something wrong with the keg, a warm, dark stream poured thickly into the glass. As it hit the bottom, it threw up a wave of unpleasant scent, like copper and earth. It wasn't as repellent as I was expecting it to be, but it was a heavy, cloying smell that pervaded the room.

With that, every head turned our way. Lestat and his buddies were practically salivating as they leaned over the bar towards me, but everyone else was simply watching with interest as I topped off the glass. There was movement in the corners of my vision and I looked up to see that the two Invicti posted to the bar had put themselves either side of the group I was serving, issuing a warning to them by their presence alone. The Anne Ricites backed off a bit, still watching me keenly.

One of the Invicti, whom I recognised as the willowy, red-haired woman from the broadcast in Paternoster Square, looked over her right shoulder at me with a rueful expression.

"Apologies," she said. "We're not all this unrestrained. These three are relatively new."

I nodded an acknowledgement back at her as I placed the glass on the bar for Lestat to take. With a cautious glance at the red-head, he grabbed the glass and walked quickly off to the terrace with his entourage to share it with them. The desperation and the clandestine nature of his retreat made the whole transaction rather unsavoury. I felt sullied by the experience.

"They have made you uncomfortable," the beautiful redhead observed.

"I would rather their desire were less overt," I replied.

"I can assure you that the elder among us find it just as distasteful as you," Sol chipped in from my left.

"Emilia, this is Genevieve," he continued, indicating the red-head, "and her companion is Carmen."

The second of the women was small and Hispanic with a ferocious glint in her eye. She had a hard set to her jaw framed by black curls that tumbled to her shoulders. She had the look of a woman who had been wronged and was determined to take out the insult to her pride on the rest of the world. Or maybe it was just me. I wondered whether or not I should take it personally.

Great, I thought, yet another intimidating Silver female.

"Hi," I said to them both brightly, immediately kicking myself for opening with such an inane greeting. "I'm Emilia."

I felt hopelessly outclassed and outgunned, like they could see my every imperfection and were judging me for it. I was acutely embarrassed, but tried to act like I didn't care. Carmen simply eyed me coldly, tipping her head slightly to acknowledge my introduction. I felt a bit better when Genevieve smiled at me, apparently warmly.

"They're here to keep an eye on the bar," Drew said, approaching the bar from my right, "to keep an eye on you, make sure you're safe."

I turned my head away from him, grabbing a cloth from under the bar and using it to wipe down the counter, even though it was already clean. He must have got the message, because after a few seconds I saw him in my peripheral vision moving across the dance floor away from me.

I looked up and saw Sol walking after him.

"Wow," Genevieve said to me as she propped up the bar, "frosty. What's the boss man ever done to you?"

"Boss man?" I asked her, confused that she thought I'd been cold to Sol rather than Drew.

"The Secundus. He's in charge of the Invicti, so he's our boss as far as I'm concerned."

"It's nothing," I said to her with a smile.

"Whatever you say. I'm not going to mess with the human carrying the Primus's mark."

I sighed. I'd forgotten about that.

The club quickly became busier and more and more vampires were coming up to the bar for drinks, but I'd still overestimated how much I'd be needed. It seemed like people didn't have a lot of tokens to throw around or maybe no one was interested in more than one blood drink a night. Either way, the demand seemed to slacken off after thirty minutes or so. There wasn't much demand for alcohol either, though I served a few shots of this and that.

Sol slipped away at some point during the rush on the bar and, although I could see the Invicti posted around the room, there was no sign of Drew. I hoped he had left. He didn't belong here, not in this place where memories of Jeff and Sarah embraced me.

Just as Laila had predicted, I didn't see a single other human. Apparently, socialising wasn't a high priority for those who had enough freedom to come to the club in the first place. I wondered what they were all doing, or being required to do, reflecting mournfully that I probably had it easy.

There was a general air of expectation in the room, as if everyone was waiting for something to happen. I guessed it had to be the evening's show, but I had no idea what to expect. The Silver seemed to feel the anticipation and those who were out on the terrace came back into the room, everyone congregating in front of the stage to my right as I looked out from the bar. The terrace wall slowly descended, shutting out the moonlight and hiding the fires burning across the city.

The Silver stood immobile, staring towards the stage with eerie stillness. I had never been more aware of their otherworldliness. Humans would have scratched their chins, tucked loose hairs behind their ears, shifted their weight from foot to foot and chatted casually, passing the time before the lights went down. When the darkness fell on the Silver they each stood frozen, intent on the stage like grim and beautiful statues, silver eyes blazing in the strobes.

The music stopped.

For at least ten clear seconds we all stood in silence in the dark. I could feel the intensity of their concentration directed to the stage and my head was drawn redundantly towards the right.

As I stared, a faint glow began to rise from the floor of the stage, gradually increasing in brightness until it threw a spotlight up onto the ceiling. There was an illuminated circle about three feet in diameter in the centre of the stage, which appeared to originate from some kind of light beneath a translucent cover.

The light snapped off again, leaving a flashing oval burned into my retinas.

The music cranked up, snapping out into the darkness like a gunshot. I remembered that Laila had said there would be another human in this room tonight and, horrified, started to suspect what their role might be.

As the room's sound systems pumped, the inverted spotlight on the stage began to glow once more, but this time its light was distorted by a figure. The rasping beat of the music ratcheted up as the beautiful shape of Laila was illuminated, grinding her hips and raising her arms in the spotlight until they pointed at the ceiling.

The effect of the upwards lighting was peculiar and disturbing. I could see the sides of her legs all the way up, the undersides of her arms, the curve of her breasts, her chin and the line of her brow, but her eyes were hidden in the shadow of her cheekbones. I only recognised her when she dipped her head to the light.

She was wearing an outfit not dissimilar from my work outfit: a half corset that ended just a few inches below her bust and the shortest shorts I had ever seen. It was difficult to tell from the silhouetting effect of the spotlight, but I thought they looked like underwear. She rolled her hips as she perched on five-inch stilettos, bending over before using the angle of the heels to sweep her body forward, leading with her head as she threw her loose hair backwards and pushed her chest out, rising to her full height.

She stretched out her left arm, beckoning to a shadowed figure at the side of the stage that walked forward at her signal. Here was the human: a young man, dark-haired, tall, early twenties, devastatingly handsome, wearing only a pair of dark trousers. He had an excited, but cocky, grin on his face. He thought he was in control.

Maybe he had a crush on Laila, but whatever reason he had for being there I couldn't believe this was going to play out like he imagined it would.

Laila took his left hand and swung him around in front of her on the spot, so he was illuminated from below, facing the audience. She ran her hands around him, laying her hands palm-down on his stomach. Slowly, she ran her right hand upwards, past his chest and along his neck, tipping his head backwards until she was cupping his chin in her hand. She moved her other hand to his shoulder and slowly pushed him down onto his knees. She was so tiny that, even with her skyscraper heels, she was only a little taller than the human on his knees.

With a predatory glance at the crowd, Laila swooped down and fastened her teeth into the neck of the human, who tensed and shuddered. After only a moment she lifted her head from his neck, the blood pouring down her chin in a dark stain. She grabbed the human by his handsome mop of hair and, stepping off the spot, pulled his head back so his head was angled over the light and silhouetted on the ceiling.

Gradually the light around the outline of his head began to change colour and I realised that his blood was falling onto the translucent cover, turning the light red as it shone through it. The colour pervaded the room, the blood filtering the only source of illumination.

The Silver were transfixed.

As we watched, a Silver discreetly crept across the stage and helped the human to his feet, leading him off to the right.

But Laila hadn't finished her performance.

Bending to the light, she was bathed in red as she pressed her palms into the blood then applied it to the exposed areas of her body before bending again to the light, all the time moving to the beat of the music. As she lifted the blood, she left smears and patterns on the spot that translated into peculiar lighting effects on the ceiling and in the room as a whole, the light progressively changing from red-hued to pink to clear, bright white.

It was gruesome yet mesmerising.

The strobes kicked in and the volume of the music ramped up. The Silver started to move to the rhythm, eyes still fixed on Laila. She loaded her hands once more with blood and stroked it across her face, before disappearing to the back of the stage behind the spotlight.

As the music built to a climax she ran through the light and threw herself from the edge of the stage, arms spread out to her sides. The audience converged on her too fast for my eyes to track. In milliseconds she was buried within a writhing mass of Silver.

Seconds later they withdrew, leaving Laila free to sashay up to the bar, her skin completely clean. Licked clean, in fact.

I was stunned. I didn't know what to make of her performance. It had been powerful, but I couldn't decide if it had been sexy or grotesque. Either way, she clearly knew her audience.

"Give me a pint," she demanded, extracting two chips from her cleavage and tossing them onto the bar.

I obligingly collected the chips and deposited them in their receptacle before pulling her a pint. I had become much more accustomed to the smell and it wasn't really bothering me anymore. What was bothering me was the atmosphere in the room. It was thick not just with heat but also with the feral scent of bodies packed together. It wasn't an unpleasant smell, but for some reason it was upsetting me.

I wrinkled my nose as I put the pint down on the bar in front of Laila.

"It's a ritual of ours," she shouted at me over the music. "You smell the pheromones."

"What?"

She shook her head at me as if I wasn't worth her time and, taking her pint, walked away across the dance floor, manoeuvring her way through an increasingly-large group of dancers.

"That scent," a voice said from my left.

Drew. He was leaning with his back against the bar, talking at me over his shoulder without looking at me.

"The one that's making your head fizz and your blood surge," he continued. "Vampire pheromones."

Great. That made me feel so much better, especially coming from Drew. I ignored him, serving a bottle of beer to a tall, leggy blonde with the most elaborate eye makeup I had ever seen.

"Seriously, Emmy?" he asked when the customer had gone. "You're not even going to talk to me?"

"Leave me alone, Drew."

He turned round to face me, leaning over the bar.

"You say that all the time, but you never mean it."

"I do now," I replied fiercely, fixing him with a glare, "and I always have, you just never gave enough of a damn to listen to what I want. You never gave a damn at all."

He looked surprised at my outburst.

"That's not fair," he replied.

"Isn't it?"

"Is this about Sol?" he asked, his brow wrinkling in anxiety. "You know it's just the kiss. It'll wear off tomorrow afternoon."

I snapped.

"This has nothing to do with Sol! It's you that's the problem. We're all just throwaway humans to you."

I was getting worked up, desperately trying to keep a lid on it so I didn't cry in front of him. I couldn't bear to look at him as the grief writhed in my stomach. I wanted to punch him until my fingers broke.

"I'm just trying to keep you safe," he said at a volume that, with screaming industrial metal in the background, was the equivalent of a whisper.

"Bollocks," I replied vehemently, "you're just trying to get me to give you what you want. And what about my friends, Drew? You know, the dead ones? Do you think I can just forget that, get over it and pretend it never happened?"

He hung his head.

He'd manipulated me and lied to me. He'd taken Jeff and Sarah away from me for no reason at all. Whatever might have been between us, however conflicted I felt about him, there was no way I was letting him close to me again.

"Just leave me alone," I said bitterly.

I walked away from him to serve a customer and when I turned back, he was gone.

CHAPTER XX

The rest of the shift was a nightmare. There was a huge rush on the bar after Drew left, apparently incited by the evening's blood-licking. By the time the place emptied out at what must have been about four in the morning, I was red up to the elbows with blood from various spillages over the course of the night.

When Genevieve finally shut the door after the last stragglers, I breathed a huge sigh of relief. She was the only Silver left in the bar. The rest of the Invicti had left with the crowd. The music shut off and the main lights came up. Time for clean up duty.

"It won't be this busy every night," Genevieve assured me with a smile, "it's just because this was the grand re-opening. You know, the ritual and all. It draws a crowd."

I nodded, yawning in exhaustion as I started a circuit of the room to collect the empty glasses and bottles.

"Don't worry about those," Genevieve said, stepping towards me. "I'll do a quick clean up, it'll take me half the time, and we've got cleaners to sort the rest out in the morning."

I smiled, touched by her kindness.

"Thanks, Genevieve."

"You can call me Viv," she said with a grin. "Genevieve's a bit of a mouthful."

I went back behind the bar and cleaned up the spills.

"By the way," Viv added, "the Primus is waiting on the terrace for you."

The club wall was still in place, but there was a doorway set into it that I guessed must lead onto the terrace.

"Oh," I said.

I wasn't sure I wanted to see Sol. It had been a bit of a difficult night. I still hadn't forgiven him for the 'uniform' and now I knew he hadn't been telling me the whole truth. But, unlike Drew, at least he'd never outright lied to me. In fact, he'd been brutally honest at times. Nevertheless, I wasn't sure I could deal with him right now. It had been a very, very long day and I was sick of the drama.

"Well," I said decisively, moving towards the staircase, "he'll be waiting a long time then."

She raised a quizzical eyebrow at me as I shoved open the door. I was too tired to do anything but sleep right now. Sol could go swivel.

"Night, Viv," I called over my shoulder.

"You're living dangerously, Emmy," she shouted after me with a laugh.

I smiled wryly to myself as I climbed the stairs to the dormitories. How could I live anything other than dangerously in this place?

When I got upstairs the lights in the dorms were out and almost every bed was filled with a sleeping figure. I was starving after a night of running around behind the bar. I had only eaten once so far today and if I didn't eat something soon I felt like my stomach would implode.

I decided to wash first and then eat. I couldn't imagine feeding myself when I was this dirty.

I took off my boots then crept along to my bed at the end of the line. Pulling my rucksack out as quietly as I could, I reached in to pull out some food, clean underwear and one of Jeff's oversize T-shirts. I managed to find some deodorant and a tube of lipsalve in my handbag, but otherwise had no other toiletries. I grabbed what I had and, leaving my boots by the bed, tip-toed back out of the dorm again into the shower room.

There was a stack of mismatched towels in the corner of the room. They seemed clean enough, so I grabbed one and set the shower running in the first stall. The water was pretty loud, but there wasn't much I could do about that. There was no way I was getting into my bed with blood all over me. I set my things down on a chair opposite the shower stall and stripped off my uniform and underwear before stepping gratefully under the water.

It was boiling hot and beautifully cleansing. The water immediately turned red as I rubbed at my arms to encourage the blood to detach. There was a bar of soap in the cubicle, together with some shampoo and conditioner, so I washed myself thoroughly head to toe as quickly as I could.

I towelled myself dry then, quickly applying some deodorant and lipsalve, slipped on my clean underwear. As I went to grab the T-shirt my heart sank. In the dark, I'd picked up the T-shirt Drew had lent me instead of one of Jeff's. Left without another choice and telling myself it was hardly worth getting picky, I slipped the T-shirt over my head.

Drew's musky scent of leather and wood shavings enveloped me, bringing back the memory of the night on the scaffolding, the night of the Revelation, when he had saved me from the Weepers. I shuddered in pleasure at the smell and hated myself for it.

Hanging the wet towel on a line of hooks opposite the cubicle, I walked out into the kitchen and crammed a couple of granola bars into my mouth, washing them down with two big glasses of water. I felt instantly better, but overwhelmed with exhaustion now my hunger had been dealt with.

I gathered up my things and crept back into the dormitory. Stowing them under my bed, I sighed with relief and slipped between the sheets.

The bed was firm but comfortable and the sheets smelled

clean. I closed my eyes and exhaled, relaxing tension from my body that I hadn't realised I had been holding. As the sheets settled, a waft of scent drifted up from the T-shirt I was wearing and, just like that, I was tense again.

"Hey," a feminine voice to my left whispered.

I looked around in alarm and saw a pretty girl of about twenty in the bed next to me, her face dimly lit by the light from the window.

"You're Emilia, right?" it continued.

"Erm, yes," I whispered into the near-darkness. "Who are you?"

"My name's Alice," she answered.

"Oh," I replied, not exactly sure what she expected of me at this juncture.

"I work in the club too," she continued in an animated whisper, "only I'm down on the ground floor. Isn't it just the best place to be right now? It's so cool. I can't believe we get to, like, hang out with the Silver."

"Alice," I said.

"Yes?" she replied excitedly.

"Vampires aren't 'cool'. They're killers. We're nothing to them but food and entertainment. Now shut up and go to sleep."

There was a moment of blissful silence.

"Hypocrite," she muttered.

"What did you just call me?" I replied indignantly, struggling to stop my voice from rising.

"Everyone knows you're the Primus's pet."

She spat the word like it was an insult, though I suspected she was probably jealous. There had been awe in her voice when she first said my name and she clearly idolised the Silver.

"I'd rather not be," I whispered back in irritation, "so you can drop that tone."

"Whatever," she replied petulantly.

I said nothing and rolled over to face the window, hoping she would shut up so I could get some sleep. I started dropping off almost immediately, a warm blanket of exhaustion wrapping around me.

"At least they notice you," Alice whispered quietly.

I didn't think that was something to aspire to, being noticed by the Silver, but I ignored her. If Drew hadn't noticed me, maybe Jeff and Sarah would still be alive. Then again, maybe I'd be dead. But that wasn't enough to absolve him. You couldn't trade off lives.

I didn't know how to reconcile the Drew who had saved me with the Drew who had killed Jeff and Sarah in a rage. He wasn't the man I thought he was. But then he wasn't a man, was he? He was Silver. And, as Ben had told me, the Silver only refrain from taking what they want when it's more fun to make a game of the chase.

Sol had never pretended to be a hero, never pretended to feel anything for me. He'd been honest about his desire for my blood and had told me openly that he was waiting until I offered it to him. He'd as much as admitted that he was in it for the challenge.

But Drew, he'd pretended he cared. He acted like it meant something, like he felt something for me. He'd lied not only in word, but also in the way he'd touched me and the way he had acted towards me. And he was still pretending, still telling me he was trying to keep me safe. He'd pulled off a grand deception to make it seem like he gave a damn.

Lifting my hand to my neck, I ran my fingers along the strip of lace surrounding it.

I wondered whether or not Sol would be right about tomorrow, whether I'd still feel the same when the effects of his kiss, his mark wore off. Regardless, I wasn't about to let myself get chewed and spat out again in the kind of terrible violation Ben had hinted at. It was in my interests to keep Sol close, to get the benefit of his protection for as long as I could, but I wasn't going to cross that line.

How long would he continue to offer me his protection when he worked that out? If there was nothing in it for him, I imagined I would soon be relegated to the ranks of the rest of the humans: monthly blood donations, no protection from casual vampire snacking. No protection at all. Falling from Sol's good graces might even make me more of a target for the Silver social climbers.

Lestat and his buddies would probably take the opportunity for revenge if they could. I'd better try to keep my temper under control to avoid making any more enemies. Even if they were on the bottom rung, they were still miles ahead of me in terms of power and strength. I'd been an idiot to taunt them.

I seemed to be managing to achieve idiocy on an almost hourly basis at the moment.

Sighing in resignation as a hot wave of shame overcame me, I wrapped the blankets closer around me and, after a few more minutes' pointless self-recrimination, fell deeply asleep.

CHAPTER XXI

Monday

The next day I woke late, so late that only three other beds in the room were occupied. I assumed the sleepers were all night shifters, like me.

I noted with guilty relief that Alice's bed was empty and made up. I wouldn't have to deal with her this morning. Or did I mean this afternoon? I had no idea what time it was.

I grabbed the pair of shorts from my backpack and pulled them on then padded out of the dorm barefoot into the kitchen area. And found Alice.

She was sitting at the table, slouched over a bowl of Cheerios, already wearing her work uniform. It was no more demure than mine.

"Morning," I said, heading for the fridge.

"Afternoon, actually," she replied in a surly tone of voice. "It's just after four."

I turned to her in astonishment. I'd slept for nearly twelve hours? Not like I hadn't needed to catch up, but still.

"Shit," I said. "Do you happen to know when I'm supposed to start work again?"

"We all start at seven," she said in a patronising tone of voice, as if I were an idiot. "Didn't you get the induction at admission?"

Admission. Surprisingly, my mind hadn't been on work assignments during admission. I don't think Sol's had been either.

"Erm, admission was a bit… rushed," I said, turning back to the fridge with a sigh.

Sol's kiss. It would have worn off by now, so I'd have to face him today. I looked contemplatively at the mark on my right wrist: Sol's brand. Regardless of the fact that the mark had faded, I still carried the brand and the choker. I still 'belonged' to Sol.

But would I still want him without the mark?

I wasn't sure how I felt about it. The sensible part of me hoped that I'd feel nothing at all, so we could part ways safely without any risk of my being brutalised in some sort of feral encounter. Another part of me, the part that was desperately clinging onto reality with its fingertips, wanted to feel the same way as I had yesterday, just so there'd be something in this new world that wasn't a lie, some emotion that was genuine.

I'd thought I'd lost everything. Then I'd lost Danny, then Jeff and Sarah. Yesterday I lost Drew, or rather I realised that he'd never been what I thought he was. I'd been made to feel safe by the version of him that didn't exist. I'd aligned myself with a mirage.

If I still wanted Sol then, even though I knew he felt nothing for me, even if I had to keep my distance to stop myself from getting hurt, physically, at least it would be real. At least I'd have that feeling.

The hard truth that I was trying, and failing, to get myself to accept was that I was on my own. I couldn't trust anyone.

But I wanted to, because I felt so bereft and alone that I wanted to scream. And I couldn't deny that, in this dangerous new world, putting myself close to the Primus was not an awful plan.

I pulled the milk out of the fridge, wondering where it had

come from. It was in a glass milk bottle and it looked fresh. Maybe the Silver had the supply chain sorted out even better than we first thought. But then, it had only been a few days. Grabbing a bowl from a stack on the side, I poured out some cereal and covered it in milk. I pulled open some drawers until I found a spoon and, returning the milk to the fridge, took my breakfast (or dinner, I suppose) to a seat opposite Alice at the table.

We ate in silence for a couple of minutes.

"So," Alice said, feigning disinterest but clearly dying to talk about it, "I heard you came in later than the rest of us?"

"Yeah, I'd been hiding out. So what happened to you?" I added quickly, eager to shift attention away from me.

"Well," she started, clearly keen to talk about herself, "I was at Uni on the evening it happened, in the library. This guy, this stunningly beautiful Silver guy, he came in and, like, carried me and this other girl out. It was scary, but sort of exciting. And they brought us to the safe house and admitted us, and I was there till yesterday, when I was brought here."

She paused and shrugged, apparently disappointed not to have had a more eventful time.

"That's it, really."

No wonder she was so starry-eyed. She hadn't seen the Weepers. She hadn't seen anyone die. All she knew was that a handsome Silver had swept her off her feet, literally. Could I really blame her for her attitude?

She reminded me of myself as I had been a few days ago, when Danny had yelled at me, just a couple of floors below where we were sitting now, for sympathising with the vampires. I still thought he'd been right, but maybe we'd gone about things in the wrong way.

"What's the choker about?" she asked. "I heard some of the Silver talking about it in the bar last night."

I snorted with laughter.

"I guess you'd call it my dog collar," I replied. "It means no one else but Sol can drink from me."

Her eyes widened at me in amazement.

"Wow," she said, "so you, like, feed the Primus?"

"No!" I said, horrified. "I don't feed anyone, thank you very much."

"Some of us don't have a choice," she answered quietly.

Chastened, I bent my head to my cereal and carried on eating. My cheeks flushed with shame. It had been a thoughtless thing to say.

We finished eating in silence then I carried my bowl to the sink and washed it up. As I was doing so, the door to our dormitory opened and the stragglers slipped out: two young teenaged girls and an older woman. They looked like a family.

I had a couple of hours to kill and I wasn't sure how to pass the time. I didn't really know anyone here but Alice, and we hadn't got off to a great start. I smiled vaguely at her and headed back into the now empty dorm room.

The afternoon sunlight was streaming through the open window, casting a sunbeam onto my bed. As I got closer to it, I saw that there was a fluffy ball curled up tightly at its foot. It was the kitten from the alley.

I crept up to the window slowly, taking care not to disturb her, and reached out to stroke her head. She was worryingly docile, not skittish like cats normally are with unfamiliar people. She opened her eyes sleepily and looked up at me, but her eyes weren't focussing properly. When I stroked my hand the length of her body I could feel her bones protruding through her skin.

She was starving.

I reached under the bed and pulled out my backpack, fishing around in the tins until I found the small, foil-sealed cans of tuna I had been looking for. Ripping the lid off one, I placed it on the bed by her face, hoping she'd sit up to eat it. She didn't move.

After a few minutes, I lifted out a small piece of fish and offered it to her on my fingers. Tentatively, she licked it into her mouth. I repeated the action several more times until she got a taste for it and, rising unsteadily to her feet, put her face in the tin.

I sighed with relief. I didn't think I could have coped with a dead kitten on top of everything else.

She was a beautiful little thing with a well-groomed coat. She must have been someone's pet, so used to getting food from a tin that she was unable to look after herself in the wild. Good thing I had plenty of tuna.

"What's that?"

Alice had returned to the dorm and was walking towards me.

"I found her on my bed," I said. "She's not been eating."

"Oh, the poor thing!" Alice gushed. "Do you think we'd be allowed to keep her?"

"I don't see why not," I replied. "I've got loads of food in my bag that she can have. It should keep her going for a while."

Alice stood by the bed and watched the kitten with delight.

"Can I... can I stroke her?" she asked.

"Of course," I replied, "but go gentle."

She reached out a hand slowly and stroked the little cat gently as she wolfed down the tuna. When she finished the tin, Alice turned to me.

"Should we give her more?" she asked.

"I don't think so. If she hasn't eaten in a while it might make her ill."

Alice looked at the kitten quietly for a moment. The kitten looked back and mewed pitifully.

"What shall we call her?"

I laughed.

"Whatever you like," I replied.

She looked serious for a moment, her pretty brow wrinkling in thought.

"Phoenix," she said decisively, "because she sort of looks like fire in the dark, and because she's survived."

I nodded.

"It's a good name."

"And we can call her Nixy for short!" she said with glee.

I rolled my eyes as I stroked Phoenix gently, sitting on the bed next to her. She settled back down to sleep.

"You want to play cards?" Alice asked after a moment. "I made a deck when we were in the safe house."

"Sure."

Alice grabbed a stack of pieces of paper from under her mattress and sat down on the other side of Phoenix, dealing out a hand. We played gin rummy and whist with scrappy cards made from lined note paper and biro, taking it in turns to choose the next game. We actually had a lot of fun.

When the woman and her two teenaged daughters returned from the showers, they cooed over Phoenix and joined us for a few games. After another hour or so we let the girls, Jane and Mia, feed Nix (as she had then come to be known).

As we played, I pulled out a few other tins from my bag and we all feasted on tinned peaches and lychees, eating them with our fingers.

The girls were quiet to start with, but eventually they started to open up. They hadn't been in the safe house with Alice. They lived out in Kent, or at least they had done, and had only been bussed in the day before. They'd lost their dad to a Weeper attack on the night of the Revelation, but the Silver had arrived in time to save the rest of them.

The girls thought the Silver were heroes walking among us, but their mother was sceptical and edgy. Mia and Jane were unmarked, no tattoos and no cuts on them. Maybe there was an age threshold for all this craziness. Their mum carried the same marks I did, but she was also fingering a puncture mark in the crook of her elbow that was surrounded by an ugly bruise. She'd been 'donating'.

Her eyes were haunted and she eyed me with suspicion. I wondered whether she thought I'd be reporting back to Sol.

All three of them worked the night shift over in the Palace, chambermaids to the Silver. They left together just after six to get to work. Jane and Mia had to be practically dragged away from Nix, so I felt like our dorm might have found a new mascot.

Alice and I were just starting another game of cards when Laila walked in with Cam trailing behind her.

"I am leaving the premises for the evening," Laila said to us abruptly, "and the Invicti are in charge until I return."

"Hey, Emmy!" Cam greeted me enthusiastically.

I couldn't help but smile back at him. He was such a sunny character.

Alice looked between us, a little awestruck.

"I will leave them in your care, Cameron," Laila said imperiously. "Please look after the club in my absence."

With that, she turned on her heel and walked back into the stairwell. I found her terse manner disconcerting, but I guess she just didn't think we were worth more of her time than was absolutely necessary.

"Hey Cam," I said, "how are you doing?"

"Good thanks."

He grinned and, after a second's hesitation, strode forward and pulled me into a bear hug. The paper cards fell from my hand with the movement.

"Woah, it's good to see you too," I said, giving him a quick squeeze before pushing him away.

"I'm just really happy for you guys."

I wrinkled my brow in confusion.

"Who? For me and Alice? Because of the kitten?"

Cam looked uncertain, flicking his eyes to Alice. She took the hint and, smiling obsequiously, went into the kitchen, closing the door behind her.

"No, you and the Secundus."

"Cam," I replied, "I hate him. Why would you be happy for us? There is no 'us', never has been. I don't even want to speak to him."

"But his scent, it's all over you. And Tommy told me…"

He trailed off into silence.

"I'm wearing his T-shirt," I replied, "he lent it to me a few days ago. What did Tommy tell you?"

He just shook his head at me.

"Why aren't you talking to him?" he asked, looking at me

in concern.

I think it was probably the first time I'd ever really seen him with a serious expression on his face.

"He killed my friends," I said bleakly, "for no reason at all. I can't ever forgive him that, Cam."

"He wouldn't do a thing like that for no reason," he replied, looking at me intently. "He cares about you, Emmy."

"That's a load of bollocks and you know it. You Silver don't really give a shit about any of us humans, you just find us tasty and entertaining. Don't try and tell me different."

"We're not all like that," he said, sounding hurt, "and Drew definitely isn't like that with you."

"And how can I possibly trust anything you say?"

Cam looked at me like I'd punched him.

Guilt rolled in my stomach. He came across as so kind-natured that I couldn't bear to hurt his feelings. But he wasn't human. Did he even have feelings? Or was this all fake?

"I want to," I said in a conciliatory tone, "but you're Silver. Don't you get it? For Christ's sake, Cam, you're the reason I got caught in the first place. You're why I'm here."

"I know, but you're safer here than out there."

"So you say."

He sighed.

"Look," he said, "will you talk to him at least?"

I shook my head.

"Is it Sol?"

"No it's not bloody Sol!" I yelled in frustration. "It's nothing to do with him, Cam. You can smell it, right? The mark?"

He nodded.

"So is it there?"

He sniffed the air a few times and, a look of resignation on his face, shook his head.

"That's the end of that, then. I need to get changed for work. I'll see you there."

I pointedly indicated the door and Cam took the hint, shaking his head before stalking off and out of the dorm room. When he was gone, I quickly shrugged out of my shorts and T-shirt and wriggled into my uniform. I zipped on the flat boots again. They were practical and comfy and they toned the outfit down a bit.

Walking out of the dorm, I went in search of a toothbrush. Alice smiled at me as I passed her on my way to the bathroom. She was walking in the other direction, doubtless off to check on Nix before changing into her work clothes. It looked like I might have repaired some fences with her, at least.

There were a few cheap toothbrushes in plastic wrappers in a cup in the bathroom so, with huge relief, I tied my hair up then cleaned my teeth and washed my face. I was ready for another night behind the bar.

I assumed I was working the same room tonight and, as I entered the first floor bar to see Cam leaning against the bar, that assumption was proved correct.

"Last night was a longer shift than normal," he said to me as I entered, his tone all business, "because it was the weekend and because it was the first night. Laila wants to open this room seven till midnight on week days and seven till two in the morning Friday to Sunday."

"Okay," I answered, not sure how to act around him now his puppy-dog persona was absent.

"We're opening earlier downstairs, but closing earlier too, so normally you'll be working there in the afternoons. You're on in twenty minutes. No stage show tonight."

I nodded back at him. He made to walk past me to the door, presumably to get the rest of the Invicti.

"Cam…" I started, reaching out for his hand.

"Look," he interrupted me, "I know this has all been pretty hard for you, but you're acting like we're monsters. We're not, Em. I'm not. Drew isn't. I know Tommy can be a shit, but even he's a good guy at heart."

"That may be true as between the Silver, but I'm human. I haven't heard great things about the way Silver treat their human pets."

He looked down and shook his head.

"Yeah, it's true that a lot of humans have suffered at the hands of the Silver, but we're trying to change that. Some of us are evil bastards, but the majority of us are just trying to do our best in a bad situation. In that respect we're no different from you. We just have a different perspective on things."

"There are lines that can't be uncrossed, Cam," I replied steadily.

"I know that," he said sadly, "but sometimes there's no choice. I don't know why Drew did what you say he did, but I trust him more than I trust any other Silver. You should give him a chance."

"And Sol?" I asked.

He looked back at me, wrinkling his brow in consternation.

"He has a reputation for… brutality, but I'm not sure how much of it is true. He wouldn't have got to be Primus if he hadn't at least appeared to regard humans as an inferior race. Be careful."

I exhaled heavily. I remembered Sol's comments about humans being cattle. At least he'd never lied about his stance.

"I care about you, you know," he added with such a hurt expression that something twisted in my chest.

To hell with it. I threw my arms around him and buried my face in his chest.

"If you don't want to see Drew then I'll keep him away for tonight," he said as his arms wrapped around me and squeezed me tight.

"Yes please," I replied gratefully.

"But you have to promise me that you'll talk to him soon. You need to give him a chance to say his piece."

"I've done that, Cam," I replied, "but okay. Just give me some time to settle in."

"You can have a couple of days," he said, breaking away from me and heading towards the door, "but I can't guarantee I'll be able to keep him away from you for that long. In fact, it'll be a miracle if I can."

"Okay," I smiled at him.

He flashed me a big, welcome grin then ducked through the door. A short reprieve was better than nothing.

I got to setting up the bar, checking the gas and making sure we were fully stocked. It looked like I was on my own again. A few minutes later, Cam returned with some of the Invicti in tow who stationed themselves around the room. There were fewer of them tonight, but I was pleased to see that Viv was among their number. She smiled at me and gave me a finger wave as she walked across the room.

I reflected on the fact that if the Silver included people like Cam and Viv they couldn't all be murderous bastards. Could they?

Ben walked in too and offered me a tip of his head in greeting as he stationed himself at the other end of the bar. The lights and music started up almost immediately and a Silver I didn't recognise opened up the doors to let the customers in. As he did so, the wall slid up to reveal the terrace. It looked like it would be staying open tonight.

The night passed quite quickly because I was busy at the bar, despite the fact that there were only about two hundred Silver in tonight. I handed over a lot more alcohol than the night before, but it didn't really seem to have much of an effect on the Silver.

In a quiet moment, I walked along the bar to where Ben was standing.

"Get you a drink, Ben?" I asked.

"Yeah, please. A Peroni would be good," he answered with a smile.

I cracked the top off a bottle and handed it over the bar to him.

"Quiet tonight," I said.

"I think this'll be about average," he replied. "There aren't that many of us here at the moment, but we like to go out most nights. It's important for us to see each other, to bond, to be together. We're pretty sociable, but we don't seriously pair up that often so we like to hang out with other people."

I wondered whether this was what Sol had meant when we

talked about touch being special, sacred. Maybe he'd been talking euphemistically. It would make more sense. Cam certainly hadn't held back on the touchy feely. Scanning the dance floor, I noticed that although there were a lot of Silver touching, none of them were kissing.

Maybe that's where the line was. Drew had never kissed me. Though he had… licked me. That had felt pretty intimate. I shuddered as heat coursed through me and forcibly changed my train of thoughts, noticing that Ben was eyeing me with amusement.

"Thinking happy thoughts?" he asked.

I remembered what Tommy had said about vampires' sense of smell and, with a brief look of disgust at Ben, left him laughing to himself as I walked to the other end of the bar. Stupid vampires.

For a few hours I got lost in the monotony of my job. The music was pretty decent and most of the clientele were polite enough. Lestat and his friends were back in tonight, but they kept themselves to themselves, the model of courtesy when they came to the bar for drinks.

It was coming up to eleven when all hell broke loose. I was just handing a pint of blood to a Chinese girl when there was a colossal crack from the dance floor. I put down the glass as everyone spun to the centre of the room to see what was happening.

The main lights came up and the music cut out, the open wall dropping down to close off the terrace. There were several blurs of movement from the corners of the room that were too fast for me to follow and a wind whipped through the club like a tornado, lifting people into the air, glass smashing to the floor. The movement seemed to converge in the middle of the dance floor for a second and then there was a sickly crunch.

It all happened in the blink of an eye.

Everything went still.

Viv was standing in the middle of a circle of Silver, blood splashed up her right arm and onto her chest, her foot on the neck of the body of a Silver boy. His head was caved in at the side and his eyes stared blankly up towards the ceiling. It looked like Viv had punched through his skull.

"Does this boy have a mate?" she asked the assembled Silver.

There was a general shaking of heads.

"Then I shall deliver him back to the Palace. The club will close now until tomorrow."

Without another word, she slung the body over her shoulder. The Invicti ushered everyone out of the room and within a minute or so it was empty save for me and Ben. I was left feeling completely redundant.

"What happened?" I asked Ben in confusion.

"The boy had too much blood, got himself all fired up and tried to pick a fight. The Invicti stepped in and, well, you saw for yourself."

"But... his head..."

"He'll be fine in a few days. We can heal from almost anything," he said with a smile, moving towards the door. "I'd better go run damage control. I'll leave you to close up."

As the doors shut behind him I looked around the room with a sigh. There was a lot of broken glass from the fight. I thought I'd better clean it up now rather than leave it all to the cleaners.

I grabbed a broom from the tap room and swept up the glass that was scattered in a pool of blood in the centre of the room, scooping it into a dustpan. I dumped it all in the bin behind the bar and went to gather up the unbroken bottles and glasses from round the room. There weren't that many. Most of them had ended up in the pile on the floor.

I was just about to turn on the glass washer when I realised that I hadn't checked the terrace was clear. The wall had come down pretty quickly and there could still be glasses, perhaps even Silver, out on the balcony.

I nearly just turned around and left for the dormitories, but I'd barely been awake for seven hours and the thought of shutting myself away again wasn't very appealing. I took a deep breath and carefully opened the door in the moving wall, letting a cool breeze waft into the room.

Stepping out, I glanced around and saw that I had been right on both counts. There were a number of glasses, mostly empty but some half-full, standing around on the tables on the open terrace. And there was Sol, sitting at one of the tables nearest the precipitous, unguarded edge of the terrace, gazing out over the city.

He turned as he heard the door open and smiled at me slightly.

"Sol."

"Emilia," he replied. "How are you tonight?"

"Fine."

I felt unsure and nervous, the knowledge that his mark had now faded thrumming between us like a taut string. I had no idea what I was feeling for Sol because I was wound too tight to get a proper read on my own emotions.

I walked away from him, picking up a glass on the table nearest to the door.

"Would you like to discuss what is upsetting you?" he asked solicitously.

"No, thank you," I said, too politely.

This was Sol. I was never polite to him and he knew it.

"It will continue to upset you until you confront it. Do you feel any different? Have your feelings towards me changed at all?"

"I don't want to know, okay?" I snapped at him, turning to face him. "Either way, the outcome is the same. I don't want to become a victim of your brutality."

I walked from table to table, stacking the pint glasses in my arms as I went. I felt his eyes on me as I moved, tracking me from step to step.

"You've been listening to rumours, Emilia."

"And should I ignore them?" I asked quietly. "Everyone tells me that humans and the Silver don't have relationships. That the Silver can't feel anything for humans. Are you telling me that's a lie?"

I glanced at him over my shoulder.

"You know it is. You feel that it is."

I shook my head at him.

"I can't trust my feelings, that much at least has become clear."

"And what makes you say that?" he asked.

I said nothing, unwilling to talk to him about Drew's betrayal.

"My Secundus," he said, divining my thoughts, "he has hurt you?"

"It's none of your business, Sol," I said, picking up another glass to add to the stack in my arms.

"That's not true," he said. "I care for you, Emilia, and you are under my protection. If anyone hurts you…"

"Just stay out of it, okay?" I interrupted him. "It's done, it's over and nothing can fix the past."

He tipped his head at me in acknowledgement.

"As you wish."

And there it was, that was what made Sol special. He accepted that I knew what I wanted and he gave me enough respect to let me have my way. Sometimes, at least. It was old-fashioned and modern, all at the same time. I looked at him in exasperation. He wasn't making this easy.

"If I asked you to leave me alone, would you?" I asked him, thinking of the many times I had asked the same of Drew.

His brow furrowed slightly before smoothing out again.

"If that is what you truly want, then yes. But I would count it a favour if you would continue to wear the choker, to ensure your protection."

He had taken my words as a dismissal and, standing from his seat, he made his way towards the door back into the club.

"I shall not approach you again unless you ask for me," he said quietly, before ducking through the door and closing it behind him.

I was left on the terrace alone, not sure what to do next. I hadn't expected him to leave because it hadn't been what I was asking. It had been a hypothetical question. I hadn't meant to give him his marching orders. I wondered if he had realised that and made a tactical play.

With a sigh, I returned to my task.

I thought I'd collected everything from the terrace when I noticed two final glasses standing on the table farthest away from me, right on the corner of the terrace. Balancing the increasingly precarious stack of glasses against my hip, I carefully moved to the edge of the terrace and added the last two glasses to the top of the pile.

As I straightened, a strong gust of wind caught my side, spinning me off balance and tipping me towards the ledge. I fell backwards, throwing the glasses into the air above me, and there was an odd moment of weightlessness before gravity drew me downwards. I had a strange sense of déjà vu as the glass fell around me, shattering on the ground before driving itself into the flesh of my arms, legs and face.

But, unlike the night I met Sean, this time I didn't stay on the floor.

The backs of my thighs and calves hit the terrace, but my hips and upper body fell backwards into the void, tipping me over the edge. The air streamed past me as my body whipped into an unintentional dive.

I opened my mouth in a scream, but the movement had taken my breath away and all that came out of my mouth was a strangled cry.

This was it. I was going to plummet headfirst into the pavement and end up dead, even though I was only one floor up.

A pressure tightened around my left ankle like a vice, jarring my injured knee and leaving me swinging in mid air. I looked up towards my feet, the world in reverse, and saw a hand wrapped around my foot. Behind that was Sol's face.

"I've got you," he said soothingly as he stood from where he was crouched on the edge of the terrace, lifting me upwards and scooping me into his arms as he did so.

"Shit," I said, clinging to the front of his shirt in a death grip as he held me close to him, one arm under my knees and the other under my shoulders.

I saw him looking around the terrace with a fierce look on his face then I just closed my eyes and leaned my forehead against his chest until my breathing stilled. His fresh, spicy scent enveloped me and, together with the adrenaline pumping round my system from the fall, set me on fire.

Sol looked down at me in surprise, his nostrils flaring.

"You came back," I whispered, looking up into his eyes as I ran a hand around the back of his neck.

"I heard you cry out," he replied, bending down to touch my feet to the ground.

I put all my weight on my right leg, just using the toe of my left boot to balance. There were little cuts all over the exposed skin of my arms, legs and face, but I couldn't even feel them.

"Sol," I said as he straightened, wrapping my other hand around his neck to pull his face down to mine.

I wanted him badly.

He'd just saved my life, so I told myself he had to be a good guy. He had to care about me.

Even if he didn't, I wasn't sure I cared.

He lit a fire in my veins and I wanted to burn up in its flame. I wanted to forget all the awful horror and betrayal that had happened over the past few days: Danny, Jeff, Sarah... Drew. I wanted to lose myself in his eyes, lose myself in his touch. I wanted to surrender to him, to give myself over to him, to do what my body was screaming for him to do.

I wanted him to blank out everything else, to remove me from myself. I didn't want to be me. I didn't want to care. I just wanted something simple, something fierce, something physical to cut through the emotions that were constricting my heart.

Let him hurt me. I welcomed it. Let it be brutal.

His lips brushed over mine and he met my eye.

"You're certain?" he asked.

Instead of answering, I pushed my lips hard against his and

ran my right hand through his hair, fisting it between my fingers and using it to pull him closer to me. He responded immediately, opening his lips against mine and driving his tongue into my mouth.

The fire flickered under my skin. I moaned in the back of my throat and pushed my body closer against him.

In a flash of movement, my back was up against the wall of the club and my legs were wrapped around him, his hand under my thighs to keep me in place. He growled low in his chest as pulled away from me slightly and looked down appraisingly.

"This is what you want?" he asked, his ice-blue eyes staring into mine, the silver threading in their whites glinting in the moonlight.

"This is what I want," I replied breathlessly.

"What do you want?" he challenged me in a gravelly voice, grinding his pelvis against me so I could feel the hard length of him pressing against my core.

I gasped.

"I want you, Sol," I replied fiercely, grasping his hair in my right hand as my eyes bore into his.

With my left hand I reached between us and unzipped his trousers, reaching inside to release him, stroking his length as I did so. He shuddered and my desire ramped up a notch.

"And I want you to bite me," I added, "now."

He didn't wait to be told again.

His pupils flared and the growl in the back of his throat rose to a roar. With a quick flick of his right wrist he reached beneath my skirt to tear off my underwear then plunged inside me. At the same time, he raised his other hand to my throat and tore the choker from it before burying his face in my neck.

I felt his teeth tear into my skin and threw my head back against the wall, closing my eyes as I cried out in pain and abandon. My body tensed rigid and I gritted my teeth in agony as tears welled in my eyes.

But then, as the drug in his kiss kicked in, came the pleasure. I felt a tugging through my body as he drew the blood from my veins; a fizzy, electric sensation that sent tingles across the surface of my skin and banked flame in my core.

The breeze that blew lightly across the terrace caught a few loose strands of my hair and whipped them across my face. Opening my eyes, I stared up towards the stars that glinted above our heads.

As Sol drew the blood from my neck, the pleasure built up within me, rising higher and higher, and I had to move.

I wrapped my arms around his neck and, bracing my lower arms against his shoulders, I began to lift myself from him, riding the waves of the pulls he was taking from my neck. The feeling of him inside me, the spicy scent surrounding me, made me feel like I was floating on a cloud. I was dizzy with excitement and desire.

But things were obviously moving a little too quickly for him.

He put his hands on my hips to still me and, bracing my back against the wall, pushed into me in a tantalisingly slow rhythm.

I groaned as he teased me with gentle, languorous strokes, matching them with the movement of his tongue on my neck as he lapped at my skin. Then he twisted his hips, nearly sending me over the edge.

"Sol…" I breathed, needing him so badly my head was spinning, "please…"

He drew his head away from my neck and licked his lips as he looked me in the eye. Then he began to move faster, deeper, making me feel every inch of him as he brought me to the precipice of excitement.

I threw my head back against the wall and, just as I reached the pinnacle, he brought his mouth down towards my other shoulder and plunged his teeth into my throat. I screamed and climaxed, convulsing wildly against him. His hips jerked deeper into me and, pulling his face away from my neck, he tipped his head back and roared into the night, a feral exclamation of possession and dominance echoing in the sea of empty buildings that surrounded us.

The world went away.

I floated high, disappearing into a warm cloud of escape and release.

Cupping a hand around the back of my head, he tipped my face gently around to his, pressing a series of kisses against my lips as he moved slowly within me, prolonging my spasms until I collapsed against him with my arms around his neck, my legs still locked around his hips.

"You'll come back with me tonight, Emilia," he said, moving his lips against mine as he stroked a stray piece of hair away from my face.

I was too blissed out to argue. I closed my eyes and moved my head sideways so my cheek was pressed against his shoulder.

"Call me Emmy," I whispered, a contented smile spreading across my face. "It seems silly to stand on ceremony after... that."

"Emmy, then," he replied, a smile in his voice.

He gently unwound my legs from around him and draped my knees over his right arm. There was a zipping noise as he re-fastened his trousers, then he wrapped his left arm around me and moved towards the edge of the terrace.

"Sol?" I asked, still too zoned out to think straight. "What are you doing?"

"I'm taking you home," he replied. "Don't worry, you're safe."

I closed my eyes as he stepped off the edge of the terrace. I had a moment of anxiety then he landed in a crouch on the ground below. A second later, we were just inside the door of his apartment on the fifth floor of the Palace.

I looked around me in bewilderment, taking in the four familiar seating areas laid out in front of me.

"What the hell?"

"We can move pretty quickly when we want to," he said, looking down at me with a slight smile. "I thought you'd probably prefer not to be seen, and I'd rather keep this between the two of us for now. I don't want to make you into even more of a target."

He gently put me down on one of the low sofas in the seating area to my left, the same seating area he had sat in the last time I had been here.

"And then," he continued, "there's my Secundus."

He raised an eyebrow as he sat down next to me on the sofa and gathered me into his arms.

"What about him?" I asked, as if I didn't know what he was getting at.

"What is he to you?" he asked. "I imagine he would not be pleased to know what just transpired between us."

"And would that really have stopped you?" I asked, involuntarily nuzzling my head into his shoulder to breathe in his scent.

He brought his hand around to tip my face up to his so I was looking him in the eye.

"How much of what just happened was about me," he asked quietly, "and how much was about him? What is he to you?"

I flushed, angry that he was pushing me, but mostly ashamed that he had called me out.

"I don't know," I replied.

"I'm not used to playing second fiddle to my own Secundus," Sol said with a warning tone in his voice.

"Funny," I said with a sarcastic smile.

"I'm serious," he replied.

"Do you want me to tell you he's nothing to me? He killed my friends and I'm never going to forgive that. I want nothing to do with him, Sol. I've told him to leave me alone, and I meant it."

"But there was something between you?"

I shook my head in denial.

We'd never even kissed. It had been nothing, less than nothing. But he'd made me feel safe, made my heart sing.

Shit.

Sol looked at me sceptically. He knew it was a lie, but he

let it go.

"Anyway, I can't see how it's any of your business. It was just sex."

"Maybe so," he replied, raising an eyebrow at me, "but I don't intend to share you. You're carrying my mark again now, Emmy. I might not have heeded it so much before tonight, but I will see it properly enforced from this point on."

"And what does that entail?" I asked in trepidation.

"No Silver other than me will so much as touch you without my permission, neither deliberately nor accidentally. Especially not Drew. You will be inviolate, except by my hand."

I couldn't believe it. I gawped. It wasn't like I wanted to sleep around the Silver, but the presumption burned me. And what about Cam? Was Sol going to fly off the handle at his bear hugs?

"You are fucking kidding me, Sol," I said in a rage, pushing away from him. "How dare you presume to tell me who can and can't touch me?"

"It is for your protection," he replied in a reasonable tone of voice.

Protection? Shit. We hadn't used any of that. Sol caught my panicked look.

"We can't procreate with humans, Emmy, and we don't suffer from disease."

"Oh," I said, relieved, then glared at him as I resumed my train of thought.

He sighed slightly, clearly hoping I would have dropped the subject of the mark.

"It's to keep you safe, Emmy."

"Bollocks," I replied, getting unsteadily to my feet, "it's to control me. To keep me in a cage. I won't let you do that to me. You're not going to make a slave of me, Sol."

Without warning, the pain I had been blocking out with the help of Sol's kiss came rushing back, stinging through the cuts on my exposed skin and aching into my knee.

"I had gathered that," he said as he stood, catching me as

I tottered sideways on my injured knee. "I won't force this on you, Emmy, but will you think on it overnight?"

I pouted back at him, unappeased.

"Please?" he asked, taking my face in his hands and looking into my eyes.

I tried to resist, but my balance was screwed up by my knee so in the end I decided just to go with it.

"Fine," I replied with a sigh, "but I'm not your sex slave, so you can forget this 'inviolate save for you' nonsense right now."

He moved his hands under my forearms to support my weight, carefully avoiding the cuts along their length. He looked at me in concern.

"As you wish, but only if you will stay here tonight and let me tend to your wounds."

Oh dear. I wasn't sure I liked the way this way going. Drew's 'tending' to my wounds had been decidedly exciting and, now that reality was sinking back in, I was increasingly unsure that having sex with Sol had been the best idea in the world.

It had been amazing, but I hadn't been expecting anything to change between us as a result. It had been oblivion for me, a chance to step out of myself. To Sol, I wasn't sure what it was, but he seemed to be viewing tonight as having given him a right of possession. I didn't want to encourage that.

"Is this going to be some kind of Silver licking thing?" I asked with trepidation.

Sol looked at me in surprise.

"No. Why would you think that?" he asked cagily.

He obviously suspected that I might know about the Silver healing thing Drew had used on my arm, but he didn't want to ask me outright and then have to reveal it to me if it turned out I knew nothing about it. Interesting.

I remembered Tommy's reaction to seeing the 'band aid' on my arm. He seemed sort of horrified. And what had Drew said about that? That humans and Silver didn't usually do what we had done together? Maybe he had been talking about the healing and not about the intimacy we had shared.

Not that the healing hadn't been an intimate experience in itself.

Probably best not to tell Sol about it.

"Well," I said, "you know, the blood and all."

He smiled his slight smile at me, his suspicion apparently allayed.

"No, Emmy," he said, "I'm going to run you a bath and clean you up. With my hands."

The way he said it was thick with sexual tension. Suddenly, I felt a little nervous. I was here in his apartments, alone with him, and I was going to have to get naked in front of him if he was going to get me clean in the bath.

It was one thing to have a mad, lustful encounter on an open-air terrace after a near-death experience. Undressing deliberately for him, making myself that vulnerable... it was an entirely different proposition. It required trust, something I didn't know whether I was willing to give.

"Sol," I said, "I'm not sure I..."

I shifted uncomfortably, blushing and looking away from him.

"Emmy," he replied softly, "I wish simply to clean and bind your wounds. You bathe alone, if that is what you wish."

I gratefully offered him a small smile.

With that, he swept me up into his arms and carefully carried me up the spiral staircase on the left. It was a beautiful piece of architecture, intricately carved in several different colours of wood. It was wide enough that Sol could carry me comfortably, but not wide enough to allow two people to walk abreast.

When we reached the top of the staircase I saw that there was another small seating area on the landing, set to the side of a single door that led off it to the left of the double-height room's central window. Sol opened the door and carried me through, shutting the door again behind us.

It was another breath-taking room. Another huge window occupied most of the wall to the right with a low window seat running its length. A four-poster bed sat against the far wall, flanked by beautiful rosewood bedside tables.

There was a seating area immediately to the right as we entered, with a sofa, a couple of armchairs and a low coffee table. A discrete sliding cupboard was set into the wall nearby, which I imagined contained a flatscreen television.

To the left was a desk with a chair on either side of it and, behind that in the far corner of the room, a wardrobe and chest of drawers. Between the bed and the wardrobe was a door that I supposed led to the bathroom.

Sol carried me over to the sofa and, careful to avoid touching my wounds, laid me gently along its length.

"There is glass embedded in a number of these lacerations, Emmy," he said, "but I can extract it for you, if you will let me."

That didn't sound like it was going to be fun. I nodded at him and settled back onto the sofa cushions.

"Just do what you have to," I replied.

He went into the bathroom and returned a minute or so later with a glass bowl full of steaming water, a pair of tweezers and a stack of towels. Kneeling next to the sofa, he placed the bowl and the towels on the coffee table then, grabbing one from the pile, gently slid it under my closest arm.

He took my hand in his and applied the tweezers to a splinter of glass protruding from the largest of the cuts on that arm, extracting it carefully before depositing it on the coffee table with a plink.

"While I do this," he said, "we need to talk about what happened on the terrace."

I so didn't want to have that conversation.

"Sol, can we just leave it?" I gritted out through my teeth, pain lancing through me as Sol pulled another piece of glass from my arm. "It was sex, okay? It doesn't have to mean anything."

He raised a sardonic eyebrow at me.

"I was referring to the fall, but since you raise the subject, perhaps we should discuss the sex."

"What about my fall?" I asked, ignoring him. "I got caught off balance by a breeze. It was stupid."

He shook his head at me, but kept his eyes trained on his work.

"No, Emmy. It wasn't an accident. There was a scent on you, the scent of another Silver."

"I hate to break this to you," I replied, "but there were about a hundred of them in the club tonight."

"You misunderstand," he said. "You know that our touch has meaning and that emotion can seal that meaning, leaving a scent mark."

I thought of the mark made by his kiss. The desire, the bloodlust, marked me with his scent.

"Yes," I said.

"But there are different types of scent, as many as there are emotions. When we mark in lust, we leave our own scents behind because that is the purpose of the mark: to stake a claim, to give notice that you are possessed by one Silver and that Silver alone."

I wrinkled my brow in irritation, not sure I liked the sound of being possessed.

"But," he continued, "if a mark is made in another emotion, it leaves behind the intent but no trace of the Silver who made it. Tonight, a Silver touched you in a rage, but I couldn't tell you who that Silver might be. You're someone's target."

"That's ridiculous," I replied. "There was a fight in the club tonight. There must have been loads of rage flying around the place. I'm not surprised I smell of it."

"It is not that random. A scent mark attaches only to its intended object. You mentioned a breeze on the terrace?"

"Yes," I said. "I was picking up a couple of glasses from a table on the farthest corner, but I was blown off balance."

"You have seen the Silver when they move at speed?" he asked, looking up into my eyes.

I nodded thoughtfully. That could have been it. It could have been a Silver zipping past.

"Someone tried to kill you, Emmy."

Shit.

Who the hell would want to kill me? I was pretty sure I hadn't pissed Drew off that much, but then he had apparently killed Jeff and Sarah in a temper. I guess I couldn't rule it out.

It was a sobering thought.

Sol removed the remaining glass in silence as I pondered this. Most of it was in my arms, although there were a couple of shards in my legs. There had been no glass in my face, but I gathered from the way he examined me that there were a number of cuts. When he had extracted it all he scooped me back into his arms and carried me into the bathroom.

I sighed with pleasure as I looked around the room.

There was a large tub on the right that Sol had already set running with hot water and steam filled the room. On the left was a separate shower and twin sinks. Sol carried me across the room and set me down on the closed seat of the toilet as he turned off the taps in the bath.

"I have business to attend to tonight so the apartment is yours, but if you need me just dial zero on the phone next to the bed and ask for me. I'll have some food brought up while you're in the bath."

He was letting me have some space and, although I was grateful, I secretly felt a little disappointed that he wouldn't be here.

"Please feel free to sleep here. I would prefer that you do, but I realise it is still early for your schedule," he continued, "so is there anything further you require by way of entertainment? There are some films in the bedroom's seating area."

I thought about the romantic novel I had left in the suite next door, but I was too embarrassed to ask Sol for that. Anyway, it would be ridiculous. I'd find enough to do here.

I shook my head.

"Emmy, just ask," he said, realising I was holding out on him.

"There was a book in the suite next door," I said

reluctantly.

There was a whooshing noise as he did his impression of The Flash and a second later he was back in front of me with the book in his hand.

"This one?" he asked, offering it to me.

I was touched by the gesture, despite myself.

I smiled at him and nodded, taking it happily. A steaming hot bath and a book. Was there anything better?

"Thanks, Sol."

"You are most welcome, Emilia," he replied, with the nearest thing to a proper smile of happiness that I had ever seen on his face.

He took my hand and, almost awkwardly, raised it to his lips, pressing a kiss into my palm. I realised in surprise that he was uncomfortable, unsure how to act around me after tonight, not knowing how far he could go. Perhaps we should have talked about it, but we didn't. He left quietly, closing the bathroom door behind him.

I stood unsteadily and hobbled across to the door to turn the lock, then turned to look in the mirror covering the wall behind the sinks. I was an absolute state. My hair looked okay, sort of dishevelled but passable. My face… yikes.

I braced my hands against the counter top as I leaned forward to get a better look. I had one cut running from the top of my right eyebrow across my forehead towards my hairline. Dried blood was caked on my skin so it was hard to tell what other cuts there might be in that area. There were a few smaller grazes on my cheeks and chin, but only one other large cut: a line running nearly from the right corner of my mouth to the outside of my right eye. If the trajectory of the shard had been fractionally different, I would have lost the eye.

I hadn't realised what a close call it had been.

A dark spot on my neck caught my eye and I ran my fingers over it: the wound from Sol's bite. A frisson of excitement ran through my body at the memory. It was a circular mark, a bruise with a cut running in a curve along one edge. There was a similar mark on the other side, although this one was larger, the cut deeper.

How the hell was I going to hide them? I hoped they'd fall under the line of my choker, assuming I could retrieve it from the terrace, but one was significantly higher than the other so I thought it unlikely. Either way, it looked like they were going to scar.

I looked down at myself to take in the other injuries. There were a lot of scrapes and cuts, but none of them was deep enough to require stitches. I'd been phenomenally lucky.

Breathing a sigh of relief and sending up a prayer of thanks to a god I didn't believe in, I untied my corset and let it fall to the floor, slipping off my skirt and ruined underwear. Finally, I unzipped my boots, holding on to the counter top for support.

The skirt and boots had come out of the incident unscathed, but the corset was a bit shredded. I'd need something else to work in tomorrow. Well, later today. I thought it was probably about one in the morning by now, not that I was intending to sleep for another five hours or so.

I sat in the bath until the skin on my fingers went wrinkly then washed my hair and body, paying special attention to each of the wounds. By the time I'd towelled off, they actually didn't look too bad. The two big cuts on my face were the worst of the lot. A shame, but I wasn't particularly vain and, in this new world, I guessed it didn't matter too much what I looked like.

Everyone would be much more interested in what I tasted like, I thought darkly.

I didn't have any clean clothes to wear, so I just tied a bath sheet under my arms and stepped out into the bedroom, using a smaller towel to dry my hair as I limped across the room. My knee was feeling better than it had been, but I still couldn't walk properly on it. I hoped it would heal up overnight because I was getting sick of being carted around by vampires.

Well, actually it had been kind of nice with Sol, I admitted to myself reluctantly.

I walked over to the seating area to find that a tray had been put on the table, a cloche covering a plate. I lifted it to reveal a huge steak with thin-cut chips and garlic fried greens. Steam drifted up from the plate, bringing a heavenly smell with it. I immediately started salivating.

I lifted a second cloche to find a wedge of caramel cheesecake. My heart leapt in my chest. I had all the creature comforts I could wish for and, for the moment at least, I was able to push my worries out of my head and pretend the world was as it used to be.

Settling happily into one of the arm chairs, I balanced the plate on my knee and devoured the meal. When I had polished off the lot, I looked around and saw with delight that there was a kettle and some mugs on a table by the desk on the other side of the room. I hadn't had a cup of tea for ages. I was gasping.

It took me about five minutes to make because I had to hobble to and from the bathroom to fetch some water and, once I'd made my cup, I had to limp very slowly to avoid spilling any. I was glad that no one was there to witness the clown show.

Finally, I settled myself on the sofa, stretching my legs out along its length, and cracked open my novel, cup of tea in hand. It was just what I needed. Sighing with contentment, I sank into the story.

CHAPTER XXII

Tuesday

I must have fallen asleep because, although I remembered finishing the novel, I awoke some indefinable time later to find myself being lifted upwards.

I stirred and turned my head, only to bury it in a warm smell that was a mixture of frozen waterfalls and Christmas.

"It's just me, Emmy," Sol's voice whispered above me. "You fell asleep on the sofa."

I opened my eyes and blinked up at him.

"What time is it?" I asked.

"About eight in the morning," he replied.

I couldn't have been asleep for very long, maybe an hour or two.

"I've spoken to Laila and you're not working tonight," he continued.

"We get nights off?"

"One a week," he replied softly, "and yours is Tuesdays."

He leaned forwards to throw back the duvet then settled me gently onto the bed on my back, pulling the covers over me.

"I'll grab some clothes from the suite next door for you," he added, turning to leave.

"Stay," I murmured sleepily.

He hesitated, pausing by the door.

"What?" he asked, although I knew he had heard.

I was tired and warm and I wanted to feel his arms around me.

"Stay. You sleep, right?"

"Yes, Emmy. We sleep."

"Then come to bed."

He moved slowly towards the other side of the bed then, leaning down to untie his laces, kicked off his shoes. He lay down next to me, lying on top of the covers.

"Sol," I said, turning to face him, "why are you suddenly so shy? Just hold me."

"I don't want to make you uncomfortable, Emmy," he said. "When we got back here, you were... uneasy. If it was a mistake, I have no wish to repeat it."

I shook off my somnolence, furrowing my brow in affront. He didn't want to repeat it? What the hell?

"Then why did you bring me here?" I said, my voice rising.

"If, Emmy. If it was a mistake. I didn't say I thought it was, but I worry that you consider it to be so."

He reached out his hand and placed it on my cheek.

"Your heart isn't in this," he said. "You seem intent on self destruction and you're using me as the instrument of your downfall."

He was right. I was throwing myself on a pyre. I was looking for oblivion, not redemption.

"Does it matter?" I asked.

"Perhaps not," he replied, "but you know I only take what is freely given to me."

"And I know what I want," I whispered back to him, "even if I'm not sure why I want it."

I leaned forward and pressed a light kiss to his lips. He looked into my eyes then studied the marks on my face, tracing the line of my cuts across my cheek and forehead with the tips of his fingers.

"I'm sorry, Emmy," he said sadly.

"Why? It's not your fault I got hurt. If it wasn't for you I would have died."

His brow furrowed in concern.

"They'll scar," he said sadly.

"I know, but it's not the end of the world."

"It doesn't upset you?"

"It could have been worse, Sol. An inch to the side and I'd be wearing an eye patch."

A hint of a smile crossed his face. He was always so controlled that even his amusement was muted. I reflected that the only time I'd seen him as himself was on the terrace, roaring with possessive fury. The sound had called to something in me, something that wanted to respond. The memory caused a yearning to curl within me.

"You need to sleep," Sol said, clearly sensing my desire, "but if I am still what you want when you wake, then I will be here."

With that, still lying on top of the covers fully clothed, he wrapped his arms around me and rolled me onto my side, enveloping me in his warmth.

My body unwound next to him, relaxing in his embrace, but my mind was racing. Was I making a terrible mistake with Sol? I felt like I'd lost touch with who I was, but I just didn't care.

It had been a weird week. I seemed to be pinging from poverty to luxury every day, one moment eating fruit from a tin and the next having food brought up to my room while I lay in the bath. And I couldn't remember that last time I had sustained so many injuries.

I contemplated the bizarre situation in which I found myself. How had this happened? Less than a week ago I'd just been living my life quietly. Now I was by turns a vampire sex object and an object of such loathing that another vampire had tried to kill me.

But maybe that was giving myself too much credit. Maybe

the vampire who had tried to kill me couldn't care less whether or not I lived or died and had just been having fun. Maybe he just wanted to watch my body crumple into the pavement to see what it would look like, to see if it would make a pretty pattern, to paint the street with my blood.

Or maybe to see what would happen next, like a child devoid of empathy pulling the legs off insects to see what they'll do.

Maybe it had been Drew. I didn't really know what he was capable of and who was to say he wasn't a complete sociopath?

I didn't know what to believe.

Whether I was a sex object or a test dummy, I was disposable. Replaceable. Meaningless.

A cold thought to send me off to sleep.

CHAPTER XXIII

My sleep was filled with disturbing dreams, of Danny and Sarah, Drew and Sol. In the moments before I fully roused from sleep, my mind projected a slideshow update onto the backs of my eyelids: the face of the bloodied man, Drew's eyes gazing up into mine as he laved his tongue along my arm, Danny's neck snapping with a sickly crunch, Sarah's head turned towards the ceiling at an unnatural angle, Sol staring hungrily into my eyes on the terrace as he demanded *This is what you want?*

You know, the highlights. Thanks, brain.

I woke to find Sol's arms still enveloping me, but he was now under the covers behind me, his arms circling me with warmth. I murmured gently as I stirred, turning towards him to press my face against his chest.

I raised my hand to place it on his chest and realised that my towel had unwrapped from around me during the night. I was completely naked under the covers.

Shit.

I wasn't ready for this. I grasped the covers to my chest.

"Erm, Sol?" I whispered to him.

"Did you sleep well?" he said softly, pulling me more tightly against him.

"Yes," I said uncertainly, "but I appear to be... um... naked."

His eyes snapped open and he looked down into my eyes, registering the fact that there was a lot of me pressed against him. A growl escaped from the back of his throat.

"And what exactly is it that you would like me to do?" he asked in a gravelly tone.

He brought his face forward and brushed his lips across my own, raising a hand to my neck to trail across one of the marks he had left there last night. My skin pulsed under his fingertips. I wanted to feel his teeth sink into me again. I wanted him to take me again, to mark me and own me in body if not in soul.

But I felt exposed, vulnerable, and that's not what I wanted. It was too much. I wanted to be in the dark with him where I could lose myself in him, but I didn't want him to see me, to find me. Panic bloomed in my chest.

"I think I need to leave," I said quietly.

He looked at me in a brief flash of disbelief and dismay before a shutter fell across his face, locking out any emotion.

"Of course," he said in detachment, gently extracting his arms from around me without disrupting the covers.

He slipped quietly out of the bed, still wearing his clothes from last night, and left the room. He returned a few moments later with a pile of clothes, which he left on the sofa in the seating area.

"I have business to attend to, so you may take your leave at your leisure," he said coldly.

"Sol..." I started, sitting up in the bed as I clutched the covers to my chest, but I had no idea what to say.

"There is no need to explain, Emilia," he said, turning towards the door.

He was back to addressing me formally again and I couldn't deal with it.

"I'm feeling weak," I blurted out, "and raw. After last night. I can't stand for you to see me like that. You read me like a broken, open book, and I don't want that."

He stopped and looked at me. I dropped my eyes to my lap as shame flooded my cheeks.

"You want to hide with me in the dark?" he asked.

I pushed my hair away from my face so I could meet his gaze.

"There's no refuge in my world, Emmy, no safe place. Everywhere you go you are perceived, if not by sight then by scent. I can protect you from a physical threat, but I can't shade you from scrutiny any more than I can shield you from your own desires."

He was right. Everyone would know. They'd scent his mark on me again and they'd know. They'd see the bite marks.

Last night felt like it had happened to another person and I wasn't sure which of us was real.

"No one can make you weak," he continued, "but your denial weakens you. You must learn to accept it, either to embrace it or to fight it. I won't create a fantasy around you to transform what we did, what you revelled in, what you pleaded for, into something you can stomach more easily."

I stared down at my hands.

"Your shame can't remake the past," he added softly "any more than it can remake you."

When I looked up again he was gone, the door closing silently behind him.

He had an uncanny knack for calling me out. If I ever had any hopes of manipulating him, I'd been a fool. He'd see it coming a mile off.

Would I have taken our encounter back if I had a chance to live last night again? I didn't think so. But I wished it had ended differently. I wished it wouldn't bare itself to everyone who saw me. I wished I could keep it between the two of us.

At the heart of it, maybe I wished I didn't want him at all, but that wasn't in my control. I could only choose what to do with my desire.

Sighing heavily, I rolled out of the bed and into the bathroom, grabbing the pile of clothes as I went. I noticed with satisfaction that my knee was much less painful this morning so, although it still twinged when I stepped on it, it shouldn't be necessary to limp along like an old lady.

I brushed my teeth quickly then put on the clean underwear, shorts and T-shirt that Sol had provided. My boots were still in the bathroom from last night, so I zipped my feet into them and gathered my tattered uniform from the floor.

With the heat of embarrassment burning my cheeks, even when I was on my own, I threw my torn underwear into the bin in disgust.

Time to face the world.

Sol's apartment was silent as I left the bedroom and climbed down the spiral staircase to the seating areas. There was no sign of him so, not eager to get into another discussion about last night, I slipped quietly out of the apartment door and along the corridor to the staircase that led down to the atrium, my uniform in my hand.

There began the worst walk of shame of my life.

It was just coming up to three in the afternoon and the hour clearly marked some kind of shift change because the Palace was teeming with Silver. As I reached the mezzanine level they passed me frequently, noting the scent then raising their eyebrows at the bite marks on my neck. I quickly pulled out the hair tie that held my hair in place and arranged it over my shoulders, shielding my neck from view on both sides.

I was beetroot red when I finally reached the foot of the grand staircase, but the torture wasn't over yet. Tommy met me at the bottom of the stairs and gestured over his shoulder towards the private dining room in which Drew had spoken to me a couple of days previously.

I shook my head at him. I was desperate to get out of the building and back to the club.

"Emmy, I need to talk to you about this."

"No, you don't," I replied abruptly, "it's none of your business."

"Yes it is," he insisted, following me as I started to walk across the atrium. "You let him renew the mark? Are you crazy?"

"Stay out of it, Tommy," I hissed, whirling round to face him.

As I did so, I noticed too late the bigger problem that had crept up on us from behind.

Drew. He was glaring at me ferociously, silver sparkling harshly in his irises.

"Piss off, Tommy," he said through clenched teeth.

"Drew, are you sure…" Tommy began.

Drew turned on him with such a look of rage on his face that Tommy fell silent for a moment.

"It's your funeral," he said to Drew as he held up his hands, "but touch her and we're all in trouble. He'll have your fucking head on a stick."

Sighing in disgust, he turned and walked away, leaving Drew and me glaring at each other in the centre of the room.

He gestured patronisingly towards the private dining room.

"Seriously?" I hissed at him. "You expect me to go back into that room with you so you can scream at me some more about how shitty my choices are? I told you to leave me alone, Drew, and I meant it."

"Emilia," he said in a carefully-controlled voice, "if you don't come into that room with me then I'm going to have to carry you in there by force, which will cause your boyfriend the Primus to rip my head off. Which option would you prefer?"

I glared steadily back at him.

"It's a pretty fucking close call," I replied, narrowing my eyes at him, "but on balance I think I'll go for the head-ripping."

Drew ran his hands through his hair in exasperation.

"Please, Emmy."

"You have three minutes," I said, stalking towards the room at the base of the staircase.

I opened the door and held it for him as he walked in behind me, shutting it securely after he had passed. I had expected him to weigh in immediately about how I was insane to have let Sol kiss me again, but he surprised me.

"How did this happen?" he asked, indicating the latticework of cuts lining my face.

"The terrace at the club," I said. "I fell. Well, Sol thinks I was pushed. He saved me."

"Oh?" he said, a pained expression crossing his face.

"What?" I asked him in irritation. "If you've got something to say just say it."

"You're sure he isn't the one who pushed you?"

"You're his fucking Secundus!" I replied, horrified. "How could you think that?"

"Emmy, I've told you before that some of us view humans differently. He probably didn't think there was anything wrong with it. It got him what he wanted, didn't it?" he said with an unattractive sneer.

I couldn't believe Drew's hypocrisy, talking about vampires who viewed humans as disposable when he was among their number. I didn't believe him for a second. Sol didn't have to tell me about the scent he detected on me. He could have left me believing it was an accident if he had been behind it.

Nonetheless, I flushed at the insult as rage banked within me, my eyes filling with angry tears.

"You have no idea what you're talking about."

"Don't I?" he replied. "What did he do, Emmy? How did he convince you to let him kiss you again?"

"He didn't," I replied steadily, even as a teardrop rolled onto my cheek.

I cursed and dashed away the tear with my sleeve. My emotions were simmering so close to the surface over the past few days that I couldn't keep them in check.

"Then why didn't you stop him? You could have called and I'd have been there in less than a second," he said, misunderstanding entirely.

I shook my head as another tear slipped out, wanting to explain, but his expression suddenly darkened. Striding towards me, be brushed my hair behind my shoulders and looked at the marks on my neck in disbelief.

"I'm going to fucking kill him," he gritted out through his teeth, reaching behind me for the door.

"No, Drew," I said in frustration, laying my palms on his chest to push him backwards, "you don't understand. *I* kissed *him*."

He looked at me in incomprehension.

"And... the rest?"

"I told him to bite me. I asked him to do it, Drew," I said, finally admitting it to myself as well as to him. "I wanted him to do it."

He paused for a moment then laughed at me bitterly.

"Did you fuck him?"

I flushed to the roots of my hair with anger.

"Well did you?" he shouted at me.

"Yes!" I yelled back at him, clenching my fist around my tattered uniform. "I fucked him! I fucked him and I begged him to bite me! Is that what you wanted to hear?"

The colour drained from his face.

I turned away from him, tears streaming down my face, and leaned back against the wall, sliding down it until I was sitting in a ball on the floor with my head in my hands as I wiped away the tears.

I guessed the whole building would have heard that.

We stayed like that for several minutes, neither of us knowing where to go from here. Finally, Drew walked over to me and knelt on the floor in front of me.

"I'm sorry, Emmy."

I didn't reply.

"It shouldn't be upsetting," he said quietly. "It should be beautiful. If it makes you cry he's doing it wrong."

"I'm not a child, Drew," I replied with vitriol.

Impulsively, he reached out and cupped his hand around my face, tracing the lines of my cuts with his thumb.

"Will you let me heal you?" he asked.

"Yeah, right," I replied, laughing darkly. "I'd be wandering around the place with silver lines across my face. If Silver were allowed to heal humans then Sol would already have done it."

"No, Emmy, he wouldn't. He can't."

I raised an eyebrow at him.

"Besides," he continued before I could ask what he meant, "I couldn't care less. I'm already touching you so I'm a dead man anyway. Just let me do it, Emmy."

He cupped my face in both my hands, gazing meaningfully at me. But for me, there was no meaning to be found in his emerald eyes. I pushed his hands away.

"I'd rather scar," I hissed at him, rising to a crouch as I made to leave.

As I did so, the door opened and slammed closed again in a fraction of a second.

Sol was there, helping me to my feet. I smiled at him gratefully, genuinely glad to have him there to remove me from this nightmare encounter.

"That's the last time you touch her and live," he said to Drew as he wrapped an arm around me.

"What the hell are you doing, Sol?" Drew asked, rising to face him with a thunderous expression.

The gloves were clearly off. All the deference I had seen Drew show towards Sol a couple of days ago had evaporated.

"If you won't let me protect her," he continued, "then can you at least try to do a better job of it yourself?"

"She is well," he replied sharply, "and no longer any of your business."

"You fucking bit her!" Drew spat indignantly.

"And what exactly is your objection to that? Is it that I broke her skin? That I sullied her flesh? Or that I did so where you were denied?"

"Sol," I interrupted, not wanting to find myself in the middle of a vampire fight, "can we just skip the pissing contest and leave?"

"Primus," Drew said, his face contorting with pain, "I'm begging you not to do this."

"And I'm telling you no, Secundus. Emilia has, I believe, made it clear to you on a number of occasions that she has no wish for your company. She has the right to make that decision. Whatever there may be between Emilia and me stands outside of that."

Drew looked at me with pleading in his eyes as I stood at Sol's side.

I shook my head and looked at the floor, unwilling to engage with the man who had killed my friends in cold blood.

"I'm sorry, Drew," he continued, a hint of compassion in his voice, "but you know that if you lay a hand on her again I'll have to act or risk my position. I need your word."

Drew hung his head and swore under his breath.

"You have it for as long as your mark remains. But," he said hesitantly, "would you let me heal her?"

A moment of silence fell as Sol looked at Drew with outrage in his expression.

"You know why I can't allow that," Sol replied, glancing towards me. "It surprises me that you would even ask."

"Besides which," I interrupted, glaring at Sol for his presumption, "I've already said no."

Sol snapped his gaze from me back to Drew.

"She knows?" he asked Drew incredulously.

I remembered the whole taboo thing. Perhaps I shouldn't have let on.

But Drew gave an almost imperceptible shake of his head, so subtle that in a human I wouldn't have even thought it meant anything. There was something they weren't telling me. Again.

"I've healed her before," he said hesitantly.

Sol went still beside me, his jaw clenching.

"You surely don't expect me to overlook this," he said, shielding me with his body as he moved towards Drew, wound tight with controlled rage. "You ignore my mark and deny my claim."

"Your claim?" I yelled indignantly, stepping out from behind him.

"Primus," Drew said in a bleak tone, "it was the night of the Revelation. There was no mark on her and I left none myself."

Drew looked over to me and met my eye, his brow furrowing ruefully.

"Much to my regret, Emmy," he added softly.

"Enough, Secundus," Sol growled at him.

"That's enough from both of you," I interjected, my patience wearing thin. "You think all that matters is the mark? So what I think and feel is irrelevant? You talk like I'm not even in the room."

"Emmy…" Sol said, turning towards me, but I cut him off.

"No, Sol," I snapped. "I choose who gets to touch me, not you, not your mark."

"I realise that," he replied quietly.

But I'd had enough. I'd gone through anger and out the other side. It wasn't that I wanted anyone other than Sol to touch me. It was a point of principle. I was riding my high horse right out of the building.

"Fucking arrogant vampires," I muttered as I wrenched open the door, stepping out into the atrium.

I strode across the marble floor, no doubt with a face like thunder, trailing the scent of Sol's mark behind me. My speed was blowing my hair away from my shoulders, exposing my neck, but I couldn't care less. Who gave a shit what they thought anyway?

As I exploded through the front door of the Palace I bumped into a familiar face.

"Hey, Emmy!" Cam greeted me cheerfully as he walked up the steps towards me.

Then he noticed my fierce expression and the smile dropped from his face. He turned and fell into step beside me as I stomped across the road to the club before pausing outside the door. I didn't want to go back inside, but it was officially my day off and I had nothing to do until late tomorrow afternoon.

I stood outside the door for a few seconds thinking

through my options.

"You want to talk about it?" Cam asked.

I shook my head, realising a fraction of a second too late that it was exactly the wrong thing to do if I wanted to hide the bites or the mark. I looked up at Cam, watching his face as he registered the bites and scented the mark in shock.

"Oh," he said.

"Yeah."

"And Drew?"

"Shouted at me," I replied. "Then he and Sol shouted at each other for a while and I got pissed off and left. Hell, they're probably still at it."

"Are you okay?" he asked me, concern in his voice.

I laughed out loud. I couldn't remember the last time someone had bothered to ask me that. It made me feel like a real person again. Then the laughter got a little hysterical and I had to stop myself so I didn't end up crying again.

I looked at Cam apologetically and his brow creased in anxiety.

"It's been a tough week," I said with a wry smile.

"I know what you need," he said, brightening.

I raised an eyebrow at him.

"You need a night off," he replied, eyes twinkling, "and as I understand it, that night is tonight."

"It's not much use having a night off when there's nothing to do with it," I complained.

"Go put your stuff away," he said, indicating the work clothes I still held in my hand, "then come and meet me in the main bar."

"What are you planning?"

"Wear something pretty."

He was holding out on me.

"I don't have anything pretty, Cam," I said, thinking ruefully of all the beautiful clothes Drew had left me in the suite in the Palace.

As soon as the thought flashed into my head I berated myself for it. I didn't need to be bought with looted designer labels.

"Unless you haven't noticed," I continued, "we're living in a post-apocalyptic war zone. I'm thankful to be clean. Pretty's setting the bar a bit high."

"Fine," he said. "If you can't manage pretty then wear something slutty."

I rolled my eyes. I wasn't relaxing in my work uniform.

"Indulge me," he asked with a smile.

I couldn't help but smile back as I headed into the club.

"Five minutes!" he shouted after me.

I walked quickly past the main bar, where Alice and a couple of guys were serving drinks to the late afternoon crowd. Rushing up into the dorm, I pulled my clothes out of the rucksack under my bed and surveyed the options. The best I could come up with was my old work shorts and a strappy black T-shirt. It'd do.

I changed quickly, finishing the outfit off with my omnipresent boots and my old leather jacket. It wasn't pretty and it wasn't particularly slutty, but it was sort of edgy. Frankly, it was comfy so I didn't really care.

I came back downstairs to find Cam at the bar ordering up a line of shots. I immediately thought of Danny, of his birthday drinks, the coloured shot glasses bringing the memories back to the surface. Cam reminded me so much of him sometimes, but he didn't have Danny's intractable nature, his fierce and unyielding sense of injustice.

Cam saw me walk in and smiled up at me, gesturing grandly to the alcoholic feast laid out before him. Just another way for me to lose myself, to hide in the dark. I welcomed it with open arms, grinning back at him.

"Race you," I challenged him as I picked up the first glass.

Unsurprisingly, I lost.

CHAPTER XXIV

A lot of hours later, we were still in the bar. We'd had a lakeful of shots and I was feeling distinctly merry.

Cam had got hold of a pack of real cards and we'd got a couple of the other Silver involved in a drinking game. They had to take three shots for every one I drank because they seemed to process the alcohol a lot better than humans. Without a handicap I would have been under the table after the end of the first round. I'd been worried at the quantities they'd be drinking, but I'd been assured that alcohol poisoning and liver damage were not of any concern to the Silver.

The other players were Ed and Carrie, a couple of young Silver who were friends of Cam's. They both worked in the Palace and they seemed nice enough from the idle, mostly alcohol-related chit chat we had exchanged.

Ed was a tall, dark-haired guy with a beard and glasses. He was the only Silver I had ever seen wearing glasses, so I guessed it must be an affectation: geek chic. Carrie had short, brown hair that lay in curls around her face, which was pleasant and round, with big brown eyes.

Neither of them seemed to think hanging out with a human was weird, or that it was any different from hanging out with one of the Silver, but they'd been a little intimidated by Sol's scent mark.

They loosened up after about a pint of vodka.

I was trying to get one of the playing cards to stick to my forehead with the exaggerated care that comes with diminished faculties. It wasn't going well, but it was apparently necessary for the purposes of the game, though I no longer understood why.

"Oh, fuck this," I yelled, throwing the card violently down onto the table, "let's just go upstairs and dance."

"Yeah!" Carrie agreed enthusiastically. "C'mon, Eddie."

"I'm not sure that's a great idea, Em," Cam slurred.

He'd come off a little worse than the rest of us in the game and it was starting to show.

"Come on!" I said, grabbing his hand and dragging him off his chair.

He moved a little unsteadily, so I wrapped his arm around my shoulder and walked him towards the stairwell. Ed and Carrie went ahead of us and it was just as well. It took us a good few minutes to reach the top. When we did, Viv was standing outside the doors that led through to the bar and dance floor, her arms crossed over her chest.

"What do you think you two are doing?" she asked, clearly unimpressed.

"Having fun?" Cam replied, a goofy grin plastered across his face.

Viv rolled her eyes and spoke into a microphone attached to her collar.

"Oh no," Cam said, looking at me in fake panic, "she's calling for back up."

We both giggled hysterically. It seemed pretty hilarious in our inebriated state.

"You're a fucking idiot, Cam," she said. "What are you doing wrapped around Emmy? Are you insane? I can smell the Primus's mark from here."

"Lighten up, Viv," he replied. "We're just hanging out. We're not in the least bit attracted."

"Yeah," I chimed in, "he's not in the least bit attractive."

We both started laughing again.

Viv just shook her head at us.

"I'm not letting either of you in here. Emmy, go upstairs and sleep it off before someone sees you two together like this."

The door at the bottom of the stairs opened and I turned around, wobbling a little, to see Sol walking up towards us.

"Too late," I said sullenly. "Captain Killjoy's already here."

His face was carefully composed, but it was evident that he was furious from the way he was controlling his expressions, not letting any animation creep into his features. It looked like we were in trouble, but I was so tanked I was finding it hard to take anything seriously.

"Cameron," he said frostily, "please remove your hands from her."

"Are we going to have to have this argument again?" I asked Sol in irritation.

But Cam had already raised his hands in surrender. He promptly fell over backwards onto the stairs above us. I snorted with laughter and knelt beside him to help him back to his feet, but he wouldn't let me help.

"Cam," I slurred at him, "stop being a dickhead and let me help you up."

He just shook his head at me.

"Forgive me, Primus," he said to Sol.

I couldn't believe what I was hearing.

"Why the hell are you apologising to him? I get to choose who I touch. It's got fuck all to do with him."

"You don't understand it, Em," he replied, using the banister rail to pull himself carefully to his feet.

With one last apologetic smile at me, he walked unsteadily back down the stairs and through the door into the main bar. Viv followed him down. I hoped she would make sure he got back to his bed safely.

When they had left I rounded on Sol, nearly throwing myself off balance as I did so. He caught my arms to stop me from falling, but I snatched them away in disgust.

"This is getting really tedious," I growled at him.

I could see that he was barely managing to control his anger.

"You bear my scent mark," he gritted out through his teeth, "my bites on your neck, and you walk into a room full of my people and wrap yourself around one of my Invicti? Do you have any comprehension of the damage that has done to my reputation?"

"Oh, fuck your reputation, Sol," I snapped. "Just tell them you ditched me and I was drowning my sorrows. I don't give a shit."

He sighed and looked at me in resignation, pressing his lips together.

"You make me look weak," he said quietly.

"Well you make me feel weak," I screamed at him, the alcohol fuelling my rage, "so do us both a favour and leave me alone!"

"As you wish," he replied, "but would you consent to staying at the Palace while you sleep it off?"

I snorted sardonically.

"Emmy, a Silver tried to kill you last night."

Before I could answer him, the door to the bar opened behind me and Ben walked out into the stairwell. He looked between me and Sol with interest.

"Primus?" he asked. "Can I help? Genevieve said…"

"Yes," Sol interrupted. "Please escort Emmy to her dorm."

Ben nodded at him deferentially and turned to me.

"I might be a bit tipsy," I slurred, "but I'm perfectly capable of getting to my bed on my own."

"I'm aware of that," Sol replied, "but Ben will ensure that you remain there."

I shot him a hot look of irritation and, thinking bed would actually be welcome, decided to file my anger away for later and argue with Sol about it when I was a little more coherent. Without another word to either of them I turned and climbed the stairs to the second floor.

CHAPTER XXV

Most of the beds in the dorm were full when I crept in, desperately trying not to stumble and make a racket. I saw with satisfaction that Nix was curled up happily on Alice's bed. She raised her head at me in a sleepy greeting.

Ben followed me to my bed, standing by the window.

"What?" I hissed at him. "You're going to watch me undress, are you?"

Raising his hands in a gesture of surrender, he turned to look out of the window, showing me his back. He opened it wide and leaned his hands on the sill, looking out into the night. The breeze it let in was wonderfully refreshing to my drink-addled head.

I quickly unzipped my boots and wriggled out of my shorts and T-shirt, pulling one of Jeff's big T-shirts over my head in its place.

"Okay," I whispered, pulling back the covers and sliding into bed. "I'm where I'm supposed to be. Now get out of here."

"Sorry, Emmy," he whispered back, "but I'm going to have to guard the door."

I rolled my eyes at him in the moonlight as he leaned forward to close the window. He turned to look at me over his shoulder.

"If I leave this window open," he asked, "will you promise not to do something crazy, like try to shin down the drainpipe?"

"If I tried it in my drunken state, I'd be a pavement pancake," I replied. "Leave it open. It's too hot for closed windows."

Reluctantly, Ben left the window as it was and walked back across the room to the door, shooting me a warning glance before shutting it behind him. The moment he did, I relaxed back onto the bed, my muscles sighing in relief. Unfortunately, it was short-lived.

With the removal of distractions, like trying to stand up straight and speak in words of more than one syllable, the pain from my injuries came rushing to the forefront of my perception. My cuts burned, my forehead and cheek on fire. On top of it all, the bed was beginning to spin.

Shit. I really didn't want to have to run through a dorm full of sleeping people on my way to throw up the just deserts of my alcohol-fuelled evening. I extracted my left foot from the covers and put it on the ground to stop the bed from moving. It wasn't wholly effective, but it was certainly better.

I still spent the next hour fighting nausea, my knee screaming in pain that wasn't helped by the necessity of having my foot on the floor.

Note to self: vodka bad.

Worse than the nausea was the fact that I was starting to get a nagging feeling of guilt in the pit of my stomach. I wasn't proud of the way I had treated Sol tonight. Or earlier today.

I hadn't considered how my behaviour tonight would affect his status, and it was becoming increasingly apparent to me how very precarious the political situation was amongst the Silver.

Worse than that: I hadn't even treated him like I would have treated a human being. I'd denied him the entitlement to have his sensibilities respected because of who he was, because of what he was. I was demonising him because he was Silver.

I'd used him when I needed to lose myself and that's not something I would have done to another human. I had assumed that the stories I had heard about him were true, that he felt nothing for humans and used humans like disposable snacks. But that wasn't how he had treated me. He had treated me with respect and I had afforded him none.

He may feel nothing for me, but I denied him the capacity to feel anything. I was right to be cautious, but I had to acknowledge the contradiction in the fact that I had considered him good enough to sleep with, but not good enough to be capable of caring about it.

That was just so wrong.

The moment of self-awareness brought a flush of shame to my cheeks and left me trying to stifle the guilt squirming in my stomach.

When I finally managed to fall asleep, it was fitful and uncomfortable, interrupted frequently as I woke for no reason I could determine. Every time it happened I had to spend what felt like hours getting back to sleep, but it couldn't have been that long because outside the window the world remained filled with the night sky.

The last time I woke I crushed my eyes shut in desperate denial. I was not awake. I was fast asleep, so terribly tired that I was going to doze off again immediately.

The minutes passed.

I remained awake.

I sighed with frustration and opened my eyes, rolling over in the bed to face the window.

And froze.

There was a figure crouched on the windowsill, silhouetted in the moonlight barely two feet away from me. A metallic, earthy smell filled my nostrils and I backed away in horror, pushing myself up the bed until I was in a sitting position with my back against the bedstead.

I knew that smell.

It was the smell of Weepers.

I carefully stepped off the bed sideways to put it between us, moving very slowly, my eyes glued to the Weeper as I went. Crouching down on the ground, I groped into my rucksack, trying to locate something I could use as a weapon.

Just as my right hand closed around something solid, the Weeper stepped down from the sill and started moving steadily towards me, moving a hand to its face as it did so. The moonlight fell on it as it turned and I saw it was a young guy, heavily muscled but streaked in grime and gore. His hand was holding a piece of material to his face, which he seemed to be smelling.

With horror, I recognised it.

It was that fucking shirt again, the paint-stained shirt I had left at Drew's apartment. That he had left on the VIP bar after killing Jeff and Sarah. How the hell had it ended up in the hands of a Weeper?

I didn't have time to regret again my decision to leave the shirt behind at Drew's because the Weeper was nearly on me. I stood quickly, bringing with me the makeshift-weapon I had found in my backpack: my precious bottle of gin.

The Weeper was walking towards me with determination, ignoring everyone else in the dorm. No one was stirring. I hadn't made a sound and his footfalls were gentle and deadened, eerily so for a man of his size.

There was no way I was going to be able to distract him. I suspected he had been tracking me, or that he was at least using my scent from the shirt to zero in on me and no one else. I backed towards the wall of the room. He was going to crush me like a bug.

Deciding that a proactive approach was more likely to be successful than waiting for him to corner me, I darted forward and swung the bottle of gin wildly at the side of his head. It shattered, spraying alcohol over us both and, by some concerted effort on my part to keep hold of it, leaving me holding the broken bottle neck. Unfortunately, most of the bottle itself had shattered away and the small tube of glass with which I had been left was not going to be particularly helpful in a fight.

The Weeper staggered to one side, but after a second's disorientation he began moving forward once more. What a waste of good gin.

People began to stir in their beds around us, roused by the sound of the bottle breaking. Not good. The last thing I wanted was for them to get caught in the crossfire. This Weeper was only aiming for me. At least, he was at the moment. He'd probably lose interest and turn on the rest of them once he'd dispatched me.

I had to concentrate on making sure he didn't get to eat the main course, so he'd be in no position to move on to dessert.

"Get out of here!" I yelled at them. "Go fetch the Invicti!"

There were screams and exclamations of panic, running footsteps and crashes as furniture was disturbed. I couldn't see what was going on because my eyes were fixed on the Weeper. I hoped they were all getting out, but I didn't dare look away.

I sized him up. I had no idea how you went about killing a Weeper, or if it was even possible. I cursed myself for failing to ask Sol when I had the chance, but I honestly hadn't thought much about the Weepers since admission. I had been concentrating on the Silver, which I thought in retrospect was probably unhealthy in more ways than one.

Gambling that the Weepers' weaknesses were much the same as humans', I ran at the Weeper, catapulting myself into him as I raised the bottle neck to his face, aiming for his eye. He reacted slowly, not managing to get his hands up in time to protect himself. With a grotesque noise, I plunged the weapon into his left eye and forced it home, the glass fracturing in my hand as I did so.

The Weeper screamed, an inhuman screech of anguish and frustration, high-pitched and keening. It raised the hair on my arms and the back of my neck. My sense of horror grew as I heard the howl answered by other voices from the city outside the window, echoing through the night.

They were communicating, calling to each other like a pack, perhaps even like a hive.

I snatched my bloodied hand back and, cradling it against me, stumbled over the bed next to me, heading for the door. The Weeper followed my movement with his remaining eye then started moving towards me, away from the window. The injury didn't seem to have discouraged him at all.

I looked around the room desperately as I ran for the door, trying to identify a weapon. As it happened, I didn't need one.

True to his word, Ben had stayed outside the dorm. As soon as everyone but me was out he came running through the door. I could see the other humans huddled in the kitchen area, peering through the door to watch.

"Shit," he said, before turning to speak into the microphone on his collar. "Viv, get up to the dorm, we've got a Weeper."

She was beside him in a flash. The two of them ran at the Weeper, one going for each arm, and pinned him to the floor. He snarled and writhed, blood-specked foam rising from his mouth. He kept his eyes pinned on me, clearly irritated at having his fun interrupted.

Drew joined them a second later and, registering my presence, flashed me a look of panic. He made to move towards me, but Viv saw that his attention was distracted and interrupted him.

"Boss," she yelled, "we could really use your super-strength here!"

Reluctantly, he turned away and wrapped his arms around the Weeper from behind, pinning his arms to his sides.

All three Silver bundled the Weeper back to the window. Viv jumped through it and Drew followed with his arms secured around the Weeper in a vice-like grip. I guessed they didn't want to take him out past a gaggle of humans and risk someone getting bitten.

I looked at my old Parker's shirt where it lay in a heap on the ground, dropped by the Weeper in the attack. How had he got hold of it?

Ben turned towards me.

"You recognise the shirt?" Ben asked, noticing my interest.

I nodded.

"It's mine. From when I used to work here, before. He had it in his hand."

"Well," Ben said on a sigh, "that would explain why he zeroed in on you."

It didn't explain how he got hold of it, though.

"How did he even get into the safe zone?" I asked. "How did he get this far?"

"The system isn't infallible," he replied. "It can't be. There's too much ground to cover. But you're right: he shouldn't have been able to get so close. We'll follow his trail back, work out where and how he broke through our line."

"What then?"

He shrugged.

"We'll do whatever it takes to make our defences stronger. It won't happen again, Emmy."

"Well," I said, "thanks for coming to the rescue anyway."

"I'm just sorry it took me so long; I didn't realise what was happening. Though," he said with a smile, "you were doing pretty well on your own."

He was indulging me. Another three seconds and I would have been a Weeper too, infected.

"I'm going to have to tell him," he continued.

I furrowed my brow at him, confused.

"The Primus," he said. "Viv has probably already let him know."

"Really?" I asked.

"Yes, really," said a voice from the doorway.

There he was, right on cue: Sol.

He looked a little dishevelled, which was unusual for him. His normally wrinkle-free shirt was crumpled and there was more than one hair out of place on his head.

He walked up to me and, noticing my bleeding hand, a panicked expression flooded his face.

"Are you bitten?" he asked me frantically.

"What?" I asked, slightly dazed from the adrenaline.

He took my wounded hand in his.

"Did it bite you?" he repeated.

"No," I replied, shaking my head, "no, this was on a bottle. I used it to defend myself."

He nodded, but the concern remained etched on his face.

"About earlier," I said to him.

"I'd rather argue elsewhere…" he replied in a low voice.

"No," I interrupted him, "I wanted to apologise. I'm sorry."

His eyebrows raised in surprise.

Behind him, Ben indicated that the humans could return to their beds and they began to shuffle in, whispering amongst themselves. I didn't know any of them. I knew both of the Silver in the room and none of the many humans.

I felt like a hypocrite for judging the Silver so harshly yet apparently choosing to form closer friendships with them than I had with any of the humans with whom I shared a dorm room. I'd only given Alice the time of day because it was she who engaged me in conversation. They all looked at me with either awe or suspicion. Not a great starting point for forging friendships.

"Emmy," Sol said to me, looking down at my hand, "this is a serious injury. We must tend to your wound. Will you come back to the Palace where we can treat it properly?"

It was actually very painful, much worse than the cuts from last night. It was still bleeding, an ugly wound that I couldn't bear to touch, and I thought it probably needed stitches. There was some glass stuck in there too, so it looked like I was in for another extraction session.

"That would be good," I replied.

Sol put an arm around me, sending a ripple of whispers around the room. I was starting to become irritated at being made to feel like a sideshow by my own kind. I tried to ignore it.

Sol detected my discomfort and picked me up in his arms. In a second, we were outside the club on the street. I noted the thoughtful gesture, thinking that it was further demonstration of why I might have been wrong about the Silver. Well, Sol at least.

I shot him a grateful smile.

"What will happen to him now?" I asked as Sol set me back on my feet.

"The Weeper? They'll take him outside the barricade."

"Then what? Will they kill him?"

"That would be the ideal," he said, lowering his voice, "but we have yet to determine an efficient method for exterminating the Weepers."

"What?"

"There is little that can kill the Weepers, short of minute dismemberment, but each piece of Weeper flesh remains impregnated with the Weeper infection. If we pursued a hasty campaign against the Weepers, the infection would inevitably be dispersed into the air and the water supply."

My eyes went wide. There'd be no humans left uninfected.

"I tell you this in the strictest confidence," he continued. "You can imagine the panic this information would cause if it were disseminated. I don't wish you to think that we are not concentrating our efforts on the matter, because we are. We have people researching everything from how to contain Weepers remains to how to cure Weepers. Either would solve the problem."

"Shit," I replied.

"So how exactly are you proposing to protect us?" I asked as we began walking across the road to the Palace.

"You've seen our strength," he replied, "and you know that the Weepers avoid the Silver. Rest assured that we can protect you more than adequately."

"Sol, I very nearly became one of those things tonight."

"All is well," he replied with a stern, tight-jawed expression.

I decided not to argue. I didn't want to rile him up, but I didn't have as much confidence as he did in the ability of the Invicti to protect us all. If a Weeper could break into the second floor of the club, who knew what else they might do?

Who knew what other possessions out in the wasteland beyond the barricade might be stumbled upon and used by the Weepers to track living humans? That must have been how my shirt ended up in their hands: cleared from the club and dumped beyond the barricade, like the bodies of my friends.

We walked up the steps from the street to the door of the Palace. Dawn was just starting to glow on the horizon. I was feeling the ill effects of too much alcohol and a horrible and short night's sleep, all chased down with the adrenaline crash from the Weeper attack. My hand was throbbing, burning around the edges of the wound. I just wanted to get it sorted out and sleep, but the thought of the pain I'd have to go through to get to that point was a little intimidating.

I was going to have to suck it up. I needed a clear head and having the scent mark wasn't going to help that, so I needed to forgo his magic, pain-removing kisses for now. I guessed that the last mark must have worn off a few hours ago now.

CHAPTER XXVI

Wednesday

Pushing the doors open ahead of me, Sol ushered me through to the atrium as I cradled my hand against me. The Invicti raised their eyebrows at our entrance, though I couldn't tell whether it was because the scent of my blood was filling the room or because Sol had put his arm around me again.

I wondered if the two were, actually, related; whether Sol was being particularly protective and publicly affectionate to avoid any blood-drinking incidents. His presence had to act as a deterrent and I imagined that the open wounds would probably rile the Silver up. After all, the fresh blood had been the focus of the 'ritual' on the opening night of the club.

That being the case, I must be Silver catnip. I hadn't stopped bleeding since the Revelation.

But then maybe his increased solicitousness this morning was because his mark had now faded. He had to find another way to make his claim on me known. The thought irritated me.

He guided me across the marble floor to the library, the admission room. I wasn't sure I wanted to go in there alone with him, not in light of what had happened last time we were there together.

I needn't have worried.

When he opened the door the effusive Silver from our last visit was firmly in residence, although her behaviour towards Sol was a little cooler. Maybe she didn't like the idea of him socialising with a human. Maybe she thought he was sullied by my touch. Maybe it was exactly the opposite, given the apparent sexualisation of blood-drinking in Silver society, but maybe she objected to him using me as anything other than a giant juice box.

Either way, she ignored me completely.

"Rena," Sol said in acknowledgement.

"Good morning Primus. How can I assist today?"

Sol turned towards me.

"Emilia has suffered an accident and her wounds need seeing to. Would you kindly oblige?"

She pressed her lips together, clearly holding back her irritation.

"Of course, Primus. Just let me collect the necessary implements."

Turning her back to us with a smile at Sol, she walked into one of the cubicles and I shot a concerned look at him. I was incredibly uncomfortable with the idea of this Silver woman, who clearly disliked me, sticking a needle in me.

"Rena is the best nurse we have, Emmy," he replied to me quietly then, raising his voice, added: "she will take good care of you and ensure you suffer no pain because you are under my protection."

Clearly having taken note of this thinly-veiled threat, Rena was decidedly more cheerful on her return to us, albeit artificially so.

"If you would care to follow me?" she asked brightly.

I followed her into the cubicle, Sol close behind me, and she indicated that I should sit on the couch. As I did so, she stood in front of me, reaching out to take my hand in hers. It was a mess.

"I need to remove the glass and clean the wound before I stitch it, and I'm afraid it will need rather a lot of stitches. You may find this less disturbing if you look away," she said.

Taking her advice to heart, I turned away from her to the left. Sol was now fully in my line of sight where he stood next to me by the couch. He sat down beside me and, taking my uninjured hand, leaned down to whisper into my ear.

"I could take the pain away, Emmy."

The first time he had kissed me I hadn't realised what it had meant and I felt like he had tricked me into it. The second time I had kissed him for all the wrong reasons, using him as a vehicle to vent my frustration and unhappiness. If it happened for a third time, it was going to be because it meant what the Silver thought it should: that I was his, but also that he was mine.

I wasn't ready for that and I wasn't sure he was either.

Maybe I was just using that as an excuse to myself to avoid having to face the real reason I was holding back: was that kind of bond something I would ever want from him? Maybe it had all been a mistake.

"No, Sol," I whispered back. "Not this time."

I shot my eyes towards Rena and he dropped the subject. Whispering had been pointless anyway since, with the way Silver could hear, she would have picked it all up anyway. Nevertheless, it gave us the illusion of some kind of privacy.

"Okay," she said, "I'm going to extract the glass then clean the wound up. It's a bad cut so I'm going to give you some anaesthetic."

I gritted my teeth as the needle slid in, concentrating my attention on the spines of the books lining the library and on the chandelier above my head. After a minute or so the whole area felt pretty numb and, after a quick check to make sure I couldn't feel it, Rena started seeing to my hand.

"How did this happen?" she asked as she worked.

"Weeper attack," I replied. "I defended myself with a bottle."

"I see," she replied, returning to her work.

It was a tortuously lengthy process. Although I couldn't feel any pain, I could feel pressure and tugging on my hand as she removed the glass and sewed up the wound. It was an uncomfortable sensation and, in my dishevelled state, I was finding it hard to cope with.

A few minutes into it Sol wrapped his arm around me, noting my discomfort, and nudged up close to me so I could rest my head on his shoulder. By the time Rena finished I wanted nothing more than to go back to sleep.

"All done," she said finally. "There was a lot of glass in there, but I've got it all out."

I turned back to see that my hand was neatly dressed and bandaged. Shards of bloody glass sat in a metal bowl on the rolling tray to Rena's right.

"You've got twenty stitches," she continued, "which I'll remove when it's healed. I'll give you some more bandages to take away so you can keep it clean. You have checked her blood, Primus?"

"Of course," Sol said.

I flushed slightly at the realisation that the marks on my neck were on full display, my hair pushed back behind my shoulders.

Yep. He'd checked my blood alright.

"Well," Rena said, looking at the bite marks whilst trying not to make it too obvious that she was doing so, "if you have any problems let me know, but otherwise come back when it's good and healed."

"Thank you," I said with a small smile.

"Thank you, Rena," Sol added graciously, helping me to my feet.

"You're very welcome, Primus," she replied, simpering.

She made it perfectly clear that this was a favour to him, not to me. I would have thought the vampires would have been concerned to keep their food supply healthy, but apparently not.

Sol escorted me from the library, his arm around me once more, and out into the atrium.

"I have spoken to Laila and she understands that, with your injury, you are unable to work this evening."

"I bet she was delighted," I replied sarcastically.

Sol offered me his characteristic half-smile, an expression I had come to associate with him and that he was always wearing in my head when I thought of him.

"You will stay here tonight," he decreed.

I was reluctant. I didn't want to go back to his apartment, neither to relive my shame nor to bring more down on myself. My anxiety must have shown in my face.

"The suite next to my apartment is still available if you would be more comfortable there, but I must insist that you remain here for the next few hours at least."

I looked at him quizzically. What was so special about the next few hours? Was something going on outside that I was unaware of?

I agreed anyway, mostly because I wanted a soft, comfortable bed and the prospect of a bath was appealing.

It was also nice to think that I had a place to hide out, not just from the Weepers and the judgemental eyes of the Silver, but also from my fellow humans. I didn't seem to be making many friends and the idea of returning to the dorm didn't really appeal.

Here I was, hiding again.

One day soon I was going to have to face up to everything, but there was so much I wanted to bury: my dead friends, the horror of my new life, the Weeper attacks, my encounters with Sol and, of course, Drew. That was the thing I'd been shoving down from the forefront of my mind whenever it surfaced, what I had used Sol to escape from: the murder, the betrayal, but mostly my feelings for Drew.

They tugged at me, no matter how hard I tried to ignore them.

Now was not the time to let them rise to the surface. I could deal with them tomorrow, or later today as the case may be. Either way, not till I'd had some sleep.

Sol guided me up the stairs to the fifth floor, my feet

dragging and my thighs aching by the time we reached the top. I was incredibly thirsty, no doubt the hangover kicking in, and my calves were burning with lactic acid. I couldn't wait to get back to sleep.

As we crested the top of the stairs into the familiar corridor of the fifth floor, we were greeted with an unpleasant, but half-expected, surprise: Drew. Of course he was here. His eyes blazed as he took in the sight of Sol's arm around me, my head leaning against his shoulder.

He sighed heavily beside me.

"Secundus," he said.

"Primus, I had to check... to see..."

"I understand the impulse," Sol replied, "but, as you see, she is well."

"And the blood?" Drew asked.

Sol's eyes cut to me before returning to look at Drew.

"Of that," he replied, "I am not yet certain."

"What?" I asked.

"You haven't told her?" Drew asked, incredulous. "Why isn't she in quarantine?"

"Is that what you want for her?" Sol challenged him. "To put her in that kind of danger?"

Drew looked at me miserably.

"I told Rena I had tested her," Sol said quietly, "but that was untrue."

I turned to Sol, shrugging off his arm and crossing my own in irritation. I raised an eyebrow expectantly, awaiting his explanation.

"I didn't wish to risk being overheard, so I have waited until we were away from those who might be listening," Sol said. "Please come inside where I can ensure your security and I will tell you everything."

Sol walked towards the end of the corridor, opening the door to his apartment. I wasn't going to sleep there, but I decided not to argue about talking in his apartment. I didn't want to put him off telling me what was going on.

"Primus," Drew said as we reached the door, "I'm not

leaving you, or her, unprotected. In the circumstances, I think I'd better come with you. In fact, I think I should probably insist."

"I might have guessed that you would," he replied. "Very well."

Sol held the door open wide and I stepped through, followed closely by Drew. I glanced at him suspiciously over my shoulder.

I didn't know what his game was. He acted like he cared, but how could I believe that after what he'd done?

Just like that, I was into the realms of things I didn't want to think about. I could see that he was interested in more than my blood from the intensity of his attention, his oddly solicitous behaviour. I wasn't going to admit it to myself until I had no other option.

I walked towards the low seating area to the left and descended the few steps leading down to it, settling myself onto one of the sofas. Sol took the sofa opposite me and, to my consternation, Drew sat down next to me. Sol cast a disapproving glance in his direction but said nothing.

"Emmy," Sol said, "you cut your hand fighting the Weeper."

"Yes," I replied. "I know that."

I wasn't sure where he was going with this.

"You told me about the bottle, that you stabbed the Weeper and cut your hand in the process."

"Spit it out, Sol," I replied irritably.

But he couldn't seem to work out how to phrase what he wanted to say. It was the first time I had ever seen Sol, master of erudition, struggle for words.

"What he's trying to tell you," Drew said, "is that you don't have to be bitten by a Weeper for the virus to be transmitted. If the Weeper's blood got into your system, you could still be turned."

There had been blood everywhere. I had no idea what had been mine and what had been the Weeper's, but it was entirely possible that the Weeper's blood had got into my wound. I felt… numb, unsure how to react.

"Oh," I said.

"There's a way we can make sure you never become a Weeper…" Drew said quickly.

"Enough, Secundus," Sol interrupted. "If you wish to have my leave to remain then you'll hold your tongue."

With a rebellious look, Drew fell silent.

"So," I said, "what now? Do you need to do a taste test?"

"You're making jokes about this, Emmy?" Sol asked incredulously.

I shrugged back. What else was there to do?

"I can't test you," Sol continued, "because too much time has passed now since the potential infection occurred. If Weeper blood did enter your bloodstream, it will be too dilute for me to detect it. I should have tested the wound site back in the dorm, but…"

"But what?" I asked.

His eyes flicked towards Drew, who sighed.

"He didn't want to let on to Ben that you might be infected," Drew said, "because he would have killed you immediately just to be safe."

I looked between the two of them in confusion.

"It's not just Benedict," Sol said.

"No, but he's pretty merciless in his approach to the control of the Weeper plague. He's also vehemently anti-human and he hardly makes a secret of it."

I couldn't make sense of that. He wasn't describing the Ben I knew, who had always been kind to me.

"No," I replied, "that can't be right. Ben's not like that with me at all, besides which he was there. He saw my wound and he must have known I'd got it from stabbing the Weeper. If he was going to kill me then he would have."

Drew shrugged.

"I don't know," he said, "maybe he didn't connect the dots, but it doesn't sound like him. I'm honestly surprised he even talks to you."

"You exaggerate," Sol interjected dismissively.

I fell into a thoughtful silence. Something was wrong in this picture, and I wasn't willing to take Drew's word that it was Ben who was the problem. Apparently, Drew and Ben didn't like each other much.

"And quarantine?" I asked after a minute or so.

"It's what it sounds like," Drew replied. "We put the potentially infected in there. Most of them end up dead, if not because they turn then because they take their own lives or get attacked by those who are turning. We try to keep them apart, but Weepers are deceptively strong. It's hard to keep them separate and we can't dedicate many Silver to look after quarantine."

"It's beyond the barricade," Sol added ominously. "I thought it better to bring you here, to oversee you myself for the quarantine period."

"And how long is that?" I asked anxiously.

"Usually about six hours," Drew replied, "so we've got five to go. You'll know you're safe in seven."

As if he hadn't processed what he was saying until the words were out of his mouth, Drew's face fell. He set his jaw and looked at me with determination.

"I can stop it, Emmy…" he began.

"Secundus," Sol interrupted in a snarl, "I have warned you once, but I will not warn you again."

Drew turned to face him with a violent expression.

"You'd rather sit here and do nothing? Just wait for the plague to take her? I can't do it, Sol. I can't just sit around and watch it happen."

"What you are suggesting," Sol replied with gravity, "is not only forbidden, but also bound to fail."

"And you think it's not even worth trying? You think Emmy's not worth the risk?"

"I think it would be wiser to approach the situation optimistically," Sol said, "instead of assuming that the worst will come to pass."

I looked at Sol sharply.

"I'm getting really sick of you both talking about me as if

I'm not here," I interjected irritably.

They both looked at me.

"Explain," I demanded. "Now."

Sol shook his head at Drew, but he turned to me with a defiant look.

"The Weeper infection can be drawn out of your blood and any remaining trace of it eradicated," Drew said, "but we'll need to get Silver blood into your system for it to work. It means that a Silver has to bite you and you'll have to drink blood from a Silver in return. There is also a... side effect."

He looked away for a second before fixing his gaze on mine.

"The process might make you one of us," he continued. "It could make you Silver."

Silver? A vampire?

Did I want that? I'd be much stronger, a member of the new elite race, but that kind of twisted power could be undesirable, corrupting. My mind flashed relentlessly back to the image of Sarah's body, crumpled unnaturally on the mattress like a puppet with cut strings.

Drew, however human he might appear, however gentle he might pretend to be, was capable of that kind of violence as a Silver.

If I were the sort of person who could do that to a human being, even if I no longer was one, I wouldn't be Emmy anymore. I would have lost myself completely, beyond any nihilistic hedonism I might have indulged in Sol's arms.

No. I didn't want to be Silver.

I shook my head.

"It's your decision," Drew said to me sadly.

So when it mattered, he would let me choose.

"Will you tell her what you have omitted?" Sol asked him irritably.

"Why bother? It would hardly change her mind," Drew said bitterly as he stood.

He walked across the room until he stood at the panoramic window of the apartment, looking out over the city.

"You two have issues," I said to Sol jokingly. "What didn't he tell me?"

"The… circumstances have to be right for the transformation to Silver to take effect. In some cases, things go wrong. There is no guarantee."

I'd definitely made the right decision.

CHAPTER XXVII

I couldn't sleep. With difficulty, I'd had a quick shower with a plastic bag over my hand to keep the dressing dry and I'd eaten some toast to try to settle my hungover stomach. Now here I was again, lying in bed exhausted but unable to sleep.

Sol had insisted that I take his bed while he and Drew remained downstairs. Despite Drew's angry expression, I couldn't be bothered to argue and, frankly, I was looking forward to falling asleep wrapped in the smell of Sol. I briefly wondered whether it might be the scent that was stopping me from sleeping, but I was kidding myself.

I was terrified.

I didn't want to turn into one of those mindless monsters. Ironically, the thing that scared me most was the concept of losing myself, of turning into something anathema to who I was.

If I got out of this alive, I was going to have to think seriously on that, to decide whether I had lost or found myself in Sol. The fear I was feeling now was very different from the fear I felt about him.

With a few hours to go until I was in the clear, I gave up. Shrugging into a pair of shorts and a T-shirt that Sol had brought from next door for me, I left the bedroom and headed downstairs. Drew and Sol were arguing in hushed tones.

"...will have to get over it," I heard Sol say.

I paused at the door, intending to go back into the bedroom and leave them to hash it out, but instead I stood and listened guiltily.

"I know that... know what it means for..."

I couldn't make out all of Drew's response.

"Why?" he continued. "You've... knew what had happened... lifetime of this, Sol."

"Yes, but we have bigger problems right now," Sol replied before looking up to the mezzanine, "and an eavesdropper."

Busted.

I walked up to the rail edging the mezzanine and looked down at the two of them. They were standing at opposite sides of the seating area where I had left them earlier in the day.

"I can't sleep," I said with a shrug, moving to walk down the spiral staircase. "I see you two have managed to refrain from killing each other in my absence."

"Just about," Drew said, grinning at me.

I frowned and looked down at my feet as I reached the bottom of the stairs. His cheerfulness felt forced and it made me uncomfortable. Things had to be bad.

"You think I'm going to turn," I said matter-of-factly as I collapsed onto a sofa.

"No, Emmy," Sol said, sitting down next to me.

He took my left hand in his and squeezed it gently.

"Well," I replied, "since I've got nothing to do but wait, perhaps you could distract me?"

Sol's eyebrows shot up.

"...by talking to me," I added pointedly.

"What would you like me to talk to you about?" he asked.

"I don't know. Anything. Where did the Weepers come from? How long have you been Silver? Have you always been? Were you born that way or what? And how did you get to be Primus?"

I hadn't realised quite how many questions I had until I started listing them all. I realised I knew practically nothing.

"I was once human," Sol replied, "like you."

I looked at him expectantly, but he said nothing else.

There was a knock at the door and Drew looked quizzically at Sol.

"It will be Adrienne," Sol explained. "I'm meeting with the former leaders of the safe houses that we have consolidated here in London. We are to discuss the assignment of new roles to each of them."

"To soothe their egos?" Drew asked with a wry smile.

"Precisely," Sol replied. "Emmy, I'm afraid I must leave you in the care of my Secundus for an hour or so."

I balked a little at this, unsure I wanted to be alone with Drew.

"I understand your consternation, but Drew will ensure your safety. Without laying a hand on you," Sol added, looking pointedly at Drew.

"Fine," I replied dismissively, aiming for nonchalance and probably failing.

Sol stood and leaned down to press a kiss into my hairline whilst Drew looked on fiercely. Sol noticed his reaction and turned to him.

"I appreciate your situation, Secundus," Sol said to him gently, "but though your protective instincts towards Emmy may serve my purposes at present, please bear in mind that challenging my mark also challenges my sovereignty."

Here we go again.

"She doesn't bear your scent mark anymore," Drew replied with a smile, "or your necklace."

"Will you two pack it in?" I sighed in exasperation. "Sol, I'm not going to let him touch me and you know I find this whole line of conversation insulting, so just stop."

"As you wish," he replied. "But nevertheless, I'd be happier if you'd wear this."

He reached into his pocket and extracted my choker. He must have retrieved it from the terrace, or maybe it was a new one. Either way, here he was with another dog collar.

Sol handed the choker to me and pressed a kiss to my cheek in a proprietary fashion. It was starting to make me feel uncomfortable, but I didn't think it was worth objecting, particularly not in front of Drew.

"Please wear it," he asked.

With that, he walked to the door to the apartment and opened it, pausing on the threshold.

"Just an hour," he said to me, "then I'll return."

I nodded at him with a smile then he stepped through the door, closing it behind him. I stared after him and willed the time to pass quickly so I wouldn't be alone with Drew.

He walked across the room to the sofa and took Sol's seat next to me.

"You care about him," he said.

I shuffled away a little, curling myself up into the corner between the back and the arm of the sofa.

"It's complicated," I replied dismissively, looking away.

We sat in silence for a few minutes, then the floodgates burst as if he couldn't keep his thoughts to himself anymore, as if the words he wanted to say were dying to be spoken.

"What did I do?" he asked me plaintively. "How did I drive you away, to him? I thought it was that I'm Silver, but you let him touch you. You let him…"

His eyes flicked to the bite marks on my neck.

I'd not only let him.

Drew bit down on the words as they tried to escape. I could see the rage building in his eyes then subsiding as he forced it back down, the silver threads glimmering in the forest-green of his irises.

I gritted my teeth and glared at him, willing him to drop it. We'd had this conversation before and it hadn't ended well.

He paused and took a breath.

"Is it serious?" he asked me with a pained expression on his face. "Do you love him?"

It wasn't love and I knew that. I also thought it was unlikely it ever would be, but I wasn't going to share that with

Drew. I didn't want to encourage him, particularly as I was confused enough about my feelings for him already. It didn't matter what I felt for him. The things he'd done...

"Is it any of your business?" I asked indignantly.

His face fell. He was clearly taking my evasive response as a sign that Sol and I were a long-term fixture. I didn't correct him.

"Why?" he asked. "I know you felt something for me."

"You're a monster," I replied in a voice devoid of intonation.

He looked at me in confusion and I looked away.

"Sarah. Jeff..." I trailed off, staring blankly into the middle distance.

"Why do you blame me for their deaths, but not Sol?" he asked in incomprehension. "I'm not the only one who decided that humans who resist subjugation should be treated as a threat. We both did, together."

"They didn't resist, though, did they?" I replied acerbically.

Drew's brow furrowed in uncertainty.

"Why would you think that?" he asked suspiciously.

I shook my head and laughed bitterly. It had been Ben who had told me, of course. I didn't know what was going on with the pair of them, but I wasn't going to debate this with him. Did it really matter if they'd resisted or not? Either way, they were dead at his hands.

"Forget it," I said.

"Emmy..."

"Will you just drop this subject?" I said, my voice rising in irritation. "You keep talking to me as if I'll change my mind if only you say the right thing, but it's not going to happen. I'm just not interested and I never will be. Okay?"

He dropped his eyes from mine. My chest constricted at his agonised expression, but it had to be said. I needed him to leave me alone. I couldn't repeat this conversation ad infinitum. It kept dredging up my misplaced feelings for him and I was torturing myself with them.

I couldn't bear the fact that I wanted him, the murderous

vampire who'd killed two of my closest friends. It felt so right to be close to him and that admission was eating me up.

I stood and walked away from him towards the TV area at the back of the room. I didn't want to talk anymore and I didn't want the drama. I just wanted to ignore the thread of Weeper-transformation anxiety that was worming through me and switch off in front of the television.

I grabbed a film at random, an obscure horror film I'd never heard of, and inserted it in the DVD player. After several minutes' frustrated attempts to make the DVD player, television and speakers all function correctly, I finally located the correct remote control to switch it on. I could feel Drew watching me, but I was damned if I was going to ask him to help.

When the film was rolling, I threw myself down onto the sofa and curled my feet under me, wrapping myself up in a blanket that was thrown artfully across the seat. I stared fiercely at the screen as Drew silently sat next to me, the couch depressing with his weight. He said nothing.

However much he might think that Sol was as culpable as he was for Sarah and Jeff's murders, there was a considerable distinction to my mind in having decreed that rebels should be killed and in actually carrying out that order. Drew knew what they were to me and he'd channelled into their deaths his rage at not having located me.

But maybe Ben had lied about Drew's rage. Where would that leave me?

I sighed heavily. A lot had happened today and I needed to sleep on it. Hell, maybe I'd wake up a Weeper and not have to worry about any of this anymore.

As I finally relaxed, exhaustion overwhelmed me and my head began to nod. I was fast asleep before the film had a chance to get scary.

CHAPTER XXVIII

I woke up on the sofa with a crick in my neck, the TV screen in front of me switched off. I sat up and looked around, wondering what time it was.

"He's not back yet," Drew said from behind me, "and you were asleep for a good long while. It's late afternoon."

I turned round to see him walking across the room towards me, a steaming mug in his hands. I detected the wonderful and welcome smell of coffee and my mouth began to water.

Just an hour, Sol had said. I wondered what had gone wrong.

Drew set the mug on the coffee table in front of me and indicated with a gesture of his head that it was for me.

"Thank you," I said stiffly.

"You're not a Weeper," he replied with a small smile.

"Apparently not."

I should have been relieved, but I just felt hollow. I'd woken up with all the problems I'd gone to sleep with and now I was stuck alone in Sol's apartment with Drew. I looked at my bandaged hand and wondered if I could move it enough to manage a shift at the bar after all. The thought of spending the night here with Drew was not appealing.

No, I thought, that was a lie. I desperately wanted to spend the night alone with Drew, which was precisely why it was a bad idea. Self-preservation kicked in.

"I want to work tonight, if Laila doesn't mind me working one-handed."

"I'd offer to heal it, but you'd say no again," he said as he sat down next to me, tracing the lines of the cuts on my face with his eyes.

"Yes, I would," I replied softly.

He sighed, clearly picking up on the fact that he was straying onto dangerous ground. I thought he would persist and take us right back to the drama of last night, but he surprised me by changing the subject.

"Food then," he said. "Can I make you something? Pancakes and bacon, perhaps?"

I looked at him incredulously, my eyes widening.

"You can make pancakes?" I asked.

"They're my favourite," he replied with a grin as he stood from his seat. "I've already made the batter so you may as well share them with me."

I was a little thrown by this, but I smiled despite myself. Pancakes and bacon were my favourite breakfast. Or late lunch, in this case.

"Maple syrup?" I asked.

"Of course."

I picked up my coffee and followed him towards a double doorway by the dining table, leading out of the side of the main room of the apartment. It opened out into a small but well-appointed galley kitchen.

"Where's Sol?" I asked.

Drew's face darkened as he opened the door of the fridge and pulled out the bacon. He turned to face me.

"Things didn't go well this morning with the former leaders of the safe houses. There are some political issues Sol needs to smooth over."

He grabbed a jug of pancake batter out of the fridge and I looked at him with concern in my expression.

"Don't worry," he added, "Sol's fine. He knows what he's doing."

He spoke the last words on a growl in a leering tone, as if the comment was directed towards Sol's relationship with me, rather than the former leaders.

I watched as Drew put the bacon under the grill then put a frying pan on the heat. Once it was up to temperature, he poured the first batch of batter in to cook.

"How do you get away with this level of insubordination?" I asked. "Aren't you supposed to support him? I would have thought he'd stamp down on any sedition of the sort you've been engaging in."

"Normally he would."

"So he lets you off because you're his Secundus?"

"No," he replied. "There are... extenuating circumstances, of which he's aware."

That made no sense to me.

"These are the circumstances that you and Sol keep avoiding telling me about?"

"Those are the ones," he confirmed.

"I wish the pair of you would stop talking in riddles and give me a straight answer for once," I sighed in exasperation.

"Maybe one day," he replied with a rueful smile.

He flipped a pancake.

"The truth is," he added, "he pities me."

"Why?"

"You know why," he replied in a meaningful tone, "at least in part. I'm not spelling it out for you."

I could understand there being an element of competition between Sol and Drew in relation to me, but I couldn't imagine the outcome of that competition being so significant as to cause Sol to pity Drew. However much I might flatter my ego, it just didn't follow that winning the affections of a single human would be worth overlooking a threat to the political stability of the British faction of the Silver.

There had to be something else going on here.

"You wanted answers last night," he continued, "about the

Silver, about Sol and how he was made, how he became Primus. Do you still?"

I shrugged as I watched him dish out the pancakes and bacon onto two plates.

"Sure, if that's all you're willing to talk about."

"It is," he replied, "for now."

He grabbed both plates and some cutlery then walked out of the kitchen to place them on the dining table in the main room. A wonderful smell rose from the plates. I settled myself quickly into one of the chairs.

"Wow," I said in admiration, "this looks amazing."

"Dig in then," he replied.

He sat down opposite me and smiled as I eyed the meal eagerly.

"So?" I asked. "Spill it."

He smiled indulgently.

"Sol is a very old vampire, turned Silver millennia ago."

"Was he one of the first?" I asked.

"I'm not going to tell you anything unless you eat the food I've slaved over for you," he replied, raising an eyebrow.

I rolled my eyes at him, but tucked in.

The food was delicious. I hadn't realised until I took the first bite that I was absolutely ravenous. I demolished my plateful in a few short minutes as Drew ate at a more sedate pace, looking on with amusement.

"We don't know who the 'first' Silver were," he said, placated now that I had eaten. "We think there have always been Silver, but there have never been many of us and we were scattered. We didn't know about the others. The small groups of two or three of us that used to exist each thought that we were the only Silver in the world."

He stood from the table and walked into the kitchen, returning with two glasses of orange juice. He put one down on the table in front of me.

"Eventually, we started to hear about each other as the Silver spread. There's no need for us to reproduce because we're practically immortal, but we have grown in numbers recently."

"Why's that?" I asked as I took a welcome gulp of juice.

"Mostly because more of us have worked out how to make Silver from humans, but before you ask that's not something I'm going to talk about."

I huffed out a breath in exasperation. The question had already been on my lips.

"What about you?" I asked. "When were you made?"

"I wasn't," he replied. "I was born this way."

I looked at him in confusion.

"That can happen?" I asked.

"Oh yes. Silver can have children, but only rarely. My mother and father were both Silver."

"Are they here too?"

He shook his head.

"I'm not going to talk about that, either," he said sadly.

Guilt flooded through me as I realised I'd touched a nerve.

We sat in silence for a few minutes as he finished his meal. I was surprised that he'd opened up at all and realised I'd become used to seeing him in a confrontational setting. It had been a few days since we'd had a conversation without him pushing me or challenging me. Or without me challenging him.

I drank my coffee and juice, looking at the last scrape of maple syrup on my plate.

"Would you judge me if I licked the plate?" I asked.

He shook his head and chuckled. My stomach flipped.

I hadn't heard him chuckle for what seemed like an age and it caught me off guard. Here we were, a picture of domesticity, and it gnawed at my heart. Everything felt real and right in a way that nothing had for days.

For the first time since my admission, he was himself, the man who had made me feel safe as my world crumbled around me. He was the man, not the monster. I hadn't realised how much I'd missed him, how much I missed that feeling, and it upset me.

With everything he'd done… it was so wrong for me to

feel the way I did.

He saw the look on my face and frowned.

"What?" he asked.

I shook my head in distress.

"What's wrong, Emmy? What did I do? I'm trying to back off…" he said desperately.

"I'm sorry," I replied as I got to my feet. "I have to go."

He stared at me in incomprehension.

"But…" he said.

"Please, Drew. Just don't," I said.

I ran up the spiral staircase to Sol's bedroom and pushed my feet into my boots, gathering up my things. I had to get out of here before I said something stupid or, worse, did something I'd regret.

He'd made me feel comfortable and I'd let myself forget what he was, what he'd done.

As I turned to leave, he appeared at the door to Sol's room.

"Please will you talk to me about this?" he asked.

I couldn't even bear to look at him. An agony of loss rushed through me. I'd let myself believe for a moment that he was the person I had met on Thursday night, the person I'd thought he was before Jeff and Sarah were killed, and now I was losing him all over again.

I wished it wasn't real. I wished he hadn't…

But wishing wouldn't bring Jeff and Sarah back, and it couldn't change him into something he wasn't.

The betrayal crashed back down onto my shoulders and I pushed past him and back down the stairs, running through the apartment to the door.

He beat me to it in a whirlwind of movement.

"Please," he begged as he held the apartment door shut in front of me, "talk to me."

He reached out his other hand to take mine, but I jerked away before he touched me.

"There's nothing you can say that will make it better," I whispered, my eyes fixed on the door.

Slowly, he moved his hand to the door handle and pulled

it open, standing aside to let me through.

"Thank you for the meal," I whispered before rushing through the door and along the corridor, plunging down the stairs without looking back.

CHAPTER XXIX

After a quick change of clothes into a work uniform, I tracked down Laila in the first-floor bar and arranged to work tonight after all.

So here I was, my hand and knee all bandaged up, cuts all over my face and bite marks on my neck, working in the main room of the club. Alice was chatting up Bed-head Vamp at the other end of the bar. She'd really come into her own over the past couple of days. The Silver clientele seemed to love her and she was lapping it up. I just kept my head down and prayed I'd get through the shift without more drama.

I was hanging out with the wrong crowd if I wanted a quiet life. Getting embroiled with the Primus and his Secundus was hardly a recipe for tranquillity.

I needed to start hanging out with my own kind and make some human friends.

"Two bottles," a blonde woman demanded, her hand glittering with diamonds as she laid her tokens in my hand.

The rings on her right hand alone must have amounted to about a million pounds' worth of jewels. I supposed she'd probably had a long time to amass her wealth and accrue interest on it. Not that money mattered anymore.

I dropped the tokens in the box behind the bar then, one-handed, popped the tops off two bottles, setting them down in front of the glamorous blonde.

I looked the length of the busy bar, Silver queuing three-deep to buy drinks, and noticed in irritation that Alice was still chatting up the vamp with the affected hairstyle, jutting her hip provocatively towards him.

"Alice!" I shouted over the blaring music. "Get your butt in gear and pour some fucking drinks!"

She rolled her eyes at me with a smile and reluctantly moved to serve another customer.

Alice and I were getting on well, but I wasn't sure I saw the point of even trying with the others.

The problem was that all the other humans in the dorm had been at the safe house together whilst I'd been out in the city and here at the club in my ill-fated attempt to escape the rule of the Silver. The irony was that I seemed to get on with the Silver much better than I got on with the humans here.

However much of an effort I made to fit in with the humans, I still felt like I was outside the clique. Odd, then, that Alice envied me for my position in the Silver clique. I was displaced and disenfranchised in this new world. I needed to find my niche, the place that was mine, the one Sol had told me to look for when we first met. But did it even exist?

"Emmy!" the happy figure of Cameron was my next customer.

"Hey Cam," I replied with a smile.

"So, I'm sorry about the other night," he said, rubbing the back of his neck in an subconscious gesture of discomfort.

"Why?" I asked.

"For leaving you," he replied. "I should have stayed, but… he's the Primus and I'm sort of sworn to do as he says."

"I know," I said with an encouraging smile, "and it's okay. What can I get you to drink?"

He grinned, happy that all was forgiven.

"No alcohol," he replied, "ever again. Can I get a bottle?"

"Sure," I said, taking his proffered token and cracking a bottle of blood open for him.

"I'm going to have to catch up with you later," I said, indicating the crush in the bar, "when things have calmed down a bit."

"No problem," he replied as Tommy pushed through the crowd to where Cam stood at the bar.

The queuing customers around him made various noises of dissatisfaction until they saw it was one of the Solis Invicti who was doing the pushing.

"Emmy, I need a favour," Tommy yelled at me over the music as he reached us.

"Little busy at the moment, Tommy," I said, serving a couple of bottles to another Silver as I spoke.

"I've got the former leaders of the defunct safe houses in the VIP bar and I could really do with a waitress," he continued unperturbed. "One of them is kicking up a fuss because he wants his drinks served by a woman, but the only wait staff in there are guys."

I served two more Silver while he spoke and was onto the third as I replied.

"Wait a minute, you want me to go in there and serve drinks just so some sexist bastard can have his preconceptions validated by having a woman perform his menial work for him?"

Tommy looked at me in embarrassment.

"Actually," he said, "I think he wants to watch your ass walking around the room in that tiny skirt."

I glared at him.

"C'mon Emmy," Cam interjected with a grin, "not a man in the world could blame him for wanting to watch that."

"Shut up, Cam. You're creeping me out."

I definitely didn't think of him that way and I was pretty sure he didn't feel that way about me either. He was just pulling my leg.

"I'll give you Chris in return," Tommy said, naming one of the human barmen, "and he can deal with this crush for you."

I was reluctant. I actually enjoyed working the bar best when it was busy like this and I'd certainly much rather be here than in the VIP room, being leered at by some petty former leader.

"We're trying to resolve a fairly difficult political situation," he continued, "and this would actually really help."

He looked at me with a hint of desperation in his expression.

I didn't reply and instead left him hanging as I served a few more customers.

"I'll be there the whole time to make sure they don't mess with you," Tommy promised.

"Tommy…" I groaned.

"Please?"

I sighed.

"Fine," I huffed, "but you owe me one."

"Great! Cam, go get Chris," he said, and they both disappeared in a flash before I could change my mind.

I served a few more customers before Chris came to replace me. He was a nice enough guy in his thirties, balding with pale hair, but we hadn't exchanged more than two words.

I left the main bar's customers in his care and pushed my way through to the VIP bar. I'd been avoiding the place. This would be the first time I'd worked this bar since the Revelation, the first time I'd been in the room since I was there with Ben.

I opened the doors and waited for the awful memories of Jeff and Sarah to come flooding back, but I was surprised. As the doors swung shut behind me, the thumping beat from the main bar was blocked out and replaced by what I thought of as cocktail music. The bar had been rearranged with new furniture and fresh paint on the walls. They'd even carpeted the floor.

I breathed a sigh of relief and took in the room around me.

There were far fewer seats now, the tables arranged in booths around the edges of the rooms and spaced in such a way that each had far more privacy than had been the case previously. Even the bar had been moved. It was now an enclosed, circular structure in the centre of the room that was accessible from every side. The new arrangement meant there was double the space for the new booths.

It was neatly done and I was impressed. I wondered idly whether it had been Sol's idea.

There was a single barman in the centre of the circular bar, spinning around as he poured and passed drinks to a waiter who was taking them to the tables. Apparently the VIP bar was now all about the table service, which had never been the case back when the club was Parker's. I guess Sol's was catering to a more demanding clientele.

I walked up to the centre of the room and the barman met my eye in relief. He was human, built like a rugby player with a nose that looked like it had been broken about five times, but he had a friendly smile in an expressive face.

I was interested to see what the male employees in the VIP bar were required to wear, but I was disappointed: boring black trousers and T-shirts.

"You're Emilia?" he asked.

"That's me."

"Thank god," he replied. "I was starting to lose all hope of calming things down in here. I'm Josh."

He extended his hand to me and I shook it over the bar.

"Call me Emmy," I replied.

"Good to meet you, Emmy. I need you to take the tables in the back half of the room," he said, indicating the space behind him. "Sam has the front half."

There were only about fifteen tables in the whole room, so I didn't think it was going to be much of a trial. In fact, I couldn't really work out why they needed three members of staff to serve the drinks here. One would have done the job, two at a stretch.

My confusion must have shown on my face, because Josh elaborated.

"Thomas didn't tell you, did he?"

I raised an eyebrow.

"This isn't just waitressing, Emmy," Josh said.

I panicked. What the hell were they asking me to do here?

"It's nothing too unsavoury," he continued, "so don't worry, but they want you to shmooze a bit. Serve some drinks, engage people in conversation, make sure everyone has a good time. Entertain, but not so you're the centre of attention. Think of it as hosting and you won't go far wrong."

"Seriously?" I asked incredulously.

"I'm not sure why you're so reluctant. Humans are falling over themselves for the job. Alice would just about kill for it."

"Why?" I asked, bewildered.

To me, it seemed worse than working the bar. At least in that role I could escape as I worked, zoning out as I mindlessly served drinks and took tokens with the music pumping around me. I wasn't keen on the concept of pressing skin, of getting involved in people's conversations.

He shrugged.

"Alice just has a hard on for the Silver. To the rest of us, it's the perfect opportunity to get yourself noticed, to make connections with the Silver, to improve your position."

"That's not something I'm looking for," I replied, thinking that between Sol and Drew I was in enough of a pickle as it was.

"Well, Thomas has made sure it's going to find you. Start at this end," he said, indicating the first booth in my section, the one that was closest to the bar, "and work along to the back corner. After you've done a first pass and introduced yourself then you can go with the flow, but keep an eye on everyone's drinks as you circulate."

"Okay," I said with a deep breath.

"Oh, and I imagine this goes without saying, but no one pays in the VIP room. Don't ask for tokens."

Josh gave me an encouraging smile and turned away to clean a load of dirty glasses that a waiter, who I supposed must be Sam, had deposited on the bar.

As I walked towards the first table, I saw Tommy enter the room out of the corner of my eye. He took up a position by the door, ostensibly keeping the riff-raff out of the VIP area.

I shot him an irritated look for having dropped me in it. I was way out of my comfort zone here and I guessed he'd probably known that.

He flashed me an unabashed grin and crossed his arms over his chest. He'd got what he wanted so he couldn't care less. He'd probably been worried to ask Alice in case she drooled on the clientele.

Bastard.

There were three Silver sitting at the first table, two men and a woman. All three looked to be in their early thirties, though of course that probably meant nothing to the Silver.

The woman seemed to be the one with the power here. She had dark hair cropped close to her head and wore no make up on a face that was all hard lines and judgement. She was dressed severely but expensively in dark trousers and a dark T-shirt that covered her from neck to wrists. The fabric was rich and stiff with beautifully intricate embroidery on the sleeves, which came down into points on the backs of her hands.

The two men were dressed in a similarly plain manner, but they wore less tailored clothing in softer cotton: T-shirts and khakis that gave them the air of bodyguards. Perhaps that's what they were.

I felt incredibly out of my depth and exposed. What the hell was I supposed to be doing here? I felt inferior. I gave myself a quick mental slap around the face. We are only constrained by the boxes we make for ourselves.

"Good evening," I said to the woman, faking a confident smile.

I withered a little when she simply stared back at me with a supercilious expression on her face.

"Would you like a drink?" I persevered.

"Are you offering your own wrist?" she replied.

If I had been flustered before, it had been nothing in comparison with this.

"Er…no…"

Obviously I wasn't going to let her drink from me, but

what was I supposed to say? Did they do that sort of thing here? I'd seen Silver drinking from humans across the road at the Palace, but I'd never seen it here at Sol's.

I really, really didn't want to watch it again, particularly now I'd experienced it for myself. The pain, the terror, the excitement… it was a heady mix that filled me with ambivalence.

I was spared the embarrassment of having to find a way out of this by the fortuitous arrival of Sol. So this is where he'd been.

He was dressed to impress in a beautifully-tailored, navy suit with a white, open-necked shirt underneath. He looked outstandingly handsome, the blue in the suit fabric setting off his eyes.

"Cleo," he said to the woman, rolling the name off his tongue, "this is Emilia."

He put his arm around my shoulders and pulled me close to him. The message was clear: this one's mine. His fresh, spicy scent elicited no desire as it wrapped around me. Instead, it washed me in an oppressive feeling of guilt that lodged in my chest. My skin itched where his flesh touched mine.

I expected that his gesture would raise eyebrows in such rarefied company, but the woman Cleo let her eyes rest on the bite marks at my neck. Drew had been right. They thought I was Sol's toy.

In some ways, maybe that was for the best.

"I'm afraid we only offer blood from the vein at the Palace," Sol continued. "The atmosphere here is too… charged to ensure the safety of our human subjects."

"A wise precaution," Cleo allowed.

I wondered how sincere she was. It was impossible to tell from the tone of her voice.

"In that case we will have three glasses, in champagne flutes for preference," she added.

I nodded dutifully and smiled as I turned away to the bar to fill their order, slipping out from under Sol's arm as I did so. Unfortunately, and inevitably, he was quicker than me.

"Not so fast," he said into my ear in a barely audible whisper that hissed through his teeth.

He turned with me, grasping my wrist in his hand as his back shielded us from Cleo's view, and walked us away to a more secluded corner of the room.

"I understood that you were safe at the Palace in the care of my Secundus," he said quietly, his eyes flashing.

"I got bored," I said with a shrug, faking nonchalance.

"This is not a safe place for you," he replied, his jaw clenching in frustration. "These former leaders are ill-disposed towards me and by your association with me you are a target. A Silver has already tried to kill you. Now you are putting yourself in the line of fire once again, particularly as I note you are without your choker."

My hand flew to my neck. The choker was gone. How had I managed to lose it since the start of my shift?

"Look, Sol," I said, irritated at my carelessness, "nothing's going to happen. You're here, Tommy's here, everything's fine."

"Nevertheless, you are without my choker, without my mark. I suppose you would not permit me to reinstate the latter?"

I shook my head quickly. I felt like I was only just getting my head straight.

"Tommy's looking out for me. It's fine."

Sol paused, his jaw setting with determination as his bright eyes hardened.

"I have no need of your permission," he said darkly.

I snatched my hand out of his grip, horrified.

"In that case," I hissed, "I have no desire for your protection."

His expression remained tense but his eyes softened slightly, willing me to relent. I glared back. It was never going to happen.

Not wanting to dwell on the incident, I turned away from him and made my way to the bar. Josh looked curiously back to where Sol stood in the corner of the room as he set up a tray of champagne flutes for Cleo's table. He helped me get a hold on it with my injured hand and I took it over to the table.

I wasn't feeling much like schmoozing, but I smiled brightly as I placed the glasses of warm blood on the table in front of each of the vampires.

I spared a moment to have a quick look around. There were only five other tables in my part of the room, so I thought I'd better do a quick sweep to get other drink orders before trying to 'entertain'.

Three of the tables were occupied by Silver couples, each of whom ordered blood in various forms. A single Silver man sat at the fourth, already nursing a pint of warm blood.

The final table was raucous with four young Silver men. I was surprised to see that one of them was the peacock from the other night whom I had branded as Lestat. The one I had mocked. Extensively.

Oh dear. It couldn't be a good thing that he'd turned up here.

Of the other three, one was clearly a little older than the rest. I had no idea what that meant in Silver terms, but he seemed to be the leader of the little group. He had ostentatious clothing: a colourful, tailored suit with detailed embroidery and a thin neck tie. He was dark-haired and handsome, but with an air of overt arrogance that made him faintly repellent.

The remaining two were clearly underlings in the same way as was Lestat. Both were of affected appearance, one with a waxed moustache and the other with a carefully-maintained beard. Both made me instantly suspicious. It was the way their eyes seemed to slide off sideways without looking at my face.

I took an instant dislike to the entire group. Concern twisted in my chest as I struggled to suppress my discomfort.

"Good evening," I said, forcing a smile.

"So," drawled the apparent leader, "you're the human I've heard so much about. When I asked for a waitress I had no idea they'd be sending you."

Of course. This was the prick who'd requested a woman to serve his drinks for him. I should have guessed.

"I'm Charles," he added with a leer.

I should have played up to him, engaged him in sparkling and intriguing conversation, but I had a very bad feeling about him. This wasn't someone I should be inviting to take an interest in me.

"Can I get you some drinks?" I asked, pointedly ignoring his comments and failing to introduce myself.

He grinned back at me unpleasantly as the other three sniggered in complicity.

"A drink from the Primus's pet human?" he replied. "How could I resist?"

The comment was loaded with innuendo. I decided he was deliberately misunderstanding my offer. He had surely heard Sol's comments to Cleo and knew I was off the menu.

I surreptitiously glanced across the room to see if Sol was still here, but there was no sign of him. I was on my own. I'd just have to brazen through.

"Great," I replied brightly, resisting the urge to rise to the bait. "We have warm blood on tap or cold bottled, or any array of alcoholic and non-alcoholic drinks."

Resting one arm on the table top, he leaned towards me. He reached out and caught my uninjured hand in his, turning it palm upwards to bare my wrist.

"On tap?" he growled, stroking his thumb along the tattoo denoting my blood type.

I tried to pull away from him, but his hand was locked around mine. He leaned forwards, his lackeys cackling like hyenas as he did so.

Shit.

Just as I was beginning to panic, he abruptly released my hand and sat back in his seat.

"We'll have four pints," he said, his manner changing seamlessly to adopt a more business-like tone.

Confused, I looked over my shoulder to see that Tommy

had just skirted round the edge of the bar and was watching us.

Sighing quietly with relief, I turned from the table and headed quickly back towards the bar to give Josh their order. As he poured the drinks, Tommy leaned casually against the bar and spoke to me gently under his breath.

"Are those guys giving you trouble?"

I shook my head a fraction.

"I think they're just trying it on. I'm okay."

He gave me a small nod and pushed away from the bar, carrying on to complete a quick circuit of the room before returning to his place by the door. Although I was indeed okay, I was still glad he'd been here.

Josh handed me a tray of drinks for Charles's table and, cautious after the appearance of Tommy, they made no comment as I placed the drinks in front of each of them. However, Tommy's proximity didn't stop Charles from giving me a distinctly predatory look as I leaned over the table.

The guy completely creeped me out.

I walked away quickly, returning to Cleo's table to see if I could rustle up some entertaining chit-chat.

It was an unmitigated disaster. Cleo didn't want to talk to me and I ended up making awkward comments about the weather for a couple of minutes before giving up. It was painfully embarrassing and my cheeks were burning crimson as I excused myself.

I had a little more luck on the next table, mostly because the lady vampire occupying it seemed to find my flushed face enticing. I tried not to think about it and concentrated on asking lots of questions about her and her companion's employment.

They'd been based in Wimbledon so they hadn't had far to travel.

"I loved the tennis," she said to me, her eyes roaming over my face as I leaned up against the side of the booth. "When I was younger I worked as a ball girl, but as time went on I simply took any position I could to be close to the action.

Finally, I ended up as an umpire."

She sighed nostalgically.

"It was delightful. I had a perfect position to watch the players moving, smell the sweat and hear the blood pounding. I shall mourn its loss."

It was a peculiar and slightly disturbing perspective, but it made me think. I had never considered that the Silver would have suffered along with the humans, though obviously not to the same extent. It was the first time I had ever thought about what the Silver had lost in the Revelation. This was a new world for them too.

"Is there no hope to rebuild?" I asked.

"Eventually," she said with a small smile, "but I doubt it will be in your lifetime, my dear."

After a little more small talk, I excused myself to move to the next table.

"Hey, Emmy," Josh called out to me as I walked past the bar. "You used to work here before the Revelation, right?"

"Yup."

"So you know the tap room?"

I nodded.

"I've lost three barrels in the past twenty minutes and I've no idea what's going on back there. Sam tried to sort them out, but he just ended up covered in blood and beer."

He frowned, apparently remembering the image.

"It wasn't pretty," he added. "Could you have a go?"

I almost asked why Josh couldn't do it himself, then I realised he didn't want to end up drenched in blood like Sam. He was delegating the shitty job to me.

I would have protested, but I was frankly in no rush to see Charles again.

"I'll give it a try, but I've got to warn you I'm no expert."

"Thanks," he said with a smile. "Sam's cleaned up so I'll get him to cover your tables till you get back."

The tap room in the VIP bar was in a cellar accessed through a door in the back of the room. It was tiny and cramped, but when the club was Parker's we had all used it as a refuge if we needed a few minutes off the floor. It was an oddly secluded spot in the middle of a sea of noise. It wasn't pretty, but it was quiet.

As I approached the door, I found myself increasingly eager for a moment of tranquillity. I was fumbling my way through this hosting gig well enough, but I didn't think I was impressing anyone. I didn't enjoy it and consequently I wasn't very good at it.

I walked down the concrete steps and into the cellar, turning the corner at their foot to walk towards the barrels. Checking the lines, I could see there were a couple of blockages. We'd have to get the pipes themselves changed. They just weren't built to carry a liquid as viscous as blood. The lines also weren't heated and it was cool in the cellar, so the blood was starting to coagulate in the tubes.

Not good.

I needed to talk to Josh about it, and probably Sol as well.

As I turned to run back up the steps, I heard the lock turn in the door at the top. Fear rising, I peered round the corner to see that the key to the tap room door was no longer in the lock where it usually lived.

I ran frantically up the stairs and depressed the door handle repeatedly, but it was no use. The door was locked and the key was nowhere to be seen.

I peered through the keyhole, wondering if the key was in the outside of the door, but I could see clear through into the VIP bar.

I took a calming breath. Maybe the key had been on the outside of the lock and someone had decided to make the cellar secure. It could have been an accident.

Alternatively, and far more likely, Charles and his buddies had decided to mess with me.

Either way, I could shout loud enough so the Silver would hear me. This was going to be embarrassing, and someone might have to break down the door to get to me, but it wasn't the end of the world.

I breathed out in resignation.

As I lifted my uninjured hand to thump on the door, a hand covered my mouth and I was jerked roughly backwards at breathtaking speed. There was a rush of movement and I found myself backed up against the barrels, silver-threaded eyes boring threateningly into my own.

Charles.

I froze. I couldn't think of a way out of this one.

If I screamed, would any of the Silver in the bar above me even hear? I knew they had enhanced hearing compared with that of a human, but was it enough to hear me over the pounding music and through the floor of the club? I didn't know.

"Finally," he crooned at me, "a bit of privacy. By the way, if you make any noise louder than a whisper, I'll snap your neck. I'd rather we weren't interrupted."

As he spoke, he brushed my hair away from the left side of my face, pushing it over my shoulder to expose the bite mark on my neck.

"Normally I don't like being second to the party," he continued, running his fingers over the wound, "but I suppose I can make an exception in this case."

Shit.

My mind was racing, frantically trying to figure out a plan. He could kill me in a second if I tried to scream or escape. My only option was to try to talk him round.

"Sol will kill you," I whispered.

"We're harder to kill than you think, little human," he replied with a rapacious grin. "Besides which, I can't see or smell any mark on you other than the brand of your safe house. The Primus has no claim on you."

He was right, but that wasn't the whole truth. Sol considered me to be under his protection and wanted me to carry his mark, though I didn't know for what purpose. Regardless of whether or not it was something to which I would submit again, things weren't over between us yet. At least, if they were then he didn't yet know.

Deceitful as it was, I decided to go for broke. I needed to

get myself out of this situation alive.

"I have a choker," I said quietly. "As far as the Primus is concerned, I belong to him."

"Ah, but that's not how you feel, is it, my human friend?"

He pushed me gently downwards until I was sitting on the rim of a keg and started to pace around the limited space of the tap room.

"You see," he continued, "I was watching the two of you together earlier in the bar. You're stifled under him, desperate to shrug off his touch, yearning to throw off the yoke. I've been asking myself whether he is the sort of Silver who would take what he wants by force, and I don't think it's his style."

He sat down abruptly on the barrel next to me, resting one ankle on the knee of the opposite leg, and leaned towards me.

"Our dear Primus is a politician," he continued. "He wants to win people over, convince them with his beautifully-crafted arguments so they dig their own graves, smiling happily in the knowledge that it was their decision to do so. He doesn't manipulate by stealth, he bares to us the ugly truths we'd rather not face and in doing so predetermines our choices. A true student of the Socratic method."

This guy apparently loved to listen to the sound of his own voice. However, it was in my interests to keep him talking so I said nothing to interrupt his flow.

"No," he said, "our Primus would make you want his protection. Then he'd make you want his love, not to mention his teeth in your neck. He'd want you to beg for it."

His eyes flickered briefly to the bite on the exposed side of my neck as he spoke.

"Did you beg, little girl?"

I would have blushed madly had I not been white with terror.

He was right, for all his limited charm. Sol was playing a game with me, drawing me along to the conclusion he wanted me to reach. I'd always known that to be the case, but I'd let him do it because it was what I had wanted.

Who knows how differently things might have played out

if it hadn't been for Drew, if he hadn't killed Jeff and Sarah? I doubted that I would have been so driven by the urge to erase myself, to burst through the vacuum in my chest, to feel anything that wasn't grief, if it hadn't been for that betrayal.

Maybe everything would have played out the same regardless.

"But something's gone wrong for our dauntless leader. Here you are with the impression of his teeth on your skin," he said, leaning over to trace the wound with his fingertips again, "and yet you don't love him. You refuse his mark. You step back from the brink. You reject him after the fact.

"Though fascinating, it's something of a disappointment for me personally," he sniffed. "This would have been a more satisfying experience if I were taking away the Primus's prize, but no matter."

"What I think doesn't matter," I breathed. "I belong to Sol."

He laughed at me, a high, barking laugh that seemed inordinately loud in the enclosed space.

"You think he doesn't know how you feel? You give too little credit to the powers of mental and sensory perception of the Silver."

He leaned in towards me threateningly, his face inches from mine.

"He knows, little girl."

Shivers ran down my spine as I felt the heat of his breath stroking my face. I suppressed the urge to wipe its memory away with my hands.

"Regardless," he continued, "you don't carry his mark or his choker, so no one could blame me for drinking from you. And if, by some horrible accident, I should happen to take more than you can survive…."

With no further warning, he plunged his head towards my neck and sank his teeth into it, breaking through the skin over the existing wound. Excruciating pain burst from where his fangs lodged in my skin, radiating through my entire body until I felt paralysed with agony. Every movement I made only increased the burning in my veins.

It was nothing like it had been with Sol. The first few seconds, perhaps, but this was something completely different. I felt like I was going to pass out.

Pain ached and screamed through my body again and again, cutting along my limbs as he pulled the blood from me. It seemed to go on for an age, as brutal as I had been warned that it would be.

A fuzzy haze had settled into my head when I felt Charles' teeth pulling out of my skin. Maybe he'd decided not to kill me after all.

I snapped back to semi-consciousness as a figure loomed in front of me. It wasn't Charles.

"Tommy?" I murmured.

"Fuck," he replied. "This looks bad."

"How did you find me?" I asked in a whisper.

"Drew… he said he… well, never mind. We found you and that's what matters."

Cam thundered down the stairs and popped up at Tommy's side.

"Holy shit, Emmy," he shouted at me. "What the hell were you thinking by letting that creep get you alone down here?"

I wrinkled my brow at him. I was too out of it to be having an argument about this.

"For fuck's sake," another voice said from the stairwell, "don't blame the victim. She wouldn't have come down here with him willingly, right Emmy?"

Ben came into view as I nodded weakly.

He was apparently my valiant defender.

That didn't seem right, I thought vaguely.

He strode across the room towards me and gathered me up in his arms.

"I'll take her over to the Palace and get her seen by Rena," he said in a tone that would admit no compromise.

There was a mumbled response I didn't hear, and that was the last thing I knew before the lights went out again.

CHAPTER XXX

I awoke shivering, the wind whipping at my hair and lashing it across my bare shoulders. I was lying on a hard, gritty surface with the sharp edges of stones sticking into my face and limbs where they touched it.

Everything hurt. There was a burn in my muscles and a chilly ache in my veins, thudding with my heartbeat. My eyelids felt like they were glued shut, but I forced them open with difficulty.

There was nothing to see but the ground, a poorly-illuminated concrete surface. I moved my arms with difficulty and tried to use them to push myself into a seated position, but there was no strength in them. I had to content myself with simply rolling onto my side so I was looking at something other than the ground.

I was on an open rooftop with darkness all around me, but from the small amount of illumination I could just make out the edge of the roof about ten feet ahead of me. There was a crescent moon tonight so there was very little light, except a faint glow that seemed to be rising from buildings in a single area in the distance ahead of me.

That had to be Sol's, I thought.

So where was I?

"You're awake," said a voice behind me.

I rolled painfully over onto my other side and saw that I wasn't alone on the rooftop. Terror shot through me. I didn't immediately recognise the voice and all I could see was a figure moving in the shadow of a building on the other side of the roof.

I was completely incapacitated. There was no way I could defend myself, or even run away, should the need present itself.

"Who's there?" I croaked.

The figure moved closer to me, stepping into a patch of moonlight.

"Ben? What's going on? I can barely move."

"I know," he replied. "Don't worry. Soon you won't be moving at all."

He smiled at me in a detached way, no emotion reaching his eyes.

My mind flashed back to the last time I had seen that smile, to the crunch of Danny's neck as it snapped in Ben's hand. That was what had bothered me about Ben, though I'd never put my finger on it before now.

He was the sort of creature who could kill without feeling because in his mind he was a superior being to humans. We didn't matter. We were things, not people. This was the Ben that Drew knew, the Ben who considered humans to be insects.

The realisation settled uncomfortably in my chest, sending a frisson of dread to my stomach. It was the apathy, the complete indifference. Killing Danny was a chore, an insignificant task that had to be completed. A box ticked and forgotten, discarded from his concern immediately.

Apparently I was next.

Fear should have been sending my heart into overdrive, pumping the blood round my body, but there was just a slow, irregular thudding in my chest. Something was really wrong with me.

"I don't understand," I whispered.

"No," he replied, "I don't suppose you would."

"You're pathetic," he sneered. "Just because one or two Silver are weak enough to treat you as an equal, you think that we're all sensitive and caring. Your association with the Primus is the only reason that the Silver have treated you as anything other than meat. We're not human, we're Silver. We're stronger, better, and we have our own rules to abide by. Your human morals are of no use to us."

He laughed again, an insidious sound full of derision and devoid of mirth.

"But you're going to make yourself useful. You're going to help me bring your boyfriend to his knees," he said.

I was cold all over, pins and needles running along my limbs.

"What's wrong with me?" I gasped.

"Charles nearly drained you dry," he said without emotion. "You're dying."

He spoke as if he didn't really care either way. There was no light in his eyes, no connection. I was just a broken toy, a tool to get to Sol.

He was going to stand there waiting until I died. I felt like a science project, like he was watching in purely intellectual interest to see how long it would take me to die so he could record his findings and report accordingly. Maybe that's what he was actually going to do.

"Why?" I asked.

He laughed.

"Power," he replied. "Why else?"

I looked at him in confusion. I couldn't see how letting me die was going to get him what he wanted.

"I'm third in line. With Drew out of the way, I'll be Secundus. Hell, the way Sol has been carrying on with you I might even make it to Primus. That was an added bonus," he said with a smirk.

I was completely bewildered.

He walked towards me, looking down into my bemused expression.

"Cara Alton," he whispered in a voice so eerie it made my skin tingle. "What a gift she was."

I exhaled a shuddering breath.

I wanted to ask what he meant, but my exhausted body felt like it was sinking into the ground and I couldn't muster the energy to speak. I couldn't even feel the cold of the wind anymore.

He crouched down to the ground beside me and, as I followed his movement drowsily with my eyes, he reached out to take my wrist. He was taking my pulse.

"We have some time yet," he whispered.

He sat back on the ground, crossing his legs in front of him, and smiled.

"Well, as I have a captive audience, why don't I tell it a story?"

His manner was oddly manic, cheerful and excited.

"Once upon a time, there was a human girl called Cara. By all accounts she was nothing special, a simple country girl with a boring life in a boring town among boring people. Young, not particularly pretty, and doubtless tedious company. One day, she met a Silver who fell in love with her.

"Humans don't know about this, but when Silver fall in love it's written on their faces for the whole world to see. Well, more accurately, it's etched into their irises: an extension of the silver tracery in the whites of our eyes."

My eyes widened.

I'd seen a Silver with silver in his irises. More than that, I'd stood and watched as the silver permeated them.

Drew.

Ben saw my reaction and clapped his hands together.

"Bingo! Our very own Secundus. But wait, there's more."

Ben leaned towards me dramatically as if he wanted to impart secrets to me. I would have flinched backwards had I the strength to do so.

"Our kind sometimes silver when they first meet someone, sometimes not until years later."

Surely it wasn't me?

But as soon as the realisation came to me I knew it was the truth. Suddenly Drew's aggression towards Sol made sense, as did the fact that Sol let him get away with open insubordination when it came to me. Sol knew.

And Ben knew too.

"Cara's Silver had known her for years," he continued, "had lived next door to her parents all of her life. One day, she came home from college for the first time in a couple of months. As soon as he saw her, he silvered for her.

"He stole her away and professed his feelings for her, only to find that she loved him too, had always loved him. His silver eyes turned gold.

"But Cara's Silver was young, inexperienced, and was overwhelmed by the feeling. When he bit her, he couldn't hold himself back. He craved her and, confusing his love and bloodlust, drained her until she lay cold in his arms.

"When he realised what he'd done he was distraught. In desperation, he tried to bring her back, tried to heal her."

He paused for a second and took my pulse again before continuing.

"You see, Silver have a gift to give only to the person for whom they've silvered. If they're hurt, their Silver can close their wounds. Even on the brink of death, contact can bring life back to their beloved, whether human or Silver."

The 'band aid'. No wonder Drew had wanted me to keep it to myself.

"But for Cara, it was too late. The life had already left her body and, try as he might, his attempts to revive her did nothing but leave a shining silver handprint on her body.

"The Silver were revealed as a result of the actions of that one foolish boy. On the back of that incident, those Silver who had been agitating for change forced the hand of the others, sending evidence of Cara's supernatural abduction to the media. They chose to come into the open, to battle their way to supremacy. Because of him, we fought and died, losing nearly our entire food source in America because he silvered for a human.

"One human girl to take down an empire," he whispered.

"The Silver aren't meant to love humans. We're meant to feed from you, fuck you if we feel like it, but if a Silver cares for a human there's something wrong with them. Your kind are so easily broken, so disposable. A Silver who loves a human, a Silver who uses a human for anything but food and ravaging, is a Silver risking their life for meat. That Silver risks us all.

"For one of our kind to silver for a human is an aberration, a defect that we will stamp out."

At last, everything made sense. Sol pitied Drew because he had silvered for me. For a human.

Ben took my right arm in his, bending the elbow to look at the wound Drew had healed. There was nothing there, not even a scar.

"When you were with our esteemed Secundus in the square that morning, I saw him speaking to Tommy. I saw the horror on his face.

"I saw that Drew had silvered. I saw the silver mark on your arm and I knew: it was you. The Secundus had fallen in love with you, an insignificant human with nothing to offer one of us. He may have had no control over it, but a man such as that shouldn't be the second-in-line of this realm of Silver. If the people knew…"

He shook his head and giggled, apparently enjoying himself.

"And here's the kicker, my little human," he said, leaning closer towards me with a leering grin, "as Cara died, so did her Silver. Within minutes, he hardened and desiccated until he was nothing more than dust on the breeze. The great tragedy of the Silver bond: we live together, we die together."

No, I thought. Please no. Not Drew.

"We Silver are almost impossible to kill," he continued, "but to take out the Secundus, all I need to do is let you die."

No.

A single tear slipped out of the corner of my eye. Despite everything he'd done, I couldn't bear the thought of Drew dying. It was too much to process that he'd die because of me, because he loved me.

Ben laughed again.

"Delightful, isn't it? But it gets so much better!"

He wrung his hands together in joy.

"I needed some time to make the right allies, insinuate myself into the right circles, so I had some fun with the self-righteous prick whilst I waited for my moment. After the broadcast that day he went out looking for you. I snuck into his apartment and found your shirt, which was helpfully marked not only with your scent but also with the name of the club where you used to work, where you were stupid enough to hide out."

Oh no.

A slow, sickening smile spread across his face.

"I knew you were still in there. I heard the cameras moving even if Drew was too stupid to make the connection. I guessed you'd be waiting for a quiet moment to make a break for it so I stayed behind at the Palace for the last broadcast. I was there watching when you and the boy left the club."

He leaned in to whisper into my ear.

"They even opened the door to me."

A wave of horror swept over me. Jeff and Sarah.

"You were so willing to believe it was Drew that I probably didn't even need to leave the shirt there. I was sure he'd deny it, but you were so sure you never even asked him the question, did you?"

He was right. I'd never asked if it was him. I'd assumed.

"But, moral to the core, our valiant Secundus still took responsibility for it. It was his order to kill any rebels, after all. Of course, your human friends didn't have time to resist."

It wasn't Drew. He hadn't killed them. My soul soared with elation before reality crashed me back down to earth. Ben had killed all three of them to get to me: Sarah, Jeff and Danny. To get to Drew and Sol. And I was going to die here in the furtherance of his goal.

Ben leaned back and looked up at the stars with a

contented smile on his face.

"After that, it just got better. For some reason, the Primus took an interest in you. Maybe he was trying to separate you from Drew, but I think I'd done a pretty good job of that already. Then the little incident I devised on the terrace just pushed you closer towards him.

"Nice show, by the way," he leered.

Disgust rolled through me. He'd been there, watching. Just when I thought I couldn't feel any more ashamed about it. If I'd had enough blood left in me, I would have been blushing.

"After that, I got to watch the Secundus agonise over the image of his beloved fucking the Primus. Better than that, letting him bite her."

He sighed.

"I couldn't have planned it better. I'm sure I can spin your illicit liaison with the Primus into a reason to depose him. After all, he does seem to care for you, a fact that will be all the more apparent after you're dead.

"My pet Weeper wasn't quite as efficient as I'd hoped at taking you down, but Charles played his part to perfection. He was supposed to be the end of you, but you've been such fun I thought I'd give you another chance.

"So here we are, miles outside of the barricade, for your very last chance. Well," he added with an amused expression, "sort of. As soon as I leave, the Weepers will arrive. Either you'll be eaten alive or, if you die from blood loss before they properly go to town on you, you'll get turned into one of them."

His eyes twinkled with excitement and he giggled again.

"I'm not sure which outcome I'm rooting for. Obviously it would be nice if you died so I'd have a guarantee that the Secundus would be dust, but I admit I'm intrigued to see what would happen if you were turned instead. Would he still die? Or would he live in heartbroken torment until the demise of your Weeper self?"

He grinned, his eyes wide and manic.

"Exciting times!" he exclaimed.

As he spoke, he jumped to his feet and spun on the spot.

"Very soon, all this will be mine: your broken world, your burning city. Things are going to change for the Silver under my rule."

I didn't doubt his conviction. His eyes gleamed with megalomania.

He leaned down towards me and took my pulse one last time.

"Our time is up," he declared as he straightened, "and your fate awaits you, whatever it may be. I must leave before your dinner guests arrive to find that their food is cold. It's been a pleasure, believe me."

He bowed to me sardonically and, in a rush of air, he was gone.

I was alone on the windy rooftop, the darkness cocooning me as my breathing slowed. My eyelids fluttered and fell shut as I lost even the strength to keep them open.

I lay in silence for a few minutes as sensation began to leave me. I could no longer feel the wind on my skin and the ache in my body was lifting away. I seemed to be floating above myself, dizzily moving upwards from where I was moored to the earth.

I was vaguely aware of a rustling noise behind me at the edge of the roof. The Weepers had come to claim their meal. I had no energy to open my eyes, let alone turn round to watch them come. Probably for the best, I thought in resignation.

I hoped I'd pass out before they reached me. It was looking like a very real possibility.

I hoped I wouldn't wake up as a Weeper.

If I did, would I remember who I was? The husks I'd seen walking around didn't seem to retain any human intelligence. They appeared to be guided by animal instinct, driven by their senses, but were their conscious minds trapped inside those shells? Were they buried deep, dissociated from themselves, unable to control their own bodies? Unable to do anything but watch the show?

Would I remember being me, being Emmy?

"Emmy?" the echo sounded in my head.

I was distantly aware of being rolled onto my back. The Weepers had reached me, then. Thankfully, I didn't seem to be able to feel anything.

"Emmy!"

It was loud. I wished my brain would shut up and let me fade away in peace.

"Open your eyes, Emmy."

I finally registered that the noise wasn't inside my head, but I couldn't open my eyes. I didn't really want to, anyway.

"She's dying, Primus," another voice said.

I wondered for a second who was dying, then I realised the second voice was talking about me. This wasn't news. I felt like I'd been dying for hours.

"I need to get her to Rena," the first voice replied.

"I don't think Rena can help. She's too far gone."

My head was spinning and a beautiful kaleidoscope of colours was playing intermittently on the inside of my eyelids, splashing like fireworks. There was no pain, just a lightness that set me adrift. I felt free.

There the sound of a weary exhalation.

"Get Drew," said the first voice.

"Primus?"

"Get him!"

I let go, soaring into the sky above me.

CHAPTER XXXI

Thursday

I woke up in another weird place, unable to tell where I was. I thought back to the last thing I remembered and was surprised I had woken up at all. A few seconds later, I wished I hadn't.

Everything hurt. Pain shot through my body, starting on the left side of my neck then thudding through every part of me, forcing its way through my veins. My face twisted into an involuntary grimace.

"Emmy?" a voice asked.

I tried to open my eyes, but the light around me was blinding. I scrunched them shut as a hand slid into my own.

"Take your time."

After a couple more attempts, I managed to open my eyes and focus. I was in the bed of the guest suite at the Palace and there was someone sitting in a chair to the left of the bed.

Sol.

"I'm sorry for what you have been through," he said. "It was Benedict?"

I was surprised he needed to ask. Surely he would have

revealed himself by now?

I tried to speak and failed, so nodded instead.

"We assumed that to be the case when you didn't arrive safely to Rena."

He looked down at his hands.

"I imagine that he told you about the Silver bond?" he added.

I nodded.

"And he told you it doesn't always happen immediately? That more often than not the Silver are bonded over time rather than instantly?"

I didn't want to have this discussion with him. It was veering into dangerous water.

I cleared my throat.

"Drew," I whispered with difficulty.

Sol's face darkened and guilt raced through me.

"You wish to see him?"

I nodded.

There was nothing wrong with my wanting to see him, I told myself, knowing it wasn't the whole truth. Still, I wasn't going to be a coward about admitting it, so I forced myself to meet Sol's eyes.

"You can come in, Secundus," Sol said, not even raising his voice.

The door on my right opened and Drew walked in hesitantly. He'd obviously been waiting outside.

He walked over to the bed and stood there awkwardly.

"You're awake," he said to me pointlessly, apparently unsure what to say.

"It was Benedict," Sol confirmed to Drew as he stood from the chair, "and he told her."

Drew took a deep breath.

"So you'll exile him?" Drew asked.

Sol looked uncomfortable.

"I won't discuss this here," he replied, shooting a glance in my direction.

"She has a right to know."

Sol sighed in resignation.

"You are well aware that I'm not in a position to exile him."

Drew narrowed his eyes at him.

"He was going to let her die, Sol."

"And what do the Silver care for the life of a single human?" Sol retorted.

It was a harsh response, but from what I'd seen of Ben it did seem to be a reasonable comment.

"But it was directed at you, at your rule. You know what he wanted. You marked her, Sol," Drew said through gritted teeth. "You gave her your protection and he trespassed on that. Isn't that a legitimate enough reason to keep the Silver happy?"

Sol shook his head sadly and looked at me.

"I'm sorry, Emmy. You must understand that if I give any indication that I care for you then that will be the end of everything I have worked for. They would perceive it as weakness, as a risk, and I would be deposed. I won't allow a puritanical dictator like Benedict to supplant me."

He paused.

"In any case," he added, "it appears that our association is at an end."

"Sol…" I whispered, but he held up a hand to stop me.

"We need not discuss it now," he said gently.

"You can't just let him get away with this!" Drew raged. "She's not safe with him still out there!"

"What choice do I have?" Sol asked in a weary voice.

Drew was arguing desperately, trying to find a way to convince Sol to banish my attacker, the Silver who had systematically orchestrated my torturous death since the moment we had met.

"It would have killed me," Drew replied. "It would have killed your Secundus and therefore threatened your regime. Isn't that worth retribution?"

Sol laughed.

"Do you really wish me to make that public knowledge?

To make it known that you've silvered for a human? After the Alton fiasco? That my Secundus, the man in charge of the security of the nation, is so assailable? That he jeopardises our position with such a weakness?"

Drew's eyes flashed as he glared at Sol.

Sol was right. There was no way to punish Ben without putting Sol and his leadership at risk.

"He'll never stop," Drew said.

"Then we will find another way to control him," Sol replied. "I assure you that you are not the only person who will take pains to protect Emmy. If that is a weakness then so be it. We will find a way. We will keep her from harm."

He turned and walked away, but stopped before he reached the door.

"Secundus," he said, "you know that the fact that you have silvered is common knowledge. If you mark her, people will make the mental association. They will know you have silvered for a human, and Benedict will use the Alton precedent to remove you from your position."

His eyes flashed as he glared at Drew.

"I can't allow that to happen, Secundus. I need your support."

He looked briefly at his feet before meeting Drew's eyes once more.

"I am truly sorry," he added softly.

With that, he left the room without meeting my eye, closing the door softly behind him as he went.

"Bastard," Drew muttered under his breath.

He looked briefly down at his feet before skirting around the bed to sit in the chair Sol had just vacated. He leaned forward and looked me over.

"Are you okay?" he asked.

I performed a quick mental audit. I felt pretty good, all things considered.

I cleared my throat again.

"I felt rubbish when I woke up," I said, "but I feel okay now."

He smiled uncomfortably.

"Good."

We sat in silence for a few moments as he wrung his hands.

"So, Ben told you about the silvering?"

I nodded back at him.

"You healed me," I said, guessing that he must have done. Otherwise, how could I be alive? I looked at my injured hands and scratched arms and saw that they were healed. No trace remained. Reaching my hands to my face, I felt only smooth skin in the place of my scarring cuts. Finally, as the extent of the healing sank in, I hesitantly felt the sides of my throat. The marks of Sol's teeth were gone, removed as if they'd never been there.

The slate wiped clean.

But nothing could take the memories from me.

Drew reached forward and gently tugged the covers away from my shoulders, revealing a single silver handprint in the centre of my chest.

"You were dying, Emmy. You very nearly did die."

His face clouded and filled with pain.

"How did they find me? Tommy said something in the cellar…"

"It's the silver bond. I could feel it slipping away. It was…," he looked away in despair. "I don't think I'm ready to talk about it yet."

The silence flowed back into the conversation.

"Why didn't you tell me?" I asked quietly.

He shook his head at me.

"You didn't want to know," he replied. "I see it in your eyes. I see the battle in there, the hatred and revulsion stamping down on every positive feeling you ever had about me."

He wasn't wrong.

"I thought you killed my friends," I replied.

He looked at me quizzically.

"We did," he said in a whisper.

"I know, but you personally didn't. Ben did."

"What difference does that make?" he asked.

Not much, I guessed, but maybe enough.

"I've killed plenty of other humans, Emmy," he said despairingly. "I should have killed you that day when Cam found you by the barrier."

"You would have killed yourself," I replied.

He nodded and looked away.

"Do you wish I'd said yes to your offer the other night?" I asked him. "Would you rather I was Silver?"

He sat silently for a moment.

"No," he said quietly, meeting my eyes. "It's not what you want."

"But it would make things easier," I reasoned. "I'd no longer be at risk from Ben and consequently you'd no longer be under threat."

And his feelings for me couldn't be wielded as a weapon against him.

Was I ready to face that, the apparently unassailable fact that he... felt that way about me?

Not yet.

"No," he said, shaking his head in agitation. "We'll find another way. You don't want this and I'm not going to impose it on you."

He ran his hands through his hair and leaned back with a sigh.

"Anyway, it's not a simple process. Besides which, Sol is bringing in some... changes."

I raised an eyebrow at him, but he pressed his lips together and shook his head. He wasn't going to talk about whatever Sol was planning.

"Will it go away?" I asked hesitantly.

"What?" he replied.

"The silvering. Is it forever?"

He smiled wryly.

"No, not forever, but it'll last beyond your lifetime."

I felt helpless. I didn't know what to say to him.

"I'm sorry this happened to you," I said softly.

"I'm not," he replied.

He looked hurt, his brow furrowing. I'd said the wrong thing.

"Most Silver go their whole lives without experiencing this, Emmy. Even if I live a century this way without ever touching you, I won't regret it."

"Drew…"

"I'm not looking for anything from you," he interrupted me, "and I don't want your pity. This, the fact that you're talking to me, that's enough. If the Primus has his way then this is all it'll ever be anyway, but it's still enough. Nothing has to change."

I shook my head at him. Everything had changed.

"Please don't push me away," he said.

I offered him a rueful smile.

"I need time," I said, "to heal."

He frowned for a moment in incomprehension. He'd already healed me, of course. The silver handprint on my chest was a declaration of that fact.

But I wasn't talking about physical recovery.

"I'll leave you in peace, then," he replied, rising to his feet.

He smiled awkwardly and walked to the door, but hesitated with his palm on the handle.

"I'll always be close by, Emmy. If you call for me, I'll be there."

The door closed behind him.

I felt horribly guilty, but oddly reassured. That feeling of safety I always had around Drew had returned, no longer quite so marred by betrayal and despair.

I needed some time to grieve properly, to remember those I'd lost.

I lay back into the pillows, my eyelids closing in exhaustion.

Ben, Sol, Drew… they would be problems for tomorrow.

Do you want to read Cara Alton's story?

Join my Readers' Club and receive an exclusive short story, absolutely FREE!

www.josiejaffrey.com/subscribe

You'll also receive my monthly newsletter, including exclusive news, giveaways and offers.

***

If you enjoyed *A Bargain in Silver*, why not read *The Price of Silver*? It's Book II in the *Solis Invicti* series, and carries on right where *A Bargain in Silver* left off.

In the straits of necessity, sometimes there isn't room for freedom.

***

Please leave a review!

If you enjoyed *A Bargain in Silver*, I'd be so grateful if you would please review it. Book reviews can make a huge difference to the success of a novel, particularly those of self-published authors like me. If you have time to leave a review, even if it's just a sentence or two, then I'd really appreciate it.

***

Get in touch!

I love hearing from readers! If you'd like to contact me, you can do that through my website, Twitter, Facebook or Instagram.

ACKNOWLEDGMENTS

The author wishes to thank her brilliant girls Zoe, Vicky and Claire for guinea-pigging the first draft and for tolerating interminable book-talk.

Thanks also to my lovely sister for taking an interest, despite being somewhat thwarted by the arrival of my nephew.

Lastly, but not least, this book would never have seen the light of day were it not for the unfailing and constructive support of my husband. You are awesome.

39553605R00211

Printed in Poland
by Amazon Fulfillment
Poland Sp. z o.o., Wrocław